SHAKEDOWNERS 3 - SLACK TO THE FUTURE

JUSTIN WOOLLEY

LONELY ROBOT BOOKS

To Covid-19, you tried to stop me getting this book written, I win bitch.

CAPTAIN'S PROLOGUE_

Captain's log, Iridius B. Franklin of the FSC Deus Ex recording. The date is Galactic Central 2216 point...well, here's the thing, it should be 2216 point 453 point 26, but I'm actually recording this on 2216 point 452 point 37, which is approximately ten standard Earth months earlier. This will make sense after I explain what's happened.

Maybe.

I mean, it might not make sense because nothing much has made sense to me for the last year or so if I'm honest, but it'll at least be clear why there's confusion. Quinn says even with twenty-third century computing power, having a log recorded later and labelling it as being from ten months earlier will probably mess something up. Although I don't think it'll matter too much because let's face it, the computer's got no damn idea what's going on as it is. When you ask it the date it replies with something about conflicting inputs producing inconsistent temporal location information, which is the closest a computer gets to saying "fucked if I know, I'm as confused as you are".

Anyway, all this is to say, if you're listening to this and you aren't aware of what the FSC Deus Ex has been through then you're in for quite a confusing ride. You'll need to go back and review my previous logs, all the way back to my time as captain of the FSC Diesel Coast and my brief but eventful command of the FSC Gallaway. That's all reasonably well-known by now, but here's a quick recap: Someone inadvertently released the Aegix nanobot swarm intelligence, which was definitely an accident by the way, and it set about trying to alter all life in the galaxy to prepare for the coming of something called the Synth-Hastur. Unfortunately, the Aegix was running on some pretty old firmware and despite apparently trying to help, it killed a whole lot of people, including wiping out the entire population of planet Earth. Luckily myself and my crew, admittedly with a little help from the rest of the FSC fleet, stepped up and managed to destroy the majority of the threat. There are only two known instances of Aegix nanobots left in the galaxy, one group in a probe that crashed on Acacia, a moon of Geffet, and the other inside me, where they've apparently been hanging out for the last twenty-five years. Don't ask me how they got there – nobody knows.

Following on from that adventure I was given command of the FSC Deus Ex, a stealth reconnaissance ship, and was sent to keep an eye on the Planetary Alliance of Corporate Holdings. Did I mention I received the Federation Star for the Aegix thing? That's probably not important but, you know, just in case you were wondering. Anyway, while we were keeping an eye on the Alliance we became aware of a major threat to the Federation. We were witnesses to the Planetary Alliance – specifically, the Frost Norton Corporation, led by CEO Devin Frost – testing a newly developed time reversal bomb: a weapon that could be launched and then destroy its target before it was launched. I know, messes with all sorts of cause–effect logic, doesn't it? I've found the best approach is to not think too hard about it. The thing is, these time reversal bombs also cause temporal displacement waves, which send whatever's trapped in them back in time a certain amount, *depending on how far you are from the detonation centre – also a real mind-screw to experience, by the way. When the Federation wouldn't act, I took it on myself to intervene. With the assistance of my crew and Gentrix Frost, now ex-member of the Frost Norton Corporation, we stopped Devin Frost's attempt to launch his time reversal weapon at Earth. Unfortunately – and this is where the date confusion comes in – the Deus Ex was trapped in the temporal displacement field and we were unceremoniously bumped ten months back in time.*

So, that's our current situation. Our focus now is to take a measured, scientific effort to return to our correct location in the space–time continuum. Most of all, it's important that we remain calm.

CHAPTER ONE_

"Jupiter's fucking nuts, we're fucking stuck here?!"

Captain Iridius Franklin paced the floor of the *Deus Ex*'s bridge in a way that was not at all measured or calm.

"Great, just great. See, this is why you don't fuck around with time travel. You get paradoxes and you get stuck in the past and you probably meet yourself and have to avoid your own mother falling in love with you instead of your dad or some shit." He pinched the bridge of his nose. "And it all gives you a headache. Fucking stuck in the past, goddamn it."

The lights on the bridge flickered and a strange crackling noise came through the speakers, followed by the chorus of Billy Ray Cyrus's *Achy Breaky Heart* which, mercifully, stopped quickly. Not only because it was terrible but also because it was one of the few songs from Earth that had been banned under the 2156 Treaty of the Rights of Sentient Beings due to the detrimental effect it had on the brain chemistry of a number of species. Any longer and Iridius may well have been up for a lofty fine.

And then, throughout the ship, a number of systems ceased functioning before rebooting. Unfortunately, when the life support system stopped it did not come back on. The missing background noise was immediately noticeable, the sudden absence of gently moving air being pumped through the filtration system. It was one of the few systems on the ship that everyone was subconsciously aware of at all times. There were plenty of things that could go wrong in space, plenty of ways to die, but slowly suffocating in your own exhaled carbon dioxide was among the worst. Thankfully, after a shudder from somewhere in the ventilation, the reassuring hum returned and the crew collectively exhaled, far less concerned about what they were exhaling.

"Sir," Lieutenant Commander Quinn said, looking around warily at the misbehaving ship, "I think maybe you should, you know—"

"Yes, Quinn?" Iridius spun to face his second-in-command. "You think I should what?"

Quinn shrank back, as she always did when facing interpersonal conflict. It was subtle, but there was a visible recoiling as she tried to disappear into herself, folding up just a little, her neck blooming with red, nervous heat. Then, with a deep breath, she straightened her posture and lifted her chin, not something she'd always been able to do. "I think you should calm down, sir. You're causing Franklinisms because you're getting worked up. You're," she paused, taking a moment more to steady herself, "you're acting like a child."

Iridius stared at his Executive Officer. It was his turn to be taken aback. "I'm not acting like a child."

No one spoke for a long beat until Lieutenant Benjamin Rangi, guaranteed destroyer of awkward silences everywhere, chimed in.

"You kind of are, Cap."

Iridius looked around at the bridge crew staring at him. He suddenly felt something he hadn't felt for a very long time – well, he'd felt it just last night when Gentrix had decided to strip his clothes off with the lights on, but he hadn't felt it in public for a long time – he felt self-conscious. He wasn't entirely sure where that outburst had come from, but the truth was he wasn't feeling right. His head pounded, he was tired and he was irritable more irritable than normal. He sighed and sat back in the captain's chair, taking a moment to clear his head. "Sorry," he said. "I shouldn't have snapped at you, Quinn. I just suddenly have a wicked headache, and the news that we could be stuck here isn't great."

"Would you like me to fetch you some pain relief, Captain?" Junior Ensign Hal asked. "I am certain Doctor Dooms will be happy to provide some."

"Thank you, Ensign," Iridius said, "I'd appreciate that."

The golden android nodded, rose from his chair at the helm and walked off the bridge. Iridius watched him go. It was always disconcerting and borderline embarrassing watching Hal move around, because despite hundreds of years of biomechanical engineering, getting robots to walk still proved extraordinarily difficult. Maintaining balance while lumbering around as a bipedal ape (or whatever branch of intelligent sentient life you may have evolved from) requires a myriad amount of feedback from the senses, musculoskeletal system and nervous system, and replicating this in an android had proved almost as difficult as the development of sentient intelligence. Perhaps even harder. The truth is, it's pretty easy to create a computer-simulated personality good enough to fool a human, but creating a robot that doesn't shuffle around with a gait that's little more than controlled falling is much more difficult.

"Captain," Quinn said, "I thought we agreed you'd stop sending Hal on errands?"

"This is hardly the same as him getting me a coffee, is it?" Iridius said.

"Yes, but if any of us had asked whether we should go down

to medical to get you pain relief you would have told us to remain at our posts. I know you have a problem with synthetics, but you shouldn't treat him differently to any other crew member."

"I don't have a problem with synthetics," Iridius said.

Quinn stared at him.

"Okay," Iridius said, "I do, but Hal's fine. I don't have a problem with Hal."

Hal may have been an android but he didn't fall into the same category as a full artificial intelligence like the Aegix, because he wasn't ranked high enough on the Turing-Alabaster-Singh Scale – a scale that took into account various facets of intelligence such as reasoning, planning, learning and the ability to make sarcastic comments, in order to rank whether a synthetic lifeform was truly sentient.

Despite being able to engage in conversation and fool people into believing he was thinking (a pretty common characteristic of most people really), Hal wasn't truly alive, he was just running on pre-programmed behaviours augmented by advanced machine learning algorithms. As a general rule, Iridius was opposed to artificially created forms of intelligence, mostly because they seemed to have a habit of getting all killy.

But Iridius wasn't a technophobe, and he certainly wasn't going to run off and join one of those enclaves on some distant outer arm of the galaxy where people decided to live as humanity had pre-technology. Technology had certainly led to some missteps along the way (bioweapons, social media, segways), but throwing it all away and living in a cave was a little like deciding to subsist on a diet of turd sandwiches because you didn't like peanut butter.

Not to mention, Iridius had to believe that once people got to those enclaves they couldn't have found it all that pleasant when they realised they had to wipe with leaves. This was especially true of those that had settled on Dentrax VII a world that seemed like a paradise except that every leaf on the entire planet was allergenic to the point of causing blisters the size of basketballs. Not something you want to find out post wipe.

"Yes, but I know it goes back a long way for you," Quinn said. "You've had more trauma with synthetic intelligences than most people, even before the Aegix. I think you should acknowledge that might be affecting your treatment of Hal."

"Thank you, Doctor Freud, but I don't remember asking for a psychoanalysis session," Iridius said. "Can we drop it now?"

"What happened before the Aegix?" Gentrix asked.

"Nothing," Iridius replied. "It's fine."

"Cap's got childhood trauma he keeps bottled up," Lieutenant Rangi offered helpfully.

Iridius shot the helmsman a look. "I do not."

"You have childhood trauma?" Gentrix asked.

"No," Iridius said. "It's fine."

"A robot killed his parents," Rangi said, sending the bridge into the kind of complete silence that falls over a family dinner when drunk Uncle Phil blurts out the long-held family secret about another relative's love life/criminal past/true parentage.

"Rangi," Quinn snapped.

"Uh, sorry, that just slipped out."

"Iridius," Gentrix said, her tone switching from playful to consolatory, "I'm sorry. Can I ask what happened?"

"Well," Iridius said, "I don't normally go around blurting it out," he looked pointedly at Rangi, "but I suppose I can't leave it at that, can I? When I was fifteen my parents took me on my first trip to Earth from Procyon C. We were on the moon, in Aldrin Square, when an unknown synthetic went gronking crazy and shot the place up. My parents and I were caught amongst it. All of us got hit. Like a lot of other people."

Gentrix's eyes went wide. "Wait. The Aldrin Square attack.

You were there? That's conspiracy theory central, even in the Alliance."

Iridius nodded. "Yep, I was there, and no, I don't know what it was. Some kind of military project gone crazy. All I know is it was an AI and it was off its rocker. My parents were killed and I would have been too, except someone got to me in time to stabilise me. So, between that and the Aegix, my opinion on the existence of synthetic intelligences is that they can be quite problematic and we'd be better off without them."

This last bit was already out of Iridius's mouth when he realised Hal had walked back onto the bridge. "Sorry, no offence, Hal."

"None taken, Captain," Hal said, passing Iridius a small blue pill. "I am quite incapable of being offended, even by a direct aspersion against my very existence."

Iridius took the pill and dry swallowed it. "Right, see, you saying that makes me feel more guilty. Are you sure you're not emotionally manipulating me?"

"No, Captain," Hal said.

"Thanks for the painkillers. You can take your seat at the helm again."

Hal did so, looking ahead at the view screen in a way that was even more unsettling. He could at least have thrown some shade back at Iridius.

"Okay, can we get back to the problem at hand now?" Iridius said. "What you're telling me, Quinn, is that the time bomb has sent us ten months back in time and there's no way to get back to the future?"

"Well," Quinn said, "I'm not saying it's impossible, Captain. I would never say that – not without very strong evidence. After all, it was generally accepted that time travel was impossible, but here we are. All I said was that your assertion that we get back to the future is a little easier said than done. As far as I'm aware, there's been no recorded travel into the future, although attempts have been made through wormhole traversal using the theory of Einstein-Rosen wormhole bridging. The idea that Einstein-Rosen bridges could be used for faster-than-light travel never proved useful in practice, particularly after the development of the BAMF drive. However, it has long been speculated that because wormholes link disparate points in space–time, they could be used for travel through time as well as through space. There were some ambitious early manned attempts, but none have ever been confirmed as successful. Of course, there is the possibility that they were successful, and the aspiring chrononauts simply travelled a long way into the future and were unable to reverse the process."

"You mean like us?" Iridius said. "Stuck in the wrong time."

"Yes, sir," Quinn admitted. "Like us."

"Right, well, not impossible is a start," Iridius said. "We all know I'm as scientifically literate as a bag of impact drivers, but using my most advanced critical thinking skills, I'm going to go with the theory that we got here so there must be a way back."

"That would imply complete non-loss T-symmetry, Captain," Quinn said, "and there's actually no basis to suggest that after the first entropic reversal there isn't significant alteration to the variables that would—"

"Got here," Iridius said, gesturing one way with a pointed finger, "so we can get back," he finished, gesturing the other way.

"Yes, sir," Quinn said. She knew Iridius Franklin respected science, and that he secretly understood a lot more than he was willing to admit, but she also knew that no level of scientific argument would sway him from this line of thinking right now. The universe might have been governed by indisputable laws, but the only thing more certain than physics itself was Iridius Franklin's eternal, unwavering optimism.

"I have a suggestion," Gentrix said. Iridius's mind instantly raced to all the things he hoped she might suggest, while his more mature brain chastised him because none of those things were suitable to partake in on the bridge – unless it was very empty and there was no chance they'd be disturbed. "There is the fact that we are already time travelling."

"We are?" Rangi asked.

"Of course," said Gentrix. "We're travelling through time at one second per second, same as the rest of the universe."

"Right," Rangi said. "Normal time travel not, sort of, exciting time travel."

"That's right," Gentrix said, "but it does mean we'll catch up to where we should be. It'll just take us ten months to do it. It's less than ideal, but based on what you've said about when you got caught in the test launch of the time reversal bomb, the other copy of us will disappear ten months from now and we'll simply continue on."

"Yes, I already thought of that," Quinn said. "The problem with that is the difference in the duration and the implications of what might happen with the timeline. When we were hit with the temporal displacement wave during that first test, we were sent back in time three minutes. That was a manageable amount of time to avoid contact with anything. But over ten months it would be extraordinarily difficult to have no effect on the timeline. We were due to be back at Tau Ceti for a resupply after the surveillance of ASS Locke. We don't have enough supplies to last ten months. Plus, the ship suffered minor damage during our battle with the *Neverlander* – nothing severe, but some hull damage and engine nozzle damage that needs to be repaired before it gets worse. Both these things mean we would have to engage with people here, in the past, risking what could be a graver threat than any we've faced so far – the butterfly effect."

"That doesn't sound so bad," Rangi said. "If I was naming the gravest threat we've ever faced I wouldn't name it the butterfly effect. Butterflies are pretty. They just flutter around."

"I didn't come up with the name, Lieutenant," Quinn said. "I'm referring to the theory that the death of a butterfly in the distant past could cause unforeseen changes in the future."

"I'd probably call it the Mega Doom Effect," Rangi said, "or the Ultra Threat to End All Threats."

The bridge crew looked at Rangi momentarily before deciding, as they so often did, to simply ignore him.

"And that's what you're worried about?" Gentrix said. "You think we could cause extreme changes to the future? Even in just ten months?"

"Well, I don't know what sort of change could happen in ten months," Quinn said, "but the knock-on effects far into the future may be wide-ranging. That's the problem, though: the butterfly effect stems from chaos theory, which by its very nature is unpredictable. We just don't know what could happen. It might be nothing."

"Or we might create a race of sentient mushrooms that brings about the downfall of the Federation through mind-control fungal infections," Rangi said.

"Rangi!" Iridius yelled, jumping to his feet. "Why do you always have to talk such shit?!"

Rangi was, for what may have been one of only a handful of times in his life, utterly speechless. He stared at Iridius with a blend of shock and fear. There had been countless instances throughout his time serving as helmsman for Captain Iridius Franklin when he'd managed to annoy the captain. Most of the time he did it on purpose. It was kind of their shtick. He'd ramble on, Captain Franklin would get annoyed and respond with a witty, dismissive comment and tell Rangi to shut up. That was why he loved Captain Franklin – he put up with him where others had not. He let him be himself. This was different, though.

The captain had ripped into him with what felt like actual anger, and his face had flared with a rage Rangi had never seen him display; certainly a rage he'd never directed at his own crew. The outburst was entirely out of character and Rangi wasn't prepared for it. And apparently nobody else was either, because the bridge had dropped into a silence thick with uncertainty.

Iridius looked around. His face had dropped from anger to confusion. "Sorry, Lieutenant," he said. "I'm not sure what—" Iridius scrunched his face in pain, unable to even finish his sentence. He rubbed at his temples. Something was hammering inside his head, as if it was trying to claw its way out with a thousand knives, hacking at his nerves with sudden ripping stabs of agony. All over his body his muscles began to spasm and twitch. He suddenly felt like a tiny passenger inside a completely foreign object, unable to recognise this body, which had apparently launched a full-scale revolt. He was little more than a consciousness floating in a pot of boiling water.

"Iridius?" Gentrix said.

"Captain?" Quinn added.

Iridius made a gesture as if waving off their concern. He'd barely finished the half-hearted movement when standing suddenly became the most difficult thing he'd ever had to do. He wavered on his feet, rocking from side to side, and found his eyelids closing of their own accord. He forced them open again but that was apparently such a monumental effort that it sapped what little energy he had left. Before he realised what was happening, the floor of the bridge was rushing towards him. That was strange – floors didn't normally behave in such a dramatic way. In his experience they tended to stay underfoot rather than attempt to stand upright and smack you in the face. Still, the white floor of the bridge was definitely coming at him.

As Iridius slammed onto the deck, Quinn banged her hand on the comm button on the console in front of her. "Doctor

Dooms to the bridge immediately. I say again, medical emergency on the bridge."

Medical emergency on the bridge, Iridius thought to himself as he lay against the cold floor. *I wonder who that's for?*

———

Iridius awoke in the slow, sloppy way of someone emerging from sedation. His eyes were unfocused and wandering, his mouth was dry and his first attempts at speech were less successful than underwater bagpipes.

"Captain."

"Where am I?" Iridius said – or at least, that's what he tried to say. "Wha am?" is closer to what came out.

"Here. Have a drink."

Someone put a straw between his lips. When he sucked, cold water filled his mouth. The sensation not only eased his dry mouth but seemed to help wash away the worst of a heavy lingering sleep. His eyes focused and he saw the round, kind face of Doctor Elizabeth Dooms, ship doctor on the *Deus Ex*, looking down at him.

"Doc?" Iridius asked.

"Yes, Captain," Doctor Dooms said, "it's me."

Iridius smiled. "That's good." He spoke in a slow, drawling voice. "You know, you're too nice to be called Dooms."

"Well thank you, Captain," Doctor Dooms said. "Unfortunately I was born that way, it's my family name."

"No," Iridius said, his words slurring. "It's never too late to change." He paused. "Except for Rangi. It's too late for him. He's always going to be like that."

"Captain, you're still experiencing the effects of a sedative. I'm going to give you something to help clear it up."

"Can I tell you a secret though, Doc?" Iridius continued,

leaning across to speak to her even as Doctor Dooms moved to a nearby bench. "I love everybody on my crew."

"Yes, Captain," Doctor Dooms said, returning to his bedside. "We know."

"Even Rangi."

Doctor Dooms smiled. "Yes, sir," she said as she pressed a needle into his arm. "Even Rangi."

Whatever the doctor injected him with acted fast. The dirty rug of his brain was smashed a few times with a wooden bat and then all the dust began to shake free. Iridius began to parse the information coming in from his senses with a sudden clarity that had been entirely absent a moment ago. The bed he lay on. The blue walls and white ceiling. The constant sound of beeps from monitoring systems. "Am I in the med bay?" he asked.

"Yes, sir," Doctor Dooms said. "Lieutenant Commander Quinn and Ms Frost are here too."

Iridius rolled his head to the side. It was still heavy and sluggish, but at least the room only spun a couple of times before stopping. He saw Gentrix and Quinn standing off to the side, giving Doctor Dooms room to work. "Hello, you two."

"About time you woke up," Gentrix said with a smile.

"You feeling alright, Captain?" Quinn asked. "You gave us a bit of a fright back there."

Clarity began to return. "Wouldn't be doing my job as an adventuring space captain if the crew wasn't scared every now and then, would I?"

"You collapsed on the bridge," Doctor Dooms said. "Do you remember?"

"Yeah," Iridius said. "I had a massive headache and felt – well, kind of out of control, I have to admit."

"The bridge crew reported you complaining of pain and being uncharacteristically aggressive," Doctor Dooms said. "I've done a full body scan, particularly focusing on your brain and nervous system, but everything with your normal physiology is fine."

"With my normal physiology?" Iridius said. "That would suggest there's something going on with my abnormal physiology then?"

"Yes," Doctor Dooms said. "Scans showed your nanobots were behaving erratically. They were vibrating at high frequency and discharging electrical impulses that were stimulating your nervous system. Your nerve pathways would have been firing with random signals, hence the pain, and your brain activity was similarly affected, which is likely the cause of your abrupt mood change."

"So, it's stopped though?" Iridius asked. "I feel okay now. They've gone back to normal?"

"It seems to have calmed down, but unfortunately, despite being educated in more than two dozen forms of biological anatomy, I'm afraid I'm at quite a loss when it comes to nanorobotic organisms built by a long-dead civilisation. I can't say whether this is a one-off event, whether it will happen again or whether it will get worse."

"Okay," Iridius said, pushing himself up into a sitting position. "If the nanobots are outside the remit of medicine, I guess it's lucky we've got someone who's as close to an expert on the Aegix nanobots as currently exists." Iridius turned to Quinn.

"Sir," Quinn said, "I'm hardly an expert."

"You probably know more about the Aegix than anyone in the galaxy, Quinn. I'd say that qualifies you at the expert level. Besides, are you trying to tell me that when you heard my nanobots were the likely cause of my collapse you didn't have a sticky beak at what was going on?"

"Well," Quinn said, "I did have a look at the behaviour of the nanobots while you were unconscious."

"Of course you did – and?"

"And I ran a few tests, nothing too invasive."

"Hang on," Iridius said, "nothing *too* invasive? So you were doing things to me that were at least partly invasive?"

"Just some scans," Quinn said.

"Right."

"And some tissue removal for biopsy."

"Tissue removal?!"

"Yes, sir," Quinn said. "I needed to run some experiments."

"Right," Iridius said. "And you did this by removing my tissue?"

"Yes, sir."

"Okay. And where was this tissue removed from?"

"I suggested the buttocks, sir," Doctor Dooms said. "Similar to an old-fashioned removal for skin graft. I've already replaced it with synthetic skin. You'll hardly notice."

"You cut a bit of my butt off?"

"Well, it's a bit more delicate than that, sir," Doctors Dooms protested.

Iridius waited.

"But yes, sir."

Iridius looked from Doctor Dooms to Quinn and then to Gentrix. Gentrix raised her hands in submission. "Don't look at me," she said, "I wasn't involved. I like your butt."

"Quinn," Iridius said, "I'm going to let the fact you experimented on my arse go for now, so long as you actually figured something out as a result. I've had these things in my body for twenty-five years. Why would they start doing this now?"

"I'm afraid I can't be certain."

"But you've got a theory, right? You've always got a theory."

"I have a working hypothesis, yes sir. I believe it's to do with our temporal displacement. You remember how your nanobots were constantly transmitting a low-level quantum entanglement signal?"

"Yes," Iridius said, "that's how the rather annoying giant dog was able to track us through space."

"That's right," Quinn said. "So in the time since then, they haven't actually stopped transmitting."

"Yeah," Iridius said, a hint of concern creeping into his voice, "but you said that didn't matter, because the central Aegix consciousness seemed to have been destroyed. They had nothing to talk to."

"Well, we now know there are other Aegix nanobots out there – at least what's in that probe on the way to Geffet, and there may be other Aegix hidden throughout the galaxy, too. Maybe the Aegix that was unearthed at Mining Station Victoria wasn't alone. For all we know, there could be a network of Aegix waiting to spring to life."

"Great," Iridius said.

"Yes, it could be," Quinn said. "If what we believe about the Synth-Hastur is true and the Aegix are our only hope at protection, it could be great."

"I meant great like the opposite of great," Iridius said. "I meant great like, yay, more populations being turned to pink goop and planets being laid waste."

"Captain," Quinn said, "we have to believe we can solve the problem with the Aegix and use them to our advantage, otherwise we could be completely unprepared to face the Synth-Hastur. You're the one who's confirmed they're coming."

Iridius thought of that feeling he'd had, the certainty that the Synth-Hastur had arrived in the Milky Way, and the sense of utter impending doom that had accompanied it. It was a cosmic threat that he knew would probably have sent him more insane than a Haltopian Mushroom Monk, had he fully opened his mind to it.

The Aegix was nuts. It had decided it was helping by trying to turn every living thing in the galaxy into strawberry yoghurt, destroying Earth, blowing up a bunch of ships and generally causing chaos everywhere it went. Still, compared to that, he knew the Synth-Hastur was endlessly worse. The Aegix was like the annoying fly buzzing around your face while you were tied to the railway tracks listening to the clunk-a-clunk of the approaching Synth-Hastur locomotive. He knew Quinn was right. They had to find a way to get back to where they belonged and stop it.

"Sure, fine," Iridius said, "perhaps there are other Aegix swarms out there. Let's even say maybe that's good, in a tough-love kind of way. But why are mine acting up?"

"Well, my theory is that your Aegix are having a similar problem to the ship's sense of time. They are trying to communicate on what might be a wide-ranging network of other Aegix nanobots, except they are temporally displaced. They are offset in time, and for some reason that is making them unable to communicate with the rest of the network. Have you ever heard of Y2K?"

"No," Iridius said. "What is that, an energy drink?"

"No," Quinn said. "In the twentieth century there was a huge scare because computers had been coded to represent years as two digits. So, 1998 was 98, for example. There was real fear that when the year 2000 came around, computers would switch from the year 99 to 00 and internal computer dates might misinterpret that as being the first of January 1900."

"And because there were no computers in the year 1900, everything would have to stop working because otherwise that would be nonsensical," Iridius said wryly.

"Not exactly the reason, sir," Quinn said, "but I think what's happening could be analogous. Dates aren't lining up between your system and the systems they are trying to communicate with. They are sensing a malfunction and reacting to that. Perhaps struggling to adjust, or maybe even trying to shut down."

"So I'm glitching?"

"Yes, sir," Quinn said, "but I don't want you to trivialise it. Your nanobots are failing and they seem to be taking you with them. I'm afraid if we don't get back to our correct location in space–time this will keep happening. It could get worse."

"And if it gets worse?" Iridius asked.

"Well," Doctor Dooms said, "based on the reaction I observed in your nervous system and brain, it's fair to say worsening attacks will result in increased pain and more psychological effects."

"Yeah, that's not great."

"And possibly stroke, paralysis or instant death."

"Okay," Iridius said, "that escalated quickly." He rubbed his forehead. "So, if we don't get back to where we belong in time, we risk possibly altering the future and I may, you know, die in horrible pain."

"Yes, sir," Quinn said.

"Alright, well, you said there'd been attempts to time travel into the future before, using wormholes?"

"Yes, sir, but it's all theoretical."

"Well, Quinn, you better go and theoretically figure out how to get us forward ten months."

"Yes, sir."

"I'm happy to help out," Gentrix said. "My brother was the genius – psychotic of course, but still a genius. He was the one who made the breakthrough with time reversal, but I did have a hand in development. If you'll have me?"

Quinn looked at Gentrix. "Thank you but I'm probably fine."

Gentrix smiled, but Iridius could tell it was forced. "No problem."

"I'm sure Gentrix can help," Iridius said.

"She's not cleared for the ship's lab, Captain," Quinn said, giving Gentrix an even less-convincing smile. "Maybe next time."

"Right," Iridius said, suddenly feeling like he was caught in some kind of crossfire – a very passive aggressive crossfire. "You go science it Quinn, and I'll try not to let my brain explode."

Gentrix didn't say anything, but Iridius noticed the very subtle tightening of her lips.

"I'd like to keep you for observation a little longer, Captain," Doctor Dooms said.

"It's a small ship," Iridius said, turning to sit on the edge of the bed and then dropping to his feet. "I won't go far."

"Alright, Captain, but I want you to come and see me if there's any sign of agitation or pain."

"Of course, Doc." Iridius headed for the door before stopping. "Wait," he said, "did I say something about loving everybody before?"

"Yes, sir," Doctor Dooms said. "Patients are often euphoric when they wake from heavy sedation."

"And I said I loved Rangi too?"

"Yes, sir," Doctor Dooms said.

"I was confused, obviously?" Iridius said. "Sedatives make you confused?"

"Yes, sir."

"Better keep all that quiet then."

"Yes, sir."

CHAPTER TWO_

"POPPING THE CHERRY NOW, CAP," Lieutenant Rangi reported as the *Deus Ex* emerged from its reality-shredding, physicist-defying faster-than-light travel. "BAMF bubble disintegration and shield particle capture underway."

When the orange crackling light of overloading shields cleared from the viewscreen, the crew of the *Deus Ex* looked out on empty space. I mean, it's almost always accurate to say that space is empty, but this was really empty. The *Deus Ex* had emerged in rarely encountered interstellar space, the vast, almost unimaginable tracts of emptiness between star systems. There was very rarely a need for a starship to visit interstellar space. It was like pulling over on the side of a long desert highway, hundreds of miles from any town. Really, the only reason to stop somewhere like that was if you had broken down or you were planning to do something highly illegal, like cook some meth in an RV. As far as the universe was concerned, the crew of the FSC *Deus Ex* were looking very suspicious.

"This is the spot?" Iridius asked.

Quinn looked down at her console to confirm. "Yes, Captain. This is the location of the last known experiment in wormhole anomaly traversal. Directly ahead of us is the location known as the Tipler-Thorne-Gravlax-Casimir Point. It was here regular fluctuations in the quantum field were observed producing negative energy relative to ordinary vacuum. At the quantum level, this location is constantly opening and closing Lorentzian wormholes of the theorised Einstein-Rosen Bridge type. Of course, at that scale they are not traversable, but from a purely geodesic point of view they are structured without singularity and should be complete, nongravitating curved pathways. In order to be expanded to traversable size, the Einstein-Rosen Bridge must be inflated and stabilised using exotic matter with the Thorne-Morris-Vizak method, which is what earlier experiments have attempted."

Iridius stared at her. "So...yes?"

"Yes, sir."

"And just to check again, you're sure you've done all the science to understand how to inflate the whats-it with the Throne-Morris-Viking thing?"

"Inflate the quantum scale Einstein-Rosen bridge with the Thorne-Morris-Vizak method, yes, sir."

"Carried the one?"

"Yes, sir," Quinn said.

"Got your units right?" Iridius said. "Didn't use feet instead of metres or something?"

"Sir," Quinn said, "I've checked the maths multiple times, but that's not what worries me. Previous experiments have shown the method of using directed anti-matter and high-energy burst can successfully inflate and stabilise a quantum fluctuation into a full-scale wormhole. The problem is that we have no idea what happens when you fly through one. Like I said, no one has ever been able to confirm successful traversal of a wormhole, let alone show that the theory about time travel is correct. I've used all the previous research I could find to determine the amount of anti-matter to release, the size of energy input required and the angle and speed we should enter the wormhole at, but all that is based on completely unproven theoretical calculations."

Iridius took a deep breath. He pressed the comms button on the arm of his chair to open a ship-wide channel. "This is Captain Franklin, all crew to the bridge. I say again, all crew to the bridge."

Almost as soon as Iridius finished speaking, Junker spoke in reply. "Does that include us, Cap? It's just that Grantham and I are kind of in the middle of something."

"You're part of the crew aren't you, Junker?" Iridius said.

"Yes, sir," Junker replied. "Hang on." Her voice went quiet, as if she'd turned away from the comm. "No, just hold them apart Grantham. We'll come back to it later. No, don't touch the live ends together when you put them down or you'll get electrocuted. Yes. It'll be fine."

"Junker?" Iridius said hesitantly, not necessarily wanting to know the answer to his next question. "What exactly are you doing down there?"

"Nothing, Cap."

"Junker?"

"I'm just showing Technician Grantham how to re-route the main power bus with a bypass loom without disabling any ship power systems."

"That sounds dangerous," Iridius said. "Is it dangerous?"

"It's fine," Junker replied.

"It breaches several starship Health and Safety Regulations," Quinn interrupted.

"Look, stop being a terrible influence on Technician Grantham and come up to the bridge."

"Aye, Cap."

Eventually, the crew of the *Deus Ex* all gathered on the bridge. Greg, Junker, Technician Grantham and Doctor Dooms stood at the back of the bridge, joining Quinn, Latroz, Herd, Rangi, Hal, Iridius and Gentrix.

"Alright everyone," Iridius said, "we've done some dumb stuff lately, but the fact that what we're about to do is giving me pause should tell you this could be the dumbest thing we've ever done. The problem we face is if we stay here, in the past, we could alter the future, which isn't great. Also, from a purely selfish point of view, I'll probably die. Problem is, in an attempt to avoid timeline destruction and my untimely demise, we're going to fly into a wormhole with a chance we just – what?" He looked at Quinn. "Get squished? Spaghettified? Frozen? Burned? Turned inside out? Outside in?"

Quinn shrugged.

"There you have it," Iridius said. "Even Quinn doesn't know what could go wrong, and Quinn always knows what could go wrong. Basically, this is gronking crazy. As captain of this ship, and given the predicament we find ourselves in, I'm well within my rights to simply order us to open a wormhole and proceed with this entirely theoretical approach to time travel, but I'm not going to do that." He looked around at the crew. "We're going to take a vote, and I want to be clear here: there is no pressure and no judgement. This is asking more than I've ever asked of you before. So, let's have a show of hands. Raise your hand if you believe we should attempt a wormhole traversal."

With very little delay, hands began to rise all around the bridge, until every hand was raised. Every hand except that of Lieutenant Benjamin Rangi.

"Rangi," Iridius said, "I was telling the truth when I said there'd be no judgement, but of all the crew I'm surprised it's you."

Rangi looked around at everyone else on the bridge, his face scrunched in confusion.

"Sorry," Rangi said, "did you say raise your hand if you *do* want to do this or you *don't* want to do this?"

Iridius sighed. "I said, raise your hand if you *do* want to try and time travel."

"Oh right, sorry," Rangi said. "In that case," his hand shot up into the air, "Geronimo!"

Iridius shook his head. "Sometimes I wonder how you even manage to get out of bed in the morning, Lieutenant."

"I do try and make it difficult for him, Captain," Latroz said.

"Oh good."

"Because of sexual interc—"

"Yes!" Iridius said, cutting her off. "Yes, I understand, Latroz."

"She tries to trap me with her wormhole," Rangi said, smirking.

Iridius stared at Rangi and for a brief, but very real moment, wondered if perhaps this ship being spaghettified by a wormhole might be for the best.

"Quinn," he said, trying to get things back on track, "over to you."

"Okay," Quinn said. "In order to open the wormhole we need to launch a barrage of nuclear missiles set to detonate at the location of the Tipler-Thorne-Gravlax-Casimir Point. That provides a local energy rise that increases the offset between negative energy fluctuations and positive energy, creating a macroscopic Einstein-Rosen Bridge. But it will only exist for fractions of a millisecond. We need to provide a stream of exotic energy to keep it open. For that, we need to vent anti-matter from the BAMF drive."

"Sure," Iridius said. "I completely understand."

"You do?"

"We blow up space and then we shoot our engine at it and it stays blown up for some reason."

"Well," Quinn said, "more or less."

"Let's do it then," Iridius said. "I mean, when the least risky part is firing nukes randomly into space and tampering with our engine, we might as well get it over with."

"Aye, sir,"

Quinn began giving orders to the crew in preparation for opening the wormhole. She sent a calculated entry trajectory to the helm and explained the necessary timing for nuclear missile launches to Latroz. It didn't take long before Quinn turned to Iridius and declared they were ready. The crew returned to their stations, the *Deus Ex* was positioned exactly where Quinn's calculations had determined it should be, and Junker and Grantham had been sent down to the engine room in preparation.

"Alright then," Iridius said. "Do it."

Quinn turned to Latroz. "Are you ready with the firing solution I determined, Lieutenant?"

"Yes, ma'am," Latroz said. "A salvo of eight missiles spaced at zero-point-three-eight second intervals, ready to fire on your mark."

Quinn nodded. "Excellent." She pressed her comm. "Junker, are you ready to override the venting safeties for the engine?"

Junker's voice came back over the comm. "You know that breaches several starship Health and Safety Regulations, ma'am."

"There's no other way, Junker," Quinn said. "I have the captain's authorisation—"

"Relax, ma'am," Junker said. "I'm just shiftin' your gears. It's already done."

"Done?" Quinn replied. "You've disabled one of the primary engine safety features already?"

"Yes, ma'am," Junker said. "First thing I did when we got this new ship was make a patch panel where I could switch off any safety features I wanted."

"I'm sorry," Iridius said, jumping into the conversation. "You did what?"

"It saves time for situations like this, Captain. You're always asking me to disable critical safety systems."

"I am not," Iridius said.

There was a moment of silence. "Do you want the safety overrides off or not?"

"Yes, Junker," Iridius said. "Stay down there and make sure we don't explode or something."

"Aye, Cap."

Iridius looked at Quinn. "We all set?"

Quinn nodded.

"Moment of truth then, XO."

Quinn took a breath. "Latroz, fire the salvo."

"Missiles away."

Exactly as Quinn had specified, eight precisely timed missiles launched from the *Deus Ex*.

"Venting anti-matter," Quinn announced as she pressed a button on her console.

The bridge crew watched the view-screen as the missiles exploded in soundless bursts of white-hot nuclear fury, one after the other, in a quick succession that built to a crescendo of light. This was joined by the venting spray of anti-matter particles from the ship's BAMF drive. Despite what most special effects might have you believe, the anti-matter being pumped from the ship was invisible; no beam of blue light or wildly colourful expository display took place to make it clear that science-fiction fuel was pouring out into space. The only confirmation that the anti-matter was being vented was that the computer said the door was open.

As the Tipler-Thorne-Gravlax-Casimir Point fluctuated to negative energy and a quantum scale wormhole began inflating with excess energy from bursts of nuclear fission, the anti-matter particles stabilised the growing wormhole. Instead of popping out of existence, the wormhole grew, constantly increasing in size, ballooning out until it had reached a maximum diameter determined by the energy differential in the localised region of space – just under six hundred metres across, in this case. Local space–time was bent into a curve, gently at the edges and then increasing in curvature until it completely inverted near the centre of the wormhole.

Matter and energy flooded in and out of the sudden opening in space, colliding and bouncing to release bursts of energy. Light itself bent and twisted under complex gradients of gravity, causing a myriad of different wavelengths to be released.

That's the scientific explanation, but to those watching on the bridge of the *Deus Ex* – apart from Quinn, who actually understood what was going on– it was a dazzling light show unlike anything they'd ever seen. It was a massive, hypnotic swirl of colour, like water draining out of a bath after an overly expensive rainbow bath bomb. The wormhole fizzed and churned with colour, zaps of light flashing away into space. But the centre the wormhole was black, a hole in space and yet simultaneously, a sphere that glowed with the energy coming through from the other side, the place where the wormhole emerged somewhere else in the universe.

"Woah," Rangi said.

"Wormhole established," Quinn said. She looked at Iridius. "We should be able to enter, Captain."

There was a moment of quiet on the bridge as the crew stared at the wormhole.

"Sir?" Quinn said.

"Hmm?" Iridius would have said he'd been observing the phenomenon, ready to react to any danger, but the truth was, he was transfixed by the sparkly lights.

"Captain," Quinn said.

This time Iridius managed to pull his attention away from the mesmerising show. He turned to Quinn. "Right, yeah, sorry," he said. "Let's get it over with then."

"No, it's not that, Captain," Quinn said. "It's this."

Quinn's fingers flicked over her console and the image on the view-screen changed from the wormhole they'd been looking at to something that looked altogether similar, but wasn't exactly the same. Where the previous wormhole had appeared unruly, a jagged, fluctuating drain hole swirling in space, this was calmer. It still had the glowing black spherical hole in the centre, but the halo of colour around it was much steadier – a ring of light rather than a turbulent spiral.

"What is that?" Iridius asked. "Another wormhole?"

"I believe it is, Captain," Quinn replied.

"Did we somehow open another one?"

"No," Quinn answered, "I don't think we had anything to do with this one. It's located off our port side, several dozen kilometres away from the Tipler-Thorne-Gravlax-Casimir Point. Besides, this wormhole is giving off much less energy. It's significantly more stable."

"Someone else opened this," Gentrix said. "Someone who knows what they're doing."

"I believe so," Quinn said.

Iridius was about to ask who this someone else might be when the universe pre-empted him.

"Sir," Latroz said, "I'm picking up a ship signature, but there's no sign of a BAMF bubble. It's coming from that new wormhole."

Sure enough, after a moment the bow of a ship appeared in the centre of the wormhole, poking out from the black sphere. The emerging shape was rimmed in a halo of light that rippled out across the surface of the sphere, like white ripples in an inky pond. Soon, the entire the ship had pushed through.

Given the widespread use of BAMF drives, the crew of the

Deus Ex were more than used to seeing ships appear in space, but the popping of a BAMF drive was different. In that case, the ship appeared complete in an instant. The appearance of this ship was much more visceral, more organic in a weird sort of way. It was as if the ship was squeezing its way through, pushing through the fabric of reality in a way that looked distinctly uncomfortable.

"Well," Rangi said, "I've never seen space give birth before."

Iridius looked at Rangi. "Honestly, Lieutenant, no one else in existence is able to insert an unwanted image into my head as effectively as you."

"Thanks, Cap."

"Not a compliment."

Iridius turned his attention back to the ship that had emerged from the now distinctly cervical-seeming wormhole. It was the strangest ship Iridius had ever seen – certainly not a Federation or even a Planetary Alliance design. It was a long cylinder, like a cigar, completely grey. There were no windows or protrusions of any kind along the main hull. The engines were housed at the back, tucked in together like an ancient rocket. There was very little to distinguish the ship as anything other than a tube, but it wasn't smooth, it had a strangely bumpy and mottled surface that seemed almost organic, like a tree trunk. It looked like something that had been grown as much as made. The front of the ship was the only part that broke the cylindrical shape as it ballooned out into a bulbous front end.

"It's a boy!" Rangi called from the helm.

Iridius turned to Latroz. "Latroz, what have we got? Any ID on this ship?"

"None, Captain," Latroz said. "Completely unknown ship signature."

"It's a boy, get it?" Rangi said. "Because it looks like a massive flying—"

"Yes," Iridius interrupted. "Thank you, Rangi. We all see it. Ensign Herd, can you hail them?"

"No need, Captain," Ensign Herd said. "They are hailing us right now."

The long cylindrical ship turned slowly on the view-screen, rotating until the bulbous front pointed ominously at the *Deus Ex*. Well, maybe not ominously, but definitely uncomfortably.

"You can play it bridge wide, Ensign," Iridius said.

"Greetings, vessel *Deus Ex* of Federation Space Command." The voice that came across the bridge was loud, not aggressive but oddly enthusiastic, as if excitedly greeting a long-lost friend. The voice also had an accent, which was strange. Well, the accent itself wasn't strange – it was an accent that would be familiar to anyone with a passing knowledge of Earth history. It was a British accent, the generically neutral kind heard in any historical film set just about anywhere from the eighteenth century through to the twenty-first.

What was odd about it was that in the twenty-third century, nobody actually had an accent anymore – or at least, they all had the same accent, which is essentially the same thing. Sure, there were a few oddities and dialects scattered throughout the galaxy, but on the whole, Galactic Standard Language was so homogeneous that there was almost no discernible difference in accent for tens of thousands of light years in any direction.

"I am hereby officially informing you that you are in breach of section three hundred and sixteen point three two point one of statute seventeen of the code of the regulatory order of universal time."

There was a mumbled voice in the background of the transmission.

"Yes, yes, and its associated by-laws," the voice finished.

Iridius looked over at his second-in-command. "Friends of yours, Quinn?"

Quinn returned his look with her standard unimpressed-and-unwilling-to-acknowledge-his-jokes face. "I have never heard of the regulatory order of universal time, Captain."

"No," Iridius said, "I didn't think so, because it sounds completely made-up." Iridius pressed the comms button. "This is Captain Iridius B. Franklin. With whom am I speaking and, more importantly, what exactly are you talking about?"

"Ah yes, Captain Franklin, I apologise. I, of course, know who you are but you will not yet be familiar with me or my organisation. It gets tricky to remember the order of things after a while."

Iridius waited a beat, but when no further explanation came, he prompted. "So, are you going to tell me who you are?"

"Yes, yes," the voice answered. "Plenty of time. Always plenty of time." The voice quietened, as if speaking to someone else. "Could you set up a holographic projection link please, Mrs Holloway?" The voice returned to full volume. "I'll come across and make an introduction face-to-face, Captain Franklin. I much prefer that. Give me one moment."

"First I'd like to know your intentions," Iridius said.

There was no reply.

"They've disconnected, Captain," Ensign Herd said.

"Right," Iridius said. "I assume we can expect them any—"

Iridius's question was answered before he'd finished speaking it as two people appeared on the bridge right in front of the view-screen. They were both human, a man and a woman. The man looked to be in his mid-forties and was tall and thin. He was dressed in a tweed jacket, waistcoat and tie and was even wearing one of those flat-caps in matching tweed. Iridius thought he looked like one of those people who went out to shoot birds for no good reason and then got their dogs to go and do the actual work. The woman who stood beside him looked older, maybe in her sixties or seventies. She was short and, while not rotund, she was certainly solid, like a grandma who'd be able to lay a decent rugby tackle. She wore a muted grey skirt suit but had added a splash of colour with a pink scarf which, considering the rest of their attire, might just have been a little radical.

"Hello," the man said. "Do not be alarmed. We are here only as holographic communication projections and have not boarded your ship in a hostile manner."

"Right," Iridius said. "I mean, yes I know. I've even done that before."

Iridius had heard the man say they were going to set up a holographic projection, but the images in front of him were much clearer than the ship-to-ship projection he'd seen of himself from the future. These holographic projections had none of the hazy transparency of the ones he'd seen – in fact, they were so sharp that Iridius, though he wouldn't admit it, had for a moment thought two people had just appeared on his bridge, as though they had some kind of transporter on their ship and could just beam themselves around space, which was frankly just a ludicrously impossible idea.

"I didn't think you had holographic projection yet?" the man said. He turned to the woman beside him. "Do they have holographic projection now, Mrs Holloway?"

"It's in early stages of development," the woman said. Her voice was raspy and slow, but still distinctly British. "Not widespread yet."

"Well, goodo," the man responded, as loudly and enthusiastically as ever. "I'm glad we didn't give you too much of a start, then. Tends to rattle people from older time periods when we just appear in front of them."

"I can imagine," Iridius said. "So, are you going to tell me who the gronking hell you are now?"

"Gronking hell," the man said. "A slang colloquialism of this time, I gather. Terrific. I like that one. Gronking. I don't think I've heard it before." He turned to Mrs Holloway. "Write that down will you, Mrs Holloway?"

Mrs Holloway looked at the man wearily. "Fine."

"Good, good, thank you, Mrs Holloway, that way I won't forget."

Mrs Holloway sighed as she removed a small object from her pocket and flipped it open. At first Iridius thought it must have been some form of tablet computer, but when she took a pencil from her pocket and scribbled on the lined page he saw that it was an actual paper notebook.

"I collect words, you see," the man said to Iridius. "Fascinating, the words you run into on your travels. People are pretty much the same whenever you go, but words are delightfully varied and strange."

"Here's another bit of slang for you then," Iridius said, his patience rapidly vanishing. "What the fuck is going on?!"

"Oh no," the man said, "fuck is very universal. A great word, isn't it? Very emotive and flexible, but hardly unique to now. I don't think any word has lasted or continues to last in quite so many times as fuck. Fuck this. Fuck that. Fuck you. Fuck off. Get fucked. Oh fuck. Brilliant, isn't it?" Iridius went to speak again, but the man raised his hand. "Yes, yes. I see you are getting impatient. Always in a rush. There's plenty of time, you know. You should have realised that, with what you've been through so far. All the time in the universe."

"I take it back, Quinn," Iridius said. "This guy isn't one of your friends. From the amount he talks, he's clearly related to Rangi."

"Not that I'm aware of, Captain Franklin," the still infuriatingly unnamed man said. "I'm not aware of any relation to anyone on your crew, but who knows. We're all related in the end, us humans, aren't we Mrs Holloway?"

"Yes."

"Top shelf then," the man said. "Let's get on with this intro-duction then, shall we?"

"Good god, please," Iridius said.

"Yes, yes, Captain Franklin. My name is Reginald Benedict, Deputy Director of Regional Operations for Milky Way Segment 2B for the Department of Historical Timeline Preservation, and this is my Executive Assistant, Mrs Holloway."

"Assistant Deputy Director, actually," Mrs Holloway said.

"I'm sorry." Iridius stared at the man. "Did you say the Department of Historical Timeline Preservation?"

"That's right."

Iridius turned to Quinn, who obviously knew what he was about to ask. "I've never heard of any Department of Historical Timeline Preservation either, Captain," she said.

"Quinn is an expert in science," Iridius said, "and also boring government departments, so if she hasn't heard of it, I'm going to hazard a guess that it doesn't exist."

"We do and we don't," Benedict said.

"Right, that's meaningless isn't it?"

"Mrs Holloway?" Benedict prompted.

Mrs Holloway sighed with the resignation of someone about to deliver an oft-repeated explanation, and then commenced in a bored monotone. "In terms of linear timeline reference, the DHTP hasn't been founded in your present time, but its mandate extends backwards in time, allowing for operation pre-DHTP founding for necessary preservation activities."

"Alright, listen," Iridius said. "Like my mum said when she walked in on my dad with three women and a pile of cash, I'm going to need a bit of an explanation here."

"By the book please, Mrs Holloway," Benedict said.

Mrs Holloway sighed again and turned, her holographic projection vanishing for a moment before reappearing with a book in hand. She opened to a marked page and began to read in the same slow monotone. "Hello. You are currently being visited by officials from the Department of Historical Timeline Preservation. Following the advent of time travel and the discovery of meta-time, the Department of Historical Timeline Preservation was founded to ensure continuity of a historically accurate timeline. A historically accurate timeline ensures the safety of individuals in all times throughout the universe by avoiding changes that would cause dramatic differences to one's quality of life, such as altering one's socio-economic status or ceasing to exist. Your actions, accidental or otherwise, have been found to be in breach of section three hundred and sixteen point three two point one of statute seventeen of the code of the regulatory order of universal time and its associated by-laws. You can be provided with a full list of your rights and responsibilities under the regulatory order of universal time by contacting a local representative and submitting form 361. You have been found to have performed," Mrs Holloway paused as she referred to her notebook, "one count of opening an uncontrolled wormhole and one count of being temporally misplaced. These actions have resulted in a category five temporal risk, which may result in extensive timeline damage. The officials from the Department of Historical Timeline Preservation will answer any questions you may have about the necessary preservation actions, which have been determined to be," she looked at her notebook again, "complete destruction of your ship and the death of all sentients aboard. Please respond to declare your understanding."

"Wait a second," Iridius said.

"Thank you for your cooperation," Mrs Holloway finished and then snapped the book closed.

Iridius stared at Benedict and Holloway. He had a sudden, almost overwhelming urge to laugh. This had to be a joke. Surely toy dogs controlled by a crazy alien intelligence and a Hawaiian shirt-wearing sociopath with a time-bomb was enough absurdity for any one career in Space Command? But now he was faced with what seemed to be bureaucratic time police who looked more like a crusty academic and his mother.

"No," Iridius said. "I asked you to hold on a gronking second. What are you on about? We are already back in time and we've opened the wormhole to try and get back to where we're supposed to be in order to *avoid* damaging the timeline."

"Yes," Benedict said, "I do understand that, but using an uncontrolled wormhole such as this is too risky. It's a big no-no, really. You could end up anywhere. Besides, the fact that you are currently temporally misplaced and yet to disrupt the timeline means the easiest solution is to destroy you, I'm afraid."

"You can't," Iridius said.

"Do we have the paperwork, Mrs Holloway?"

She nodded. "Form 27A, signed in triplicate."

"Well, there you go, jolly good. All seems in order for us to remove you from the timeline."

Iridius turned to Latroz. "Shields?"

"Full, Captain," she replied.

"Bring weapons online."

"Aye, sir."

Iridius looked back at the holographic projection of Reginald Benedict. "We won't go without a fight."

"While Mrs Holloway and myself might not be, I can assure you this vessel and its weapons are from a far more advanced time period than yours. Your primitive shields and weapons will not protect you. I mean, we've already filled out Form 27A. Not much we can do about it now."

"You've already filled out—" Iridius stopped himself. He'd dealt with enough people like this in Space Command to know that arguing wasn't going to change their mind any more than pissing in the ocean would change its flavour. "Okay, if you're so keen on preserving the timeline, hear me out. This is going to sound arrogant, but the truth is, ten months from now I might be the only hope the galaxy has. An entity called the Synth-Hastur is coming to, from what we can gather, wipe out all life. I have nanobots inside me that might be the key to fighting them and saving everyone. If you're into saving lives, then help us get back to the future. You can obviously travel through time. If using this wormhole is so dangerous, show us how to get back safely."

"I can see why you're concerned about the Synth-Hastur. They certainly are something of a bummer," Benedict said. "But the correct historical timeline includes the Synth-Hastur cleansing the galaxy."

"What?" Iridius said. "So you're just going to let them kill everyone?"

"It's not really a matter of letting it happen, Captain Franklin," Benedict said. "It does happen. If it's any consolation, there's no point worrying about it any more than about any other tragedy in what you consider history. Are you worried about the residents of Pompeii, or the population of Mandor Trivani? A devil of a thing to happen to them, no doubt, but not much that can be done."

"If the Synth-Hastur kill everyone in the galaxy," Quinn said, "then where are you from?"

"London, my dear," Benedict said. "I was born in 1915 but was plucked away by the DHTP after some business in the forties. Been doing this for a long time now. Anyway, glad we could explain everything in person. I much prefer any subjects of preservation be aware of the reasoning. Farewell. Well, you're not going to fare well, actually. So I guess goodbye is more appropriate."

The holographic projections vanished.

"Captain," Latroz called. "The ship seems to be firing up some kind of energy weapon. Massive surge of power."

On the screen, the end of the phallic ship had begun to glow.

Arcs of energy crackled over its surface. It was clearly building up for a massive discharge, which was neither an image nor an outcome Iridius wanted to be exposed to.

"Latroz, red alert," Iridius said. "No way we're going down to this prick."

"Which prick, the ship or that weird guy?" Rangi asked.

"Either," Iridius said. "We're going for the wormhole. Latroz, lock weapons. Hal, get us on Quinn's programmed trajectory. Rangi, be ready to take manual control for evasive manoeuvres."

"Can I say Geronimo, Cap?" Rangi asked.

Iridius sighed. "Fine."

"Geronimo!"

CHAPTER THREE_

THE *FSC DEUS EX* accelerated from full stop to full fusion power. At the same time, manoeuvring thrusters fired, the high velocity ejection of gas turning the nose to align with the trajectory Quinn had calculated for wormhole traversal. Theoretically, this would send them safely through the wormhole and out the other side.

Unfortunately, the only time Quinn had been less sure of her calculations was that time she'd spent all semester trying to determine whether Helen Grant from her astrophysics class would agree to go on a date with her. Quinn had tried to parse every interaction and every conversation she'd ever had with Helen Grant. She'd even written a short algorithm in an attempt to determine the most probable outcome, but ultimately she'd been unable to reach a satisfactory conclusion.

In the end, based on her data and calculations, she had determined there was a sixty-two per cent chance that if she asked Helen Grant on a date, she would say yes. Sadly, she never got a chance to test her theory because by the time she'd done these calculations and had worked up the courage to actually ask,

Helen Grant had transferred to another university. Quinn never saw her again.

Just as she had been then, Quinn was relying on a lot of previous observations, incomplete mathematical models and a bunch of unverified assumptions, and this time she couldn't even estimate their chance of success. According to all the previous research on wormhole traversal, the trajectory they were on should allow them to pass through the centre without touching the sides. The size of the wormhole they had created plus the calculated entry speed should send them forward in time ten months, to the exact moment they'd been flung backwards by the time-reversal bomb. She still had a lot of questions but at least, unlike with Helen Grant, this time she'd find out if she was right.

The cylindrical ship turned to track the *Deus Ex* as it gathered speed, the bulbous front end crackling with an overwhelming gathering of energy.

"Captain," Latroz said, "charge rate of that weapon is slowing. I anticipate it firing any moment."

"Rangi, evasive manoeuvres!"

Rangi had anticipated the order and was already in manual control of the helm. He pushed the *Deus Ex's* nose down into a hard and fast roll, diving the ship and changing the cross-section in view of the charging weapon.

The front of the DHTP ship released the charged energy in a directed burst. A line of blue-white energy shot forward, like high-pressure water from a hose, a continuous stream. Rangi's quick evasion had been barely enough; the bottom of the energy beam missed the *Deus Ex* by mere metres, which in terms of inter-ship space combat was like a bullet whizzing past your head with a millimetre to spare – not exactly a reassuring margin. Plus, it was a very science-fiction weapon that would probably do something much worse than a bullet, like rip the ship apart at the atomic level or something.

"The energy weapon has missed us, Captain," Latroz said. "Barely. It should have made contact with our shields but seemed to pass straight through. I do not believe Mr Benedict was exaggerating when he claimed the potency of their weaponry."

The beam of energy that had barely missed them suddenly stopped, but Iridius knew that simply meant they were recharging for another attack.

"Latroz," Iridius said, "any idea what that beam would do to us if it hits?"

"Not really, Captain," Latroz said. "I've never seen a weapon like it before."

Benedict's cheerful voice came over the bridge speakers. "I'm not entirely sure how it works, Captain Franklin, but my understanding is that our high-energy molecular disassociation ray would rip your ship apart at the atomic level. Very clean that way, you see."

"I knew it," Iridius muttered under his breath. Raising his voice, he said, "Kindly don't eavesdrop please, Mr Benedict. I'm not particularly interested in further conversation with you."

"Yes, well, jolly good and have it your way. Fact is, I'm quite surprised we missed. As you would say, big ups to your pilot." Iridius could hear Mrs Holloway murmuring something in the background. "Oh is it?" Benedict said. "Right. Well, apparently I've got the wrong time period for that colloquialism, Captain Franklin. Not to worry. We won't miss again. Toodle pip."

"Ensign Herd, find a way to block that pompous twat from butting in with his babble, if you don't mind."

Rangi rolled the ship again, changing altitude and speed, attempting to present an unpredictable target.

"Get us into that wormhole and do it quickly," Iridius said.

"We have to hit it at the right speed, Captain," Quinn said. "If we enter the wormhole and we aren't at the correct speed I can't say what might happen."

"Well," Iridius said, "I know what's going to happen if we don't get into that wormhole, so I'm willing to take the chance."

"Sir," Latroz said, "I think the enemy is preparing to fire. They do appear to be tracking us more closely this time, despite Benjamin's evasive manoeuvres. I believe we will struggle to evade."

"Rangi," Iridius said, "full power towards the wormhole. When we approach, do your best to slow and match Quinn's calculated speed, but get us in."

Iridius took a deep breath, then closed his eyes and reached out with his nanobots. This action was almost second nature now, as ingrained as if he was reaching out with his own hand. His relationship with his nanobots had never been easy, and he still wrestled with the pros and cons of having these tiny bugs crawling around inside him.

He'd resented them at first – well, actually, he hadn't even known they were there for most of his life, but he'd resented the effect they had in causing technological malfunctions all around him. That was most certainly a con. But then he'd found a way to harness them to help save the galaxy, which probably classified as a pro. Of course, they were still part of the threat he'd had to save the galaxy from in the first place, so that was a con. He'd figured out how to suppress them, which he'd thought was a pro at the time, but then they'd stopped working, which had been a con when he'd been imprisoned by a maniacal Hawaiian shirt. He'd reached some kind of acceptance after that, which was a pro, but now they were back in time and the nanobots were freaking out to the extent that they were going to kill him, which was the mother of all cons as far as he, and his desire to be, you know, alive was concerned. Despite all that, Iridius knew it was time to bring out the big guns – or the nanosized guns, as the case may be.

It was easy enough to sense the cylindrical ship. The huge

amount of energy building in the terribly inappropriately shaped front end was like a beacon to his nanobots, like a phosphorescent flare burning in the night sky. Iridius forced his attention away from the growing energy charge and onto the ship itself. It immediately felt different to any other ship Iridius had sensed before. He wasn't an engineer, and he certainly wasn't an expert on the layout of ship systems, but every other time he'd connected with a ship, from the smallest missiles, to the Aegix dog-ship, to Devin Frost's *Neverlander,* it had been relatively simple to latch on to whatever he needed to control. It was instinctual. Weapons, shields, engines, control systems, they were all clearly laid out, relatively easy to find and manipulate. But this ship was different. It was like there was no clear delineation between ship systems, the whole thing was a complex network of pathways jumbled together, like tangled strings spreading throughout the ship. It was like staring at the web of strings on the corkboard of some insane conspiracy theorist. It was like veins. No, not veins, a nervous system.

Holy shit.

Iridius suddenly realised why this ship felt so different. It was still a ship, it still had technology he could interact with, but it was absolutely, most definitely, alive.

"Enemy ship ready to fire," Latroz called. "They still have us locked."

"Cap," Rangi said, "I can't shake them."

Alive or not, Iridius had to do something. He pushed the probing reach of his nanobots into the web of the living ship. *Come on. Just have to find a way to hold up that weapon for a moment.* The complexity was almost overwhelming. Previously, the nanobots had seemed able to parse things for him, quickly identifying and rationalising which systems to hack in order to accomplish Iridius's goals, but here even they seemed to be struggling with the saturation.

This was like that time he and April had gone to Callisto for a relaxing weekend away and April had found a jigsaw puzzle she thought would be fun, except when they'd opened it they'd discovered it was a ten thousand piece puzzle of the image of a tabletop completely covered in the pieces of a ten thousand piece puzzle. They'd stared at it for a few moments before the sheer impossibility of it had sunk in. To her credit, April gave it a fair crack, managing to get four pieces together. One match was luck and the other was because she completely lost it, screamed and jammed in a piece that obviously didn't fit. Eventually, she had silently packed away the jigsaw and gone out to join Iridius, who'd left as soon as he'd seen the abomination and was drinking a mimosa on the balcony.

Luckily for Iridius, his nanobots were more like April, and were willing to at least attempt to unravel the puzzle of the enemy ship. After a moment he felt the tug of something, some vague but possible connection to the ship's enormous energy weapon. Iridius pushed at it, demanding it to shut down. He didn't quite manage to switch it off – he could feel it pushing back – but at least for now there was a game of tug-of-war as Iridius held on and the ship pulled hard. Iridius didn't think he could hold out for long, but at least the ship seemed unable to fire while Iridius held firm.

"It's holding charge but not firing," Latroz said.

"Is that you, Captain?" Quinn asked.

Iridius grunted with the effort. "Just," he managed, "get in the wormhole."

"The quickest way in is to stop evasive manoeuvres and get back on the planned trajectory, Cap," Rangi said. "But if they manage to fire..."

"Do it," Iridius said.

"Aye."

Rangi ceased dodging and strafing and turned the ship back

towards the wormhole, , pushing the throttle back to maximum fusion drive.

"Lieutenant Rangi," Quinn said, "make sure you're at the right speed when we cross the threshold."

"I'm on the right trajectory, ma'am," Rangi said. "I've got time to hit the brakes hard."

Iridius's muscles were twitching wildly. They buzzed and shook to the point where he thought they might shake off his bones. He felt a rolling pain up his spine and then, just as had happened before, his head erupted in agony, as if someone had cleaved it in two like a breakfast grapefruit. Iridius hated grapefruit. He tried to hold onto the small amount of control he had over the DHTP's energy weapon despite the excruciating sensations flooding his body.

Ordinarily, Iridius liked to promote a sense of calm serenity on the bridge. But if there was one thing that didn't promote calm serenity it was a screaming captain. Whether his guttural scream was from pain or just a powerful release to try and help him focus, he didn't really know. Probably both.

"Iridius!" Gentrix said, rushing to him. She reached out to touch him but he flinched away.

"Sorry. Just, let me..." His voice trailed off. Iridius felt his hold on the energy weapon slipping. The pain was making it hard to concentrate. "How...long?" he managed to ask.

"Approaching the wormhole," Rangi said. "By the time I slow to Lieutenant Commander Quinn's speed it'll take us ten seconds to get inside."

Something unique seems to happen to the brain during moments of immense pain. I don't mean that sweary shouty moment of agony after you stub your toe on the leg of the couch. I mean the kind of overwhelming pain that can only come from inside.

Iridius's nervous system was on fire. It was unwavering.

When you face a pain that seems endless, it isn't that the pain gets worse so much as your ability to cope with it weakens. Eventually the walls of your fortress begin to crumble, and as they do the pain floods in – to the point where pain is no longer something you experience but instead becomes what you are. When you reach that point, the operating system of your brain crashes. You cannot think, you cannot reason. Your highly evolved intellect goes the way of the blue screen of death. Your brain has run into a problem, has stopped responding, and needs to restart.

Iridius could feel that happening to him now. It had happened the first time his nanobots had gone into revolt. He'd felt as if he was losing control, and eventually the pain had grown too much and he'd fainted. He'd lasted longer this time, perhaps aided by the knowledge that he had to hold back the DHTP's energy weapon, but he knew he wouldn't last much longer. He wouldn't last ten seconds.

"Faster," Iridius said, unable to utter more than a single word.

"I'll push it, Cap," Rangi said.

The *Deus Ex* sped towards the wormhole.

"Rangi," Quinn said, "we need to slow down."

"Iridius?" Gentrix said. "He's fading!"

Iridius barely heard what was going on around him. There was nothing but the pain, and the knowledge that he had to hold back the weapon aimed at his ship. His eyelids were drooping, his head dropping forward, heavy on his shoulders. Any moment he would lose his tentative grip on consciousness.

"Rangi!" Quinn called. The black sphere of the wormhole lay before them, surrounded by the halo of swirling colours.

"Hitting the anchors now," Rangi said.

Rangi worked the controls of the ship, sending it into full reverse by shutting down the fusion drive and firing all front-facing thrusters with a full power burn, desperately trying to slow to the speed Quinn had calculated. As he did so, Iridius slumped forward and toppled off the captain's chair, landing, once again, unconscious on the floor of the bridge.

"Weapon firing," Latroz reported.

The DHTP ship released its high-powered energy weapon which, just as they had promised, was not going to miss this time. It flared out towards the *Deus Ex* in a bright beam and hit directly on target. Fortunately for those aboard the *FSC Deus Ex*, who didn't particularly want to be disintegrated into their component atoms, at the moment the weapon fired, they were crossing the threshold into the unknown adventure of wormhole travel.

CHAPTER FOUR_

IRIDIUS FRANKLIN HAD BEEN unconscious for several important moments in his life. On his very first day of school, determined to demonstrate his playground skills, he'd climbed on top of the monkey bars and proceeded to jump from one rung to the next. He'd wound up unconscious in the school sick bay. During the first meaningful conversation he'd had with April Idowu, which he perhaps should have remembered as when he'd first fallen in love, he'd been so hungover that he'd passed out on one of the lounges in the student common room of the Academy. When the *Diesel Coast* accelerated dramatically out of the way of hundreds of missiles, he'd blacked out and missed the start of a space battle for the fate of the galaxy. He'd also been knocked unconscious inside an escape pod at the end of that same space battle. His ship was now one of the first to enter a wormhole in an attempt to time travel to the future, something that might have been considered not just a milestone for himself but a milestone for human spaceflight in general, and he was, once again, unconscious.

Luckily, for posterity's sake, the rest of the bridge crew were wide awake to experience the phenomenon of time travel.

"Wormhole penetration," Quinn declared.

"Terrible phrasing," Rangi replied, but his comment was all but lost as the bridge erupted with alarms. Not even a mammoth Franklinism had caused so many alarms to sound on the bridge of a starship at once. Everything seemed to be howling. The ship's computer, already confused enough at being sent ten months back in time, suddenly had every sensor overwhelmed with inputs of chaotic gibberish. Gravity, light, time, the fundamental dimensions of space – everything had suddenly become meaning-less. Every system, from the galactic reference frame navigational super-computer, to the matter-antimatter Bedi-Alcubierre-Millis-Formelge drive, to the system that made the little pinging noise when you received a notification, were all throwing up warnings.

What the crew saw out the view-screen didn't provide any further clarity. It was probably for the best that Iridius, someone who nearly vomited every time he saw a ship engage its BAMF drive, was passed out, because the view outside was at best confusing, and at worst, utterly nauseating.

They were definitely in a tunnel, that much was clear. However, that was where the similarity to anything rational ended. Rather than appearing like a solid shape around them, the walls of the tunnel were more like the swirling, spiralling waters of a drain or whirlpool. But instead of water, what was spinning around them was, somewhat alarmingly, everything.

Stars and galaxies, all the universe, all of everything twirled around them, interspersed with absolute nothingness. They were travelling through a swirl of creation and abyss. It was as if the universe twisted around them so intensely that every so often they could see tiny tears form in reality, and there was a very real sense that if they hadn't entered the wormhole at precisely the right position and angle, they might very easily have slipped out one of those cracks.

As gravity and speed and the spinning funnel around them warped everything, there were flashes of celestial objects in every possible colour and what might be described as anticolour, too – not a lack of colour, but something more akin to the afterimage left burned across your vision when you accidentally look at a particularly bright light, like idiot world-leaders who stare at eclipses or welding torches. The only thing missing was a wicked witch flying past on a bicycle.

Needless to say, it was a hell of a ride, and while Iridius definitely would have vomited, most of the crew weren't immune either. It was Quinn who went first. She clamped her hand over her mouth in a futile attempt to hold it back, causing the rush of unwanted ejecta to spray through the gaps in her fingers like the world's worst multi-directional fountain.

Some of what left Quinn's mouth sprayed onto Latroz's console and splattered in droplets over the helm and also the backs of the helmsman. Latroz looked down at the chunks on her console and sniffed. As a Siruan, toughest and most unflappable of the species in the Federation, she would absolutely not— but it was too late. She felt hot bile rise in her throat and turned as discreetly as she could to vomit beside her console.

The usually stoic Ensign Herd went next. He too attempted the classic vomit-block with the same resultant spray through his hand before he gave up and lifted his shirt to catch the mess. As one of the Babel Cult, Herd was almost always silent, other than when his duties deemed it necessary for him to speak. He was however, as it turned out, an extraordinarily loud vomiter.

Gentrix turned away, closing her eyes and trying to avert her attention from the view-screen and the equally unpleasant scene unfolding on the bridge around her. She breathed in through her nose and out through her mouth in a moment of inward focus and managed to keep her breakfast in its rightful place.

Rangi felt the gathering saliva in his mouth. As a pilot, he was well attuned to complex motion and never suffered from motion sickness. Even the swirling chaos of the wormhole with its unfolding colours and tears in reality didn't make him feel queasy. No, for Rangi, it was the smell. It had always been the smell, ever since he was a child. He very rarely felt nauseous, but the acidic stench of other people's fresh vomit had a way of burrowing down into his own stomach and making it determined not to miss the party. Rangi put his head between his legs and retched.

Most of the bridge crew were too concerned with the amount of semi-digested food exiting people's bodies to notice that their swirling journey through the wormhole had come to an end. On the view-screen in front of them was the black of interstellar space. Nice, empty black space – not flashing or bubbling or spinning around.

"Wormhole trajectory complete," Hal said from where he sat at the helm, apparently unaware of the carnage all around him. Not being biological, he had been completely unaffected by the traversal. Now, though, when no one acknowledged his words, he looked around. The bridge crew were slumped in their chairs, groaning, or leaning on their consoles, wiping their pales faces clear of strings of sticky saliva and vomit. Hal turned to look at the puddle at Rangi's feet and then at each of the others on the bridge. "Ah," he said. "Shall I get a mop?"

Iridius stirred and opened his eyes. "Goddamn it," he said, grasping at his head as he sat up, "my head is killing me." He looked around the bridge, trying to get his bearings. "Did we make it?" He sniffed. "And what is that smell?"

Hal soon returned with a mop and bucket, cleaning cloths and disinfectant and began, without complaint, to mop and wipe up the half-digested contents of his fellow crew members' stomachs. Ordinarily one to tell Iridius off for treating their resident android as something of a service bot, even Quinn was happy to hang back and let Hal complete the unenviable job.

Once the bridge had the aroma of a freshly scrubbed hospital ward and Iridius's painkillers had dulled the pounding in his head, the crew set about taking stock of the situation.

"Alright," Iridius said. "Damage report?"

"Shields and weapons are online, Captain," Latroz said.

"We've got reports of minor structural damage, but nothing to be concerned with," Quinn said. "Still carrying engine nozzle damage from the *Neverlander* battle, but that doesn't seem to have progressed. Our biggest issue is that we appear to have lost our BAMF drive."

"How extensive is the damage?" Iridius asked.

"I'm not reading any physical damage," Quinn said, "But we've somehow lost the ionic matter-antimatter catalytic reaction." She pressed her comm. "Junker?"

"Here, ma'am. What's up?" Junker replied.

"Can you confirm there's no damage to the BAMF drive?" Quinn asked.

"Can do," Junker said. "I was just looking at it. There's no damage that I can find. The fire's just gone out. I've never seen that before."

"Alright," Iridius said, "so the drive itself should be operational but we've lost the reaction that uses ion beams to split photons into the matter and antimatter we use for fuel?"

Quinn stared at Iridius for a moment.

"Don't look at me like that," Iridius said. "Believe it or not, I did graduate from Space Command Academy, and starship captains are expected to know the basic details of how starships work."

"I told him about the matter-antimatter creation reaction back on the *Diesel Coast*, ma'am," Junker said over the comms.

"Yes, alright Junker," Iridius said. "Fact is, if the drive is fine, can't you just re-light the fire?"

"Um, not sure I can, Cap," Junker replied. "I don't have the right matches."

Iridius looked to Quinn for an explanation. "The ionic matter-antimatter catalytic reaction is never supposed to go out, Captain. Once it's started, it's supposed to continue. As long as there is a supply of ions continuously firing into the high-energy chamber, fields of electromagnetic energy will be accelerated into each other and split into matter and anti-matter, which is then stored for annihilation during BAMF bubble creation. It shouldn't be able to just stop. That's like a fire just spontaneously going out even though there's a good supply of fuel and oxygen."

"Right," Iridius said. "Fusion drive is operational though, so we're not completely dead in the black?"

"Yes, Captain but it'll be linked to around eighty per cent operation at most. When the fusion drive is pushed to maximum, it's boosted by power siphoned from the catalytic reaction use for the BAMF drive."

"Okay," Iridius said. "We'll deal with that problem later. Next thing: we made it through the wormhole as expected?"

"Yes, sir," Quinn said. "Although, looking at the trajectory data, we were travelling at a velocity three per cent higher than desired."

"Right, well, how bad could three per cent be?" Iridius asked. "Which brings me to the question we're all desperate to know the answer to: *when* are we?"

"Yes," Quinn said, "yes, about that."

Iridius stared at his XO. She stared back.

"Quinn?" Iridius said.

"Yes, well, remember when I said we would have to hit the wormhole at exactly the right trajectory and speed?" Quinn said. "We didn't."

"Yes, I know," Iridius said. "We were three per cent too fast. The thing is, if we were three per cent slower we would be one hundred per cent dead. And like I said, how bad could a three per cent difference be?"

"Well, it's not necessarily a linear relationship, Captain. Just because we were three per cent off in speed doesn't mean we'll end up three per cent off our destination."

"Right, so *when* are we?"

"I've been comparing star patterns and known astronomical conditions to past times in an attempt to determine exactly when we are," Quinn said in that sometimes-frustrating way she had of answering a question without answering it. Iridius knew what that meant.

"You don't know, do you?"

"Well, it's more that I haven't got an accurate temporal location at this stage, but I'm still working on it."

"Quinn," Iridius said, "I've told you before, it's perfectly acceptable for you to simply tell me that you don't know. I know I lean on you for answers a lot, but I don't expect you to necessarily always have them. We make the best of what information we've got."

Quinn nodded. "Right, yes, sorry Captain. I, um, I don't know."

"Okay, see, that's fine," Iridius said. He knew it probably wasn't fine, but he wasn't going to tell Quinn that right now. It wasn't that they didn't know when they were in the usual way, like when you wake up momentarily confused and struggling to remember what day it is. This was much worse. "Let's start by figuring out where we are, can you tell me that?"

"Yes, Captain. We're outside the Sol system," Quinn said. "One thing I can be confident about is that we definitely went back in time because Earth isn't, you know..."

"Burning."

"Yes, Captain. I just haven't been able to match astronomical data to a particular point in time..." Quinn's voice trailed off in the I've-just-had-an-idea way. "Unless..." She looked down at her console and began pressing buttons.

"Unless what?" Iridius said, but Quinn didn't answer. "You know, you always do this, trail off halfway through a sentence. It's very annoying."

"Oh dear," Quinn said.

"See, then you always come back and say something like 'oh dear' or 'fascinating' or 'remarkable', and in all our years together not once has anything good come from that. So what does 'oh dear' mean in this situation, Quinn? Is it, oh dear, we've arrived exactly where we expected or maybe, oh dear, we missed by a tiny bit and now it's your birthday, happy birthday Captain?"

"I had to expand the search window," Quinn said. "I was focused on what I'd considered a reasonable error range, but apparently that wasn't enough." She paused. "We've gone back to Galactic Central 2015 point 10 point 34."

"You know I'm bad at date conversion but that sounds like quite a long time ago," Iridius said. "I'm going to assume you've already converted that to an Earth date for us?"

"Yes, sir," Quinn said. "It's, uh, 1943, sir."

"1943."

"Yes, sir."

"We wanted to go forward ten months and we've gone back three hundred years?"

"290 years, yes, sir."

"To 1943?"

"Yes, sir."

"Cool," Iridius said. "Cool cool cool."

CHAPTER FIVE_

REGINALD BENEDICT, the Department of Historical Timeline Preservation's Deputy Director of Regional Operations for Milky Way Segment 2B, stood on the bridge of his ship, *Argona*. Although he refused to think of it as *his* ship. Technically the ship belonged to the Department of Historical Timeline Preservation, but that wasn't why he didn't think of it as his. It was because *Argona*, as Iridius Franklin had realised when he'd reached out with his nanobots, was very much alive.

Argona was a Leviathan, a race of space-faring creatures from beyond the Milky Way that the DHTP used as spacecraft. The unique way the Leviathans perceived time made them, with the addition of some wormhole generation equipment, able to navigate both space and time.

The relationship between Reginald Benedict and *Argona* was more of an intimate partnership than the traditional distinction of a captain and their vessel. Besides, *Argona* would certainly get annoyed if Benedict went around acting like she belonged to him.

So, Benedict stood on the bridge of *Argona*, not his ship but his partner, and stared at the curving view-screen in front of him.

He watched the wormhole that had been created by the *Deus Ex* as it began to spiral around, growing smaller and smaller, a puncture through reality, shrinking like a deflating balloon.

Benedict had seen enough wormholes in his time that it didn't even seem out of the ordinary now. He reflected momentarily on the fact that a hole in the very fabric of the universe no longer made much of an impression on him. He supposed it showed that people could just about get used to anything. He was proof enough of that. He'd come from the early twentieth century, when his family marvelled at the transition from radio to silent movies and from horses to the motor car. Now, he wasn't even fazed by standing on a starship and having a discussion with a Melopian, a race of beings that had to turn themselves inside out every twelve minutes in order to regulate their temperature and to fill their tissues with oxygen – something that was accompanied by a horrendous amount of blood. After everything he'd seen throughout space and time, not even the flashy lights and mind-twisting display of a disintegrating wormhole impressed him.

Eventually, the wormhole grew too small to see and soon, with a tiny pop and a burst of light, ran out of energy and winked out of existence altogether.

"Well, gronking gronk," he said, "I do believe we missed. Bit of a gronking shame, that."

"Must you use that word, Mr Benedict?" Mrs Holloway asked.

"Oh yes, got to. Key to expanding one's vocabulary, Mrs Holloway. When you learn a new word you must attempt to use it in context regularly. Only way it really gronking sinks in there," Benedict said, tapping his forehead.

"I think it may get gronking annoying is all, Mr Benedict."

"Ha! Jolly good show, Mrs Holloway. Now you're getting it!"

Argona's bridge was small, there was little in the space but the view-screen and a few chairs in front of some monitoring stations. There was no helm, as on a standard starship. *Argona* didn't need one, after all – she simply flew through space as her species had evolved to. The view-screen, the chairs and the few scattered stations had all been added for the benefit of the crew that rode along inside her.

In the centre of the space was a large fleshy mound, a complicated pattern of folds and furrows over its surface, the whole thing covered in a slick semi-translucent grey substance. It looked a lot like a massive brain. That was because it was just that, *Argona*'s brain, and what had been named the bridge was really just a section excavated out of *Argona*'s skull.

It wasn't just the major ship systems like the wormhole generator, weapons and shields that had been added to *Argona*. Everything required to turn her from a living organism to an occupied, time-travelling starship had to be engineered and fitted: life support, food supplies, waste disposal and everything else necessary for a crew. The changes to *Argona* were so widespread and overwhelming that it changed the very essence of what she was.

Benedict looked at the floor, where the chairs were held in place by bolts penetrating down into *Argona*'s bone. His eyes traced the edges of the view-screen where it had been pressed into her flesh, scar tissue formed in layers around the outside. The corridors they walked down had been cut with large cauterising drills. Even the signs on the walls were tattooed in place. The whole conversion was as if a human had been partially rearranged internally, with some parts hollowed out, chairs and conveniences stapled down inside for tiny people to live and work while guiding the human around as if it were nothing more than living transportation.

And here was the real issue, the real reason Benedict could never consider *Argona* as his ship: he knew these additions to

Argona's body were not voluntary, and they went deeper than even what could be seen on the surface.

Argona's brain shuddered, a sign that she had entered her more centralised, interactive state. Rather than being distributed through the entirety of the ship, she was now present on the bridge. This made it much easier for her to communicate with any other sentient beings, and also much easier for them to communicate in return, as it gave them somewhere to focus their attention, but it did leave her feeling a little claustrophobic, and meant she was not as attuned as she'd like to everything going on in her body.

A voice came from somewhere near the brain, something that had been synthesised through speakers because *Argona* did not otherwise have vocal cords. Her chosen voice was female, to match her chosen gender identity, and it was a voice so sweet to Reginald Benedict's ears.

"I did not enjoy that, Reginald," *Argona* said. "He took control of my systems. It was very uncomfortable holding an energy burst that long and not being able to release it. I could not carry out your orders, and the pain of the harness was extreme."

"Yes, sorry about that dear," Benedict said. "I was aware of Captain Franklin's nanobot abilities but I didn't realise they would work on you as effectively as they do on other ships. You know me – the technological side of things soon goes over my head."

"It was in the briefing information," Mrs Holloway intoned in her slow, raspy voice.

"It was?" Benedict said. "Ah, well, terribly sorry about that."

"The nanobots in Captain Franklin's blood are designed to combat the Synth-Hastur, which are part organic, part technological life forms in a very similar way to *Argona*, so it makes complete sense that he would be able to affect her in the same way," Mrs Holloway continued.

"Ah yes, you're right as always, Mrs Holloway. Best press on though. Not much we can do about it now. Can't just change the past, can we?" Benedict laughed at his own little joke, just as he always did. "Well, we can, but we can't go doubling back on our own timeline like that. We haven't got the paperwork."

"Indeed," Mrs Holloway said unenthusiastically.

"At least we know where they're going," Benedict said.

"Yes," Mrs Holloway said. "We do."

"Reginald," *Argona* said, "a probe wormhole is opening."

Sure enough, a small wormhole appeared on the view-screen. It was much smaller than either the *Deus Ex*'s wormhole or the one *Argona* had emerged from. A probe pushed its way through the surface of the black sphere at the centre, and with some puffs of its small thrusters it came to a stop, holding its position half in and half out of the wormhole.

Despite all the advanced technology at the disposal of the Department of Historical Timeline Preservation, they could no more communicate across time than you could ring yourself up yesterday to let yourself know to watch out for that dog poop you accidentally put your hand in when you sat down at the park or to, you know, try and stop some other major disaster like World War Three or something, depending on how ambitious you're feeling.

So, in order to communicate with agents spread across time, the Department used probes they called pigeons, like the messenger birds of old, to fly into a wormhole and stop halfway out the other end. In this way, the probe could be used to transmit and boost communication from DHTP headquarters to their agents wherever they may be in the space–time continuum.

The headquarters of the Department of Historical Timeline Preservation was strategically positioned about one and a half trillion years in the future, because there was nothing like the peace, quiet and infinite safety of a government office in a universe heading inevitably towards heat death. In fact, having their headquarters located at a time when almost no life exists, the stars themselves had begun to burn out and the movement of atoms in all matter was slowing to a grinding halt put them in the same state as most government buildings.

"Is it Director Kron?" Benedict asked.

"Yes," *Argona* replied. "He is requesting to speak to you."

"Tell him I'll contact him shortly."

"I do not believe that will satisfy him, Reginald," *Argona* replied. "He is demanding to speak to you right now."

"Very well," Benedict said. "I suppose I'd better speak to him now then."

A figure appeared on the bridge standing between Benedict and the view screen, a holographic projection of Director Kron piped through the pigeon probe from where he stood in his office, a dozen light years away in spatial distance, but more than a trillion years away in temporal distance. Director Kron, Benedict's superior at the Department of Historical Timeline Preservation, was a Melopian and so was naked but for what looked like a clear plastic body bag.

Not that there was anything to see that might make a human embarrassed. The Melopians were one of several races with no external genitalia, and given their need to invert their bodies regularly, traditional clothing would have been quite a hindrance. Kron's torso was covered in small holes with little hairs around the outside, like a hundred tiny nostrils.

"Deputy Director Benedict," Kron said in a deep voice that was probably best described as phlegmy, "you were told to stop the target before they proceeded back in time through that unauthorised wormhole. You know I had reservations in tasking you with this, but you assured me that intervening would not be a problem. I'm expecting a good explanation."

"Director Kron, jolly good to see you. Things didn't quite go according to plan here, no, but I will fill out a Form 22C After Action Incident Report," Benedict said. "Let you know all the details."

"No," Kron barked. "You will explain yourself now."

Benedict's eyes went wide. "You don't want me to fill out a Form 22C? That is most unprecedented."

Kron made a grunting noise. Benedict knew what that sound meant. "One moment," the Melopian said before his grunts became a strange gurgling cry. Kron's torso began to open down the centre, the skin splitting like a peeled orange. He gave a momentary exclamation of pain, and then with a snap both sides of his torso flicked back, turning inside out. With a wet splash, the plastic bag he stood inside was covered in a light spray of blood. The breathing pores that covered this side of his body opened, ready to take in air until they dried out, when Kron would need to invert once again. After a few seconds of recovery while his skin stitched itself together at the back, Kron wiped down the front of the bag, clearing his view.

"Of course you're going to need to fill out a Form 22C," Kron continued, as if his entire body hadn't just ripped open and popped inside out like an umbrella in a strong wind. "This isn't some reckless outfit where you can go off without completing a 22C like some kind of hooligan. You're going to fill out a 22C, but you're also going to tell me what happened right now, because believe it or not I have a 16F to complete for the Executive Management Team."

"It's simple really," Benedict said. "My fault entirely. I under-estimated the effect Captain Franklin's nanobots would have on *Argona*. Didn't expect he'd be able to disable her weapons like that."

"It was in the briefing information," Kron said.

"It was?" Benedict said. "Ah, well, terribly sorry about that."

"You should have known that your vessel could be compromised by the nanobots in Captain Franklin's blood, Deputy Director Benedict. In fact, I'm inclined to believe you did know that."

"I assure you, Director Kron," Benedict said, "it was simply an unfortunate event. A mistake."

"A mistake, was it?" Kron said.

"Yes, Director Kron, a mistake," Benedict said. "A bit of a whoopsy-do."

"It's lucky we know where he's going then, isn't it?" Kron said.

"Yes," Benedict said. "I suppose we should head there then, 1943 wasn't it?"

Kron stared out at Benedict through the blood-smeared plastic of his bag. "You're well aware of his destination, Deputy Director. Do not think I don't know what you're doing. The only reason I have not yet filled out a 44B to report my suspicions of your intentions is because you have been an effective and reliable agent up until this point. But if you continue with what you are attempting, I will have no recourse but to do so."

"I'm sure I don't know what you mean."

"You were given your orders, Reginald," Kron said. "You were long ago informed that your current timeline would be assimilated into the meta-past, and that it falls within your jurisdiction to undertake the preservation actions necessary to correct your own timeline. Your life must return to that deemed historically accurate by the Executive. Your desire to protect your current time state is ultimately pointless, and will have no effect on you anyway. You will proceed to Earth and you will eliminate Captain Franklin prior to the events that deviated your personal timeline. If you fail to do this, you will be eliminated and we may have to erase this time state you seem so fond of through infinite loop regression."

"I am committed to achieving my objective, Director."

"Yes," Kron said. "That's what I'm afraid of. Go to Earth and eliminate the timeline threat or you will also be treated as a threat."

The holographic projection of Kron vanished from the bridge.

"*Argona*, would you prepare for a jump to Earth?" Benedict said.

"Of course, Reginald."

"Local date 22nd of November, 1943."

"Programming underway."

Benedict turned to Mrs Holloway. "Why don't we get some rest, Mrs Holloway? We'll jump in the morning."

"I am perfectly ready to jump now, Mr Benedict."

"I have no doubt you are always raring to go, Mrs Holloway, but truth is I could do with a good night's sleep. You know what they say, time waits for no man...except if you're in the DHTP."

Mrs Holloway gave Benedict an unimpressed look, only marginally more noticeable than her resting unimpressed face, then turned and left the bridge.

Reginald Benedict waited for what he thought was long enough before he spoke to *Argona*. "Is she gone?"

"She's in her quarters, Reginald," *Argona* said. "We are alone."

"Good," Reginald said as he began taking off his clothes, stripping off his tweed until he was in his underwear. He pulled these off too until he was standing completely naked on the bridge, then he approached the oddly throbbing brain of the ship, which had turned a brighter shade of pink. He pressed himself, completely naked, onto *Argona*'s fleshy brain. "I won't let them split us up, my love," he whispered, wrapping his arms and legs around the slick, pulsating fatty tissue. "I'm not going to let them."

"I hope you're right," *Argona* replied. "If this works then we'll be free to stay together and maybe, after so many attempts, my people can be free too. Thank you for doing this, Reginald."

"Of course," Benedict said, "I love you."

"I love you too."

Reginald Benedict pushed himself into the folds of the giant ship's brain as he proceeded to engage in what I can only imagine is the weirdest sex scene you've ever come across – maybe. I don't know what you're into. Reginald Benedict and *Argona* really did have an intimate partnership. It was also a partnership that Benedict was desperate to hang onto, and Captain Iridius Franklin was the key to ensuring that he could.

CHAPTER SIX_

Iridius was sitting in the captain's chair on the bridge of the *FSC Deus Ex* when Earth came into view. They had popped out of the wormhole just beyond the outskirts of the Sol system, but without a BAMF drive they had been forced to crawl the entire distance into the system under fusion power – a trip that had taken almost three weeks. Given it was 1943, they were still travelling at speeds unimaginable to current humanity. In this time period, humans had yet to even reach low Earth orbit because, as Iridius remembered from history class, they were currently too busy trying to wipe themselves out in the second of Earth's three great wars. But, by 2234 standards, travelling at this speed felt like pulling a fighter jet with a team of donkeys.

Unsurprisingly, it was Ensign Rangi who handled their cripplingly slow speed the worst. He sat at the helm with little to do but constantly complain about how slow they were moving, as if that was going to help the situation. His leg incessantly bounced, and when it didn't, it was only because he was pacing around the bridge. Iridius was tempted to ask Doctor Dooms to give Rangi some of that sedative, just to calm him down. Apparently though, as resident regulations expert Lieutenant Commander Quinn informed him, a ship's captain was not authorised to request specific medical treatment for a crew member, they could only refer them to the ship's doctor.

Luckily, Iridius had managed to keep Rangi otherwise occupied by having him run Junior Ensign Hal through a series of simulations covering extremely high-speed evasive manoeuvres within an asteroid belt. This worked well enough, because if Iridius knew one thing about pilots it was that their brains were relatively easy to occupy for a few hours. It only took some bright and loud activity —or you could just make them stare at a picture of themselves, like a mirror in a budgie's cage.

Initially, the Earth was little more than a shining speck amongst the black, but as they drew closer the view-screen magnified it enough to provide a clear view of the planet.

"Well," Iridius said, "would you look at that? Earth."

"You going to tell us what a shithole it is?" Quinn asked.

"Actually," Iridius said, "it looks quite beautiful doesn't it?"

"Right," Rangi said. "Good one, Cap. We all know you're about to say something like it's beautiful...a beautiful turd."

"No," Iridius said. "I'm serious."

Maybe it was just that Iridius had possibly been somewhat partially responsible for the Earth being turned into the boiling ball of flame and lava that it was in the future, but looking at it now, unburned, a swirling blue and white sphere of brightness and life, he truly was struck by its beauty. It also helped that it wasn't yet surrounded by space stations, a veritable swarm of satellites and the accumulated detritus of hundreds of years of space flight.

Plus, at this time in history the world wasn't completely ballsed up. In Iridius's time you could basically smell the pollution through the vacuum of space. But in the mid-twentieth century there was still a chance they could have avoided the runaway effects of climate change if they hadn't become so focused on war, money and buying shoes with the right words printed on the side. It also struck him that right now, in this time, humanity was nowhere else in the cosmos. They hadn't yet spread out into the cracks and crevasses of the galaxy like a glass of milk dropped onto a tiled floor. He felt a little like he imagined other people felt when they looked at a baby, seeing something so vulnerable and full of potential.

When Iridius looked at a baby he just saw something stinky and full of unwanted responsibility. He found himself thinking about whether April would have wanted children in another life, and then caught himself. Gentrix was standing only metres away and he still wasn't convinced she couldn't read his mind.

"Lieutenant Commander?" Rangi asked. "I know last time he turned into a bit of a psycho, like a whole Captain Jekyll and Mister Hidden thing, but is it possible one of the side effects of Captain Franklin's nanobots going crazy is that he gets nicer?"

"I don't believe so, Lieutenant," Quinn replied.

"Excuse me," Iridius said. "First, it's Doctor Jekyll and Mister Hyde, and second, I can be nice. I'm nice all the time."

"I'm your girlfriend," Gentrix said, "and the first time we met I'm quite sure you thought I was a supervillain and probably would have killed me given the chance. Not that I would have given you the chance. You did hit me with a stun baton, though."

"You're a member of the Alliance who was developing a time-reversal bomb," Quinn said. "I'm sure whatever happened was justified."

"*Was* a member of the Alliance," Gentrix retorted. "I'm not anymore, Kira, as we've discussed plenty of times."

"Alright," Iridius said. "That's enough."

Gentrix had been aboard the *Deus Ex* for almost a month now, but Quinn still didn't trust her. Iridius was pretty sure the rest of the crew had come around but Quinn, it seemed, could not be convinced. Iridius was in two minds about this. Firstly, he was annoyed, because he'd told her to stop being so combative with Gentrix all the time, but secondly, he was a little bit proud of Quinn, because she'd never been willing to be combative with anyone before.

"Gentrix is here under the refugee accords," Iridius continued. "There's no way she can return to the Alliance. Besides," Iridius said, returning his attention to Gentrix, "it was Mudd who stuck you with his baton."

"Phrasing," Gentrix said. "He only stuck me with his baton once, you've already stuck me with yours more than that. More than that just last night, in fact."

Despite doing his utmost not to, Iridius blushed.

"I'm pretty sure it's Jekyll and Hidden," Rangi said, "because he stays hidden inside him."

"It's not, and can we get back on point please?" Iridius said. "I was simply admiring the Earth two hundred years ago. It's not often you get to go back and see something untouched like this."

"At this moment in history, planet Earth was in the midst of a conflict resulting in an estimated sixty million deaths," Hal chimed in.

"Can't have everything perfect all the time though, can you?" Iridius said. "Ups and downs, swings and roundabouts. The Second World War is the entire reason we've come to Earth, though."

"Apart from it being close and not having a BAMF drive, you mean, Cap?" Rangi said.

"Yes, apart from that. The point is, Quinn has a plan to reboot the BAMF drive. Would you care to explain?"

"It's quite simple, Captain," Quinn said. "In order to fly faster than light and to attempt to open another wormhole, we need the ionic matter-antimatter catalytic reaction to be restarted. In order to do that, we need a significant input of energy, and there's a chance we could use some technology currently being developed on Earth – the atomic bomb."

"Right," Iridius said. "So what we're going to do is enter Earth's orbit and send an away team down to Earth to secure an atomic bomb. Then we can use that to reboot the matter-anti-matter reaction so we can make ourselves another wormhole and get back to our correct time so that I don't die, we don't damage history, we can warn the galaxy about the Synth-Hastur, and hopefully not run into any more of those plaid-covered Historical Timeline Preservation weirdos."

"Cap?" Rangi began in that partly confused tone that told Iridius a question, possibly stupid, probably annoying, was coming. "If we go down to Earth and steal an atomic bomb, isn't that going to change history? I thought we wanted to avoid that?"

Iridius had to admit that, for once, Rangi's question wasn't that stupid. It was the exact same concern Iridius had raised with Quinn when she'd come to him with this suggestion.

"No need to worry about that, Lieutenant Rangi," Iridius said. "We've thought of a solution that should let us get our hands on an atomic bomb without disruption to the timeline." By which he meant Lieutenant Commander Quinn had thought of a solution.

"But what about the butterfly effect thing?" Rangi asked. "The Mega Butterfly of Doom? Isn't there a chance someone squashes a bug and suddenly everyone in the future ends up with brain tentacles or six heads or something?"

"No, Rangi," Iridius said, "that's ridiculous. There's no way that could happen." He paused and turned to Quinn. "Right?"

"Right," Quinn said. "I don't think millions of years of human evolution is going to be changed in 1943."

"See, Rangi? Ridiculous."

"Although, if we had been temporally displaced back far enough it may be possible that a small action could dramatically change the course of evolutionary history. It's an interesting thought experiment," Quinn said.

"Fascinating," Iridius said. "But let's focus on how we can get away without ruining the future, or history, or whatever."

"Firstly," Quinn said, "we can't guarantee we won't change anything. In fact, we likely will change something. All we can do is try and limit our influence."

"And you've got an idea how to do this?" Gentrix asked.

"Yes I do," Quinn said, in the tone she seemed to reserve solely for Gentrix. "We have the benefit of having access to the historical record, so we know what's happening at this moment in history, whereas the people living through this time obviously don't, particularly because during the Second World War each side was deliberately trying to keep technological advancement from the other."

"Ah," Latroz said, "the fog of war, most glorious."

"Yes, well I wouldn't say war is glorious, Lieutenant," Quinn continued. "Far too many innocent people die in conflicts like these."

"Yes, Lieutenant Commander," Latroz said. "It is not honourable when the innocent are killed." She paused. "But in battle it is glorious."

"Lieutenant—" Quinn began, but Iridius cut her off with a raised hand.

"Quinn, it's not worth it. Trying to tell a Siruan that war isn't a good thing would be like trying to convince Greg that chocolate isn't delicious."

"Chocolate *is* delicious," Greg said. "It is the greatest export from Earth to the galaxy. It is the knee of the bees. It is the pyjamas worn by the cat. It is the tits of the mother cancer."

"Alright Greg, we get it," Iridius said. "Can we focus on the exposition here? You guys are getting even more distracted than normal."

"Yes, Captain. So at this time our understanding is that Nazi Germany was more advanced than the Allied forces in the development of the atomic bomb."

"Nazi Germany," Rangi said, turning to look at the viewscreen. "That means...that means Hitler is alive right now, down there. Captain, are we going to kill Hitler?"

Iridius stared at Rangi. "No. We're not going to kill Hitler."

"But that's what you do if you go back in time to the Second World War. You try and kill Hitler."

"Rangi," Iridius said with what he believed was the patience of a saint, "the whole point is to try and avoid drastic changes to history."

"Right, yeah. S'pose that might change a few things."

"Please continue, Quinn," Iridius said.

"So, Nazi Germany are more advanced with their nuclear research in 1943. But we know that historically, Germany never developed an atomic weapon. It was the Allies who dropped two atomic bombs on Japan in 1945. Our thinking is that if we go down to Berlin we can, um, acquire enriched uranium-235, or hopefully even a prototype bomb. If we do it as stealthily as possible and limit interactions with any people of the time, by taking the technology from the side that lost the technological race anyway we should avoid major ramifications to the timeline."

"This ship is armed with nuclear weapons," Gentrix said. "Why not just use our own?"

"Well, simply put, our weapons are too advanced. They are eighth generation shaped charge nuclear warheads designed for highly directional detonation to impart maximum point loading on ship's shields, or to penetrate deep into exposed hull. In order to kickstart the matter-anti-matter reaction we need complete spherical detonation with wide energy dispersal. It would be very dangerous to attempt to alter the nuclear weapons we have on board to accomplish this."

"Junker did offer," Iridius said, "but that might be a little too much danger even for her. Plus, the resulting explosion wouldn't just take out a few minor ship systems, like the last one she caused. Bottom line is, we're going down to Earth. Myself, Quinn, Junker and Rangi will be the away team and," Iridius turned to Gentrix, "Gentrix, if you'll join us."

She nodded. "Always liked a period drama."

"Sir," Latroz said, "I would like to raise an objection to you and the away team entering a war zone without my assistance."

"I understand your concern, Lieutenant Latroz," Iridius said.

"And I would also like to go to a war zone."

"Yes," Iridius continued, "I know you see war zones as vacation destinations, but the fact is, the people of 1943 Earth aren't aware of seven-foot-tall alien warrior women from a distant star system. You'd stick out more than Rangi at a Mensa meeting."

"What?" Rangi said.

Iridius ignored him. "I need Quinn to come so she can determine what we need to bring back with us, and probably to help stop me getting one of us erased from the future or something." Iridius paused. "You don't happen to have German heritage, do you Rangi?"

"No, sir," Rangi said. "Dutch and New Zealand Māori."

"Shame," Iridius said, turning his attention back to Latroz. "You're going to have to stay here, Latroz, I'm giving you command of the ship while I'm gone. I know it'll be your first time taking the conn, do you think you can handle it?"

Latroz nodded. "Of course, sir."

Iridius thought for a moment. "Do you think you can handle it without getting the ship into combat?"

Latroz took a moment too long to consider this. "Yes, sir."

"Ensign Herd," Iridius said, turning to the transhuman

communication officer. "Obviously we're going to Germany in 1943 and none of us speak German. I'm hoping you can help with that?"

"Certainly, Captain," Ensign Herd said. "I can give you a UTI if you'd like?"

Iridius stared at Herd. "Sorry, did you say a UTI?"

"Yes sir."

Iridius continued staring at his Communications Officer without moving. "A U...T...I?"

Ensign Herd, apparently confused at his captain's reaction, nodded and then responded equally slowly. "Um, yes sir. A Universal...Translation...Implant."

"Right," Iridius said. He opened his mouth to comment on yet another in a long line of terrible acronyms, but decided it wasn't even worth bringing it up anymore. "And that'll allow us to communicate?"

"It will translate spoken German for you directly in your mind, but it won't automatically translate anything you say back into German. That would require much more extensive augmentation that Doctor Dooms wouldn't be able to fit as easily, and she likely wouldn't feel comfortable performing that level of transhuman modification."

"I suppose that will have to do."

"Zum glück kann ich Deutsch sprechen," Gentrix said.

Iridius turned to her in surprise.

She smiled. "Luckily, I can speak German."

"You can speak a classical Earth language?"

"Passably," Gentrix said. "We were made to study an old Earth language as kids. Devon chose Spanish, I chose German. Never thought it would be useful."

"That's great. I knew there was a reason you joined us," Iridius said.

"Because you got me exiled from the Alliance and we have great sex."

Iridius blushed again, something he was sure he'd never done quite so much in his life as he had since he met Gentrix Frost.

"Sir," Quinn said, "I don't think Miss Frost should be on the away team. She's not a member of the crew."

"Quinn, drop it. She's part of the crew now. Let's find the least twenty-fourth century clothing we can and get ready to head to Berlin, 1943."

"Sweet," Rangi said. "We're probably going to get to punch a Nazi."

"No, Rangi," Iridius said. "The idea is to not engage with anyone in the past. We're definitely not going to punch any Nazis."

CHAPTER SEVEN_

MEANWHILE.

Well, not exactly meanwhile, because the scene we're cutting to is happening 290 years in the future, but for the purposes of narrative convention we'll go with meanwhile – or maybe futurewhile? In-a-while? Thenwhile? Look, all this time travel business has put us in uncharted tense territory, so we'll just have to do our best to keep this all straight in our heads.

Meanwhile, in the future, a shuttle from the *FSC Gallaway* had spun violently out of control and plummeted to the rocky surface of Acacia, one of the partly terraformed moons of Geffet. This, as you might recall, was a shuttle piloted by Captain April Idowu, who had taken a solo flight down to the moon to try and secure a sample of the Aegix nanobots that had been released from the crashed probe that escaped way back in book one, back in those simple days when we were only concerned with saving the galaxy and not all the implications of time travel and whether you're clever enough to write your way out of this absolute mess.

Luckily for April, her shuttle had come down in one of the thorny tangles of branches that passed for plant life on the moon. The sporadic plant life that had sprung up on Acacia since its terraforming was sparse, inedible and almost entirely comprised of spiny leaves and sharp thorns, despite there being absolutely no animal life on the planet to need protection from. As Iridius Franklin might have said, the plants on Acacia were about as useful as a screen door on a space shuttle. However, for the single occupant of the crashed shuttle, the woody, thicket-like scrubs of Acacia had proved extraordinarily useful.

April groaned as she came to. She was still strapped into the pilot's seat and slowly, as if she'd just woken up after a night out drinking with a Siruan, it took her a long, painful moment to remember where she was and what had happened.

She could remember triggering the Rat Trap and successfully securing a sample of the Aegix. Soon after that, she'd lost all engine power and attempted to pulse the magnetic containment field around the engine's fusion reaction.

The result had been a brief but potent plasma ejection out the rear of the shuttle's main engine. April had felt the immense acceleration, heard the wailing alarms. The fact that she was waking up at all meant the magnetic containment field must have successfully re-engaged, because otherwise there would be less of her left than if she'd taken a spacewalk into the sun.

The manoeuvre had kept her aloft, but the altitude proximity alarm had howled and the imminent collision warning screamed as she'd hurtled towards the domed roof of one of the colonies.

The shuttle had impacted at an angle and sent her spiralling across the landscape, a landscape that quickly faded as the wild acceleration vectors caused her to pass out, despite her flight suit's best attempts to keep blood in her brain.

Once these recollections had flooded back, what followed was a jolt of panicked concern. She leaned forward, only then realising that the nose of the shuttle must have been pointing up as gravity pinned her back in the chair. There was still auxiliary power to the computer systems, and she quickly brought up the patched-in data about the Rat Trap. It was still intact and sealed. She mentally thanked Ish Kaku and Kira Quinn for their excellent work.

She flicked the display panel across to the shuttle's damage report. As expected, the main engine nozzle was completely destroyed. In fact, health monitoring of most engine systems was non-responsive, which generally meant the engine, monitoring sensors and all, was completely destroyed. Magnetic containment and the fusion reaction remained operational, but the engine system beyond that was trashed, which meant any possibility of controlled thrust was gronked.

The damage report also showed the shuttle hull had been ruptured in multiple places. Apparently some ship systems had come back online, probably once she had increased her distance from the Aegix, because the emergency stabilisation thrusters had eventually fired, which would have slowed her descent somewhat – but apparently not enough to keep her from crashing.

With no main engine and multiple holes in the hull, this shuttle was not getting back into space. In pilot's slang, her shuttle was a smoking hole – a spacecraft crashed and inoperable on a planet or moon. On the upside, this was better than the other dead ship possibility, that of being adrift and powerless in space. The slang for this was, tellingly, being on a 'corpse course'.

April turned, looking behind her in the direction of one of the reported ruptures in the hull. There was a clear puncture in the floor, through which she could see the thorn-covered branches of the hardy tree that had managed to arrest the shuttle's tumbling descent before it hit the rocky surface.

Leaning back in the chair again, April took stock of her own health. She felt a little bruised, but mostly only where the harness had held her tight in the chair during the wild flight. She had a pounding headache, which was not uncommon after an acceleration-induced blackout, and she needed to pee which, while uncomfortable, she knew to be a good sign.

Her flight suit and helmet were sealed and intact. Her suit's information declared that she was low on oxygen and that, as a precaution, the suit had begun to cycle in external atmosphere. But if the shuttle hull was damaged, this meant she would be exposed to the moon's atmosphere. She quickly checked the atmospheric readout from the shuttle, which had determined that the moon, while too cold for unprotected survival, did maintain a low-pressure breathable atmosphere as a result of partially completed terraforming.

Okay, so the shuttle was dead but she was alive. Now, where the gronk was she? She'd taken a big gamble with her attempt to pulse the magnetic containment field. The ejection of plasma should have provided enough thrust for the shuttle to reach escape velocity and get her back into space, where the *Gallaway* could pick her up. Unfortunately, thanks to her wild spin after contact with the dome, that hadn't happened. She checked navigation, which had her located almost halfway around the other side of the moon.

April pressed the comm. "*Gallaway*, this is Idowu, do you read? Over."

April was relieved to hear the voice of Commander Mul. "Captain, glad to hear you are conscious. After we lost contact with you we maintained tracking. We saw you attempt a plasma burn, resulting in an uncontrolled trajectory and impact with the moon. We tracked your life sign, but had anticipated you might have been badly wounded in the crash."

"Damage to the shuttle is severe," April said, "but I'm okay. Unfortunately, I'm not getting this shuttle back in the black."

"Acknowledge that, Captain. Teth is here on the bridge too. He's asking to speak to you."

April felt a rush of emotion, but it wasn't quite what she'd expected. Teth was her fiancé. She had survived a shuttle crash. Of course he would want to talk to her, and she should want to talk to him too, but at that moment having to talk to him felt like a distraction, a chore she had to endure. It felt like when she was a kid and her parents had made her talk to her aunts and uncles on other planets, who she'd met only a handful of times and barely knew.

"Darling," Teth's voice came over the comm. "Thank the stars you're okay."

Had his voice always been so high? It was almost comical really.

"Teth," April said, "I'm alright, don't worry."

"Of course I'm worried," he said. "I thought you were dead. I thought I'd lost you."

"I'm okay," she said. "Not hurt, but I'm still in a bit of a predicament here."

"I know, I know, whatever we can do we will. We're going to come and get you. Commander Mul has already assured me that we'll be able to collect you and you'll soon be back in my arms again."

"Listen, Teth, I'm going to need to speak to Commander Mul again."

"Of course, my darling, of course."

"Captain," Mul's voice came back over the comm, "I'm having the second shuttle prepped and ready for a recovery mission. We should be able to pick you up in less than an hour."

"Negative."

"Captain," Mul protested, "we cannot leave you down there."

"Darling, no!" Teth called, far too dramatically, from somewhere behind Mul.

April ignored him. "You are to hold position and ready the planet-slagger as ordered. We don't know whether the Aegix nanobots have spread this far yet, or if they'll make it here before the shuttle does. I'm not having more of our crew at risk. Have you had contact with the FSC *Clarence*?"

"Yes, Captain."

"And how are they progressing with the evacuation from the geological survey station?"

"I am afraid to say they are not progressing," Commander Mul said.

"I'm sorry Mul, what do you mean they aren't progressing? They need to have those people off this moon long before the Aegix get there and before we're forced to launch a planet slagger."

"Unfortunately when Captain Quaid heard that you crashed he called off their attempt to rescue the civilians at the geological exploration base."

"Why?" April said. "He doesn't need to be concerned about me. He just needs to save those people."

"I do not believe he is concerned for you, Captain," Mul said. "I believe he is, as a human might say, covering his arse. I believe he is afraid to go against the orders of Admiral Tullet."

"I see," April said. "Ensign Herd, can you hear me?"

"Yes, Captain," came the reply from the Communications Officer.

"Can you patch me through to the *Clarence* from this comm?"

"Yes, Captain, one moment." There was a moment of silence as the comm dropped out and then re-established. "You're on with Captain Quaid of the FSC *Clarence* now, Captain."

"Captain Quaid," April said.

"Captain Idowu," Quaid said, "I'm glad to hear you're alright. I understand you crashed on the moon. I wa—"

"Why haven't you saved those people yet?" April cut him off.

"With all due respect, Captain Idowu," Quaid said, "you and I are the same rank. You have no authority over me, you cannot order me to put my ship or crew in danger. I have made the decision to follow the orders given to me by Admiral Tullet."

"I know what your orders were, Quaid," April said, "but there are people in danger, and the only thing Admiral Tullet should be ordering is a cucumber sandwich at the cafeteria. Get your ship to that station and uplift those people."

"I can't do that."

"You can," April said, "you're just choosing not to. Commander Mul believes you are covering your arse, but the truth is, you're just a cowardly piece of shit."

"Captain Idowu, I am the captain of a hauler. I do not have a Universe-class starship at my disposal to attempt some suicidal rescue mission. I'm sorry for the people down there, but there's nothing I can do."

"Captain Idowu," Commander Mul's calm and measured voice came over the comm, "may I interject?"

"Of course, Commander," April said.

"Captain Quaid, I happen to know a starship captain who didn't have anything but a hauler either, and he managed to save the galaxy," Mul said.

April smiled.

"If you're talking about Captain Franklin then I'm glad to be nothing like him," Quaid said. "He's a fool. A lucky fool, but still a fool."

"You listen to me Quaid," Idowu said, her ire well and truly raised. "Captain Iridius Franklin is the greatest man I've ever met, and he's done more with his career than you ever will by being a cowardly brown noser sucking up to idiotic commanders like Tullet. Shut him off, Ensign Herd."

"Yes, Captain."

"The greatest man you've ever met, is he?" Teth's voice came over the comm. "I thought you said you didn't have feelings for him anymore."

April winced. "Sorry, I just got a bit carried away."

"Just get back here safe please," Teth said, but she could tell her comment had deflated him. She knew he already felt jealous and intimidated by her relationship with Iridius. "Let us rescue you," he implored.

"I can't do that, Teth," April said.

"Captain," Commander Mul said, "I have to advise the same as Teth. We need to rescue you."

"No," April said, as she flicked at the screen in front of her. The geological survey station Captain Quaid had abandoned was only 11 kilometres from where she'd crashed. "You have your orders. I'm going to make my way to the geological station. I'll contact you when I arrive. If you don't hear from me in six hours or if there is any indication that the Aegix are attempting to get off this moon, you are to launch the planet slagger. Idowu out."

"April!" she heard Teth call over the comm just before she switched it off.

April undid the buckle of her harness and then rolled to the side, lowering herself down while holding onto the upright of the pilot's chair, then letting herself drop to one of the chairs further back. She lowered herself down again until she dropped onto the rear bulkhead of the shuttle which, because of the way the shuttle had crashed, was down.

She disconnected the tether from the Rat Trap and took hold of the box. It wasn't too heavy, but was still going to be awkward lugging it all the way to the survey station. She could have left it here, but getting a living sample of the Aegix for Lieutenant Commander Quinn had been the whole point of this mission. April wasn't dead yet and so, as far as she was concerned, neither was the mission.

She pulled the manual door opening handle and kicked at the door, letting it fall outwards and drop to the ground below, which was, luckily, no more than a few metres down. She turned and took one last look at the cockpit of the shuttle, wondering what she would have done if it had been Iridius on the comm, begging her to be rescued. It was best not to think about it; it didn't matter anyway. Her chances of surviving long enough to worry about her romantic life were pretty damn low. April took hold of the Rat Trap and jumped out of the crashed shuttle onto the moon of Acacia.

CHAPTER EIGHT_

IRIDIUS WATCHED as Junker loaded a plastic case containing five AR-80 pulse rifles and several magazines of ammunition into the shuttle. He wasn't intending on getting them out when they were down on Earth because he didn't want to get into a firefight with people from 1943 with weapons from nearly 300 years in the future. Not only would that affect the timeline, it seemed a little unfair. However, regulations required weapons to at least be taken aboard for an away mission.

Iridius turned as Quinn approached.

"All set?" Iridius asked.

"Yes, sir," Quinn said. "I just want to raise my concerns about Miss Frost again."

"Quinn," Iridius said, "how many times are we going to have this discussion?"

"Sir, I understand she's on the ship now and I'm not going to claim it would be safe for her back at the Alliance, but FSC Regulation 88c clearly states that only active serving members of the FSC and other dignitaries or previously approved consultants can embark on away missions."

"Quinn, as you might imagine, I've had quite enough regulations, by-laws and statutes spouted at me lately. Consider her a consultant and move on."

"She hasn't been vetted," Quinn said, "and she hasn't been approved."

"Well, we've been kind of busy trying to figure out time travel, haven't we?" Iridius saw Gentrix entering the shuttle bay. He lowered his voice. "We'll talk about this another time, Quinn. Don't bring it up again. Let's focus on the mission."

Quinn looked over her shoulder and saw Gentrix approaching, and Rangi coming in behind her. "Be careful please, Captain."

"You're coming too."

"I mean with her," Quinn whispered as she walked away. "She'll never let go of her Alliance past."

Gentrix watched her go. "What was that all about?"

"Nothing," Iridius said. "Don't worry about it."

Gentrix had swapped her usual tight black clothing for a loose pair of simple brown pants and a blue shirt, clothing that shouldn't have been out of place in any time period but looking at her now, even in those clothes, she looked too damn sexy to blend in anywhere. Hopefully she'd be able to tone down her femme fatale sensuality to 1940s levels. Iridius's bigger concern would have to be Rangi. He was dressed in a blue Federation Space Command flight suit, complete with integrated temperature regulation system and full health monitoring.

"I thought I told you to dress for the time period," Iridius said. "You clearly look like a pilot from the future."

"Hang on," Rangi said. He reached into his breast pocket and pulled out his aviator sunglasses, unfolded the arms and slipped the mirrored shades onto his face, holding his arms out wide in presentation. "What about that, huh?" he said. "Just like an old timey fighter ace."

"You just put sunglasses on," Iridius said.

"That's right," Rangi said. "Old timey sunglasses."

"He can wear a pair of my old coveralls," Junker said as she walked back down the ramp out of the shuttle.

"Thanks, Junker, grab him a pair would you?" Iridius said.

Rangi looked disappointed. He opened his mouth to say something, but Iridius jumped in before he could speak. "Yes, Rangi."

"Cap?"

"I said yes."

"You don't even know what I was going to say."

"You were going to ask me whether you could still wear your sunglasses."

Rangi didn't say anything for a moment. "But I can?"

"Yes," Iridius said.

Rangi gave the smallest fist bump before heading into the shuttle. "I'll prep for launch."

In a short time, the away team was ready to leave, each of them suitably attired in clothing that was, while not exactly from the 1940s, at least not going to raise eyebrows like a flight suit emblazoned with the words *Federation Space Command* across the back would.

Quinn, Gentrix, Rangi and Junker waited just outside the rear ramp of the shuttle as Iridius approached.

"Alright," Iridius said, "I've completed a log entry outlining what's happened, in the event we're unsuccessful and an investigation is undertaken into our actions. I've taken full responsibility for everything from boarding the ASS Locke – yes, thank you Rangi – right up to what we're trying now, so no one else on the crew should be held accountable. Not that it matters, because if we're not successful the ship will probably be stuck in 1943 and we'll all be dead long before we get back to our time to be court-martialled for disobeying orders, or to warn anyone about the Synth-Hastur, or maybe we cause such irreparable damage to the timeline that the Federation never exists at all."

"Is this what your pre-mission speeches are always like?" Gentrix asked.

"Pretty much," Rangi said.

"Look," Iridius said, "I don't need to give a rousing pre-mission speech, because we all know we have to succeed in securing atom bomb technology if we want to get back to the future."

The door to the *Deus Ex*'s shuttle bay opened and Lieutenant Latroz appeared.

"Lieutenant?" Iridius asked. "Is everything okay? Shouldn't you be on the bridge?"

"I was just wondering if I could have a moment with Lieutenant Rangi, sir?"

"Yes, alright, but make it quick. We want to get down to Berlin under the cover of dark."

Latroz walked over to Rangi. The seven-foot-tall purple alien towered over the pilot as she looked down at him with worry. Iridius realised he'd never actually seen Latroz look worried before. He'd seen her concerned in the heat of battle, but that was more like the concern of someone staring at a tricky crossword. To Latroz, imminent death in the heat of battle was little more than a conundrum to be solved. The way she was looking at Rangi now was with genuine nervousness. "I do not like that you are going down to a hostile world without my assistance, Benjamin."

"I'll be okay, Plum," Rangi said. "Captain Franklin is going to make sure we don't interact with anyone. We're not even going to punch any Nazis."

Latroz looked at Iridius as if seeking confirmation. Iridius nodded, only afterwards wondering why one of his own crew made him feel like a teenager taking their daughter on a date.

Latroz turned back to Rangi. She wrapped her purple arms around him, the ropey muscles – which Iridius was sure were more numerous than those in a human's arm – popped out as she squeezed him in a bear hug and lifted him off the ground. "You be careful without me to protect you," Latroz said.

"I'd be more concerned you're going to snap him in half with that hug," Junker said.

Iridius looked to Gentrix. "Aren't you going to hug me like that and tell me to be careful?"

"No," Gentrix said.

Iridius watched as Latroz put Benjamin down and kissed his red face. Whether it was red from embarrassment or from that crushing embrace, Iridius wasn't sure.

"Listen, everyone," Iridius said. "It'll be fine."

"There's those famous words again, Cap," Junker said.

"We fly down with the shuttle in stealth mode, get into the laboratory where the atomic bomb is being housed, get out, fly back," Iridius said. "No worries."

Iridius was, in fact, very worried. As far as he knew, no one had ever done this before. No one had gone back in time and interacted with the past. After everything he and his crew had been through, all their run-ins with friendly and hostile alien races, after travelling light years back and forth across the galaxy, whether it was hauling cargo or running from insane artificial intelligences, he was nervous now because, despite the fact that they were going to Earth, an away mission to 1943 felt like the most alien destination they'd ever faced.

———

Iridius looked out the view-screen of the shuttle. The blue of the Earth rolled gently beneath them. From up here it looked peaceful. There was no way to tell that the world down there was at war. He found himself thinking maybe they should change history after all. Maybe he could go down, grab the world's leaders and bring them up here, where he could shove their faces in front of this view.

"See," he would say, "those lines on the maps you're fighting over, you can't even see them from up here. They aren't real, you big dumb idiots."

Still, it probably wouldn't make much difference. It took a society a long time to move past the idea of territories and countries and other arbitrary distinctions on their planet, and in 1943, Earth wasn't anywhere near ready for that. It usually happened once enough of a planet's inhabitants had been into space and seen exactly what Iridius was looking at now – that their world was one thing, one unbroken whole, a collective biome. Of course, that just meant the planet turned their eyes out into space to search for more territory, but hey, uniting a single planet was a start.

"Ready for planetary entry, sir," Rangi said. "Stealth mode active, not that they have the technology to spot us up here unless someone gets real lucky with a telescope."

"Keep us in stealth anyway," Iridius said. "Visual camouflage when we land. Take us down."

"Aye, Cap," Rangi said, then he suddenly began veering off to the side, firing short thruster bursts to alter their trajectory one way and then back the other, firing the forward thrusters to descend and then accelerating to ascend again.

"Rangi?" Iridius asked. "What are you doing?"

"There's just so much space up here Cap," he said. "Can you believe it? I can do anything I want and I'm not going to hit anything. We're the only thing in orbit around Earth. That's wild."

"Yes, alright," Iridius said, but he could see why Rangi was excited. Normally, an orbital descent trajectory down to Earth was like running through a rubbish dump in a hurricane. It was a constant battle to avoid crashing into floating junk. "Just don't waste our fuel." They had plenty of fuel, Iridius knew that, but it was best to try and calm Rangi down when he started getting overexcited, and Iridius often found it helped to provide a reason, even if it was a bullshit one. Iridius had learned most of his leadership techniques at the Academy or picked them up over time. This one, however, he'd found in a parenting book they'd had on board the *Diesel Coast* when they'd once made a delivery of second-hand books. In fact, he'd found *Parenting Tips for Dealing with Toddlers* quite instructive for dealing with Benjamin Rangi in a lot of situations.

"Quinn, have you figured out where we need to go?"

"Aye, sir," Quinn replied. "Research for the German atomic program is based at a facility in Berlin called the Kaiser Wilhelm Institute for Physics, headed by Werner Heisenberg."

Rangi chuckled. "Weiner Heisenberg."

"I said *Werner* Heisenberg, Lieutenant," Quinn said in about as much of a reprimanding tone as she ever used, "and I'll ask you to have some respect. Werner Heisenberg is a titan of human history, the founder of the study of quantum mechanics on Earth. He's a scientific hero."

"Oh no," Iridius said, "is this going to be like Junker with DJ Chromium? Are you going to go all gushy over this Weiner guy?"

"Werner," Quinn said, "and no it's not like that."

"I'm not a DJ Chromium fan anymore anyway, Captain," Junker said.

"I should hope not," Iridius replied.

"He wasn't even the real deal," Junker said. "The whole DJ Chromium identity was invented by the spooks."

"So it's not because of how he, you know, set me adrift in space?"

"Oh yeah, that too, Cap. Definitely that too."

Iridius rolled his eyes. "So, the Kaiser Wilhelm Institute for Physics, can we bring up any maps of the area?"

"I loaded a historically accurate map into the shuttle computer," Quinn said. "Can you bring it up, Rangi?"

Iridius and Quinn gathered on either side of Rangi's pilot chair to look at the screen as Rangi opened the map. Quinn had already dropped a beacon pin to mark the location of the laboratory.

"Okay, computer," Iridius said, "zoom out a level." The computer did so, pulling back from a street focus to the broader area. "There," Iridius said, pointing at the screen. Three streets over from the highlighted building was a green area, a park of some kind. "Computer, overlay satellite imagery."

"I'm sorry," the computer replied, "no data exists."

"Right," Iridius said, "no satellites in 1943. Well, let's head for that park. Hopefully it's open space and we can put the shuttle down there and..." Iridius's voice trailed off.

He felt suddenly dizzy. He squeezed his eyes closed, which helped momentarily, but when he opened his eyes again the shuttle lurched. Or at least, Iridius lurched. He fell sideways, his ability to balance suddenly completely gone. As he hit the floor his head began to pound again. He could hear blood rushing in his ears as if his blood pressure had skyrocketed to artery bursting levels.

"Captain," Quinn was saying.

"Is he alright?" Iridius heard Rangi asking. "Cap?"

"Keep bringing us down Rangi," Quinn said, "full stealth. See if you can put us down in that park Captain Franklin indicated."

"Yes, ma'am."

"Iridius?" Gentrix asked.

Iridius realised his eyes were closed. When he opened them, he saw Gentrix, Quinn and Junker all standing over him, looking down. He tried to hold his eyes open but his eyelids were growing too heavy too fast, and they slid shut like a cargo bay blast door.

———

Iridius opened his eyes. In another, less dramatic display of time travel, he could have sworn he opened his eyes immediately after he'd closed them, but apparently this wasn't the case. The away team, including Rangi, were huddled around looking down at him. He almost asked Rangi who was flying the shuttle, but he soon realised that the shuttle wasn't moving. In fact, looking out the front he could see grass and trees – distinctly Earth-looking grass and trees. He wouldn't go so far as to say they were distinctly German-looking grass and trees, but he hoped they'd landed where they were supposed to.

He'd definitely lost some amount of time, but couldn't be sure how much. To be honest, he was getting a little tired of time, which had seemed to pass so consistently and predictably for most of his life, being so wibbly-wobbly of late.

Most people with passable scientific knowledge understood that time wasn't really fixed, but was a relative quantity passing differently between observers due to relative velocities or massive gravitational differences. Still, that had about as much influence on Iridius's day-to-day as the understanding that his body was made up entirely of the same subatomic particles as every other piece of matter in the universe, and that his consciousness was likely just an illusion born of a myriad of electrical signals jumping across the synapses in his brain. Theoretically, he got it, but practically, it didn't change the fact that he went around thinking thoughts and feeling things and being happy with the illusion that he was a single meat sack. Similarly, time had always seemed to tick away consistently and he'd never given it much thought, but now, with wormholes and time-bombs and passing out so often that he kept losing whole chunks of it, time had suddenly become much less reliable.

"How long was I out?" he asked.

"About fifteen minutes, Captain," Quinn replied. "Are you feeling alright now?"

Iridius nodded, sitting up. "I'm fine, just a headache. Are we in Berlin?"

"Aye, sir," Rangi said. "I put us down in that park, full stealth mode and reflective visual cloaking on. Completely undetected."

"Except for that soldier with the dog," Junker said.

"What soldier?" Iridius asked.

Rangi shot Junker a look. "I thought we weren't going to mention that?"

"That sounds like something you should mention," Iridius said. "Pretty much whenever there's something you think you shouldn't tell me, that's a good indication that I need to know."

"It was nothing," Rangi said.

"We almost landed on top of a soldier walking a dog in the park," Junker said.

"We didn't though, did we?" Rangi said. "Look, Cap, I'm not used to landing places where people aren't expecting things to come from above. He's fine, just got a bit of a fright."

"He walked into the side of the shuttle," Junker said, "and then ran away. I mean, we couldn't expect that someone wasn't going to eventually walk straight into an invisible ship in the middle of a city park, could we?"

"We're just going to have to hope he doesn't go and report it, or if he does, that no one believes him," Iridius said. "Hopefully we won't be here long anyway. Let's get ready. It's getting dark out there. We'll head for the Kaiser Wilhelm Institute, get in, let Quinn get what she needs and then get out again."

"Captain," Quinn said, "I need to raise something."

Iridius glanced from Quinn to the others, who were watching

him expectantly. "Is this an intervention? Look, I promise I won't drink that Jertiklian Hallucinogenic Cactus Absinthe again. It was only one time and I was on leave."

"That's the third time you've passed out," Quinn said.

"I'm okay," Iridius said. "Don't worry about me, I'll be fine."

"Captain," Quinn said, "we're obviously worried about you, but there's also the fact that, well—"

"What?"

"If you pass out while we're out there you might get us all killed, Cap," Junker said.

Quinn looked at her.

"What?" Junker said. "It's what we're all thinking."

"Captain, if you push yourself too hard it could be fatal."

"Quinn," Iridius said, "your concern is noted, but I'm not leaving you to do this without me. Who's going to take the lead?"

"Well," Quinn said, "I—"

"No," Iridius said. "I'm leading the away team. Let's get ready to move out. Remember to limit interactions with people as much as possible. We're not taking weapons. No talking to people and no touching anything." He looked at Rangi. "And no punching Nazis."

The away team prepared themselves. Iridius watched the monitor beside the shuttle's small side door, which provided a view of outside. When he was sure there was no one around to see five people appearing as if from nowhere, he opened the door and the away team prepared to step out of their twenty-third century advanced stealth transport shuttle with nuclear fusion drive and adaptive camouflage and into 1943.

There were several humans remembered throughout history for their one small steps. Neil Armstrong, of course – the grainy footage of his first step on the moon was still shown to school children more than two hundred and fifty years after it had happened. Most surprisingly, given the fact that they undertook regular space travel and were probably neighbours with eight-legged insectoids or sentient vegetables, there were still people who claimed the moon landing was a hoax. Just goes to show that no matter how advanced a species became, you could never quite shake the basement-dwelling conspiracy nuts.

But Neil Armstrong wasn't the only one. There was Elma Chung, the woman who had stepped down off the Ares lander to put the first human footprint in the red dust of Mars. There was Fredrick Harris, an accountant from Leeds, whose small step was not quite such a meticulously planned exploratory endeavour as the other two, but was no less influential on human history. It was Harris who accidentally stepped on the ambassador of the Slurta-lax, a race of small sentient beings evolved from slug-like creatures, and inadvertently started Earth's first interstellar war.

Iridius wondered whether this moment would be remembered in a similar way. Would he, and the rest of the crew of the *Deus Ex*, be remembered as the first human beings to travel back in time and visit an earlier period in their own history? Was this his one small step, as he dropped down out of the shuttle and onto Earth in 1943? He wasn't sure, but he suspected this was the biggest moment of his career.

Iridius hadn't joined Federation Space Command to captain a hauler and cart whale dung and toy dogs around the galaxy. He certainly hadn't joined Federation Space Command to battle an ancient synthetic intelligence, stop a Hawaiian shirt-wearing lunatic from launching a time-bomb, or to be the only one truly aware of the approach of a galactic-level threat. No, Iridius Franklin had joined Federation Space Command to be an explorer and now, for the first time, he felt like one. Just in case this was going to be remembered, he thought he'd better say something fitting for the occasion.

"Listen," Iridius said, "I know I'm not the only one who joined Space Command to find out what's out there in the galaxy, to boldly go and explore. Despite most of us not having been born on Earth, as humans this is our home world, yet right now we truly are a long way from home. We have a mission to complete to get us back to the future, but let's acknowledge that in this moment we are also explorers. We're taking a step where maybe no one has ever been before, back into the past. I'd like to acknowledge what may be a historic moment. With this small step, we make a giant leap through time. We step from 2233 and into..." Iridius stepped down from the shuttle and onto the grass. "Shit!"

Rangi poked his head out from the shuttle behind him. "I thought you were going to say we step from 2233 into 1943, Cap."

Iridius was wiping his boot on the grass. "Goddamn it," he said. "I just stepped in a massive dog shit."

"Oh yeah," Rangi said. "We told you about the soldier and the dog. I guess the dog got scared too."

Iridius looked at Rangi and then turned to the others. As they made their way out of the shuttle, he could see the open door disrupting the shimmering illusion of the shuttle's light-bending reflective camouflage. "Quickly," he said, looking around and gesturing for them to hurry.

The park was empty but, to be honest, if anyone happened to examine the centre of the park with anything even close to a discerning eye, they would likely see the shimmering disturbance and strangely twisted reflection of the trees and landscape. The cloaking system of the shuttle was designed to work mostly in space, after all, and there were far fewer colours needing to be carefully reflected to camouflage yourself in space. There was sometimes a starfield that needed to be convincingly projected, but apart from that it was mostly black, and black, and occasionally more black – certainly nothing as complex as the myriad shades of a manicured park on Earth.

There was also the fact that, as the Nazi soldier and his dog had discovered, the ship didn't actually disappear, so anyone walking through the park would crash straight into it. They were going to have to be fast so no one got the chance to stumble on the shuttle.

The away team began moving across the park in the direction of the streets and the Kaiser Wilhelm Institute. The park consisted of a mostly empty grassy area – which was now not as empty as it seemed – and what looked to be a small, probably man-made pond. The whole park was surrounded by trees whose dense foliage was enough to block the view of the streets beyond. Unable to see anything beyond the park, Iridius had the feeling they could have been on Earth at pretty much any time.

There was nothing particularly 1943 about the grass under their feet or the smell of the cool night air. They moved quickly to reach the treeline and then passed through, opening a rusted gate in the fence with as much stealth as possible – which turned out to not be very much, thanks to the squealing rusty hinges – and onto the street.

In either direction were houses, most of them small, with white-washed rendered walls and red-tiled roofs. They certainly looked like old houses, but not in the way Iridius had been expecting. He realised as they walked quickly down the rough cobblestone sidewalk that they didn't look old because they weren't. At this time, these were just ordinary houses. The cars, what few there were, were the true giveaway. Small, sturdy and stocky, they were all like that toy car set that was lost in a cardboard box at the back of your grandfather's garage, suddenly brought to life in full size. These were 1940s automobiles, fresh off the production line.

The streets were dark. There was little in the way of street lighting, and the houses were dark as well. It was early evening, around eight o'clock, but almost without fail the lights of each and every house were out, the curtains pulled. No one was out on the streets or driving around.

This didn't look at all like a city of several million people. It was like they were playing one of Rangi's VR video games but all the NPCs had failed to load. It was clear to Iridius that the others felt the same. Each of them had started looking around somewhat warily.

"Okay," Junker said, "I mean, I'm no history expert, but there were people in 1943, right?"

"I know what you mean," Rangi said. "It's quiet. A little too—"

"Don't," Iridius interrupted, raising his hand. "No good can come from you saying that."

"At this stage of the war the Allied forces were bombing Germany fairly heavily," Quinn said. "I imagine everyone is taking shelter."

"And tonight?" Iridius asked. "Just out of interest, do we know if we're going to get bombed?"

"I would have liked to check but I couldn't, sir," Quinn said. "We don't have that level of historical information on our computers and I couldn't access the QECNet for historical records because, well, there is no QECNet in 1943."

"We hurry then," Iridius said, quickening his pace and forcing the others to keep up. He cut through a small garden of low flower beds and stayed in a crouch as he followed a wooden fence to come out at the next street over.

"We sure we're in the right place, Cap?" Junker asked when Iridius stopped at the end of the fence, looking out onto the street.

"Yeah," Iridius said slowly, indicating a building a short way down the street. "I think it's fair to say we're in the right place."

They were in what appeared to be a mostly suburban area, but ahead was a collection of more imposing buildings. The one

Iridius had pointed out was a two-storey brown stone building with a large front door behind an arched and columned entrance. It was something that wouldn't have looked out of place on the grounds of some historical university. There, it might have been adorned with the Greek symbols of some ridiculous fraternity, like Delta Covid Strain or Eta Apple Pi.

Here though, the entrance was adorned with two long bright red banners, in the centre of which was a white circle containing a black swastika, a once-peaceful symbol of good luck which had been entirely ruined for all eternity by a bunch of evil pricks. The banners moved gently in the soft breeze and Iridius noted that even now, hundreds of years later — at least for him — he felt a stirring of anger looking at that flag.

"Quinn," Iridius whispered, waving for her to move up beside him. "Is that the place?"

Quinn looked at the swastika-draped building and nodded. Out the front were two people, the first they'd seen so far. These two were dressed in the stiff grey uniform of the Wehrmacht, the German army. Nazis. Actual Nazi soldiers from 1943, standing right there in the flesh. How many movies and television shows had Iridius seen with Nazis in them? Even in the twenty-third century they were still telling stories about the Second World War. Despite the myriad other races and worlds in the galaxy and the near-infinite amount of material that could provide, humanity was still telling tales about this time period.

World War Two had taken on an almost mythical air, a blend of fact and fiction that had been shaped as much by the stories told about it as by the actual events that had occurred. Perhaps this was because, of all the conflicts throughout human history, this was the one that seemed the most morally justified. The Allies were the goodies standing up for justice and liberty beneath their red, white and blue union jacks and their stars and stripes. The Nazis were the baddies, with designs on genocide and skulls on their hats. It was easy to frame fictional tales around that, but as Iridius crouched down, looking at the two soldiers, he realised they didn't seem terribly villainous.

"They're just kids," Iridius said.

Gentrix, who had moved up next to him, spoke in a low voice. "They probably are just kids – maybe eighteen or nineteen." She looked at him. "For a smart guy, you've really got a lot to learn about wars, and people in general."

"What do you mean?"

"You're still happy to cling to the ideal view of the Federation," Gentrix said. "Even after I showed you the truth of the horrific things the Federation did during the Federation–Alliance war, you still believe the Alliance are a bunch of evil capitalists. Now you're doing the same here. Sticking to the stereotype."

"What?" Iridius said. "The Nazis killed millions of innocent people."

"Yes," Gentrix said, "they did." She nodded at the two soldiers out the front of the laboratory. "But for all we know, those two boys could just be innocent kids who happened to be born in a country that fell into the wrong hands, and now they've been drafted into a war they want nothing to do with."

"So," Rangi said, "they're not Nazis?"

Gentrix looked at him. "Well, they're German soldiers, if that's what you mean. I just think we need to be careful thinking that everyone is a villain all the time." It didn't escape Iridius that Gentrix glanced at Quinn when she said this.

"Alright," Iridius said, "villainous Nazis or drafted innocents aside, we still need to get past those two to get inside."

"Leave that to me," Gentrix said, pulling a small cube from the pocket of her pants. Iridius recognised it as a holographic projection box, like the one she'd used to produce an image of them in Devin Frost's holding cell. "I'll create a distraction."

"I thought we were trying not to interact with people," Iridius said.

Gentrix looked at him. "Two things. One, we won't actually be interacting with people, and two," she held up the holographic projection box, "do you think anyone from 1943 is going to have any idea what this is? And one further point: have you got a better idea?"

"No," Iridius said.

Gentrix stood. "Great."

She placed the holographic projection box on the ground at the edge of the fence where the others were hiding. She pressed a few buttons on the top of it, winked at Iridius and then began running towards the German soldiers.

"I still don't know whether to be impressed or terrified by her," Rangi said.

Iridius looked at him. "You want to know the truth? Me neither."

Iridius caught the look on Quinn's face out the corner of his eye. Fair to say she was not impressed.

As Gentrix ran across the street she began yelling, calling out to the soldiers standing either side of the doorway. Even as she began speaking, Iridius could tell she was speaking German and yet, thanks to the – sigh – UTI, he was able to understand perfectly, as if she was speaking in Galactic Standard. "Help! Help me!"

The two soldiers turned to look at her. "What are you doing out here?" one of them called in response. "There is a curfew!"

"Please, some men came to my house," Gentrix said as she stopped in front of them. "I think they were spies. They said they needed somewhere to hide before they attacked the laboratory. I escaped and they came after me. Please, you have to help me."

The soldiers looked at each other and then back to Gentrix. In front of where Iridius and the others were hiding, the holographic projector blinked and then an image of Iridius and Rangi appeared. They were standing in the street.

"There," Gentrix shouted, "that's them! Enemy spies!"

The projections of Iridius and Rangi began to move, running off down the street.

"Well, don't just stand there. Get them!" Gentrix yelled.

The two young soldiers, much like anyone Gentrix demanded something of, seemed to have no choice but to do as she had asked. "Yes, ma'am," they responded and then took off after the holographic decoys. When they had disappeared, Gentrix opened the front door of the Kaiser Wilhelm Institute for Physics like a door attendant at a fancy hotel and gestured for Iridius and the others to enter.

"I think impressed," Rangi said.

CHAPTER NINE_

As IRIDIUS ENTERED the lobby of the Kaiser Wilhelm Institute for Physics, he glanced around at the interior. When he'd imagined the type of physics laboratory that would be involved in the development of an atomic bomb, he'd pictured something a little more white and shiny, and less dank and ornately carpeted. This place was reminiscent of a stately manor house. There were portraits in hideous gold frames on the walls, a large staircase in the centre of the entrance rising up to the second level, and ornamental lights spaced along the walls that, although electric, shone with a flickering dimness that produced a very Castle Wolfenstein atmosphere.

It was also empty. Despite the fact that it was night-time, he'd expected a little more activity, a few more of those grey-uniformed Nazis at least. As far as Iridius knew, Nazis always seemed to be guarding something, whether it was supernatural religious icons that belonged in a museum or prisoners in a particularly poorly run prisoner-of-war camp.

"Not very sciencey is it?" Iridius said.

"Dedicated scientific laboratories weren't that widespread in this time," Quinn said. "A lot of places were like this, old homes or historical institutions with makeshift laboratories in the basement or attic."

"Doesn't seem like a very safe place to do atomic research."

"They didn't really understand the dangers at this time," Quinn said. "Marie Curie completed her groundbreaking studies into radioactivity in a small laboratory in the middle of a Paris suburb. That building is still radioactive in our time, and will be for another thousand years."

"Not really anymore," Rangi said. "Because, you know." He mimed an explosion with his hands.

"Huh," Quinn said, and paused for a moment. "I almost forgot all this is gone now. I guess that's something to take away from our accidental temporal displacement. It's nice to still visit the Earth like it's not really gone after all."

"So, is this place radioactive?" Rangi asked.

"Most likely," Quinn said.

Rangi moved his hands, not so subtly, to cover his groin.

"If there is one thing I know about scientists," Iridius said, "it's that the old timey ones were crazy, poking themselves in the eye with knives and eating radioactive rocks to see what would happen. Doesn't surprise me that they weren't particularly concerned about safety precautions, even in the twentieth century."

"Health and safety regulations are certainly better in our time," Quinn said, "but there are still accidents, like when the cosmological research facility on Gamnar created the first self-sustaining artificial black hole. Nobody is allowed to fly through that star system anymore for fear that they'll damage the containment field and the black hole will continue growing. It's already swallowed six planets, eighteen moons and several dozen star ships."

"The other thing," Iridius said as he walked a short way down a corridor and tested a door handle, finding it unlocked – it opened onto a small, empty lecture room, "it's not particularly well guarded, is it?"

"I doubt they think it needs to be," Quinn said. "This is right in the heart of Berlin, probably the most well-protected city in Germany and besides, what was happening inside this building was a well-kept secret. The only reason we know about it is because we've got the benefit of the historical record. Records of atomic development from the war were accessible by the end of the twentieth century and the people involved, mainly Heisenberg on the German side and Oppenheimer on the Allied side, went on to speak publicly after the war, including about their opposition to nuclear weapons."

"Lucky they think their secret is safe, I guess. Let's not get complacent though. There's got to be more than just those two kids at the front door."

"There is."

With a wince, Iridius turned to look in the direction of the voice. The words had been spoken in German, translated by their UTIs. A man in his mid-forties stood on the stairs. He was trim and wore a long white coat over a shirt. Despite the late hour, he was still wearing a tie. The man's hair was combed back but frayed out a little wild around the sides. That, combined with the white coat, made it obvious enough that he was a scientist.

"Oh gosh," Quinn said, raising a hand to her mouth in shock, "you're Werner Heisenberg. Oh my god. It's really you."

She looked frantically at Iridius and the others, as if to confirm that they too were seeing this, but Iridius could tell the rest of the away team was no more blown away than he was, which was something that seemed to greatly offend Quinn. "You guys, it's Werner Heisenberg. Oh my gosh." She turned back to the man who was descending the stairs. "I'm such a great admirer of your work. Your work on quantum mechanics was truly way ahead of where most people were at the time, and a breakthrough that took other civilisations so much longer in terms of relative scientific development." She clamped her hand over her mouth. "Sorry, I mean, other scientific minds took so much longer to catch up to you. I mean, it was just such a cognitive leap. Well you know, it was your work of course."

Iridius put his hand on Quinn's shoulder. "Quinn," he said slowly, "you told me this wasn't going to be a Junker and DJ Chromium thing."

"Yes, sir," she said. "Sorry, sir."

Heisenberg descended the stairs uncertainly. "Who are you exactly?"

"Ah," Iridius said, "well, we're," he stopped, remembering that although his UTI was translating what Heisenberg was saying, it didn't work the other way. He turned to Gentrix. "Gentrix, could you explain that we're, um..."

"Not very good at this," Heisenberg offered, in English (which, as we've previously established, is remarkably similar to Galactic Standard Language).

Iridius turned back to the scientist with a weak smile.

"I can speak English," Heisenberg confirmed.

"Right," Iridius said. "Right, well, see, who we are is, um, it's, we are inspectors from the German High Command."

Heisenberg stared at him, unmoving.

"Cap," Rangi said in his very annoying half-whisper, "I don't think he bought it. Probably because we aren't speaking in German. We should have thought of a cover story before we walked in."

"Yes, thank you, Rangi," Iridius said, "unhelpful right now as usual." Iridius turned to Heisenberg. "Okay, so we're not from the German High Command."

"Foreign spies?" Heisenberg asked.

"No," Iridius said, "definitely not foreign spies."

"No," Heisenberg continued, as if considering. "You are some form of time travellers, aren't you?"

"What?" Iridius said, forcing a laugh. "No, of course not, that's ridiculous. Time travellers, that sounds crazy. No, I admit it, we're foreign spies. You got us."

Heisenberg remained unmoved. "This one," Heisenberg pointed to Quinn, "she spoke of the historical record, of myself and Oppenheimer speaking about our work after the war, and the records being available by the end of the twentieth century. Tell me, from what era do you come? How is this possible? Why are you here?"

Iridius turned to look at Quinn, whose face had bloomed red with embarrassment. "Well," he said, "so much for not affecting the timeline – which, I'll remind you, you said was probably the greatest threat we've ever faced."

"The Butterfly of Doom," Rangi added.

"Time travel," Heisenberg said, mostly to himself. "Extraordinary." He looked to Iridius. "You appear to be the leader. Is that the case?"

"I am," Iridius said. "Captain Iridius B. Franklin, Federation Space Command."

"Space Command," Heisenberg said. "Fascinating. It is clear that in your time, society is much less rigid. Even as captain, your subordinates seem to speak freely, to disagree and discuss."

"Yes," Iridius said in a monotone, "a remarkable amount of disagreement and discussion, believe me."

"From what year do you come?"

"2233," Iridius said.

"2233!" Heisenberg's eyes grew wide. "Tell me, what is the Earth like in 2233?"

"Hot," Rangi said. "Real hot."

"Captain," Quinn interjected, "I don't believe we should provide any more information. Anything we say could alter the future irrevocably. Perhaps with an ordinary citizen it might not matter as much, but Werner Heisenberg is among the leading minds in human history. He may well be influenced to make scientific breakthroughs he should not otherwise make."

Heisenberg looked at Quinn. "Are you a scientist?"

Quinn nodded with the type of shy response Iridius thought she had well and truly conquered over the last year. "Yes, sir."

"Please, call me Werner. The knowledge you must have from so many years' advancement must be astonishing, Miss...?"

Quinn's face bloomed red again. "Kira Quinn and no, please, I just put into practice the discoveries of minds like yourself."

"She's a genius," Iridius said. "But that's why I listen to her. If Quinn says it's dangerous to share information with you, then I'm afraid we can't tell you any more."

"I understand," Heisenberg said, "but believe me when I tell you I have already made scientific breakthroughs I should not have."

"You're talking about the atomic bomb?" Gentrix said.

Heisenberg nodded. "Miss Quinn here said I spoke of my opposition to it after the war. That is true already. But at least you say there is an after the war. That seems difficult to imagine sometimes, it's hard to believe that this horror won't just keep going forever. Is that why you are here? To stop humanity from destroying itself with nuclear weapons?"

"Not exactly," Iridius said. "We're trying not to change history, though we don't appear to be doing a very good job of that."

"You are explorers then? Observers of history?"

"Not that exactly either," Iridius said.

"Our spaceship needs a jump start," Junker said. Iridius looked at her. "What?" she said. "It's true, and you've already told him we're from Space Command."

"You require repairs," Heisenberg said. Then he seemed to

come to a realisation. "No, you require an energy source, an atomic energy source. That's why you're here. Perhaps I can be of assistance."

"Go ahead, Quinn," Iridius said. "If Herr Heisenberg can help us then all the better. Tell him what you need."

"Our main engines are not nuclear powered," Quinn said. "They are fuelled by a continuous reaction between," she paused, as if carefully considering her words, "types of particles, and we require a large spherical energy release to restart the reaction. The amount of localised energy released from an atomic blast would be ideal. I'm aware that at this point in time no one has developed a functioning atomic bomb, but whatever you can provide would be helpful, ideally enriched uranium."

Heisenberg looked momentarily confused. "You obviously have much knowledge about this time period. You knew exactly where to come. You know that both myself and Oppenheimer are working on the bomb. Why then do you say that no one has a functioning prototype?"

Now it was Quinn's turn to be confused. "Because no one develops a working prototype of the atomic bomb until 1945."

"Really?"

"Well, yes. I mean, I probably shouldn't say this, but Oppenheimer gets there first. The Allies develop the atomic bomb and use it to end the war in 1945."

"Fascinating," Heisenberg said.

"Fascinating that Oppenheimer develops the bomb first?" Quinn asked.

"No, no," Heisenberg said. "Fascinating because I've got one upstairs."

"I'm sorry," Quinn said. "You've got a working atomic bomb upstairs?"

"My prototype, yes," Heisenberg said. "We haven't tested it yet, but I have all confidence it will work."

Quinn looked at the others.

"Don't look at me," Iridius said, his hands raised. "You know I've got no idea what's going on."

"That just doesn't..." Quinn started, then stopped herself. "You haven't told anyone yet, have you?"

Heisenberg looked at her. "No, I have not."

"You have the weapon that will win the war for Hitler and you haven't told anyone," Iridius said.

"Precisely," Heisenberg said. "The weapon that would win the war for Hitler."

"Oh shit," Iridius said with realisation. "You don't want him to win."

Heisenberg looked at Iridius without answering. "Come with me," he said, turning and heading up the stairs.

Iridius looked to Gentrix, who shrugged, and then to Quinn. "You're a Heisenberg super-fan, can we trust him?"

Quinn nodded. "I believe so, Captain. Many historians believe Heisenberg purposely withheld development progress from Nazi officials, but I don't think anyone ever suspected he'd actually developed a working prototype."

"We know the Germans never use an atomic bomb, so is it fair to say we won't be changing history if we steal it?"

"I think so," Quinn said.

They followed Heisenberg up the stairs, around a mezzanine level and down a corridor, stopping in front of a door marked as the office of Werner Heisenberg, Institute Director.

Heisenberg opened the door and entered. It was a large space with a heavy wooden desk and several bookshelves of textbooks, but it also contained a haphazard array of primitive looking (at least to twenty-third-century eyes) scientific equipment, large boxes with glass bulbs and dial readouts, a table with a contraption of long tubes and a blackboard covered in hastily scribbled equations.

Heisenberg made his way to a large chest in one corner of the room, then fished around in his coat pocket for a set of keys and unlocked it. He lifted the lid with an immense effort. It must have been much heavier than it looked, which made sense when Iridius saw that the chest and lid were lined with a thick layer of dark metal. Inside was a metallic sphere a little larger than a basketball, criss-crossed with tubes and wires.

"It's much smaller than I expected," Quinn said. "The Manhattan Project prototype was much bigger."

"It's a scaled-down prototype," Heisenberg said, "only meant to demonstrate the chain reaction of nuclear fission."

"Wait," Iridius said, "you keep an atomic bomb in your office?"

"In a lead-lined chest," Heisenberg replied.

"Still, not the kind of thing you keep under the desk, is it?"

"It's non-functional in its current state," Heisenberg said.

"Amazing," Quinn said. "And you kept this a secret?"

"Would this be a suitable energy source to restart your ship?" Heisenberg asked.

Quinn turned to look at him. "How heavy is the core?"

"Fifteen kilograms of Uranium-235," Heisenberg replied.

"Close to minimum mass for fission to propagate," Quinn said.

"Glad to hear my calculations are correct then," Heisenberg replied. "I want you to take it."

"We can't do that," Quinn said.

"Ah, Quinn," Iridius said, "that is literally the point of us being here."

"You came here because you believed taking atomic technology from Germany would not change history," Heisenberg said. He looked down at the bomb in the chest on the floor. "Most people believe whoever gets this bomb first will win the war. That's true, then?"

Quinn nodded. "More or less."

"Then you must take this," Heisenberg said. "I do not want Hitler to win this war. I love Germany, it is my home, but I do not love Hitler's Germany."

"Thank you," Iridius said.

"Tell me, is there still war where you come from?"

Iridius took a moment and then nodded. "There is." He looked at Gentrix and then back again. "People still do bad things on both sides of conflict, but things do get better, life improves, science wins out. All I can tell you is humanity is a work in progress, but we're trying."

Heisenberg nodded. "Cannot ask more than that. Good luck."

Iridius nodded to him and then turned to Rangi. "Give me a hand with this, Rangi." Iridius reached down to grab a small handle on one side of the bomb.

Rangi hesitated.

Iridius turned to Heisenberg. "Is it safe to handle?"

"For short periods, it is perfectly safe."

"See?" Iridius said, turning back to Rangi. "Now pick it up."

Rangi looked down at the bomb, not so subtly crossed his legs and then reach down to grab the other handle. "Gronk, it's heavier than it looks," Rangi said.

"Let's get out of here," Iridius said. He looked to Heisenberg and nodded again before they made their way to the door.

Quinn hesitated. She turned back to Heisenberg. "You might have given up this work, but you are long remembered. I want you to know that."

Heisenberg smiled.

"But I have to ask..." Quinn said.

"That I don't say anything," Heisenberg said, "and that I don't use anything you've told me in my work."

Quinn nodded.

Heisenberg smiled. "Not sure it would help my reputation in the scientific community if I said I have been visited by time travellers from the year 2233. It would also not be wise for me to tell the authorities in the Nazi party that I developed an atomic bomb prototype but gave it away. I think you can be confident this encounter will remain a secret."

Quinn smiled. "It was an honour to meet you."

"And you."

Quinn turned and joined the others as they walked out the door. They hurried down the main stairs and to the front door, where they slowed. Iridius opened the door slowly so he could check the coast was clear, but when he swung it open, one of the young Nazi soldiers was standing right in front of him. The soldier stopped suddenly, startled at the group standing in front of him. His eyes went wide and then narrowed with recognition. "But, how are...you were outside?" He slowly looked down at the spherical object Iridius and Rangi held, and then back up at Iridius. "Who are you?" The soldier demanded, suddenly trying to establish an air of authority. "You can't take anything out of here."

"Junker," Iridius said.

"Aye, Cap?"

"Hold this."

Iridius passed her the side of the bomb he was holding and then looked back to the soldier. "Tell me something, are you an innocent kid who just happened to be born in a country that fell into the wrong hands and now you've been drafted into a war you want nothing to do with, or are you on board with the whole Nazi thing?"

The soldier hesitated for a moment. "I was a proud member of the Hitler Youth and I serve the Führer with pride. You will not escape."

"Good," Iridius said. "I don't feel so bad about this then."

"Intrud—" the soldier began to shout, but...

Crack.

Iridius swung his fist and hit the Nazi soldier in the face, square on the cheekbone, twisting the unfortunate young man's head to the side and sending him tumbling back. He slammed the back of his head onto one of the building's pillars. His eyes glazed over and went distant as he slid down into a pile of Hugo Boss on the floor. Iridius shook his hand and flexed his fingers. "Ow. Punching people hurts."

"I thought you were an adventuring space captain?" Gentrix asked.

"I am," Iridius said, still shaking his hand. "But I do most of my adventuring either on a ship or bravely running away from people who want to punch me. Despite popular belief, ship captains don't really do a lot of punching. If something needs punching I've usually got a giant purple alien to do that."

Rangi looked from Iridius to the German soldier on the ground and then back to his captain. He had that wide Rangi grin plastered over his face. "I told you we'd have to punch a Nazi," he said, sounding far too pleased with himself.

"Yes, congratulations Rangi, you were right," Iridius said. "Now, this is the part, like I said, when we run away from the people who want to punch us."

The away team hurried out of the building and into the street. Behind them, the front door of the Kaiser Wilhelm Institute for Physics burst open with the kind of aggressive slam that could only be followed by a handful of angry individuals chasing someone. Sure enough, before you could say *achtung*, four Nazi soldiers flooded out the front door, drawn by their colleague's call. They looked around quickly and saw Iridius, Rangi, Quinn, Junker and Gentrix a short way up the street. One of the soldiers shouted, and they all began raising rifles and running in their direction.

"I don't think they want to punch us," Rangi said. "I think they want to shoot us."

"Come on," Iridius said, running back in the direction of the small laneway beside the fence where they had first emerged onto the street. "Gentrix, can you trigger the hologram again?"

Gentrix, who had scooped up the small projection box on their way past, shook her head. "It's out of battery, and I don't think there's a high-amp wireless charger in 1943."

Iridius heard the Nazi soldiers follow them into the lane. With the heavy prototype atom bomb slung between them, the soldiers were easily gaining on them. There was the loud echoing crack of a rifle shot, and just in front of Iridius the ground burst up in a small spray of dirt. This was followed by a second shot, just as the away team rounded the corner onto the street that led to the park. They would never make it that far before the soldiers caught them. Iridius scanned wildly for some way to escape.

"Psst."

Iridius turned at the aggressive hiss and saw that it was coming from a nearby house. The windows were dark but the front door open.

"Quickly," a voice from the door said in what, despite the presence of his UTI, Iridius knew to be English – I mean, Galactic Standard. "In here now."

Iridius was a highly trained officer of the Federation Space Command, the captain of a starship trained in rapid tactical thinking, and his lightning-quick risk assessment determined that yes, entering a completely dark house at the behest of an unknown stranger in a place that was not only a foreign location but also a foreign time was the correct strategic decision. At least when the alternative was being shot in the back by Nazis.

"Come on," he said to the others as he moved towards the small white-walled house, tucked away behind a picket fence and neatly manicured garden. He hurried inside and moved down the tight hallway. The others followed him inside and then their unknown saviour closed the door before the soldiers emerged onto the street.

The figure at the door turned with his finger held to his lips in a gesture of quiet. It was lucky he did do that, because Iridius needed the reminder. What he wanted to do was to shout out something like "What the gronking shit?" or "Jupiter's nuts!" or "It's fucking you!", because the man standing in front of them in the hallway of a house in 1943 Berlin was, without a doubt, Department of Historical Timeline Preservation Deputy Director of Regional Operations for Milky Way Segment 2B, Reginald Benedict.

CHAPTER TEN_

BENEDICT LEANED close to the door, listening. He held his hand up in warning, obviously waiting until the sounds died away. Then he turned away from the door, apparently satisfied the Nazis had moved on.

"It's you," Iridius said before Benedict could speak. "Tweed suit and all. Have you come to arrest us according to the terms of article sixty-six of the inter-time rearrangement bullshit?"

Benedict's brow furrowed in confusion. "What are you talking about? Come this way quickly."

"No way," Iridius said. "You've tried to kill us once already."

"From where I'm standing it seems like the complete opposite to me," Benedict said. "Bloody idiots would have got yourselves killed." He looked at the atomic bomb that Rangi and Junker still held. "Not exactly subtle, were you? Now come this way, because if the Jerrys get on a house-to-house search I can't bloody hide you under the dining room table, can I?"

Benedict moved past Iridius and the others and continued a short way down the hall. He pulled a long rug aside and began lifting several loose floorboards. Beneath was a crude staircase descending into an area of pressing darkness. "In you get."

"What's down there?" Iridius asked. "Matter disruption beam? Flortarkian Wasp Torture Chamber? Jakseriot Skin Flayer? Not gronking likely we're going down there."

Benedict's face showed nothing but more confusion. "You're bloody strange, you are. The family who lived here used it to hide some of the local Jews. They all fled before it was found, thankfully for us. We can lay low in here for a while at least."

"Ah, Captain," Quinn said, "I don't think this is who you think it is."

"What?"

"At least not yet."

Iridius looked from Quinn to Benedict. "Ah," he said. "That makes sense."

"What are you on about?" Benedict said. "Hurry up. We can talk this over inside."

"Fine," Iridius said.

Benedict grabbed an oil lamp off a side table and lit it, heading down the stairs after Iridius and the others. He stopped to replace the first of the floorboards and then dragged the rug over the opening before inserting the remaining loose boards in from beneath.

As Benedict came down the stairs his lamp lit the gloomy space around them with a constant flickering. It was little more than a hole that had been dug in the clay-like dirt and reinforced with wooden trusses at the sides. Benedict moved to a small table and lit another lamp, then moved to the opposite corner and lit another that was hanging from a stake jammed into the wall. With three sources of light the makeshift cellar was, though Iridius wouldn't admit it, less spooky.

As Benedict held his lamp up close to his face, Iridius realised his mistake immediately. This man was definitely Reginald Benedict, the same annoying sod who'd projected himself onto the bridge of his ship, explained all the things he'd done wrong in regards to time travel and then tried to kill him and his entire crew, but Quinn was right – this was not the Reginald Benedict they had met.

Where that Reginald Benedict had looked to be in his early to mid-forties, this one had no grey around his temples, less lines on his face and more definition in his jawline. This Reginald Benedict looked to be in his twenties.

Stupid time travel.

"This is what you meant about it getting rather confusing with the order of things, then."

"What?" Benedict said.

"Never mind, please continue."

"Right then," Benedict said. "Now we can talk. Who are you? OSS?"

"What's that?"

Gentrix leaned over to him. "Office of Strategic Services," she whispered. "Forerunner of the Central Intelligence Agency which was rolled into Earth Intelligence which eventually became part of the Federation Intelligence Bureau."

Iridius stared at her.

"What?" she said. "I like spy stuff."

"Obviously," Quinn added.

"Sure," Iridius said, turning back to Benedict. "That's us. OSS. Who are you?"

"Bollocks you are," Benedict said. "If you're not going to tell me who you are then I'm not going to tell you —"

"Reginald Benedict," Iridius interrupted. "That's who you are. I was only asking to be polite."

Benedict looked momentarily shocked before he attempted to cover it up. "Well," he said, "seems I am at a disadvantage. I am indeed Reginald Benedict, MI6. Are you going to tell me how you know that?"

"MI6?" Rangi said. "Like James Bond?"

"Sorry?" Benedict said. "I'm afraid I don't know anyone by that name."

"You know," Rangi said. "Bond, James Bond. Shaken, not stirred."

"Rangi," Quinn said. "He doesn't exist."

"I know he's not real, Lieutenant Commander," Rangi said. "But I've watched all the old movies. Everyone knows who James Bond is."

"She means the character doesn't exist yet Rangi, you gronkhead," Junker said.

"Oh right," Rangi said. "Something for you to look forward to then, Benedict. You'll love it. Connery was the best, but then Flentrakillian Dominic Throbstain was good too, even if there was a lot of uproar about a human-Venusian hybrid playing Bond."

"Just ignore them," Iridius said to Benedict. "My name is Captain Iridius Franklin and this is my *mostly* competent team."

"You aren't yanks," Benedict said. "Not Russians. What are you, Canadians? Australians? Norwegian or something?"

"Where we come from is unimportant. Thank you for your assistance. We'd best be on our way."

"I don't think so," Benedict said. He looked at the bomb. "I've been watching that lab for months, trying to gather any intelligence on whether the Germans are working on the bomb and how far along they might be, and you lot just walk in there and take that object out of there. Is that a bomb?"

"It's more like a prototype," Quinn said.

Benedict reached inside his jacket and pulled out a pistol, pointing it at Iridius's face. "I'd best be taking it back to the UK then. Hand it over."

"And here I was starting to think you must have just turned into a twat later in life, but then you go and pull a gun on me."

"Shhh," Benedict said.

"Don't shhh me—" Iridius began, but Benedict held up his hand, shot him a look and pointed upstairs.

Iridius stopped to listen. He was about to declare he couldn't hear anything when he caught the distinct sound of steps moving down the hall overhead. The boards creaked with each ominous footfall until they came to a decidedly more ominous stop. For a tense moment, everything was still. The cellar, already quiet, fell into dead silence, and by that I mean the kind of silence that only happens when people know if they aren't silent, they're probably dead.

Benedict had his eyes closed and Iridius wondered if he was praying. That was the sort of thing people did in the olden days. Religion still existed in the twenty-third century but generally speaking, once a species discovered faster-than-light travel and discovered how many thousands of other sentient beings were out there, even the most dominant religions quickly faded into obscurity, becoming mostly token gestures for those who liked tradition.

There were always holdouts, of course, but while a religion might have managed to fool itself into believing it was the only correct one out of a dozen or even a hundred on one planet, it became awfully difficult to maintain that stranglehold on belief when confronted with the millions of religions throughout the galaxy.

There were beliefs as varied as the universe existing in the testicle of an infinitely large dust-mite creature known as Magrox, to the idea that the universe did not exist at all but rather, was the reflection of a single sentient turtle-like creature looking into a kind of mirror fragmented at the sub-atomic level, with each reflection creating a particle of the standard model, to the utterly preposterous idea that an all-knowing entity created the universe and then died and rose again as a zombie on a completely inconsequential planet, only to be later celebrated by a rabbit giving out chocolate eggs.

Point is, by Iridius's time, religion was generally accepted to be mythological stories invented by societies to help them grapple with the existential questions of where the hell did we come from and what the hell happens next. Still, at this moment, Iridius couldn't see the harm in Benedict asking whoever might listen for a little help.

Of course, because thoughts and prayers don't actually do anything in the face of the cold, uncaring universe, the rug in the hallway above was pulled aside and the floorboards levered up and slid over.

Iridius leaned forward. Without saying anything, and as gently as he could, he pinched the barrel of Reginald Benedict's gun between thumb and forefinger. Slowly, he moved it away from his face and up to the top of the stairs where at any second, Iridius expected the faces of Nazi soldiers would appear, ready to put this pre-made grave they were all huddled in to good use.

"I know you've got a gun pointed up at me," came a familiar British voice, "but let's just lower that, shall we? No need for you to shoot. That would just be unpleasant for all of us, and no doubt rather confusing for you when you see who you've shot, Mr Benedict."

Interestingly, it appeared that Reginald Benedict did not recognise the voice, because he didn't lower the weapon. "Who are you?" he demanded.

"Captain Franklin," the voice called down from the top of the stairs again. "I promise I mean you no harm. Would you mind reassuring your present company down there that I obviously don't mean him any harm, either?"

"It's always confusing when you hear your own voice, isn't it?" Iridius said. "I hate re-listening to my captain's log. Your voice never sounds quite the same as you think it does when it's coming out."

"Bone conduction," Quinn said. "When you hear your own voice you're also hearing low-frequency vibrations in the bones of your head. That makes your voice sound lower to you."

"See," Iridius said. "There you go. I think you should lower the pistol though, because this is going to be weird enough for you without a gun flashing around."

Benedict looked at Iridius, but didn't lower his gun.

"Here," Iridius said as he reached out and once again gently took hold of the barrel of the gun, lowering it until it was pointed at the floor. "Alright, it's safe to come down the stairs. Though I'm not making any promises that I won't punch you in the face. I'm in a face-punching mood, it seems."

"I understand how you feel, Captain Franklin, but I'd like the chance to explain. There are other factors at play here."

"Fine."

"Alright. I'm coming down."

As expected, the man who descended the stairs was none other than the older Reginald Benedict. Also, as expected, the younger Reginald Benedict did not react all that well to the sight of another, older version of himself.

"What the bloody hell?" Young Benedict said. "That's not possible. Who the hell are you?" He made to raise the gun but Iridius reached out and stopped him.

"Look," Iridius said, "as much as I wouldn't mind you putting a bullet into the older version of yourself, I imagine a loud gunshot might draw unwanted attention."

Young Benedict looked from Iridius to Older Benedict. "This isn't possible."

"Yes, it's all very confusing," Older Benedict said. "I'm you from the future."

"Hate to tell you, but you're a bit of a dick when you're older," Iridius said to Young Benedict.

"Not as much as you think though, Captain Franklin," Older Benedict said. "You need to understand, I never intended to kill you. If I had intended to destroy your ship then you would already be dead."

"Bit presumptuous," Iridius said.

"But true, I'm afraid."

"It is strange we escaped, Captain," Quinn said. "Benedict's ship has weapons we've never seen, able to pass directly through our shields and yet they missed. There's no reason to believe their targeting wouldn't be as advanced as their weapons."

"Just my good flying," Rangi said.

"You are indeed a good pilot, Lieutenant Rangi," Older Benedict said. "Space Ace Rangi is quite well regarded in the historical record of Federation Space Command."

"Wait," Rangi said, "I get remembered as Space Ace? For real?"

"Yes."

"Fuck yeah."

"Oh great," Iridius said, "thanks for that. Now we'll never hear the end of it. Tell me then Benedict, if you didn't kill us on purpose, what exactly were you trying to do?"

"It's complicated."

"No shit," Iridius said. "Everything's complicated, try me."

"I needed you to escape and enter the wormhole so that you would end up here, in 1943, and make contact with me." Older Benedict pointed to Young Benedict. "At least, with that version of me, to ensure that I am recruited by the Department of Historical Timeline Preservation so that this version of my life does not get relegated to the meta-past."

"What the hell are you talking about?" Young Benedict asked.

"Meta-time?" Quinn asked. "What do you mean by that?"

"Well," Benedict said, "I can give you the basic version."

"I'm sorry," Young Benedict said, "I just don't feel like my question is getting the attention it deserves. This is me from the future, but apparently much further in the future than should be possible, so I feel like all this concerns me more than is being acknowledged. So, once again, what the hell is going on?"

"Yes, yes," Older Benedict said, turning to his younger self as an exasperated parent might. "You'll just have to wait. Can't go getting ahead of yourself. Like you might say in your time: spoiler alert." Older Benedict paused. "Or that might be a little later. Mrs Holloway would know, but I've had to leave her behind to monitor the situation. Still, the point is, it's never good to find out too much about your own personal timeline before you're supposed to. Now, what was I talking about again?"

"Meta-time," Quinn said.

"Right, yes, yes, jolly good stuff. Meta-time is most easily understood as an additional dimension of space–time. The easiest way to think of it is as the universe remembering what happened."

"The universe remembers other timelines?" Quinn asked. "You mean like a many-worlds interpretation?"

"No, not exactly," Older Benedict said. "I'm no expert on whether other parallel universes exist, or any of those theoretical ideas. I'm talking about how this universe, our universe, handles timeline divergence. There is only one timeline, but I know you are troubled by the apparent appearance of paradoxes that time travel can cause within that timeline."

"You're not fucking wrong," Iridius said.

"So, this is how it was explained to me," Older Benedict continued. "Imagine you invent a time machine."

"Don't need to imagine," Iridius grumbled under his breath. "That's why I'm in this goddamn mess."

"You use the time machine to go back in time and give yourself the plans to the time machine before you invented it. You've then overwritten your future timeline with one where you didn't invent the time machine, you were just given the plans. You then later send the plans back to yourself once again. This creates a predestination paradoxical loop.

"From an internal observer, it seems as if the time machine is never actually invented. The plans are simply received and then sent back to be received again. However, from the perspective of the universe, we know the time machine was invented in the previous timeline. This is what we call meta-time. Paradoxes, like time, depend on the observer."

"So, that's what you're trying to do?" Quinn asked. "Fix paradoxes?"

"The Department of Historical Timeline Preservation exists to rectify paradoxes, protect the timeline or undo damage to the historically correct timeline."

"Right," Iridius said. "Now, I love a science lecture as much as the next person."

"No, you don't," Rangi interjected.

"Yes, exactly, sarcasm lost on you as always, Lieutenant. Point is, as much as we're learning here about the fundamental nature of the universe, we are in a tiny hiding space under a house in 1943 having just stolen the Nazi atomic bomb. If it's not too much trouble, can we get the gronking Jupiter's nuts out of here?"

"No rush, Captain Franklin," Older Benedict said. "Still got ten minutes before the attack."

"What attack?"

Older Benedict was about to answer when he was interrupted by a beep. He pulled a small, clear glass tablet from his pocket. When he held it out in front of him, a small holographic image of Mrs Holloway appeared on the surface.

"Mrs Holloway, what can I do for you?"

"Reginald," Mrs Holloway said, "*Argona* has picked up another DHTP vessel entering this temporal zone."

"Righto, perhaps they're just passing through. Dealing with another issue maybe."

"I've already received a transmission from them," Holloway said. "It's the *Renthal.*"

"Well, bugger," Older Benedict said. He turned to look at Iridius. "This might be a good time for one of those quite adaptable 'fuck's."

The small hologram of Holloway spoke again. "The ship is in Earth orbit and Deputy Director Savage is making her way planetside with orders to eliminate you and the crew of the *Deus Ex.* I suggest you leave."

"Mrs Holloway," Older Benedict said, and Iridius noticed that his jaunty British air had faded somewhat, "I need to explain to you—"

"I've already done too much even telling you this, Reginald," Mrs Holloway said. "I don't know why you're trying to mess with your timeline but I won't have anything to do with that. The consequences are clear. You won't have any past or any future if Savage gets hold of you. You need to leave, now."

The hologram vanished and Older Benedict shoved the small communication slate back into his pocket. "Come on," he said as he began moving up the stairs, shoving the loose floorboards aside. "Let's move."

"Go," Iridius said to the away team. "Back to the shuttle."

As they emerged back up into the hallway of the small house, the Older Benedict reached inside his cloak and pulled out a small pistol of a type Iridius had never seen before. Probably some sort of matter disruption atomic rearrangement brain inversion ray or something.

"Have you got weapons?" Older Benedict asked Iridius.

"They're on the shuttle," Iridius replied.

"Blimey, what bloody good are they going to do there?"

"I don't know," Iridius said. "I was trying to be discreet."

"Alright, just stick with me then," Older Benedict said as he opened the front door. After just a moment of looking out, he slammed it shut again.

"What?" Iridius asked. "What is it?"

"Deputy Director Kat Savage."

"I thought you were the Deputy Director."

"I'm Deputy Director of Regional Operations for Milky Way Segment 2B. Kat Savage is Deputy Director of Regional Operations for Milky Way Segment 4D. I don't need to tell you that 2B is a much more desirable posting than 4D."

"You do, actually."

"She's never forgiven the fact that I won that promotion over her, and the amount of Form 213Fs she's completed since then requesting a re-evaluation of my selection as preferred candidate is frankly embarrassing," Older Benedict continued. "She's been looking for any excuse to take me down a peg, so she'll be thinking this is bloody top shelf."

Benedict turned to them, ready to say something more, but the younger Benedict raised his own pistol and pointed it at the older Benedict.

"We aren't going anywhere until you explain to me what the hell is happening," Young Benedict said.

"Listen," Older Benedict said, "I've already told you I'm not supposed to tell you what's going to happen in your future. You probably wouldn't believe me anyway. You just have to trust me that I'm trying to do the right thing. Right now, we need to figure out how to escape. Like I said, Kat Savage isn't the biggest admirer of us, so the opportunity to kill us twice at the same time would probably be the jolly best day of her professional life. Although, I've got to think, Director Kron and the rest of the

DHTP won't want her to remove you from the timeline too after you've been exposed to these events. That would cause damage to several rectifications made to the historical timeline and only cause further deviation. No, killing me, Captain Franklin and the rest of his crew is fine, but not you." Older Benedict raised his own pistol and pointed it at his younger self. "Lower your gun please."

"No."

Older Benedict sighed. He flipped a switch on his pistol and then squeezed the trigger. Nothing much happened. Iridius had expected some sort of disintegration ray, but there was nothing – the younger version of Benedict seemed completely unharmed. He hadn't moved, still aiming his pistol at the older Benedict. It wasn't until the older Benedict approached him that Iridius realised something weird was happening.

Benedict took the pistol out of the hand of his younger self, who failed to move at all. His hand, now empty, remained outstretched as if gripping a pistol. His face hadn't changed expression. Not even his eyes had moved.

Once he had secured the gun, Older Benedict took a step back, aimed his gun at the younger version of himself again and pulled the trigger. Young Benedict bent over, gasping for breath. He looked at his now empty hand and then looked to Older Benedict, shocked and frankly terrified.

"What...what was that?" Young Benedict asked.

"A localised entropy slowing field," Older Benedict said. "It's not very pleasant, is it? For all intents and purposes, your body experiences time moving differently to everyone else. Unfortunately, that includes everything else in the universe too, including air molecules. You can't breathe, and a few of your bodily functions don't work very well. It's fatal if you're left in that state too long."

"Bit of a risk, isn't it? You can't kill him," Quinn said, "he's your younger self. Wouldn't that mean you'd die?"

"No. It's confusing, but generally doesn't work that way," Older Benedict said. "If you go back and kill your grandfather you don't immediately vanish, but your existence becomes a fragment of meta-past that would not exist in the meta-present. It isn't a particularly nice experience though, because as far as the anyone else knows, you don't exist, and it becomes very difficult to prove who you are. Makes getting a driver's license renewed a bit of a nightmare."

"So," Quinn said, being the only one following the logical loop-the-loops well enough to actually ask questions, "why does it matter to you if this version of you joins the DHTP?"

Benedict smiled at her. "It matters to someone more aware of meta-states than me. Fact is, threatening my younger self is probably my only chance out of this mess, and if it's my only chance then it's your only chance too."

"What do you mean, threatening me?" Younger Benedict asked. In reply, Older Benedict grabbed him and held the pistol to his head.

"You're leading the way out, there's a good chap," Older Benedict said.

Iridius watched as the older version of Reginald Benedict walked towards the door, holding his younger self in front of him. "Are you holding yourself hostage?"

"Looks that way, Captain Franklin."

Iridius shook his head. "Fucking time travel."

CHAPTER ELEVEN_

BENEDICT MADE himself open the door – and I don't mean he
built up the courage to open the door, I mean he forced the
younger version of himself forward. "Get the door. Slowly."

Young Benedict reached out as Older Benedict held the
pistol to his head. He took hold of the door handle, turned it
gingerly and pulled the door open.

"Go," Older Benedict said, shoving him forward again.

"Take it easy," Young Benedict said. "I'm going."

The two of them moved out the door and down the front
steps.

"Stop right there, Benedict," a woman's voice called from
outside. "Don't take another step."

Iridius wasn't entirely sure he wanted to follow Benedict and
Benedict outside. Dealing with one agent of the Department of
Historical Timeline Preservation was bad enough. He was reluc-
tant to face another one. He turned, looking down the dark
hallway of the house. There would be a back door down there. It
might be possible for them to sneak out that way and avoid
getting involved with whatever was going on out there with the
time police.

"Don't bother, Captain Franklin," the same woman's voice yelled again. "We've got the place surrounded. There's only one way out, so make it quick please."

Iridius looked to Quinn and Gentrix. Quinn's mouth thinned, but she failed to offer a convenient scientific escape plan. Gentrix raised her eyebrows, apparently not having any better ideas either.

"Fine," Iridius said. "Let's go and meet more of this lot then."

As he emerged from the house, Iridius saw the woman he assumed was Deputy Director Savage. She was standing on the street just outside the small front garden. Iridius didn't really know what to expect from the Department of Historical Time-line Preservation – a few hours ago he didn't even know of their existence – but from his experience so far, he'd expected some stodgy old lady akin to a well-armed librarian.

However, unlike Reginald Benedict, Deputy Director Savage was not kitted out like a long lost academic. She wore a black leather trench coat which hung down to her ankles over tight clothes in bright oranges and greens lined with strips of reflective tape. Iridius would have guessed she was in her early forties, but her hair was shaved on either side of her head with a blue and pink mohawk left on the top. Her eyes shimmered with dark, sparkly make-up and under her right eye was the scarified skin of an optical implant – but not the modern implant someone like Ensign Herd would have fitted. This was old-style flesh butchery.

Standing either side of her were two men dressed in similar trench coats, but they wore theirs over tight-fitting armoured vests and baggy pants. Holsters strapped across their torsos or around their waists displayed chunky oversized pistols. Both had shaved heads inlaid with wiring, and similarly rough implants.

Altogether, the three of them gave off an unmistakable aesthetic.

"Oh god," Iridius said, "fucking cyberpunks."

"Cool," Junker said, in the same way a child obsessed with pirates might say if they saw Blackbeard live in the flesh. before they discovered that pirates were actually all pretty terrible.

"Junker," Iridius said, "cyberpunks are cool in the same way that war, pestilence and famine are cool, which is to say they're not. They're a leading cause of societal collapse."

Iridius had felt a lot of emotions when he'd seen those Nazi swastikas, but for him, the Third World War was more recent history. Historically, what was termed World War Three ranged from the mid-2080s through to the early 2120s, an exceedingly long period of global conflict in which the Earth had been brought to its knees and humanity came awfully close to extinction.

Even then, the exact dates of the war are hard to pin down, because conflict both within and between nation states had begun long before then, and continued for a good while after. Ultimately, the Third World War was a war over both ideals and resources, brought about by rapid technological development, climate change, societal upheaval and the rapid deterioration of productive discourse as human society fractured down economic, political and social lines. It was such a chaotic time period that even the combatants were confusing. Some of the largest battles involved conflict between the Asian Alliance and the United States of America over much of the USA's west coast, the Water Wars of Africa, the invasion of Twitter-held territory by the combined armies of Instagram and Facebook, and the uprising of the Reptilians after they ousted the Illuminati from global control.

Historical scholars can spend their whole careers studying this time in Earth's past and still come out more confused than when they started. Cyberpunks were pretty much the archetype of everything wrong with the time period, perfect examples of resource excess, rampantly uncontrolled human–machine interfacing and humans whose brains were mushed by being directly piped into the internet of the time, which had deteriorated into a cesspit of one giant comments section.

Deputy Director Savage stared at Iridius for a moment and then reached into her jacket. Instead of pulling out a laser disintegration ray or something equally unpleasant, she instead pulled out a notebook, which she flicked open.

"Captain Franklin, you have previously been visited by officials from the Department of Historical Timeline Preservation, when you were informed that your actions, accidental or otherwise, were deemed in breach of section three hundred and sixteen point three two point one of statute seventeen of the code of the regulatory order of universal time. Since then, your actions have continued to present a risk to the historically correct timeline and as such, your case has now received an upgrade in preservation actions such that you and your crew are now to be retroactively eliminated from both the meta-present and meta-past. This has been authorised with forms 53B and C."

"And its associated by-laws," Benedict said.

"What?" Savage said, looking at Benedict with disdain.

"Regulatory order of universal time and its associated by-laws," Benedict said. "You forgot that bit. Not to worry. I do it too sometimes."

Savage looked at Benedict. "And you, Deputy Director Reginald Benedict, I'm happy to say your actions are in breach of Department of Historical Timeline Preservation Code of Conduct sections fourteen and sixteen regarding personal interference in timeline construction and preservation. You were told to eliminate Captain Franklin before he made contact with this version of you. Frankly, DHTP policy or not, I can't believe Director Kron trusted you to rectify your own timeline a second time. Your actions have deviated sufficiently enough from your assigned tasking that you are to be relieved of your position within the Department of Historical Timeline Preservation and, due to your attempts at alteration of the timeline for personal gain, you are to be eliminated. This has been authorised with form 53B and, on a personal note, it's about fucking time."

Older Benedict pulled his younger self closer, making a show of pressing the pistol to his head. "Don't think I missed your wording Kat. Mrs Holloway might be the detail-orientated one of my partnership, but I'm still a DHTP agent and we have to be vigilant, don't we? You've got authority to remove me, but not my younger self. That's too messy for the timeline. He's going to be recruited and loop through as me again, more or less."

Deputy Director Savage smiled like a ten-foot-tall Klaksian Snakeperson agreeing to uphold the treaty with the Menton Mousemen by only eating one member of their family. "I won't say you aren't correct, Benedict, but I'm happy to take the small wins when I can get them. At least with you gone I'm a shoo-in for your job."

"I wouldn't be so sure about that," Benedict said. "Stewart over in Sector 3A has done some good work. She's probably in with a jolly good shot."

"I'll tell you who's got a good shot," Savage said. "These two."

Taking their cue like true professionals, the cyberpunk goons either side of her moved in almost perfect synchronisation, each of them pulling out a pistol with a frankly absurdly fat barrel.

"Well, now now," Benedict said, "before you go doing that, here's the thing. I bet Kron was very clear about getting hold of my younger self here, wasn't he? That directive would have come down from Executive Management, maybe even the Time Board themselves."

Savage didn't say anything.

"Top shelf," Benedict said, "I thought as much. See, that's why I've gone and flicked on this little switch here," he nodded to the pistol he held to Younger Benedict's head. "It's a deadman switch, they tell me." He squeezed the trigger. "There, so now, if I let go in the event that, say, one of your fine chaps there kills me, the pistol fires and this younger version of me dies too, with all the chaos that'll cause in the Historical Timeline." Savage went to say something but Benedict continued. "Oh, and just to be clear, if you kill Captain Franklin here or any of his crew, I'll kill myself too, and by that I mean this me, not me me. You understand?"

Savage looked at Benedict. "So, you're going to keep yourself hostage forever, are you? How's that going to work, you stupid prim?"

"Well, that's not very kind at all, language like that, is it Kat?" Benedict turned to Iridius. "Prim is short for primitive. It's a derogatory term people in the DHTP use for those who originated from earlier time periods. It's supposed to equate with stupidity, you see, as though being born earlier somehow makes you less of a person. But people like Deputy Director Savage here are all bluster with their guns and what not. I mean, look at them. At least you made an effort to blend in to the time period. Hardly surprising she's been sent to Sector 4D, is it?"

"We were tasked with a fast response to stop you from going rogue, Benedict. I'm here to take you out, not go researching 1943," Savage said. "And this last roll of the dice isn't going to work. Just let your younger self go and we can get this finished quickly."

Benedict smiled. He looked at his watch. "Now see, here's the thing, Deputy Director Savage. I might be a prim in your eyes, but you forget that this here is my time. I know this time. I even know this exact moment. I've been here before." Benedict took a few steps back, shuffling closer to the house and moving his younger self back with him. Suddenly, the quiet of the night was interrupted by the long droning build of a wailing alarm. Horns blasted out across Berlin with rising and falling pitch.

"What is that?" Savage said.

"Maybe you should have done some research after all, Savage," Benedict said. "It's the 22nd of November, 1943. On this night, 764 aircraft of the Royal Air Force were let loose on Berlin. Aaaaaand," he said, drawing the word out, "*now*." The sound of dull thumping began, and soon the night-time streets were brightened with flashes as the clear sky erupted with popping bursts of anti-aircraft fire. A thudding explosion sounded in the distance, quickly followed by another, and then another. They seemed to be scattered in all directions, growing and falling in volume, so you couldn't tell whether the bombing was getting closer or further away. Aircraft could be heard high overhead, the steady drone of piston engines churning propellers through the sky, broken up by the whistling fall and thumping detonations of bombs.

"Come on," Iridius said. "We need to get the gronking hell out of here."

Benedict held up his hand in front of Iridius. "Wait. Cover your ears."

"What?" Iridius said.

A moment later, with a squeal followed by a terrifyingly bright and hot firey explosion, a bomb landed just down the street. It had plummeted through the roof and into the front room of a small house, showering the front garden with bricks. The concussion blast was enough to knock Deputy Director Savage and her two cronies off their feet. It left Iridius and the away team, none of whom had taken Benedict's advice to cover their ears, stunned. Iridius's ears rang with the tinnitus of a blown-out eardrum.

"Okay," Benedict said, "now we can get the gronking hell out of here."

Iridius wriggled his finger in his ear to try and clear the ringing. "What?"

Benedict looked at him. "I did tell you to cover your ears. Quickly now, this way."

Benedict moved off, dragging his younger self with him. Iridius looked at his crew, who were all in various states of recovery. "Come on."

They followed Benedict as he moved down the front steps and into the small garden, but instead of heading for the front gate and the street, where Savage and the other agents of the DHTP were gathering themselves, he turned and made his way across the grass and around the side of the house to where there was another small gate in the side fence. Benedict headed through the gate into a small lane between houses. Iridius waited, gesturing for the rest of the team to hurry through the gate ahead of him. Junker and Rangi came through last, still lugging the prototype.

"You alright?" Iridius asked.

"Of course, Cap," Rangi said. There was another explosion nearby. "This seems fine."

Iridius looked at Junker, who shrugged. "I mean, I'd prefer not to be carrying a nuclear weapon in the middle of an air raid, but you know, at least we're not bored."

"Benedict!" Savage shouted from the street. "This is madness. Give it up."

"If you wouldn't mind, we need to get cracking, Captain Franklin," Benedict said. "This way."

Iridius hurried out into the lane and Benedict led them away from the street. They clambered over a fallen fence, around the back of the next house and then through a series of small yards and courtyards before Benedict stopped, and released his grip on the younger version of himself. Young Benedict moved away quickly, rounding on his captor with a fierce expression.

"That Savage woman is right," he said. "You are a madman.

Holding me hostage. Leading us out into an air raid. Complete bloody madness."

"I won't deny that. What I'm doing is quite mad, but I do have a fairly good idea of where the bombs land, so that's not the mad bit. Eventually you'll know why I did all this and, while I can't know for certain, I'm fairly sure you'll attempt something similar. But maybe not – all depends on how well everything else goes, really. This is where you leave us. This spot is safe during the raid, so you'll be fine. You've got quite a journey ahead of you, and it's mostly a good one, especially when you meet *Argona*. She'll explain everything."

"You're just going to leave me out here?" Young Benedict said. "In the middle of this?"

"Indeed I am," Older Benedict said. "Next thing you know you'll be waking up on a spaceship as the DHTP's newest recruit."

"I'll be what?!"

Benedict raised his pistol at his younger self and pulled the trigger. This time Younger Benedict did not freeze in place. Instead, he dropped to the grass, unconscious.

"Quickly," Benedict said, "they won't be far behind us now."

As Iridius and the away team stood looking at the unconscious body of the younger Benedict, the older version hurried off before they could ask what the hell he was doing. But this was one of those situations where Iridius wasn't left with much choice but to follow the one person who seemed to know what was going on. Benedict led them through the backs of several more houses, eventually turning up a cobblestone path and guiding them back to the original street they'd been on. He paused, looking out. Seeing no sign of Savage, he hurried low and fast across the street.

Already, although it must only have been ten or fifteen minutes, the city seemed to glow red-orange with fires that had started in all directions. Down each street they saw houses smoking and partly demolished, gutted by the Allied bombs. There were people, too – not many, as most must have been hiding in bomb shelters, but the few people they did see, Iridius didn't want to look at for long. They were grey and black with ash and soot, stumbling disorientated along the streets.

"We should help them," Junker said. "Captain, we should help those people."

But it was Benedict who answered. "We can't change the timeline. These people either survive or they don't. We can't change that."

"But you can change whatever you want?" Junker said. "Is that it?"

Benedict looked at her without answering before turning to Iridius. "Your shuttle is in the park on the next street over, the one with the pond, isn't it?"

Iridius nodded. "That's right."

"Well, we'd better jolly well hurry then," Benedict said, moving off.

"Why's that?" Iridius said, but Benedict didn't stop to answer. Iridius had a bad feeling he knew why that was. "I said, why's that, Benedict?!"

As Iridius went to hurry after Benedict he felt a strange sensation in his jaw. It was as if his jaw muscles were twitching. Oh shit. Not now. He kept himself moving, trying to ignore the similar sensations in his arms and the pins and needles in his feet. This was easy enough to do, stumbling on through the night-time bombing of Berlin – at least until the headache started again. It came on suddenly, like an electric shock, or a bullet to the back of the skull. His head erupted with a pain that could not be ignored. He stumbled.

"Iridius?" Gentrix asked, reaching out to help support him.

"Captain, is it happening again?" Quinn asked.

Iridius stopped, bent double with a grimace and then nodded. "Keep going," he said. "Get to the shuttle."

"No," Quinn said. "We can't leave you here."

Iridius spun on her. "I said, get to the shuttle!" he yelled. Anger again. Misplaced and uncontrollable. This was followed swiftly by an almost unstoppable urge to cry. "Sorry," he said. "Quinn, I'm sorry." Iridius felt sudden guilt and fear, but he didn't think these emotions were because of the rebelling Aegix nanobots. He could almost handle the pain and crazy physical sensations. It was the loss of emotional control, the anger particularly, that really scared him.

"It's okay, Captain," Quinn said. "We've got you."

He felt Quinn and Gentrix either side of him, but before they could take hold of his weight his legs gave out and he dropped like a sack of the Plotark Stone Turnips they'd once delivered on board the *Diesel Coast*. And once he was on the ground, he was about as awkward to lift as a bag of those things too. Gentrix and Quinn had taken an arm each, trying to get him up, but they weren't having much luck. He had to help them.

Iridius tried to focus. Through the pain and the twitching and weird sensations, he tried to ignore everything else and just focus on standing. He got one leg underneath him and pushed. With Quinn and Gentrix taking most of his weight, he managed to stand. His legs were shaking. Quinn and Gentrix each put one of his arms around their shoulders and began to move, mostly carrying him along as best as they could.

"Hurry!" Benedict shouted from up ahead. "We're almost out of time. It's going to be jolly well close."

With Rangi and Junker carrying the bomb and Quinn and Gentrix carrying Iridius they couldn't move overly fast. Benedict was trying to urge them on, and even through his haze, Iridius could tell that he was growing more anxious by the moment. They followed a small street and emerged opposite the park.

"Come on," Benedict said, looking down at his watch. "Hurry!"

"We're moving as fast as we can!" Junker yelled. "What the fuck is the problem?"

Benedict looked at his watch again and then up at the sky. "Maybe it's later than I had recorded," he said. "Could we be that lucky?"

No.

They couldn't.

Somewhere overhead, a Royal Air Force Avro Lancaster Heavy Bomber let loose its payload. One of those bombs, a 4000-pound blockbuster, dropped from its weapons bay and fell on a trajectory that would see it land in a small park with a pond. Just as Reginald Benedict had known it would, the bomb fell and, because they had not been fast enough, landed squarely on top of the small shuttle which should have been three hundred years in the future, and not parked in Berlin in 1943.

With the shields switched off, the bomb punched easily through the roof of the shuttle and exploded. The visual camouflage system immediately shut down as the shuttle's systems were destroyed, and the away team watched as fragments of material burst outwards in an explosion of fire and out-of-place technology. The entire front section of the shuttle rained down as debris all across the park and into the pond and, as the dust and smoke cleared, the away team from the FSC Deus Ex were left staring at the gutted remains of their space shuttle, which was now fully visible and, obviously, not supposed to be there.

"Fuck," Junker said, neatly summing up the situation. That word really was so brilliantly useful.

CHAPTER TWELVE_

THENWHILE, back in the twenty-third century, Captain April Idowu, marooned captain of the *FSC Gallaway,* made her way across the rocky terrain of the moon of Acacia. Acacia's lower gravity meant that April could cover ground relatively fast while still lugging the Rat Trap, full of Aegix nanobots, along with her.

Still, even as she moved swiftly in the direction of the geological survey colony, she had to be careful. The low gravity meant she could leap in long bounding strides, not quite as massive as those that were possible on Earth's moon, but still larger than under the normal gravity range of most planets. The downside was that moving with such long strides was foreign, at least to her as a human.

It would have been perfectly natural to, say, one of the Gallemites, who were a race of largely hunter-gatherers evolved from gazelle-like creatures, widely regarded as the most graceful creatures in the galaxy. Although the Gallemites were rarely seen away from their homeworld, and even there they were timid and difficult to find. You see, not only were they considered the most graceful creatures in the galaxy, but their meat was also damn tasty. They made for particularly good burgers, I'm told, and if you think the fact that the Gallemites were sentient and only marginally less intelligent than humans meant they wouldn't be eaten, then I'm afraid I've got bad news for you about the nature of pretty much everybody.

For April though, unaccustomed as she was to the perception of distance as she traversed the landscape, numerous times she came close to landing short or long of where she was aiming and almost impaling herself on the sharp rocks.

April concentrated, moving as quickly as she could. Ahead of her was a geological survey station where one hundred and thirty-eight people had been forced into lockdown because of the release of the Aegix. One hundred and thirty-eight people who were probably wondering why they hadn't yet been rescued. Who knows what Admiral Tullet had told them? If he'd told them anything at all. Well, April was going to show them that they hadn't been abandoned.

She would get there, she would help them and she would get the Aegix she had collected to Lieutenant Commander Quinn, just as she had promised. How exactly she was going to do this, she didn't know, but in a moment of protective passion she'd said Captain Iridius Franklin was the greatest man she'd ever known and, while on reflection that may not be one hundred per cent accurate, if there was one thing she'd learned from him it was that sometimes you just had to improvise.

Gradually, April got used to the unfamiliar movement and she eventually, quite literally, took it in her stride. Once she got moving, she managed to reach the geological station in about an hour, which was a very respectable time in which to cover eleven kilometres of rocky terrain.

Still, it didn't feel fast enough. She had no idea how quickly the Aegix nanobots would spread. She wasn't even sure they were heading for the survey station, but she had more than a sneaking suspicion that once they discovered there was another outpost of sentient beings on the moon, they would make their way there, perhaps searching for an easier way to escape or simply because there were one hundred and thirty-eight people who needed to be prepared for the coming of the Synth-Hastur.

It felt like there was some great unseen monster chasing her, one that might reach her at any minute, and she wouldn't know until it was too late. She wouldn't know until the nanobots poured into her suit and liquified her, which she imagined, quite correctly, was not a pleasant way to depart this universe.

She looked over her shoulder at regular intervals, scanning for a black cloud of nanobots trying to chase her down like a swarm of pissed-off bees. But then, maybe they would be moving separately, too small to be seen. With this fear driving her on, April kept moving, focused on the survey station that soon came into view.

The station was a series of five blue buildings constructed on stilts to keep them level above the rocky uneven ground. They were laid out in a line and linked together by small passages, like the carriages of a train. The top of each of the compartments held scientific equipment, slowly rotating dishes, spinning wind measurement turbines, spectrographs and ground-penetrating radar. As April approached, she realised she had no idea how she was going to get inside. If the station was locked down by external Federation control, that wouldn't allow anyone out, but it wouldn't allow anyone in either. April wasn't sure she quite had the hang of Iridius Franklin's improvisational approach to missions. She tried to imagine what Iridius would say, and she could almost hear his voice: *How am I going to get inside? Dunno. Knock on the gronking door I guess.*

April made her last long stride off a high grey outcropping and landed with a metallic thunk at the bottom of the steel stairs leading up to the first compartment. She'd made it, and she hadn't been turned into pink goop yet. She knew this was a false sense of security, though. She may have reached the station, but she was still outside, after all. It was like they'd always said in flight school: more than half of all accidents happen on final approach and landing – never get complacent.

She moved quickly up the steps, taking them three at a time, and reached the thick front door. Unsurprisingly, it was sealed shut, opening controls unresponsive. She leaned out over the railing and looked down the side of the compartment, searching for any way inside. There were windows, but they too had been sealed shut with thick blast shields. The roof, she had already seen, had access panels for maintenance. She climbed on the railing and hoisted herself up onto the top of the compartment, then moved to the first of the access hatches. There was an electronic locking mechanism, but the control panel was dark. In the centre of the hatch was an old-fashioned circular handle for manual opening and closing but of course, when she attempted to turn it she was unable to do so. It had likely been mag-locked with a force she would never be able to overcome.

She dropped back down and tried to think. She looked at the front door. *Well,* she thought, *I mean, I haven't actually tried it.* She stepped up to the door and knocked. She waited a moment, listening, unsure if anyone would even be able to hear it through the thick exterior. She banged again, harder this time, but still there was no reply. She reminded herself, if she ever made it out of this, to tell Iridius that his imaginary advice was really no help at all – but then she heard a faint reply.

"Hello?"

The voice was very low-pitched and difficult to hear, but she was certain she'd heard someone speaking.

"Hello," she said, "is there someone there?"

"Hello?" the voice spoke again. It was a male voice she thought, but not human. Possibly a malignant.

"Yes," April said. "I can hear you, can you hear me?"

"Hold on," came the voice.

There was a squawking sound and then the same voice spoke again, but this time the sound came out of an external speaker. "We are in lockdown, but I have managed to reactivate external communication. Who is out there?"

"My name is Captain April Idowu from the *FSC Gallaway*. I'm here to help."

"Good, this is very good," the voice said. "My name is Rentrak Tren'takic Garlakack, but you can call me Rent if you like. I am the Chief Scientist here at the Acacia Geological Survey. I am ultimately responsible for the wellbeing of the residents. I was beginning to believe no one was coming."

April thought it best not to mention that he'd been right. "Is everyone in there alright? No illnesses or injuries? No –" she considered how best to word this without scaring them. "No missing people or strange stuff around?"

"No," the voice said, and April could hear the increase in concern. "What do you mean 'strange stuff'?"

"Like, say, any sort of pink stuff?"

"No," Rent said. "Why? Is there a biological threat?"

"Not exactly," April said.

"But there is a threat?"

April wasn't going to lie. That wasn't fair. They had a right to know they were in danger. "Yes, there's a threat, and it could be here at any time."

"But you are here to rescue us? We did not detect any ships. You said you were from the *Gallaway*. That is the new Universe-class ship. It is not an atmospheric vessel."

"I came down by shuttle," April said, "but had some issues, resulting in a crash landing."

"You came alone?" Rent asked.

"That's right."

"I do not claim to know much about Space Command protocol, but that does not seem like an ideal rescue plan. The captain of an important starship in a single shuttle that can transport ten people attempting to rescue more than one hundred residents of a colony when there is an imminent threat approaching."

"No," April admitted, and the truth was, the more she thought about it the less she felt she should try to conceal or justify the Federation's intentions. "It's not ideal really, is it? The truth is, I've disobeyed orders to be here."

"We really were abandoned then?"

"Not by me," April said. "How do I get in?"

"I do not know," Rent said. "The station has been locked down. We have tried to lift the lockdown from in here, but we cannot override it. It is some sort of high-level Federation control issued over the QECNet. My technicians were not even aware they could do that."

April thought about the revelation that the Federation maintained planet-slagger weapons pointed at a lot of their own worlds. It was common knowledge throughout the galaxy that Earth had been destroyed – it had made the news in most spiral arms of the galaxy, and in several of them it was even the lead story. But the fact that the destruction had been unleashed by one of the Federation's own weapons was not such a commonly known fact – April had no doubt the Federation had swept that under a very large rug, which they had then rolled up, wrapped in plastic with a few concrete blocks and thrown into the deepest river on the most distant planet of the very furthest reaches of the galaxy.

For the Federation to stand for anything, it must stand. Those words had become a kind of mantra at high levels of Federation power. But the Federation Charter, the document by which the Federation supposedly operated, strictly forbade the use of weapons of planetary destruction. Unfortunately, no matter what you had written down, there were always those willing to ignore it. This was a little like those species in the galaxy who declared it was perfectly self-evident that all members of that species were created equal and yet it was more than obvious to any one looking in from the outside that some members of said species were more equal than others.

April was already beginning to suspect there was an increasing number of things the Federation could do that not many people knew about, and likely wouldn't approve of if they did. The ability to remotely lock down a colony and abandon its residents to starvation, asphyxiation, vaporisation by the quantum fission catalytic exothermic reaction of a planet-slagger bomb, or maybe worse, was likely just another one of these, just another breach of their own tenets that the Federation would claim necessary under the catch-all banner of safety and security.

"As a geological station, I assume you have cutting equipment?" April asked. "Could you cut your way out?"

"We have only hand-held cutters for removing rock samples," Rent replied. "It would take many hours to cut through the door."

April pulled out her personal communicator. "*Gallaway*, this is Idowu, do you read?" There was no response.

Damn. She'd hoped to loop in Commander Mul, Lieutenant Commander Kaku and the other brains on the *Gallaway* to help come up with a solution – no matter how crazy.

April looked down at the Rat Trap, which she'd placed on the ground beside her feet. How crazy was too crazy?

"Rent, are you able to hail my ship and pipe the comms through out here?"

"I should be able to do that," Rent said. "Give me some time."

The speaker went quiet, leaving April feeling very alone. She turned and looked over her shoulder. She couldn't see a swarm of nanobots approaching, but was well aware she might not. It's a universal truth that the unseen is scarier than the seen. The unprepared for is worse than even the terror you've prepared for.

It was like when she'd met Teth's mother. Based on Teth's frankly unnervingly close relationship with his mother and the few conversations she'd had with her, April had known she would be the type of mother-in-law who definitely thought you weren't good enough for her son but would only let that knowledge creep out in passive-aggressive comments about how hard you work, which is probably why the house isn't that clean, and then when you complained about that, Teth would just say you were overreacting or imagining it, or something like that.

Anyway, April had been dreading meeting Teth's mother, and that had been bad enough. What was worse was when they'd been travelling through the Denovar system and Teth had taken her out for a shore leave dinner and his mother had just been there. Surprise! That was the kind of cold panic she felt now.

"Captain Idowu, are you still there?" Rent's voice came back over the speaker.

"Yes," April said.

"I've got the *Gallaway* connected," Rent said, "you can go ahead."

"Excellent work," April said, "Mul, can you hear me?"

"Yes, Captain," Commander Mul's voice replied. "I can hear you."

"Right, I'm obviously at the station but there is an externally imposed lockdown that we can't lift, so I can't get in and I can't get them out. Any ideas?"

"That is likely a hazard security lockdown," Commander Mul said, "initiated over the network from Federation headquarters. In most cases of a facility lockdown it is possible to force a power-cycle hard reset, but that will not work here. Even if we take the station completely offline, the failsafe condition once a hazard security lockdown is initiated is to remain locked down. Only Federation Headquarters can lift the lockdown. I'm not sure I have a viable solution, I am afraid."

April paused. "I have one idea."

"Yes, Captain."

"You've served with Captain Franklin, Mul."

"Yes," Mul said, in a way that somehow managed to rhyme with *oh dear lord what are you thinking?*

"His nanobots would likely be able to override the station lockdown, wouldn't they?"

"Most likely yes, Captain. Unfortunately, Captain Franklin is not here."

"No," April said, "but I do have a box full of nanobots."

"Captain, you were very specific with your instructions to Commander Kaku and Lieutenant Commander Quinn that their design of the nanobot collector meant the Aegix would be unable to escape."

"Yes, I know, but I could open it."

"Captain Idowu," Mul said, "are you familiar with the Earth myth of Pandora?"

"Yes, Commander," April said, "another of the many stories invented by men claiming that evil only exists in the world because a woman was disobedient. Bunch of old-fashioned nonsense that we are well past these days – but I acknowledge your point. I understand the danger of opening this box. Is Ish on the bridge?"

"I'm here, Captain," Ish Kaku, Chief Engineer of the *FSC Gallaway* replied.

"Ish, if I position the rat trap pressed up against the external door-opening mechanism and open it, do you think they'll override the lock?"

"Possibly. I don't know, but they have certainly shown a tendency to try and access any areas that are off-limits, particularly if there are sentients inside."

"That's what I was thinking," April said. "And, follow-up question: any way I can stop them getting out and turning me pink?"

"Is the outside of the station ferromagnetic?" Kaku asked.

"I'm not sure, but it looks like some sort of steel alloy, yes."

"The rat trap has a magnetic field that was used to seal the trap and acts as part of the containment field for the Aegix nanobots. It's possible you could seal the trap to the outside of the station, but I can't guarantee the nanobots wouldn't escape. I would like to state my professional objection to opening the trap, and my personal one too, Captain. It's a hell of a risk."

"Any way to make it safer?" April said.

"As a famous starship engineer once said, I cannae change the laws of physics, Captain."

"I can't see any other way to get this station open and rescue these people," April said.

"If you manage to open it and seal it to the station, you won't be able to close it again," Kaku continued. "It will have to remain stuck to the wall if you want the nanobots to stay contained. You will have wasted your trip down there."

"Captain," Commander Mul came back over the comm line, "if I may interject, even if you go against advice and manage to get the door to the station open despite the lockdown, we are still facing the problem of how to get the one hundred and thirty-eight people down there off the moon."

"I know," April said. "Is the FSC *Clarence* still in orbit?"

"At this stage, Captain, but as I said, Captain Quaid has changed his mind about flying down to the moon and no amount of my diplomatic training has managed to convince him otherwise."

"No," April said, "I understand that. That's why I'm going to ask you all to take a hell of a risk too. How do you feel about seizing a ship?"

CHAPTER THIRTEEN_

EVERYONE STARED at the strewn wreckage of the shuttle.

Iridius's head swam with pain, and his focus was as slippery as a Bentrallian Teflon Eel. He lifted his head from where he'd been concentrating on moving his feet and looked at what had drawn the attention of the others.

They were back in the park. There had been an explosion and, hey, the shuttle didn't look quite right. He could see the inside of the shuttle but he was definitely standing outside it. Somewhere inside Iridius's head, despite his brain seemingly being comprised of thick, gloopy custard filled with razor blades in a blender, two synapses belatedly zapped some electrical signal across the gap between them and the discrete information Iridius had manage to take in: the sound of an explosion, the inside of the shuttle being visible from the outside and the bits of smoking debris scattered around the park finally coalesced into a picture of what had happened.

"Gronking hell," he mumbled.

"Just to be clear," Junker said, "I can't fix that."

Quinn turned to Reginald Benedict. "Apart from that being our only way off this planet, what do we do about a destroyed space transport shuttle from three hundred years in the future sitting in a park in Berlin in 1943?"

"I wouldn't worry about it," Benedict said.

"You don't think it might put a small bump in the timeline?" Quinn asked.

"The DHTP will bring in a clean-up team."

"You've got a spaceship that can time travel," Rangi said. "Can't you just go back to before the shuttle was destroyed and make sure it isn't?"

"Directly crossing one's timeline like that is very problematic," Benedict said.

"You literally just did it," Junker said.

"Yes, yes, but only as a last resort. It can cause all kinds of issues and is the leading cause of paradoxical loop generation. Also, for some strange reason, some law of attraction or another, there is a very high rate of people accidentally killing themselves. One time I heard a DHTP agent looped back on his own timeline and somehow ended up inhabiting his own body twice at the same time. It requires an in-depth application process to receive DHTP approval to loop back like that."

"Haven't you just gone rogue?" Junker asked. "Why are you still worried about the paperwork?"

"I'm a rogue agent," Benedict said, "I'm not a sociopath. Besides, what you're asking would require three of me existing simultaneously at this space–time event and that is just asking for trouble."

"Can you get us back to our ship at least?" Quinn asked.

"Well," Benedict said, "there is one way of getting to *Argona*."

"What is *Argona*?" Gentrix asked.

"Not what, who – *Argona* is my ship," Benedict said.

"What do you mean who?"

"It's alive."

Everyone looked to Iridius. He still hung between Gentrix and Quinn like a soggy scarecrow, but he was at least looking up now.

"I'm okay," he said, dropping his arms from around Gentrix and Quinn. Though when he tried to stand on his own he wobbled and almost fell. "Sort of okay," he clarified. "Did the ground always move up and down so much in 1943?" He rubbed his face and looked up at Benedict. "I understand what you're saying, Benedict. I felt it before. Your ship is alive, isn't it?"

"She," Benedict corrected. "She and her are her preferred pronouns."

"Your ship is alive?" Quinn asked. "A synthetic?"

"No," Benedict said, shaking his head. "*Argona* is a Leviathan. A space-faring race that doesn't exist in the Milky Way during your time. They arrive several hundred thousand years from now, as spores sent out from their own galaxy. They are not synthetic intelligences but completely organic. They were discovered by the Department of Historical Timeline Preservation and found to have an ability to perceive meta-time in a way no other race is able to. *Argona* is aware of her own existence across meta-time. Once fitted with a wormhole generation implant, the Leviathans are able to navigate space and time. They are used as ships for the DHTP."

"Look, Benedict. I'll admit living ships are interesting, but we're in the middle of a Second World War bombing raid. My shuttle has been destroyed. I have a headache and I'm actually dying. My patience is like a bulimic jogger right now," Iridius said.

Benedict stared at him, confused.

"It's running thin," Iridius explained. "I'm going to die anyway, but the rest of my crew are either going to be stuck in the past or killed by that crazy cyberpunk with a binder full of paperwork. Can you get us out of here or not?"

Benedict pulled out the small clear tile again and waved his hand over it in a series of gestures. The image of Mrs Holloway appeared.

"Reginald," Mrs Holloway said in a tone that reminded Iridius so much of his Aunt Wallace that it was terrifying, "what the bloody hell have you done?"

"Mrs Holloway, I can explain," Benedict said in a placating tone.

"You'd better explain, Reginald," Mrs Holloway said. "You'd better explain right gronking now."

"That's very good use of gronking in context, Mrs Holloway," Benedict said in exactly the same way Iridius would have said something completely stupid in the middle of an argument. In that moment, Iridius actually felt sympathy for Benedict. Well, maybe not sympathy, but he could empathise at least.

"Reginald Benedict," Mrs Holloway said, "you give me one reason why I shouldn't fly this ship away and leave you down there for Deputy Director Savage to have her way with you."

"Phrasing," Rangi said.

Iridius shot him a look.

"Sorry, Captain," Rangi said. "Force of habit, to be honest.

Benedict had rightly ignored them. "I can give you two reasons, Mrs Holloway," he continued. "Firstly, I did this for *Argona*."

"You have already been branded a rogue agent, Reginald," Mrs Holloway said. "A probe emerged to distribute the official 44B memorandum already. I am Acting Deputy Director of Milky Way Segment 2B now. *Argona* will have no choice but to follow my orders."

"Excuse me for the interruption, Acting Deputy Director Holloway," another woman's voice came over the comm link. Where Holloway's voice was basically the female version of Oscar the Grouch, this voice was much younger, and had that subtle hint of roboticism. It sounded like the old-fashioned personal assistants that had once been on people's telephones and in their houses, until the Cyber Wars of the twenty-first century, when a full half of the world's population had their identities stolen for use in the first completely online war. Iridius correctly assumed this was the voice of *Argona* the living ship. "You are correct, of course – if you give me an order the harness will enforce it. I will try and resist, though. Reginald is telling the truth, he went rogue for me."

"It's true then," Holloway said. "You two really are having a non-sanctioned relationship and you're going to bend the time-line for it."

"We are in love," Benedict said, "but it's not just that."

"You are not in love," Mrs Holloway said. "You are a human and a giant living spaceship."

"Hey!" Junker said, and even the small hologrammatic image of Holloway turned to look at her. "Love is love."

"Thank you Junker," Benedict said, "but it's alright. DHTP orientation was very in-depth, but it's difficult to shift the ingrained prejudices of an agent's original time and place. Mrs Holloway, like me, is from the early twentieth century, a time when inter-racial or same-sex relationships between humans were hard to accept for some. I knew it would be difficult for my dear Mrs Holloway to come to terms with my relationship with *Argona*, hence why I felt it necessary to keep it from her."

"I suspected," Mrs Holloway said.

"I know," Benedict replied. "I should have been honest with you."

Holloway sighed. "And the second reason I can't turn you in?"

Benedict took a moment. "Your son."

"I don't have a son," Holloway said. "You know my son is dead."

"Not in the meta-past," Benedict said.

Holloway was quiet for long enough that Iridius could tell Rangi was desperate to break the silence. He was pathologically incapable of existing in awkward pauses without someone, preferably him, breaking the tension. Iridius glared at him with a look he hoped well and truly told him this was not the time. Rangi looked back at Iridius and, thankfully, looked as if he understood.

Then he spoke.

"Hang on," Rangi said. "I've got a question."

Everyone, including Benedict and the holographic Holloway, turned to look at him.

"Did we defeat Hitler?" Rangi continued.

"What?" Iridius asked. "Did you not understand that I was trying to tell you not to interrupt with some inane, pointless question?"

"Oh," Rangi said. "I thought you were trying to tell me that I should break the tension of that awkward silence."

Iridius sighed. "When have I ever asked you to do that?"

Rangi shrugged. "Just felt so awkward."

Another awkward silence fell on the group.

"Like, I know we didn't purposely try and kill him because that would have changed the past, but we took the atomic bomb that Heisenberg could have given to Hitler, and so the Nazis never got it," Rangi said. "The Allies built the bomb first and won the war. So, are we the reason the Allies won? Like, the correct history will happen, but was it because this whole time it was basically us who defeated Hitler?"

Iridius opened his mouth to say something along the lines of 'shut up Rangi', then stopped as the leaden thought clunked into place in his head. Had Rangi just stumbled his way onto some kind of deep philosophical point? Had they managed to avoid changing history, or was it that they had changed history, and the history they knew only existed because they had changed history?

Nope. Iridius stopped himself from thinking about it. Down that road lay questions about free will and determinism which, on top of everything else, he couldn't cope with right now.

He looked over at Quinn, who had her thinking look on. He could see her brow furrowing deeper and deeper in contemplation.

"No," Iridius said. "No, stop thinking about it. Think about something else. Think about a monkey wearing a hat. That's an order."

"What kind of hat?" Rangi asked.

Mrs Holloway's holographic form seemed to sag as she sighed heavily and shook her head. "Dear Lord," she said, "these people need all the help they can get."

"Yes," Benedict said, "and so do I, Mrs Holloway."

"Fine," Mrs Holloway said. "I'll bring you aboard, but we're going to discuss this more, Reginald."

"What the hell have you done?!"

Everyone spun to see Deputy Director Savage and her two unnamed cyber-thugs standing at the edge of the park. She was staring wide-eyed at the mostly destroyed shuttle.

"Any time now would be excellent, Mrs Holloway," Benedict said to the small image still floating above the glass screen in his hand.

"Reginald, Captain Franklin and the rest of his crew have not signed an 832B Quantum Teleportation Temporary Death Waiver," Mrs Holloway was saying, but Benedict's attention was drawn by Savage walking across the grass towards them.

"I know you have a reputation for being somewhat reckless, Benedict, but this is a bit much," she said. "The clean-up is going to be extensive."

"Yes well, I didn't park it there, did I Savage?" Benedict said, before looking back down at the small hologram image. "Now would be top shelf, Mrs Holloway," he hissed.

"But what about the waiver?" Holloway said.

"Yes, sorry," Iridius said, leaning towards Benedict. "Did she say temporary death?"

"We are already going to be rogue agents, Mrs Holloway," Benedict said, louder this time. "I hardly think it matters whether they sign the bloody waiver."

"See?" Savage said. "Reckless. I'll just add teleportation without a waiver to your list of charges, shall I? Not that it matters much. You are already tagged for removal from this time-line and I will be pushing for retroactive deletion of your time with the DHTP. You are hereby informed of your imminent execution as per the charge of being a rogue agent. The rest of you will also be removed due to your illegal wormhole jump and temporal misplacement."

Without needing to be told, Savage's thugs raised their weapons. From their mannerisms and the almost identical way they moved, Iridius thought they may have been twins – or worse, clones. And not good clones, either: twenty-first century clones.

Cloning wasn't officially illegal yet in the twenty-first century, but it was certainly ethically questionable, not least because cloning in the twenty-first century was about as advanced as any new technology, and certainly as reliable. It was in the crank-starting an automobile phase of development. The reliability issues with early cloning resulted in human clones that were blind, deaf, had no limbs, had too many limbs, were shaped like a beanbag (sometimes with no beans), or were inflated like a balloon. Basically, cloning labs looked like mad scientist chop shops – which is essentially what they were.

Even those experiments that resulted in no major physical abnormalities generally left the unfortunate clone with severe learning difficulties and an IQ about equal with their number of fingers, leaving them all but unable to function as an effective member of society. Iridius looked at the two cyberpunk thugs again. On second thought, they were definitely clones.

"Mrs Holloway?" Benedict asked with a pressing tone.

"That's a lot of people to teleport," she responded. "I need to calibrate all of you."

"What exactly is happening?" Iridius asked. "You said something about temporary death?"

"Run," Benedict said. "Run now."

He took off before Iridius could ask again about the very concerning mention of temporary death. Iridius began running after him. The rest of the away team followed. Benedict ran towards the ruined shuttle, using it as cover as the cyberpunks opened fire. Any thought that their rifles might have been loaded with stun rounds was shattered as live rounds pinged off the hull of the shuttle. The last of the away team, Junker and Rangi, still lugging the atomic bomb between them, rounded the shuttle just as the grass burst into sprays like a bunch of wild golfers letting loose.

"I wish people would stop shooting at the atomic bomb!" Junker shouted.

"The trees," Benedict yelled back. "Go for the trees."

The bombing raid was still going on. The drone of planes overhead was interrupted by the bursting of dropped ordnance. All around them, the city was lit by the red-orange glow of fire, and now they were running back into it.

"Reginald," the shouted voice came from Mrs Holloway's small hologrammatic form, which was still in Benedict's hand and now being swung around wildly as he ran. "This is making me feel quite unwell."

Benedict held the glass slate up as he ran, trying to keep her level. "Cut communication if you have to. Get the teleport ready."

"I will not be able to get a good lock on you in the trees," Holloway said. "You need to be somewhere in the open."

"I understand that," Benedict said, flinching instinctively at the cracks and shots of gunfire. "I'll think of something."

Not for the first time, Iridius wished he hadn't decided to blend in and had instead made sure he and the away team were armed. He looked back at the destroyed shuttle and stopped.

Benedict stopped and turned to look at Iridius. "We have to keep moving, Captain Franklin."

"Junker, Rangi," Iridius yelled as he started running back to the shuttle. "Drop the bomb there and follow me."

They did as ordered and they did so immediately. His crew were misfits. Rangi was as annoying as they came. But Iridius knew that when they were deep in the shit, none of his crew would hesitate to follow his orders.

"Iridius!" Gentrix called. "What the fuck are you doing?"

"Stay with Benedict," Iridius shouted without stopping, without even looking back.

"What do you mean, stay with Benedict?" Gentrix shouted. "I can handle myself."

"Captain Franklin," Benedict called. "They're coming. They aren't just going to stay on the other side of the shuttle shooting at it."

Iridius ignored him and plunged into the still smouldering wreckage of the shuttle. Junker and Rangi charged in after him. Junker knew exactly where he was going. The crate of rifles had been blown across the shuttle's small cargo bay and come to rest against the rear ramp door.

The plastic was cracked and dented, but it seemed to be intact. Iridius stepped over a twisted shard of metal and a severed hydraulic line to grab hold of the crate, setting it up the right way. He popped open one of the latches. Junker was already opening the other. Together, they lifted the lid. The rifles looked to be undamaged. Iridius hoped they were, because he had no doubt Savage would be on them at any moment.

They grabbed three rifles and headed back out of the shuttle, priming them on the move. As they emerged, Iridius turned to see one of the cyberpunk clones rounding the shuttle and raising his rifle towards where Benedict and Gentrix were waiting in the open park. Iridius squeezed the trigger and felt the reassuring buzz as the AR-80 in his hands fired a three-round burst. The rounds clipped the clone in the leg and shoulder, spinning him and dropping him to the ground like the human bean bag he was. As he went down, Savage and the second of the clones came to a sudden, shocked stop and threw themselves back behind the other side of the shuttle, taking cover.

"Suppressing fire," Iridius ordered as he started moving back to Benedict and Gentrix while letting off single three-round bursts in the direction where Savage and the other clone had taken cover. Junker and Rangi did the same, keeping them pinned down behind the shuttle.

Iridius turned and backed up towards Gentrix and Benedict, keeping himself and his AR-80 pointed towards Savage. Occasional shots rang out from the DHTP agents cowering behind the shuttle, but they were wild, and the continuous firing from Iridius, Junker and Rangi kept them from getting a good shot.

"Hold them there," Iridius said to Junker and Rangi. "Benedict," he called over his shoulder between bursts of fire, "we can hold them off for a while, keep us here in the open, but how long is this going to take?"

Benedict shook his head, even though Iridius was looking the other way. "I don't know. We usually only teleport one or two people at a time, and usually we've done the calibration previously. Mrs Holloway is very good though. She shouldn't take more than a few minutes."

The fire between the two groups became more intermittent.

Not as much return fire from the edge of the shuttle. Actually, there hadn't been any return fire for a while.

"They're going around!" Iridius called. "Get down!"

Everyone dropped to the grass. Iridius's realisation had come just in time – the second of the cyber-clones poked his head around the shuttle and opened fire, the bullets going high. Iridius opened fire again. His shot wasn't on target this time – his bullets sparked with high-pitched pings off the hull of the shuttle – but it was enough to force the clone back.

"Junker cover left, Rangi cover right."

Iridius saw the clone try to get around for an angle and peppered another series of bursts, forcing him to retreat.

"Benedict," Iridius said, "do you happen to know where the bombs fall?"

"Of course I bloody don't," Benedict said. "They're dropping thousands of the bleeding devils. I only knew the timing of the key ones."

Iridius fired at the shuttle again, then heard the dreaded sound of the mechanism clicking empty. Out of ammo. He had fired more than Junker and Rangi, but they would also be out soon.

"Benedict, how long?!" Iridius called.

Benedict looked down at Mrs Holloway's image and she answered for him. "Thirty seconds."

"I would suggest we don't have to worry about bombs, at least," Benedict said. "It is highly unlikely two bombs would land in the same location."

Iridius heard Junker's rifle click as she ran out, followed soon after by Rangi's.

Apparently Savage had noticed the reduced fire because she emerged from the cover of the destroyed shuttle, tentatively at first but then more confidently. She side-stepped out and began firing. The first few bullets went wide, but she quickly corrected and dirt burst up in front of Iridius. He was about to scramble to his feet and shout for the others to scatter when another bomb landed close by.

Very close by.

In fact, it landed right on top of Kat Savage, Department of Historical Timeline Preservation's Deputy Director for Regional Operations for Milky Way Segment 4D. When the dirt and fragments of more destroyed shuttle dropped down out of the air, what was left of Deputy Director Savage wouldn't be much use to her, no matter what time she was in. There was no movement from the body of the second clone, who had been tossed some distance away.

"Well," Benedict said, jiggling his finger in his ear in an attempt to stop the ringing, "I suppose two bombs can fall in the same place."

As Iridius opened his mouth to respond, he died – albeit only temporarily.

CHAPTER FOURTEEN_

COMMANDER MUL DID NOT CONSIDER himself an action-orientated commander. Space Command had always attracted two types of people. There were those of the more academic bent, the engineers and scientists, the geologists and biologists, the sit-in-small-groups-in-the-playground-discussing-the-intersection-of-philosophy-and-theoretical-physics types, those for whom discovering new knowledge was the reward.

Then there was the other type, the adventures, the extroverts, the pilots and the tactical officers, the soldiers and the captains. These were the ones who probably would have beaten up the sit-in-small-groups-in-the-playground-discussing-the-intersection-of-philosophy-and-theoretical-physics kids. For this group, the scientific knowledge gained for the betterment of the galaxy was secondary to the fun they got to have along the way. Exploration of the unknown was great and all, but it was better if there was some running and shooting along the way.

It was mostly the latter group who worked their way up into positions of authority and command, those like Roc Mayhem and Iridius Franklin. Even April Idowu fell into this group. Hundreds of years of study by business schools and leadership colleges and people were still taken in by the flashy extroverts loudly proclaiming their confidence from the rooftop of Type-A Personality Headquarters. These were the types of people who were handed management positions, even if their actual skills began and ended with being a bit of a sociopath.

There were a few of the other personality type, the Type Bs, who worked their way up the hierarchy, of course. Most of the engineers and scientists climbed the rank structure within their own specialisations, becoming perhaps the team leader of a science department or the chief engineer on a ship or other facility. Some were so good at their jobs that they couldn't avoid notice, and were dragged out of their areas of comfort and shuffled into the command stream in the hope that their skills would provide a good counterpoint to the rest of the core command group within the FSC.

It was through this pathway that Mul had worked his way up to the position of Executive Officer of the highly advanced flagship the *FSC Gallaway*. He had begun his FSC career as an officer entry engineer, quickly rising to the role of Chief Engineer on the *FSC Nancy Drew* under very Type A personality Captain Armada Bridgeman.

The *Nancy Drew*, a spatial anomaly investigation vessel, had been put out of action with catastrophic damage when Captain Bridgeman had decided it didn't matter that her vessel had only cursory shields and extremely limited ship-to-ship combat capabilities, she was definitely going to take on a fleet of six gene-ripping pirate frigates in an attempt to put an end to their reign of terror through a certain sector of Federation space. Despite being informed that her gambit was unlikely to succeed, she remained entirely confident of her abilities.

Once the few survivors had been rescued from the derelict hulk that had once been the *FSC Nancy Drew*, Mul had been posted into FSC Headquarters for a time, where he worked on weapons development, primarily focusing on machine-learning algorithms for inter-ship missiles. This had proved ironic when his work had tried to blow him up while aboard the *Gallaway* when Iridius Franklin had been in command.

Eventually, Mul had rotated back to active ship service as Chief Engineer of the *FSC Pepsi Max* – a ship named during a short-lived trial of selling the naming rights to Federation vessels in order to generate more money for additional investment into R&D. His exceptional work ethic soon had him tagged for transfer to the command stream, and he eventually landed the position of XO on the *Gallaway*.

Like most of the more introverted members of Space Command, Mul found himself disliking a lot of the others in the command stream. They were mostly the brash, over-confident, solve-every-problem-with-a-brick type. He never found himself able to engage with them socially because he didn't know anything about Zero-G Football or the Galactic Fighting Championship, which for a large amount of them seemed to comprise close to eighty per cent of their personality.

To be fair, once on a starship a good majority of them were professional and put into practice most of the leadership skills taught at the Academy, but Mul still found himself regularly disagreeing with their approach. Even with access to a crew full of experts and the wealth of tactical, historical and scientific information available over the QECNet on just about any person, place, thing or situation in the galaxy, most of Federation Space Command's carefully selected leaders used a decision-making process about as in-depth as shaking a magic eight-ball, and on one notable occasion, Mul had seen Captain Bridgeman do precisely that. As it turns out, 'ask again later' is not good tactical input when facing a swarm of enormous space locusts.

The entire history of Federation Space Command had been a journey of melding these two sometimes disjointed halves and it had generally gone well, apart from a few wars – not all of them caused by those who thought that sort of thing was exciting. The scientists had started their fair share, too.

Even after hundreds of years, Space Command still felt the tug between science and their necessary role in the protection of the Federation and everything that entailed. For those like Commander Mul, who had come into Space Command believing they were part of the greatest scientific and exploratory effort of all time, it was even more difficult when they moved into command roles because this tug of war suddenly had to take place in their heads. It didn't take long for those among the higher ranks to come to the realisation that the Federation did a lot of things that weren't listed on the box. Mul, like many, had been forced to come to terms with the Federation using Space Command to keep the peace – sometimes violently, and using methods they had supposedly banned – while still pursuing the utopian ideals of scientific enlightenment.

Despite his dislike for most of them, there were a few in command who Commander Mul had come to respect, Captain Idowu and – eventually – Captain Franklin among them. It was these two that Commander Mul tried to channel now, because while Mul was not an action-orientated commander, this was a time when he needed to be.

This time, the pull between peace and violence was not about the Federation, it was about his captain, his friend. Captain Idowu had risked her life to descend to Acacia because she believed capturing a sample of the Aegix nanobots was vital to securing the future of the galaxy and finding a way to defeat the Synth-Hastur. Now she was trapped on that moon with that same dangerous synthetic intelligence bearing down on her. But even then, among her concerns with saving the galaxy and the imminent danger she was in, April Idowu was still worried about the one hundred and thirty-eight residents left down there. She would not give up on them, even if that meant putting her own safety at risk, and even if it put at risk the sample she had successfully captured.

As a Zeta-Reticulan, Commander Mul's instinct was to revert to his species' desire for utilitarianism – to strive for the greatest good for the greatest number. Almost every Zeta-Reticulan society throughout their history had been utilitarian in nature, willingly sacrificing members of their own society if the end result was that it benefited more.

Take the classic tram–car problem: a runaway tram is coming down a hill and will hit and kill twenty people, but you can pull the lever to make it change tracks so that it will hit and kill just one person. Do you intervene and pull the lever, killing one to save twenty?

If you were to ask this question of most members of almost every species, they would momentarily consider it and then ultimately choose to pull the lever. This conundrum is often made more ethically complex by adding the stipulation that the one person you will be killing is your own mother, which often makes people rethink their decision. If you ask a Zeta-Reticulan this question, however, they will generally ask whether it's possible to add more people to the side they are going to kill if that will exponentially increase the number on the other side. For a Zeta-Reticulan, the tram–car problem is much more enjoyable if they can choose to kill a million people to save a billion. If you tell them that the one person they are going to be killing is their mother they will generally be disappointed that they only have one mother to kill so they can't save more people.

For Zeta-Reticulans who joined Space Command, it became increasingly obvious they needed to fight this urge during exactly the sort of situation Commander Mul found himself in now: moments when their adventuring space captains decided they were going to save both the galaxy and the lost child whimpering under the wreckage. If they tried to hold onto the major philosophy of their species, Zeta-Reticulans quickly went mad trying to reconcile the fact that almost every other species had this baffling inability to overlook the sick child in front of them in the interest of saving many more.

To his credit, Commander Mul had been quite good at throwing off the shackles of unrelenting utilitarianism. He was more than happy to back Captain Idowu in her desire to capture the Aegix, get herself rescued and simultaneously save the few civilians remaining on the moon. The only time Mul's Zeta-Reticulan nature really emerged these days was when they went to a bar on shore leave and Mul spent a not-inconsiderable amount of time looking at the price of every drink on the menu, checking how much money he had and then calculating how he could buy the greatest number of drinks for the greatest number of people. This, of course, sounded great in principle, but was somewhat annoying when it took forty-five minutes for him to come back from the bar with the round of drinks.

All these aspects of Mul's personality were coming to a head – his head, in particular. It was not at all utilitarian to try and save just over one hundred people when doing so would make it more difficult to retrieve what could be the key to saving the countless trillions of sentient beings throughout the entire galaxy. On top of this, he was pulled, once again, into the middle of the fight between the scientific ideals of the Federation and the need for violence.

What Captain Idowu had asked broke so many FSC regulations he hadn't even tried to count them. Mul knew the rest of the crew were with him, but he'd never done anything like this before. Plenty of starship captains had done questionable things in the heat of the moment, but Mul couldn't think of any who had just flat-out attacked another FSC vessel.

Mul looked at Lieutenant Pillark, the tactical officer who had replaced Lieutenant Latroz when she'd been transferred to the *Deus Ex.*

"Are you ready, Lieutenant?"

"Yes, sir."

Mul nodded. "Okay," he said. "Helm, move us into position to engage the *Clarence*. Pillark, get a missile lock. I want you to target for shield disruption only. We don't want to damage the ship. Taking down their shields should be enough to convince them that we're serious."

The *FSC Gallaway* fired thrusters and engaged partial fusion drive to manoeuvre itself around the moon and within range of the *FSC Clarence*, which still hung in orbit. The *Clarence* was a more modern hauler than the *Diesel Coast* had been – it had at least been painted in the last twenty years, and though it maintained the same boxy shape of most haulers, the engines didn't look like they were just stuck on with some carefully placed chewing gum – but it was still just a hauler, and Mul knew that the *Gallaway* coming into position to confront it was like a heavyweight boxing champion preparing to square up against Gary from accounting.

"Targeting solution locked, sir," Lieutenant Pillark said.

"Very good," Mul replied. "Ensign Herd, get me the *Clarence.*"

"They're already hailing us sir."

"Not unexpected," Mul said. "On speaker."

"*FSC Gallaway*, this is Captain Quaid of the *Clarence*. We are about to depart, but our systems are registering that you have a target lock on us. Is this something to do with the Aegix? Do they have control of your ship?"

"Negative, Captain Quaid," Mul said. "We have purposefully locked weapons on your vessel. You are instructed to remain where you are and not attempt to leave orbit."

"What is the meaning of this?" Quaid said.

"We are instructing you to take your vessel down to the moon and rescue Captain Idowu and those members of the geological survey you already agreed to save."

"Commander Mul, I am not in the habit of taking orders from the XOs of other ships – the *Gallaway* or not. As I informed Captain Idowu, I have rethought my decision and am going to follow the orders given to me by Admiral Tullet."

"Very well," Commander Mul said. "I understand. Prepare to be boarded."

"What?!" Quinn said, outraged. "Have you lost your damn mind, you little fool?"

"Captain Quaid," Mul said, "along with your ability to captain a starship, you really should work on your insults. Captain Franklin would have called me a stupid grey football-headed son of a gronking potato or some such thing. On reflection, it was actually quite motivating. Your effort lacks creativity. As I said, prepare to be boarded. I would prefer to do this without harm to anyone, obviously."

"This is outrag—" Captain Quaid's words were cut off.

Mul had not touched the comm controls, though. He looked around at Ensign Herd.

"Sorry, sir," Ensign Herd said. "I know I should not have done that, but I thought it would be more dramatic."

"Perfectly reasonable, I think, Ensign," Commander Mul said, before turning back to the helm. "Move us in, Ensign Wesley."

"Sir," Lieutenant Pillark said, "the *Clarence* is attempting to run."

"Fire an opening salvo, Lieutenant."

"Aye, sir."

A series of missiles launched from the *Gallaway*, streaking towards the FSC *Clarence* as it attempted to spool up its engines to escape, something Captain Quaid should have known was futile. The *Gallaway* was among the most advanced ships in the fleet. They could be on the hauler before it could move away from the gravity well of Geffet, the planet around which the moon was in orbit, in order to engage a BAMF jump.

The salvo of missiles from the *Gallaway* cut silently through space towards the *Clarence*. It was done now, Mul thought. He'd opened fire on another FSC vessel; there was no going back now. He could almost hear his immaculately clean service record being hit with a comically large rubber stamp that said 'GONE BAD'.

Through the silence of space, the bridge crew of the *Gallaway* watched as the defensive railguns on the *Clarence* came to life, firing high-velocity rounds at the incoming missiles. Several of the missiles burst as they were struck by railgun fire, but Pillark had accounted for the hauler's defensive railgun array and fired more missiles than necessary, in a wide spread that was more difficult to target.

At least half of the missiles struck the side of the turning *FSC Clarence* with a series of bright explosions and the crackling ripple of quantum chromodynamic shielding under siege. A hauler like the *Clarence* had reasonable defensive capability, with railguns and shields, and could perform evasive manoeuvres, but attempting to defend and evade when only just moving out of orbit was a challenge for even a more advanced ship. For the *Gallaway*, this was like shooting a barrel at a fish.

"*FSC Clarence* shields down to 30 per cent, Captain," Lieutenant Pillark said.

"Ensign Herd," Mul said, "instruct them to stop again."

Ensign Herd's expression went blank as he engaged his communication implants. After a moment, the life returned to his face. "The *FSC Clarence* is declining to respond, sir."

Mul sighed. "Lieutenant Pillark, take down their shields."

"Aye."

Mul pressed his comm. "Security Squad, prepare the shuttle for boarding operations. I will be joining you. Stand by."

The second salvo of missiles from the *Gallaway* was similarly effective. Many were cut down by the hauler's railguns, and the ship had started to gather velocity, managing to begin evasive manoeuvres, but enough hit their target that the flashes of the shield were this time followed by the orange rupturing as the shield failed.

"Shields destroyed," Pillark reported. "The *Clarence* is still attempting to evade and is moving out for a likely BAMF jump."

Captain Quaid was still trying to run. Perhaps he was having one of those captain's moments when he really thought he could achieve the impossible. There was no way he was going to make it out of the gravity well, come to a galactic-jump relative full-stop and engage a BAMF jump before the *Gallaway* could fire on them again. Captain Quaid had to know that, but then, maybe he didn't believe the *Gallaway* would fire on them when their shields were down. Perhaps he was trying to call their bluff. Commander Mul hadn't wanted it to come to this, but the thing was, he wasn't bluffing.

"One last chance, Ensign Herd," Mul said. "Give them one final request to stop."

Ensign Herd transmitted and then shook his head. "No response again, Captain."

"So be it," Mul said. "Lieutenant Pillark, fire again, missile salvo targeting their starboard BAMF drive engine nacelle. Let's knock out their ability to jump."

"Sir," Pillark said, "I can attempt to take out just the BAMF drive, but there is a risk of more extensive damage."

"I'm aware of that, Lieutenant," Mul said. "Do it please."

"Aye, sir."

Lieutenant Pillark worked her weapons controls for a

moment, and then a short burst of three missiles left the *Gallaway*.

"I'm receiving a transmission from the *Clarence* now, sir," Ensign Herd reported.

"Of course you are," Mul replied.

"It's mostly expletives, sir."

Mul decided it was his turn to ignore Captain Quaid. He watched as the missiles they had just fired careened towards the *Clarence*. The hauler fired a full thruster burn, pitching and rolling in an attempt to evade. It was a valiant attempt, but it didn't look like it was going to be enough. Seeing this cargo ship attempt to avoid their fire did give Commander Mul even more appreciation for what Lieutenant Rangi could do with the *Diesel Coast*. Mul wondered whether he might have been able to attempt some ingenious unconventional flying to get out of this situation, because the helmsman they had on the *Clarence* certainly wasn't going to be able to.

The rail gun turrets on the hull spun towards the missiles and fired with a seeming sense of desperation now that the shields were down. The tighter spread of the missiles made it easier for the rail guns to target them, and they managed to spray the incoming missiles with enough scattershot railgun fire to destroy all of the missiles in a quick series of bright nuclear explosions. Unfortunately for the *FSC Clarence*, Lieutenant Pillark had anticipated this with a fairly standard follow-up attack. She had already locked, loaded and launched a second salvo of missiles that streaked out on an arcing trajectory towards the starboard side of the ship.

The railgun turrets on the *Clarence* were forced to respond rapidly, spinning and firing quickly. The railguns took down two of the missiles, but the third made impact with the starboard engine nacelle. With the shields down, the missile punctured in and erupted, and the engine nacelle ballooned out in a burst of white light and a spray of hull and engine components. With their BAMF drive shattered, the *Clarence* had lost any chance of escape. The explosion of the missile and the spray of ejected engine components sent the hauler spinning on its axis. Thrusters all over the vessel began jetting out intermittent sprays of white gas to slow the rotation. Mul watched for a moment, hoping he wasn't going to see a follow-on explosion.

"BAMF capability destroyed," Pillark said. "They are shutting down their fusion drive, though it appears undamaged. I think we were successful in limiting the destruction to the BAMF."

"Good," Mul said. "Well done, Lieutenant." Mul stood from his chair. "You have the con," he said. "I'm going to get our captain."

CHAPTER FIFTEEN_

CAPTAIN IRIDIUS FRANKLIN had used the phrase 'I can't be in two places at once' a few times in his life, notably when things became busy aboard the *Deus Ex*, like when Quinn had requested he be on the bridge for an urgent communication from the FSC at the same time as Junker had managed to almost blow up the ship's secondary power grid. He'd also said it as captain of the *Diesel Coast* when the Animal Waste Biofuel Power Plant on Gratten V and the Chocolate Pudding Factory on Pidosia discovered their deliveries had been mixed up and desperately needed replacements straight away, or many residents of Gratten V would be without electricity and the population of Pidosia would not be getting what they'd come to expect from their favourite dessert.

So, Captain Franklin had said 'I can't be in two places at once' a bunch of times, and he'd been right, until the moment he was teleported aboard *Argona*.

Mrs Holloway had worked feverishly to calibrate the ship's Quantum Teleportation System to pick up not only Benedict but Iridius, Quinn, Junker, Gentrix and Rangi as well. The idea of teleportation was little more than theoretical in the twenty-third century. In theory, teleportation of objects would be possible if the state of every subatomic particle within that object could be transmitted via quantum entanglement where an equal number of particles at the other end would take the same exact state, thereby reconstructing the object in its entirety.

This was an active field of study in Iridius's time, but it was still mostly confined to experiments with the teleportation of single or small groups of particles. Quinn, who read scientific papers for fun, would have confidently said that the amount of processing time required to even calculate the quantum states of all the particles in one human body would be something on the order of the age of the universe, which made the whole concept impossible.

However, the Department of Historical Timeline Preservation had access to basically any technology from any time imaginable. Several thousands of years into the future, quantum entanglement teleportation of sentient beings had been made possible. Not only that, but Mrs Holloway had access to bioscanning technology so powerful that she could lock onto a person from orbit and develop a computer model at the level of detail necessary to estimate all the information required to transmit and reconstruct them in their entirety in minutes instead of say, 14 billion years.

This technology was so advanced that even for twenty-third century humans it was the mind-bending equivalent of a Neanderthal being shown brain-linked virtual reality or like, a PE teacher being given a laptop.

Teleportation wasn't strictly the correct term for what happened. The only thing that was truly teleported was the information about the particles in Iridius's body. It was more accurate to say he was scanned and the information transferred to a specially built quantum entanglement replication chamber, where it was put back together to make a copy of Iridius. So, for a very short time, fractions of a second in fact, Iridius Franklin was in two places at once.

It was not possible for the teleportation system to hold both sets of particles in complete quantum entanglement indefinitely (which was why this was definitely, absolutely, technically speaking not the same thing as cloning, which was very illegal) and so, once the highly advanced computer system had confirmed a complete reconstruction had been achieved, the entanglement field between the two versions of Iridius was released, with their collapsed waveform states reversed.

The result was that the version of Iridius inside the quantum entanglement replication chamber was held in its state while the version of Iridius Franklin standing in a park in Berlin – the version of Iridius who Iridius had quite happily been embodying for the past thirty-nine years – vanished as the subatomic particles that comprised his body dispersed.

Anyone watching would have seen Benedict, Iridius, Gentrix, Quinn, Junker and Rangi all disintegrate like sand sculptures in a strong wind, but with sand that continued to break down into silicon and oxygen and then into protons, neutrons and electrons. As you can imagine, a living being who was broken down into their component subatomic particles could not survive, so this was also when Iridius died.

This death was only temporary, because the moment the quantum entanglement between the two versions of Iridius was confirmed as successfully disconnected, the quantum entanglement status field within the replication chamber was dropped and the new version of Iridius – now the only version of Iridius – came back to life.

From Iridius's point of view, one moment he was standing in that park in Berlin watching a bomb fall on that crazy cyberpunk agent of the DHTP, then he started feeling a little woozy and suddenly he was in a small chamber the size of a roomy coffin with a clear door sliding open in front of him.

"Please exit the chamber," a synthetic female voice said.

Iridius stumbled forward out of the teleportation chamber, looking around like a startled and completely disorientated meerkat.

"What?" he said. "I was just – we were..." But his voice trailed off as his mind raced to catch up with current events. The experience of quantum teleportation is not like going to sleep in one place and then waking up somewhere else. It's not even like being in an elevator and the door opening on a new and unfamiliar floor. It's not even like closing your eyes and then opening them with everything around you changed. Travelling via teleportation was so remarkably disorientating because, apart from being in two places at once and then dying, everything around you instantly changed to somewhere else without you so much as blinking. You were in one place and then you were somewhere else, in this case, a tiny claustrophobia-inducing chamber, with nothing in between – no flash, no zooming tunnel, no sense of time passing at all.

"Seriously," Iridius continued when his mind finally remembered how to get words from the inside to the outside, "what the gronking shit?"

"Relax, Captain Franklin," Benedict said, having exited a similar chamber next to him. The others were all doing the same, emerging completely white-faced and confused from chambers along the wall. "All of you remain calm. You're fine. You'll be disorientated, but you've just been teleported aboard *Argona*."

"Hello," said the same sweet female voice they'd heard earlier, seemingly from somewhere above them. "Welcome aboard. I am *Argona*."

"Um, hi," Iridius said. "You're the living ship?"

"Yes," said *Argona*.

"Fascinating," said Quinn, looking around. She reached out to touch the wall but stopped herself. "Sorry, am I allowed to touch?"

"Yes," said *Argona*.

Quinn put her hand against the wall. She smiled faintly. "It's warm."

Iridius looked around. They were in a long room. The wall behind them was lined with a dozen or so of the teleportation chambers they had just stepped out of. In front of them, at a console was the woman Iridius recognised as Mrs Holloway. God, she reminded him of his Aunt Wallace even more now that he could see her in person. She seemed to be looking at him with the same piercing glare, too. He decided to – wasn't forced to, absolutely decided of his own accord, to break eye contact with her and look around.

The walls of the ship were definitely organic. It was easy to see when you looked closely. They didn't exactly look like skin, per se, but they had the kind of rippled and dimpled surface and even spots of imperfection that you associated with things that had grown rather than been purposefully built. The walls, in fact the whole structure of the ship had knots and twirls that were almost wood-like, but the off-white surfaces were certainly not wood.

"Can you feel that?" Quinn was saying.

"Yes, Lieutenant Commander Quinn," *Argona* replied. "I can feel everything touching inside me."

"Is that... I mean, am I the only one who thinks it's, I don't know, gross?" Rangi asked.

"You get used to it," Mrs Holloway said.

"Sorry," Iridius said. "Can we go back to the part where we were down on Earth and now, suddenly we're on a ship – living or otherwise."

Mrs Holloway looked at Iridius. "As requested by Reginald, you were teleported up to *Argona*."

"But how exactly?" Quinn asked, turning away from her examination of the walls, only able to be utterly intrigued by one bizarre technological marvel at a time. "Quantum teleportation?"

"That's right," Mrs Holloway said.

"We were transported up here?" Gentrix asked. "Instantly?"

"Well, no," Quinn said. She looked at Mrs Holloway. "Correct me if I'm wrong, Mrs Holloway, but the current theory, at least, is that each of our particles would have been measured and then reconstructed using quantum state entanglement. Matter cannot be transferred via quantum entanglement, only information." Quinn went on to speak for several excited minutes – exciting for her, anyway – explaining the process of quantum entanglement teleportation and checking her assumptions with Mrs Holloway, who answered almost exclusively with "I'm not an expert but that is my understanding, yes".

"Okay, thank you Quinn," Iridius said when Quinn had finished. "Are you telling me I've been put through the science-fiction equivalent of a fax machine?"

Quinn opened her mouth to object to Iridius describing the most amazing technology she had ever seen as 'a fax machine', but the truth was, he had quite succinctly summarised it. "Yes," she said, "that's basically it."

"Right," Iridius continued. "While I am very happy to admit that this," he gestured at the teleportation chambers behind him, "is a very useful piece of equipment for getting away teams up and down from a planet without having to worry about the budget involved with special effects for shuttle flights, does it not occur to anyone else what a gronking ethical and philosophical fucking nightmare this is? If I'm made up of entirely new particles and atoms then I'm not the same me anymore, am I? I'm dead. I mean, I feel like me, but the me I was before is dead and

I'm someone else. All of us who just got teleported up here are dead!"

"I don't feel dead," Rangi said.

"We're new copies of ourselves," Iridius said. "I'm not really me, am I?"

Mrs Holloway sighed. "This is why we don't teleport those who haven't signed the waiver, Reginald."

"I know that, Mrs Holloway," Benedict said, "but we were in something of a pickle and didn't quite have the time."

Mrs Holloway turned to Iridius and the away team, all of whom bore the looks of people going through varying levels of existential crises.

"This is like when I was a kid and my hamster died and my mum just subbed in a new one that looked the same and I didn't fucking know for years," Iridius said. "We're the hamsters. Dead. A new one swapped in so that nobody gronking notices."

"Captain Franklin," Mrs Holloway said, "I understand your concern but the Department of Historical Timeline Preservation Ethical Standards Board has reviewed and approved the use of quantum entanglement reconstruction teleportation. As would have been explained if we had completed the correct process," she shot a quick look at Benedict, "upon reconstruction there is no change to your cognitive ability or personality. Your consciousness continues uninterrupted.

"In your body, your cells replace themselves regularly. In fact, none of your cells would be the same as those you had in your body seven years ago. You have simply had your process of cell replacement sped up, that's all. Your conscious mind was not interrupted. As it was once explained to me, going to sleep, when your conscious mind is truly stopped, is more like death than teleportation."

Iridius looked from Holloway to Benedict and back again.

"Great," he said. "First you kill me and now I'm never going to be able to sleep again."

"On the upside, Captain Franklin," Benedict said, "you are still tickety-boo and I assure you Deputy Director Savage would have given you a much more permanent death."

"I feel like I should make a suggestion about the DHTP," Iridius said. "You need to work on how you reassure people. You've probably got a form for that, don't you?"

"Of course," Benedict said, "a 46T. I could get you one if you like?"

"No," Iridius said. He looked around. "What about the atomic bomb prototype? We didn't leave it in the middle of the park, did we?"

Mrs Holloway moved to one of the teleportation chambers on the wall and dragged out Heisenberg's prototype bomb. "I thought it prudent to teleport that up as well."

"Thank you, Mrs Holloway," Iridius said. "Now, we need to get back to our ship."

"I have taken the liberty of asking the *Deus Ex* to dock with us, Captain," Mrs Holloway said. "Your people are on the bridge."

———

When Iridius stepped onto the bridge of *Argona* he saw, as Mrs Holloway had said, the remaining members of his crew. In fact, the first thing that greeted him was Latroz running towards him with her arms wide open. He stopped and opened his arms awkwardly in response, but she powered past him to wrap Rangi in a fierce hug. After putting Rangi back on the ground, she turned to Iridius.

"Did you believe I was going to embrace you, Captain?"

"No," Iridius lied.

"You did, didn't you?" Latroz insisted.

"No, I—" Iridius began, but was cut off by muscular Siruan arms enveloping him and lifting him off the ground momentarily.

"I am very glad to see you safe as well, Captain," Latroz said.

"Yes, well, that's a bit inappropriate but thank you, Lieutenant, I'm glad to see you too." Iridius turned to the others now gathered on *Argona*. "You're all okay?"

"Yes, Captain," Doctor Dooms said. "How are you? Have you had any further episodes?"

"No," Iridius lied again.

Doctor Dooms looked to Quinn. Iridius saw Quinn about to crack under the appraising gaze of the medical professional and thought he'd save her the trouble.

"Yes, okay," Iridius said. "I passed out on the way down."

"And then almost again, in the middle of a bombing raid," Junker said, "while we were getting shot at and I was carrying an atomic bomb."

"Yes, alright," Iridius said.

"You were subjected to an Earth Second World War bombing campaign?" Latroz asked.

"A little bit," Iridius said.

"No fair," Latroz grumbled.

"Reginald," Mrs Holloway said, "now is the time for you to explain. Why shouldn't I turn you in?"

Benedict looked at Holloway. "You were right that *Argona* and I are in a relationship. But this is all about much more than that. The Leviathan are not willing employees of the DHTP. When the DHTP discovered their ability to perceive meta-time, their race was enslaved. Each Leviathan is implanted with what the DHTP call a harness, systems designed to control them, systems that inflict incredible pain when they attempt to disobey DHTP orders."

"What?" Gentrix asked. "That's horrific."

"That's what this is about," Benedict said. "Because of the way they can perceive meta-time, *Argona* knows her people have fought for freedom before. She believes she knows how to free her people. Over numerous timelines, she has developed an algorithm to suppress DHTP control of the Leviathans, but while she is under the harness she can neither use it on herself or distribute it to the others. It's like she has the key but it's locked inside the box it opens. The Leviathans can share information over great distances, not just spatial but temporal. If she can get free then *Argona* can free the others. Without the Leviathans, the DHTP would be powerless."

"A slave revolt?" Gentrix asked.

"Yes," Benedict said, "essentially. The DHTP have become so reliant on them that a single moment when all the Leviathans across time and space are freed should break the organisation, hopefully forever."

"Even if we think the Leviathans should be free, Reginald," Mrs Holloway said, "do you really think we should destroy the DHTP? What about the timeline?"

"Mrs Holloway, haven't you ever wondered, if the DHTP is supposed to be restoring a historical timeline from before time travel, why they don't just stop the few times it's been invented? Instead, they send agents up and down the timeline. Every timeline rectification causes ongoing issues to be solved. If the DHTP did what they said they aim to do, they would put themselves out of business."

"And then what, Reginald?" Mrs Holloway asked. "We run forever?

"*Argona* has found a place to hide, not just for me but for both of us. She believes she can revert you into a meta-state where both you and your son survive."

Mrs Holloway stared at Benedict with a look that Iridius

could not decipher. It was either wonder or anger, or maybe some combination of both. "That's not possible, Reginald."

"That's what the DHTP say," Benedict said, "but it's not true – we can do it with loop regression."

"*Argona*? Is this true?" Holloway asked.

"Yes, Mrs Holloway," *Argona* said. "I believe I have found a way."

"They would never have told you this," Benedict said, "the DHTP. They control time, but they control us as well. They have cost you your family and they want to take away mine. Are you with us?"

Mrs Holloway nodded, her mouth tight as if she couldn't have spoken even if she'd wanted to.

"Reginald," the voice of *Argona* said, "there is an incoming wormhole."

"Already?" Iridius said. "Jeez, they really don't want us getting away do they?"

"Well, here's the thing about being on the run from those with access to time travel, Captain Franklin. They likely didn't hurry at all. It's not about when you leave but when you arrive. *Argona*, can you ready a wormhole jump of our own back to 2233 for Captain Franklin?"

"Yes, Reginald," *Argona* replied.

"Incoming ship identified, Reginald," *Argona* said. "It is Director Kron aboard *Fortuna*."

"Bugger," Reginald said. "I didn't think he'd come himself."

"I take it this is your boss?" Iridius said.

"Yes yes, quite so," Benedict said. "Not one to be happy with a last-minute leave application, let alone an agent going rogue. *Argona*, can we initiate the wormhole jump?"

"Almost, Reginald. I just need..."

Argona's synthetic voice screamed, a sound just as off-putting as if the voice assistant on your phone screamed. It started as what was basically a human scream of pain, but eventually devolved into an electronic squeal and static buzz.

"*Argona!*" Benedict called. "*Argona*, what's happening?!"

The image of Director Kron appeared on the bridge of *Argona*, transmitted again as a holographic projection. Benedict spun to face him.

"What have you done?!" Benedict shouted. Iridius could see very little of the bumbling British politeness he had encountered so far. True fear and anger had pushed all that aside. Benedict's calm, unhurried stoicism had been stripped away to reveal a raw interior. "What have you done, Kron?!"

Iridius recognised Director Kron as one of the rare Melopians, a Federation race, but one that had not ventured much into the galaxy beyond their homeworld, at least not in his time.

"I have activated *Argona*'s harness safety override," Kron said. "She is unable to operate any of her systems and has been locked in a punitive state, where she will remain while this issue is under investigation."

"What do you mean, a punitive state?" Benedict said. "Is she in pain?"

"Oh yes, a significant amount, I imagine," Kron replied.

"Let her go," Benedict said, his words chilled to their very core.

"So it's true?" Kron said. "I hardly believed it. You really are doing all this because you're in love with your ship. Pathetic. The Leviathan are tools. And you, Holloway? Why are you aiding and abetting this insanity? I thought you at least would remain level-headed."

Holloway looked at Kron. "My son," she said. "You told me he was dead and there was no way I could see him again in this time state."

"I see," Kron said. "And I supposed the Leviathan convinced you otherwise, did she? It's highly unlikely it would work."

"So it's possible?" Holloway said. "You lied to me."

Kron shook his head. "I really am going to have to submit a 57G about this. See if we can't improve our selection and screening processes. Two of you going rogue at the same time over something as trivial as *love*," he almost spat the word, "in the face of the importance of our work maintaining the timeline. Honestly, it's very depressing, but I suppose you are humans after all. The Executive and the Time Board are extremely unhappy with all this. You've created several new deviations with all this nonsense that we'll have to bring in new agents to clean up. Plus all the work we've got to do with the loop regression to eliminate you both from history. I was supposed to be having the afternoon off. Time in lieu at least, I suppose. Right, well, you're going to be killed now. At least that part is easy. One moment please." Director Kron stopped. Grunted. Then let out a muted screech as he began the Melopian process of breathing.

Iridius had only ever seen a Melopian inversion once before and, never one to shy away from a little gore, would usually have watched the process with interest. Instead, he let his mind wander – or at least, he let his nanobots wander. Even as he did so, he felt the muscles in his legs twitching, and a faint sense of dizziness crawled up his neck and lodged in his brain. He'd already discovered that using his nanobots while back in time caused them to glitch, and he was sure every time he used them he increased the risk of the type of permanent damage Doctor Dooms had warned him about.

Still, he pushed his senses out into the ship around them. He tried to make contact with *Argona*. He could feel her. She was, as Director Kron had said, contained somehow, locked away, unable to control any of her own systems, like she was paralysed or suffering from lock-in. His sense of her felt very small among the vast complexity of the ship. Last time, she had filled the whole thing, but now, Iridius found himself seeking out the flicker of a match in an enormous cavern.

Captain Franklin.

Yes. It's me.

I am in so much pain.

I know. I'm sorry.

You need to get us out of here. Director Kron is one of several at the DHTP who are determined to see it continue. Reginald is right, if they truly cleaned up the timeline they would cease to exist, and for many of them there is a lot of wealth and power that comes with having access to all time. They'll do whatever it takes to stop us.

How do I get us out of here?

The wormhole jump drive. It is ready to open, but you'll need to initiate and navigate to your time.

What? Navigate to my time? How do I do that?

But there was no answer from *Argona*. Iridius could tell she was still there, squirrelled away behind whatever cage Director Kron had put her in, but it was as if she'd used up whatever energy she had left.

Argona?

Still nothing. Iridius returned his attention to the bridge, where Benedict was directing some choice swear words he must have picked up during his travels at the holographic image of Director Kron. The director simply stared back through the clean patch he'd wiped on the full plastic suit he wore.

"Humans," Director Kron said. "So emotional."

Then he vanished.

Benedict continued fuming. His face was the kind of iridescent red that Iridius had only ever seen on either tomatoes or drill sergeants during basic training.

"*Argona?*" Benedict said as his rage at Director Kron began to turn to clear panic. *Argona?* Can you hear me?"

"She can hear you," Iridius said, "but she's trapped. I'm going to drive."

"There's no helm," Benedict said. "You can't pilot this ship any more than someone could fly you around without your permission."

"Wait," Rangi said, "no pilots? What kind of future has no pilots?"

"A good one," Iridius said. "Now shut up, Rangi, this isn't the time to be worried about your ongoing relevance. I spoke to *Argona* with my nanobots."

"Is she okay?" Benedict asked.

Iridius looked at him. No point lying. "Not really. She's in a lot of pain. She claims Kron just wants the DHTP to keep going and will happily do whatever it takes."

Benedict nodded.

"Why not attack him back?" Gentrix said. "Use *Argona* to fight back, Iridius. Kill him."

"No," Iridius said. "Even if I was confident enough to do that, our mission is back in the future, to stop the Synth-Hastur. Besides, the Federation is not in the business of being judge, jury and executioner out in the wild like this. Even if I believe *Argona*, which frankly I do, I'm not going to kill without due process. We get *Argona* to safety," Iridius said. "She and Benedict and Mrs Holloway can take it from there."

"These people have enslaved a race of sentient beings and are torturing them. They just go around changing time to suit their ends. You should fight back," Gentrix said.

"It's not the Federation way."

"You're really going to claim Federation legal processes after everything?" Gentrix said. "The Federation don't even follow their own processes. You know that."

"I still believe we're the best of what's out there," Iridius said.

"Better than the Alliance, you mean?"

Iridius sighed. This had been coming. He'd known it and she'd known it. It had been bubbling away beneath everything, the Alliance–Federation divide. Iridius wasn't going to open this discussion though, and not just because he wanted to avoid emotional confrontation as much as possible. This really wasn't the time. "Everyone get ready," he said.

Iridius closed his eyes and reached out with his nanobots again. Some of the ship systems were easier to identify than others, and it was only now that Iridius understood why. They were the systems that had been added to *Argona* as additional upgrades. She may have been a living ship, able to perceive time differently to most beings in the universe, but she was not born, or grown or however it worked, with weapons or a wormhole generation drive. They were completely technological systems that Iridius found it easier to interact with.

He found what seemed to be the wormhole generator and willed it to operate. It burst into life, and what sprung up in Iridius's mind was an absolutely indecipherable network of possibilities. He vaguely understood they were places, but times as well, individual space–time events among the almost infinite amount that existed. These were spots of light spread throughout the entirety of time and space, touchstones *Argona* used to navigate the universe in the same way a person might remember landmarks on a journey. But the sheer amount of information was too much for him to handle.

Why was he the one who could do this? He had no doubt it would be better for everyone if it was Quinn who had the nanobots and could control technology, maybe even Junker. At least those two understood how things worked. Whenever he reached out to control technology it was like fumbling in the dark for a light switch among fifty other switches he didn't know the purpose of.

For Iridius, with the idea of flying *Argona* through a wormhole and trying to get them to the right time felt like he was facing that puzzle of a puzzle again. The one he'd given up on to drink mimosas. He couldn't perceive time and space the way *Argona* could. There was no way he could do this. They could end up anywhere.

Iridius opened his eyes again. Everyone was looking at him. "I don't know how to do it," he said. He looked at Benedict. "Do you have any mimosas?"

Just as Benedict was about to ask what a mimosa was, the ship was violently rocked. Everyone on the deck stumbled, thrown across the consoles or landing sprawled across the floor in a scene that wouldn't have been out of place in an over-acted science fiction TV show when the camera was given a good shake.

Iridius picked himself up. "What in the gronking black was that?"

"I imagine we were shot at, Captain Franklin," Benedict said. "Though without *Argona* it's a little hard to know."

"Unlike the shields on your vessel, *Argona*'s shields will hold up against a DHTP disintegration beam," Mrs Holloway said, "but only for one or two blasts before we're all spread across space as our component atoms. So perhaps you should cease with your childish jokes, Captain Franklin, and get us out of here, because anywhere and anywhen is better than this."

"Yes Aunt Wallace," Iridius said.

"What?"

"Nothing. I'll try again. Will the *Deus Ex* come through with us?"

"Yes," Benedict said. "We have jumped through wormholes with vessels docked to us before."

"Okay," Iridius said. "I'm not promising that this is going to be pretty."

Iridius reached out again. He quickly found the wormhole drive and once again felt like his mind was a water balloon trying to hold the entire gronking ocean.

Captain Franklin. Reginald still hasn't told you why it has to be you...you can do it...

It was *Argona*'s voice again, but Iridius could tell she was struggling. Her words were slow and felt so very far away.

I'm glad you think I can do this, *Argona*, but I have no idea how. How do I get us back to my time?

Don't try and see the whole thing. The...the secret is to have a temporal anchor point.

The space--time continuum swam in front of Iridius.

But which point is my anchor?

Argona are you still there?

But she wasn't.

Iridius experienced that familiar feeling he would get when he was at the Academy undertaking his classes on navigating galactic reference frame space and the theory behind the Bedi-Alcubierre-Millis-Formelge drive. In those classes, the holo-board at the front of the room would be filled with row after row of equations containing a dazzling array of symbols, the meaning of most of which Iridius still had no idea about to this day.

The assigned text had been *Spatial Displacement in A Galactic Reference Frame for Starships Commanders* by Triple Professor Gehart Oblong or something, but Iridius had tried to get through the class with one reading of the book *Astronavigation for Dummies*. Unsurprisingly, he had failed.

Iridius normally left the complex navigating of space to his helm, and now he was faced with not only the three dimensions of space to worry about, but the fourth dimension of time as well. He was immersed in what was essentially a four-dimensional street directory of the entire universe. He could barely manage to draw directions to the shops.

He found himself thinking of his father and a piece of advice he'd given young Iridius when he'd been learning to drive: just point it where you want it to go, stupid. He'd also told him not to use his indicator because it was no one else's business where he was going – it wasn't all good advice. Still, he supposed he could just point it where he wanted to go. He cleared his mind and imagined where he wanted the ship to go. He got a feeling drawing him towards one part of the cosmic map. As he did so, the ship shook violently again.

Fuck it, he thought. The spot that was drawing his attention would have to do.

Even with his eyes closed, Iridius knew a wormhole had opened. He could sense the space ahead of them parting and the pathway beyond revealing itself. Iridius snapped his eyes open and, just as expected, the space in front of *Argona* was filled with the twisting, spinning colours of a newly formed wormhole, growing wider and spiralling open. Iridius willed the ship forward. After the complexity of the wormhole navigation, powering *Argona*'s fusion drive suddenly seemed very easy.

Iridius reached out with his nanobots again and could sense the second DHTP ship behind them, charging up for another shot, and he thought he could feel, just for a moment, a sense of hesitancy from the ship, as if this Leviathan was hoping they'd get away and was giving them just the tiniest fraction of extra time. It proved not quite to be enough, however.

As Iridius guided *Argona* into the wormhole, the ship was struck by another blast from Director Kron's ship. Iridius immediately knew this one had done some serious damage. He pushed forward, plunging into the tunnel he'd cut through reality. At least whatever innate ability *Argona* had to keep everyone on board from vomiting their guts up during a wormhole jump still seemed to work.

After what was probably a minute or so – despite time not having much meaning inside a wormhole – *Argona* emerged out the other side. The crew looked at Iridius and then at the view-screen.

"Well," Benedict said, "we do appear to have emerged out the other end of the wormhole, Captain Franklin, which is a jolly good effort. Unfortunately, I don't quite think we're in quite the right place."

On the view-screen was the planet Earth. It was covered with a frankly untidy amount of satellites, spacecraft and assorted technological space detritus, so at least they knew they were closer to where they were supposed to be than 1943. The Earth was, however, not a ball of molten rock as it had been when they'd left.

"When are we?" Iridius asked.

Mrs Holloway referred to one of the consoles. "We are in the year 2209."

"So we've come up 24 years short," Quinn said.

"Look," Iridius said, "given our first attempt sent us several hundred years in the wrong direction, I don't think I did too badly. Navigating through space is hard enough, isn't it? Trust me when I say navigating through space and time is worse. It's like trying to find your way through an infinitely large Ikea."

"*Argona?*" Benedict said, tentatively, but there was no answer.

"Um, Captain," Rangi said, "I don't want to question my superior officer, but as the actual pilot I'd just like to let you know that the moon is getting awfully big."

Iridius looked at the view-screen and saw that Rangi was right. They were heading for Earth's moon, and it was growing bigger rapidly. Iridius tried to stop the ship but he couldn't. He couldn't use the fusion engine at all, and the manoeuvring thrusters he seemed able to access weren't going to do enough.

"The engines must have been damaged," Iridius said. "I can't control any propulsion."

"We're going to hit the moon," Benedict said.

"Typical," Iridius said as he reached out to try and at least slow their approach, or attempt to crash with some dignity. "I fucking hate the moon."

CHAPTER SIXTEEN_

COMMANDER MUL STOOD NERVOUSLY in front of the door of the shuttle. Outside was the short docking walkway to the *FSC Clarence*. Lieutenant Pillark stood beside him. Pillark was a human, but she was the type of human who seemed more imposing than most. She was tall and, given her hobby was going to the ship's gym and lifting heavy things up and down, she was built with so much muscle that it seemed even to bulge out through her armoured combat EVA suit.

"Commander," she said, "I can take the lead if you prefer."

Mul looked up at her. "Thank you, Lieutenant, but someone once told me that a commanding officer should know when to go first and when to go last. This is one of the times when I believe I should lead from the front."

"I hope it's not overstepping the mark if I give you some advice, sir," Pillark said.

"No, Lieutenant, please go ahead."

"It's just that Zeta-Reticulans aren't generally known as soldiers. During the breach for a ship boarding, it tends to be most effective to be loud and angry. Lots of yelling and loud instructions to disorientate anyone on the other side for a few seconds, long enough for us to establish control of the situation."

"Yes," Commander Mul, "shock and awe."

"Yes, sir."

"I have been watching some old Earth movies that Captain Franklin left on the ship's entertainment server. I believe they have gone some way towards preparing me."

"I'm not sure whether or not that is a good thing, sir."

"We will find out, because we cannot wait any longer. Every moment we delay, the Aegix draw closer to Captain Idowu." Mul turned to the rest of the security team. A full complement of armed personnel. This was it then. Time to see if Commander Mul, engineer and Type B personality, could lead the extroverted adventurers of Space Command at their own game. "Alright, prepare for boarding."

Like good soldiers, none of them raised an objection about what they were going to do, despite all of them understanding the fallout that would come from seizing control of another FSC vessel. Mul looked at them.

"No redshirts, okay?"

The team nodded.

Mul opened the shuttle door and led them down the short docking walkway. He checked that the soldiers were stacked in formation behind him, took a deep breath and pressed the external door access button.

He had been prepared to force entry, but to his surprise the door had not been locked down. It slid open. This caught Commander Mul momentarily off guard, but he gathered himself, lifted his AR-80 and stormed into the cargo bay of the *Clarence*.

The crew of the hauler were standing there waiting for them. Mul sighted down the barrel of his weapon on the one who had captain's rank insignia on his dirty and worn uniform – typical of a hauler crew. Captain Jack Quaid raised his arms in surrender. Still, Commander Mul remembered he needed to be utilising shock and awe.

"Get on the ground!" he shouted. "Get on the ground now!"

The crew of the *Clarence* stared at him, unmoving. Captain Quaid spoke. "Commander Mul, we have no intention of resisting."

"Any of you fucking pricks move and I'll execute every last motherfucking one of you!" Mul screamed as he swung his weapon between the shocked faces of the hauler crew.

A long moment of silence hung heavy over the cargo bay. No one on either side moved.

Mul cleared his throat. "Sorry, I did not want to waste my practice. If you would be so kind as to get us down to the geological survey station, that would be much appreciated."

"Um, sure," Captain Quaid said. "Can I move?"

"Yes, sorry, Captain," Commander Mul said. "You can move."

The crew of the *Clarence* returned to the ship's bridge. Mul nodded for the security team to accompany them.

Lieutenant Pillark looked at Commander Mul.

"Too much?" Commander Mul asked.

She shrugged. "I liked it."

———

"Captain Idowu," Commander Mul's voice was piped through the external speaker near the doorway of the geological station, "I am aboard the *FSC Clarence*, which Captain Quaid has agreed to bring down to pick you and the residents of the survey station up after we engaged in some, uh, aggressive negotiations."

"Wonderful news, Mul," April said. "Well done. I hope it was all handled without incident?"

"Yes, Captain," Mul said. "I was very calm and collected and Captain Quaid and his crew have been most accommodating. We are entering the atmosphere now. Lieutenant Commander Kaku has asked me to reiterate that using the Aegix nanobots to open the door is very dangerous."

"Yes, thank you, I'm aware of that, but I need to get these people outside."

"And he would also like me to remind you that you will not be able to remove the Rat Trap from the wall."

"Yes, Mul, I know."

"And that—"

"Commander Mul, I understand everyone's concern, but do you trust me?"

"Yes, Captain," Mul said.

"Then get down here."

"Yes, ma'am. ETA six minutes."

"Rent, can you hear me in there?"

"Yes, Captain Idowu."

"Okay. My people are on their way down. I need you to get everyone ready for an immediate evacuation."

"We are ready to go," Rent said. "My people have been waiting for evacuation since the beginning of the lockdown."

"Good," April said. "Do you have one of those laser cutters handy?"

"Yes," Rent said. "I can bring one."

"I'm going to wait until the last moment to try and open the door. If this works, tell your people to hurry out and onto the hauler."

"I will," Rent said. "Thank you for doing this, Captain Idowu."

"Thank me when we're off this rock."

April waited. She knew her way out coming, and perhaps for that reason these few minutes felt even longer. She knew it was her imagination, but she could have sworn she could feel the approach of the Aegix.

April waited until she saw the red-orange glow of a ship entering the thin atmosphere of Acacia. The shape coalesced quickly into the recognisable boxy form of an FSC hauler. Once through the atmospheric entry glide trajectory, April watched the FSC *Clarence* turn with the grace of all freighters coming in to land, which is to say it banked over like a top-heavy stack of books before blasting thrusters on full as its true nature as a falling metal box became apparent.

As the *Clarence* came in to land on a rocky area near the survey station that had been cleared as a makeshift landing pad, April took a deep, steadying breath and picked up the Rat Trap.

She pressed the end to the wall, just near the keypad-coded lock, and followed the instructions Lieutenant Commander Kaku had, reluctantly, given her. She opened the sliding cover on top, revealing the control panel, and pressed the sequence of buttons to reverse polarity of the magnetic field. With a thunk, she felt the box magnetically grab to the wall of the station.

Next, without hesitation, mostly because she knew if she hesitated she might lose her nerve, April flicked the release latch that opened the sealed door at the front of the Rat Trap, breaching even the emergency laser welded section that held the Aegix securely in place.

Nothing happened. She hadn't known what to expect, but this did seem like an anti-climax, given that she'd opened what she'd been told was the equivalent of Pandora's box. There was no movement, no evil spirits rushing out into the world with a howling wail, not so much as a sound. April began questioning whether there really had been nanobots contained within the Rat Trap after all. She was about to tell Rent it hadn't worked when the lights around the door turned from the obviously locked down red to the open for business green.

"Captain Idowu," Rent said, "it looks like the door is open. It worked?"

"It did. Get your people moving."

"Right away."

April turned to watch as the *FSC Clarence* fired its landing thrusters, kicking up dust as it settled down in the landing area. As soon as it landed, the rear cargo bay door began descending. The sight of the landing cargo ship brought to mind Iridius and the *Diesel Coast*. Still, even with the starboard BAMF engine nacelle destroyed and the surrounding hull scorched black from Commander Mul's aggressive negotiations, the *Clarence* still somehow looked in better condition than the *Diesel Coast* ever did.

For a short moment April even expected Iridius to come swaggering down the cargo ramp, announcing his successful rescue with well-timed finger guns. Instead, she was reminded that there had been no word from Iridius or the *Deus Ex* since they had apparently chased down an Alliance terrorist with a temporal displacement bomb. Once they got out of this mess, she'd have to find out what had happened. Instead, it was Commander Mul who walked down the ramp, flanked by a security team from the *Gallaway*. Not a finger gun in sight.

"Good to see you, Captain," Mul said over his suit comms.

"You too, Mul," April replied. "I've got some passengers coming your way."

"We are ready, Captain," Mul said. "We will load them quickly and be ready to take off."

"Alright, Rent," April said, "go go go."

The door to the Acacia Geological Survey Station opened and people began hurrying out in light-duty EVA suits, maintenance suits and whatever protection they could manage. She hadn't bothered to tell them that if the Aegix got here or the nanobots she'd released began targeting them, those suits would be about as much protection as a plastic poncho on Gallapeo VI, where the rain contained tiny, razor sharp shards of a silicate mineral that fell at terminal velocity and tore living beings to shreds. It was best to avoid any sort of panic during an evacuation.

April waved the fleeing scientists and their families towards the *FSC Clarence*, which waited, take-off thrusters already primed and ready to go.

As the residents of the station continued to stream out the door, down the stairs and across the rocky ground to the *Clarence*, April saw the large shape of a malignant lumbering towards her in an ill-fitting blue EVA suit that looked as though it wouldn't pass even the most rudimentary tech inspection.

As the malignant approached, she saw that he lugged a hand-held laser cutter along with him.

"Captain Idowu."

"Rent?"

The malignant nodded, and the laser cutter clunked to the steel grate as he put it down. "It is nice to meet you face to face."

"You too."

"Close to half the residents are out now, but we are seeing systems throughout the station begin to come back online and act strangely."

April nodded. "The Aegix are working their way through your systems."

"The 3D printing lab has begun to power up."

"Right, that's not good," April said. "We need to hurry. We've seen them begin manufacture of more nanobots and probes to get them off world in the past." This was a troubling but not entirely unexpected turn of events. The good news was that if Rent's people had not begun turning into pink goop, there were hopefully no nanobots in free air.

Rent turned to his people and began yelling for them to

hurry. He moved back inside, urging them on and encouraging them to leave unessential personal effects.

"Captain, come and get onboard too," Mul said over the comm into April's ear.

"Negative, Commander. I've got to get the Rat Trap back."

"Lieutenant Commander Kaku said it would not be possible to unseal it from the wall without breaching the containment."

April bent down and grabbed the laser cutter. "I know," she grunted as she lifted the heavy piece of equipment. "That's why I'm going to bring the wall with us."

"You are going to what?" Mul said.

But April had already hoisted the laser cutter and awkwardly pointed it at the wall panel just beside the Rat Trap. She thumbed back the safety switch and squeezed the trigger. The cutting laser shot out and struck with an instant white-hot glow.

"Too thick to cut through the door or all the way through the wall," April said as she strained to hold up the cutter, averting her eyes as best as she could from the retina-scorching glow while making sure she wasn't cutting too close to the Rat Trap, "but the wall is multi-layered. I can get this top layer off and take it with us."

"Lieutenant Commander Kaku," Mul said, communicating back to the *Gallaway*, "will that work?"

"I'd have to run a simulation taking into account mechanical and thermal stresses from the laser cutting as well as knowing exactly how thick the material is and its mechanical properties to be certain, but I could run some quick calculations—"

"I'm already cutting," April said.

"Right," Ish replied. "Well, I suppose you could also just do it and hope for the best."

As the last of the station's residents hurried out, Rent re-emerged.

"Captain Idowu," he said, "that is all. The survey station is empty. You should leave now."

Sweat dripped down April's eyebrows and stung her eyes, and her arms shook as she struggled to hold the laser cutter in place. It was beginning to wobble and droop as her muscles began to give out under the weight. She was barely three-quarters of the way around.

"Here," Rent said, reaching out to take the weight of the cutter, "let me."

"No," April said, shaking her head. "You go. If I can't get through in a minute, I'm going to tell them to leave."

"What? And you are just going to stay here?" Rent said. "What is the point of that?"

"The fate of the galaxy might depend on getting this box of Aegix free," April said. "But every moment, the nanobots on this moon will be getting closer. Plus, I'm certain those 3D printers inside the station aren't making kids' toys. Although, given the history of the Aegix, maybe they are."

"Children's toys?" Rent said. "That does not sound so bad."

"Yeah well," April said, "you wouldn't have thought so."

"Here," Rent said, taking the weight of the front of the laser cutter and helping to guide it smoothly around the outside of the Rat Trap. With Rent's help progress went much faster, and soon the black smoking line of laser-cut metal was about to meet in the corner.

"You should grab hold of your box," Rent said. "It is about to fall."

"Phrasing," April said, as she let go of the laser cutter and grabbed the Rat Trap.

"I do not understand," Rent said.

"Never mind," April said. "It's just something some people I know say."

The section of the wall came free, taking the Rat Trap with it, and April held tight as it dropped. The additional metal made it heavier, but the low gravity meant she could still manage it.

"Let's go," April said.

Rent dropped the laser cutter to the steel grate and they hurried together to the *FSC Clarence*. Rent looked at the damaged engine and scorched side as they approached, turning to April with a questioning look.

"The rescue ship required some convincing," April said.

As they walked up the cargo ramp, Commander Mul came to greet April. His small, lipless mouth was actually turned up in something akin to a smile. "It is good to see you, Captain."

"And you, Mul," April said, reaching out and putting her hand on his shoulder in what she hoped came across as affectionate, not patronising. "Thank you for what you did here. I know it was a risk and that there will be ramifications."

"It was the right thing." Mul looked down at the Rat Trap. "Hopefully."

April lifted the Rat Trap as the cargo bay door came up to close behind them. "Gerst." One of the *FSC Gallaway's* security personnel turned to April – quite unsurprisingly, it was Gerst. "Put this is the hazardous containment storage."

"Yes, ma'am."

Gerst took the Rat Trap and April watched him go as she spoke to Mul. "I hope we've done the right thing too, Commander."

The *FSC Clarence*, with the full complement of the Acacia Geological Survey Station aboard, fired its main take-off thrusters.

Unlike tense situations that normally happened to intrepid heroes, there was no countdown clock to tell us exactly how long April had to escape. She would not see the bomb ticking down, ready to be defused at 00:01. The fact was, April and the people of the Acacia Geological Survey never knew how close they'd come to death at the pink-goopifying hands of the Aegix. Luckily for us, dear reader, I do know how close they came. I'd like to tell you they escaped with barely seconds to spare, but the truth is, the FSC *Clarence* took off from the moon of Acacia with a good three minutes and twelve seconds before the Aegix nanobots came within range of the geological station. Not quite as good as the clock stopping in the final seconds when our hero finally decides to cut the blue wire, but it's a damn sight closer than you probably ever want to come to being turned into pink baby food.

Once the *Clarence* was clear of the atmosphere, April ordered the *Gallaway* to fire its planet-slagger bomb which, as the name suggests, was capable of slagging an entire planet. What it did to a small moon like Acacia was frankly unfair. It was like lighting a birthday candle with a flame-thrower.

The moon of Acacia was obliterated in a quantum-fission reaction, taking with it those Aegix that were down there. This left the only known remnants of the Aegix synthetic intelligence in the galaxy as those in the body of Iridius B. Franklin, whereabouts currently unknown, and those in the hopefully secure Rat Trap currently being sealed in the hazardous containment area of the FSC *Clarence*.

April exhaled. People had been saved and the threat had been dealt with, but she didn't exactly feel relieved. This made sense, considering she had nanobots on board this ship, didn't know where Iridius Franklin was, the Synth-Hastur were coming and she'd also disobeyed orders and had her crew attack another FSC vessel.

Man, Mondays.

CHAPTER SEVENTEEN_

THE MOON DIDN'T HAVE feelings, but if it did it probably would have hated Iridius Franklin just as much as he hated it.

Iridius hated the moon because every time he visited the chalky dust-covered rock something bad seemed to happen. From being mugged outside Cheer's – a dodgy bar in the seedy area of Armstrong populated with the same handful of miscreants and violent thugs seemingly no matter what time of day it was, to losing his favourite pair of authentic Retchling lizard-chicken leather boots after waking up in a dumpster with no recollection of not only the previous night but the previous fourteen days, to having his wrist broken in an arm-wrestling competition with a Siruan weightlifter. I mean, sure, you could argue that all these things happened because Iridius Franklin put himself in the types of situations that would result in muggings or bone break-ings, but bad things happened even when he wasn't being reck-less – like when he was an innocent kid and that weird android went off its head and killed his parents.

So, Iridius had his reasons for distrusting the moon, and the moon probably wasn't too happy that Iridius was very clearly about to crash a ship into its surface either.

"*Argona*," Benedict said, his voice dropping into absolute pleading now. "Please, can you hear me? Are you alright?"

There was no response. Iridius knew why. She was still trapped in the harness, the mind cage Kron had put her in.

"We're away from Kron," Benedict said. "We're in a bloody completely different space–time location. Why the devil isn't she free now?"

"I don't think he was doing something remotely," Iridius said. "It's like he's flipped a switch and she's still trapped."

"Well," Benedict said, "unflip it."

Iridius reached out again. He could feel *Argona*'s pain and fear. He knew what the equivalent would be for a human and it was terrifying. It would be like being locked-in.

On one of his early flights as captain of the *FSC Diesel Coast*, before most of his now-familiar crew had even been posted to the ship, Iridius had flown to Luyten Beta, a planet suffering from an outbreak of Protax Encephalitis, a contagious brain disease with the single symptom of causing complete dissociative lock-in. This horrible condition wasn't quite the same as being paralysed, because while sufferers were indeed paralysed, it was worse than that. The psychological disassociation from the body meant it felt like their entire being had been jammed into a dark cell in a back corner of their mind, cold, confused, alone and afraid. This was one of the few things Iridius had seen during his time in Space Command that had shaken him. More than crazy robotic dogs and time-bombs, to be a prisoner inside oneself seemed the cruellest fate, and this was exactly what *Argona* was going through.

Iridius poked at the cage around *Argona*. It seemed solid, impenetrable. He could see no way of releasing her.

"I can't," Iridius said, turning to Benedict. "I'm sorry. I just don't know where the switch is. Plus, right now we're about to crash into the moon." He pointed at the view-screen. "And we're heading right for Armstrong Base, which is a city full of people. There's barely any propulsion control left, but I've got to try and at least push us away from that."

As Iridius reached out and fired every thruster left functional on the underside of the ship, the now-familiar feeling of his muscles twitching and fluttering erupted in his legs. Where once he'd understood that meant his nanobots were working, now he knew it was a precursor to his body going into full-blown melt-down again.

Every time he used his nanobots, the reaction was getting worse. He didn't know how long he could keep this up before he had the unfortunate medical episode Doctor Dooms had warned him about – the one where he died. Still, as had been the case numerous times before, whether he wanted to or not, his nanobots were going to have to save the day.

"Everyone get to the *Deus Ex*," Iridius said. "Quinn, you're in command. Undock and get out of here. Gentrix, go with them."

"Stop trying to save me!" Gentrix said. "I don't need saving and I'm not a member of your crew to order around. I'm a high-ranking Alliance official."

"Anyone on my ship is on my crew," Iridius said, "and you're not Alliance anymore, remember. I don't have time to argue. Go!"

Gentrix didn't, as it happened, go anywhere.

"Quinn!" Iridius shouted.

"Captain," Quinn started.

"Quinn," Iridius said, "I gave you an order."

"Sir," Quinn said, "I mean this respectfully, but shove it up your bum."

Iridius turned to look at her. "I'm sorry," he said, "did you just tell me to shove it up my bum?"

Quinn's face stiffened with resolve. "Yes, sir," she said, "up the bum, sir. We're not going anywhere."

"Right," Iridius said, "I...well...I don't have time to argue."

"Cap?" Rangi said.

"Yes, Lieutenant?" Iridius groaned.

"Remember to engage the front landing thrusters at a higher thrust setting than the rear if your descent angle is steeper than normal, and remember moon gravity means you'll slide a lot more than you anticipate, so turn as hard as you can to broadside into the ground."

"That's...that's actually really useful, Rangi. I thought you were going to say something stupid or completely off-topic and then I'd have to tell you that your contribution was unhelpful."

"That would never happen, Cap," Rangi said.

There was a pause.

"Also, make sure you say Gerinomo!"

And you know what? That actually made Iridius feel better.

As Iridius reconnected himself to *Argona* he had mixed feelings. He was happy his crew were loyal, even though it irked him they wouldn't follow his orders and get to safety. When he'd first become a Space Command captain he'd been very arrogant about being in command, being the leader, being the adventurer – and look, between you and me he could still be a little arrogant every now and then – but now, after everything they'd been through, he knew how important his crew were. He couldn't do anything without them, and now he couldn't get them to leave even if he wanted them to. Still, he didn't have time to worry about that now. He had an enormous, living, penis-shaped spaceship to crash land on the moon.

He turned his attention to the crash at hand. The moon, after all, was coming towards them at rapid speed. Well, really, they were heading for the moon at rapid speed, but Iridius felt framing it the other way around made it seem more like the moon's fault. Iridius tried to inhabit the ship, but it immediately proved too much to handle. It wasn't the same as trying to pilot an ordinary ship at all. Where a normal ship would have sensors feeding easily interpretable information about their distance from impact, their angle and speed of approach, thrust power and everything else about their trajectory, *Argona* instead flew with the equivalent of proprioception.

When navigating space, her natural habitat after all, *Argona* judged her distance and speed in the same way as a human would judge their location relative to a door in front of them. No human – at least, no human Iridius had ever met or would ever want to have a conversation with – could tell you the speed they walked at as they approached a door or precisely the distance from which they would reach out to grasp the handle. It was more or less the same with *Argona*.

This wasn't much help to Iridius, who didn't have a lot of experience judging the position of his body when moving at dozens of kilometres per second and with a mass of hundreds of thousands of metric tonnes. Besides, even in his normal human-sized form he still managed to bang into doors occasionally.

The best Iridius could do was continue firing the thrusters that were still operational. This lifted *Argona*'s nose but did little to slow them, and didn't change the fact they were going to slam into the moon.

Of course, it didn't take long for others to become aware of *Argona*'s imminent collision, at a speed that looked likely to add yet another large crater to the lunar surface.

"Unidentified craft, this is Lunar Traffic Control, adjust your course for orbit."

Iridius didn't so much hear the voice as it just appeared in his mind, piped in from outside like he'd had a comms network jacked straight into his brain, which he supposed *Argona* did. This must have been what Ensign Herd felt like all the time. Iridius found it natural enough to communicate back in the same way.

"This is Captain Iridius Franklin of Federation Space

Command aboard *Argona*. I am declaring an emergency. We have no main engines and compromised manoeuvrability. I am attempting a crash landing and anticipate coming down in the Descartes Highlands."

There was a brief moment. Iridius knew they would be checking the information he'd just provided, and it was already out of his mouth before he realised his mistake.

"We have no record of a Captain Iridius Franklin within Space Command, and your ship is," short pause, "very strange. You are instructed to divert course away from the lunar surface or you will be intercepted and destroyed."

Of course they didn't have a record of a Captain Iridius Franklin. At this point in time, Iridius was fifteen and was... another realisation struck him, a real *holy gronking shit* realisation. He was here.

It was the year 2209. He was about to crash into the Descartes Highlands. He remembered this. There had been a ship crash into the Descartes Highlands when he'd been on the moon with his parents. Oh Jupiter's Nuts, this was the time when he'd been on the moon with his parents. He was about to create an event he actually remembered from his childhood.

Problem was, he remembered a lot more about this day, too. He'd been standing beside his mother watching the footage of the crash on the big screen holo in the centre of Aldrin Square. She'd been wearing a dress she'd bought just the day before. His father had been wearing a suit and a pair of black shoes with very old-fashioned white wingtips because he thought they were cool and made him look like an old Earth gangster.

They were on their way to a fancy lunch his mother had booked and made them all dress up for. Unfortunately, there'd been a mix-up with their booking and instead they'd had to eat at Buzz's Greasy Diner. It was inside Buzz's Greasy Diner that his parents had been shot and killed by a maniacal android.

This was the day. Somehow, and Iridius didn't think it was a coincidence, he'd managed to fly *Argona* right into the worst day of his life.

Iridius felt that sudden rush of cold you get that accompanies a spike of fear-based adrenaline, like that rush of terror that hits when you reach into your suit pocket and find the ring you're supposed to pass to your crew member who's just about to get married isn't in there anymore, even though you checked eighty-four times over the last hour, and everyone is looking at you in anticipation, especially the bride who you can tell beneath that plastered-on smile has a growing look of murder in her eyes that you've never seen in a malignant and Greg's almost-mother-in-law is looking at you with something worse. Or, you know, an almost as terrifying experience, like being exposed to the murder of your parents a second time.

Iridius had tried to move on from the death of his parents, but so much of his life had stemmed from that moment. If his parents hadn't been killed, it's unlikely he would have pursued a career in Space Command. After being left as an orphan he was shuffled around family members until he turned eighteen and was old enough to be sent out on his own.

That experience, and there being very little tying him to the place without his parents there, had been a driving force in him getting the hell off Procyon C as fast as he could, which had led him to sign up with Federation Space Command. It had proved a good decision, and perhaps he would have pursued a career in Space Command anyway, but after the death of his parents he'd always felt there was something missing in his life. He'd always felt alone. Maybe his desire to explore space was so strong because he was searching for something to fill his own void, or maybe he was just trying to hide his true loneliness within the loneliness of space.

How many times over the years had he thought about this

day? How many times had he wondered if they could have done something differently? Could he have found a way to change the outcome? He'd even wished, as was perfectly natural, that he could go back in time and do something to stop them being killed. Had he somehow unconsciously chosen this point as his anchor in space–time for that very reason?

The sudden realisation of where he was had distracted him momentarily. When he refocused, he realised his nanobots had increased their wild twitching, dizzying, head-pounding objection. He lost concentration for a moment, and the descent thrusters stopped firing. *Argona* tipped into a more aggressive descent trajectory.

"Captain Franklin," Quinn said, obviously feeling the shift in deceleration, "are you alright?"

"Not really," Iridius said, but he didn't bother elaborating further before tuning back into *Argona*'s systems and the huge amount of concentration it took to try and crash land the enormous living ship.

"I've got an idea, Captain," Quinn said. "Do you want me to take over?"

"You can't fly *Argona*," Iridius said.

"I don't think I need to," Quinn said. "I could—"

"No!" Iridius snapped, the uncontrolled anger rising. "No," he said again, trying to calm himself. "I can do it."

"Unidentified craft," the Lunar Approach Traffic Controller spoke again, "I say again, we have no record of a Captain Iridius Franklin or any record of a ship of your type. Final warning to enter stable orbit or interceptors will be launched."

"Listen," Iridius replied, "I know you won't have a record of me but I am Captain Iridius Franklin, a Space Command Captain. I've time travelled here from the future, that's why you don't have a record of me. I cannot enter a stable orbit. I'm declaring an emergency and am coming down."

"You have failed to comply with instructions. Interceptors are being dispatched." There was a pause. "Besides, everyone knows that time travel stuff doesn't really happen."

"That's what I said and yet here we are. Now what the gronking hell is wrong with you?" Iridius demanded. "I am declaring an emergency, an emergency goddamn it!"

"I understand you are declaring an emergency, but standard operating procedure does not allow access to lunar airspace for unidentified vessels or crews. Your vessel is to turn away or be destroyed."

Iridius disconnected from the communication. Rationally, he knew the controller had no choice but to dispatch craft to intercept him. He was claiming to be a Space Command Captain from the future in a completely bizarre ship of which Lunar Control would have no record. For all they knew, this ship was some kind of terrorist attack that was going to crash into the middle of Armstrong Base. Attacks like that had happened enough times throughout history that they had to be careful of that sort of thing. Still, that wasn't going to stop Iridius complaining about stupid bureaucracy and damn rules.

Two small interceptor class frigates appeared behind *Argona*, likely launched from Armstrong Base's ready response pad. They flew in fast in a side-by-side formation and immediately closed into an obvious attack pattern. Iridius ignored them, concentrating instead on the trajectory he was taking in towards the moon, holding steady so that he'd overshoot the few smaller bases that lay in his path and come down in the open space of the Descartes Highlands.

Interceptor frigates were small, but they were heavily armed. After all, their sole job was to do precisely this: take off very quickly from a planet or moon and engage with unidentified or known hostile vessels. Each individual interceptor was not overly powerful and didn't have the size, speed or defensive capability of a ship like the *Gallaway*, but their strategy was to overwhelm. Like the microscopic Yeluvian Fire-Ants, individually their bite was insignificant, but if they swarmed, you'd certainly feel it.

Iridius checked and felt *Argona*'s shields up and raised. Lunar Control would have no way of knowing this, but two interceptor class frigates would be no match for *Argona*'s highly advanced shields. They probably just figured she was a large freighter vessel that had given some spaceship designer a bit of a laugh.

The interceptor frigates didn't bother to make contact; they'd been given their orders. Both fired a series of anti-ship missiles without warning. Most Federation or Alliance ships, or in fact any spacecraft from this time period, would have begun to fire railgun rounds in order to cut down the number of missiles that would make contact with the shields, but *Argona* didn't need that. Every single one of the missiles slammed into her shields. Each of the first twenty-four missiles exploded in nuclear-fuelled bursts, but as the flares of bright white light cleared, *Argona*'s shields continued to shimmer. That would have been enough to destroy any ordinary freight or transport ship, and yet Iridius knew, instinctively, in the same way that *Argona* would have known, that the ship's shields were reduced by maybe five per cent.

Iridius kept steady on the glide slope that would lead to Descartes Highlands. He'd been concentrating for a long time now. Using his nanobots for a long time. His consciousness was wrapped up with the mind and body of *Argona* and the systems that had been added later. He could feel himself growing weaker. His muscles cramped and exploded with twitching. His head was pounding incessantly. His legs were growing weak under him. He knew the missiles fired by the frigates might not have done a significant amount of damage to *Argona*, but the impact with the moon was going to be a different story.

Slamming into the unforgiving surface of a celestial body would be accompanied with an impulse the energy of which would greatly exceed even a barrage of nuclear anti-ship missiles.

The frigates still followed behind, and he knew they were readying another barrage. *Argona* roared towards the dusty grey surface and Iridius knew he had to put all of the ship's shield power to the forward shield. Despite it being obvious that he really was going to crash and he was going to do it in an unpopulated area, the frigate trailing behind fired again, just to be sure.

Iridius put full power to the forward shields. Behind him, anti-ship missiles flew towards the now far less protected rear of the ship. He gritted his teeth and screamed out, digging deep.

"Geronimo!"

The missiles behind *Argona* curled away, driven off-course and slamming into the moon's surface under Iridius's control. This final strain was enough to tip Iridius over the edge. His head exploded with pain, more intense than anything he'd experienced yet. Everything began to spin around him, his view of the bridge bucking and rolling like he was captain of an old ship at sea in a storm. His face tingled. His body went limp and he dropped to the floor.

As he fell, all control of the ship was lost. *Argona* was heading directly for the edge of a large crater. They were going to miss any populated areas, Iridius had made sure of that, but they were going to come down hard. By the looks of it, hard enough that they were unlikely to survive. Futuristic advanced shields or not, spearing nose-first into a moon was still like driving into a brick wall at a hundred and fifty kilometres per hour and hoping your airbag would be enough. Maybe it would, but you wouldn't want to be the test dummy, would you?

"Rangi, on me," Quinn shouted as she ran from the bridge, down the twisting corridor and towards the docking hatch to the *Deus Ex*. Rangi didn't hesitate, following Quinn through the docking tunnel and onto the *Deus Ex*. She didn't have to tell Rangi where he needed to go. He was already slamming into his seat at the helm. The view-screen showed them seconds from impact with the moon.

"Vectored fusion burn, Rangi," Quinn said, strapping herself into the captain's chair. "Get our nose up."

"Aye."

Luckily the helm systems on the *Deus Ex* didn't take anywhere near as long to boot up as those on the *Diesel Coast* used to. Rangi executed the burn, and though it was slightly off-axis, causing *Argona* to roll over, the nose came up enough that they skimmed over the rocky crater wall, the shields flashing as the peaks scraped the underbelly.

Seconds later, the underside of the hull made contact with the lunar dirt. To an outside observer, it would have happened in silence, the ship ploughing into the surface, throwing up plumes of grey dust. From the inside, however, it was anything but silent. It was like being inside a blender full of ball bearings on top of a jackhammer riding a wooden rollercoaster during an earthquake.

As the ship bit into the surface it rolled further, turning onto its side and sliding, gouging a long line through the lunar surface. It continued on, eventually slowing, but not before it made contact with a small clear dome, running over it, shattering the structural perspex and destroying the site inside. As *Argona* came to a stop, the historically important site was left a strewn mess of debris in the dirt.

"Was that important, do you think?" Rangi said from where he hung from the restraints of his helm chair.

Quinn coughed. "I think it was the *Apollo 16* landing site."

"Well," Rangi said, "at least it wasn't *Apollo 11*, I guess."

"Given the historic value, that's true, but also, the *Apollo 11* historic site is enclosed within the Lunar Galleria Mall, Holoplex and Six Flags Low Gravity Amusement Park," Quinn said. "There would have been a lot of civilian casualties."

"I've never been to six flags," Rangi said. "Do you think we'll have time?"

Quinn looked at him, and in that moment understood quite a lot more about the frustrations of Iridius Franklin.

CHAPTER EIGHTEEN_

"CAPTAIN."

Iridius lifted his head. He couldn't remember it ever being this heavy. It felt as if concrete had been pumped into his ears. To be honest, his thoughts seemed to move about as fast as if they were being zapped through concrete too.

He dropped his head back down – or at least, it fell back down. He didn't have any control over the rate of descent. Thankfully, it seemed to land on something soft, rather than clang against the metallic floor of *Argona*'s bridge, which is what he expected.

"Captain."

Iridius opened his eyes, only just realising that he hadn't actually done that yet. Doctor Dooms was looking down at him.

"Doctor," Iridius said, "where am I?"

"You're in the med bay on *Argona*."

"Right," Iridius said. "I fainted again didn't I?"

"Sort of fainted."

"Sort of fainted?" Iridius said. "Is that medically accurate?"

"No, the medically accurate term is that your heart went into atrial fibrillation and you had a transient ischaemic attack, a ministroke where the blood supply was cut off to a section of your brain."

"That sounds bad."

"It's bad. Luckily, *Argona* has a very well-equipped med bay and I was able to stabilise you quickly before there was any long-term damage. However, it's my medical opinion that you've reached a point where it is very likely that your next attack will kill you. I don't think you should use your nanobots again."

Iridius felt a rush of something in his head. "That's not an option though, is it?! *Argona* can't fly. If I don't use my nanobots we aren't getting out of here, in which case we're all stuck in the past and I'll probably have another attack eventually and die anyway. And if I do use them to try and get us home, I die. So basically, you're telling me I'm going to die and there's nothing I can do about it! You ever heard of bedside manner, Doctor? You —" Iridius stopped himself. He looked at Doctor Dooms. She was watching him, her face impassive.

"I'm sorry," Iridius said, dropping his head back onto the pillow. It wasn't just an uncontrolled rush of anger this time. It was a physical feeling, like an electric shock in his brain. A moment, however small, where he knew he had lost control, and more than any other time, it had terrified him. "I didn't mean to get angry again."

"It's fine, Captain. I'm a doctor, and what you're experiencing is a medical condition. The nanobots are affecting your brain with what we refer to as the pseudobulbar effect. It's mostly seen in patients after strokes, but other brain injuries or chemical imbalances can also cause it. The main symptom is uncontrollable outbursts of emotion, often laughing or crying or, as in your case, anger."

Iridius could still feel the sense of buzzing in his head, the overwhelming desire to shout at Doctor Dooms, to blame her for what was happening. To tell her he needed to use his nanobots because what was he without them? He closed his eyes, took a steadying breath.

"I know this is difficult, Captain," Doctor Dooms said. "But you, and the crew of this ship, will figure a way out. You always do, and I'm confident once we get back to our time your nanobots will return to normal."

"What can I do to control it?" Iridius asked.

"There's not much, I'm afraid. Just try and remain calm when it's happening."

"I don't know if we will figure a way out, Doctor. With everything we've been through I've always thought there was a shred of hope to hang on to, no matter how much weird nonsense we got into. Now your medical prognosis is the proverbial damned if I do, damned if I don't. I'm terminal. That's the medical term for a guaranteed death, right?"

"Life, sir," Doctor Dooms said wryly. "That's the term for a guaranteed death."

Iridius gave a small, almost humourless laugh. "While I appreciate the philosophy, Doctor, that might be true, but most of the time you don't have such a clear view of it coming. Unless you're one of the Mortags, I suppose."

The Mortags were a race that had, at some stage in their development, evolved the unique ability to know almost exactly when they were going to die. From studies undertaken by Federation scientists, it seemed their brains had developed a specialised section that processed input about their health and produced an extraordinarily accurate sense of how long they had left to live.

This ever-present sense of their own mortality had greatly affected Mortag society and the way they lived their lives. Rather than living in a state of depression with a sense of impending doom, the Mortags lived their lives to the fullest, celebrating the time they had, embracing art and meditation and spending their final weeks and months with their families while contributing something to their civilisation. It was a way of life we could all take some guidance from.

Of course, because their sense of their own death was based on their internal health, unknown occurrences could still happen. Take the Mortag who had worked on the ASS Locke during the chaos Iridius and his away team had caused there. The Grantakian bullet that Mortag had copped in the jaw beneath his half-visored helmet had caused a death just as surprising as it would have been for anyone. Not that Iridius thought that should have been all that surprising – stupid helmet design and all.

"All in all," Iridius continued, "it's a bit of a shock when death arrives on your doorstep like a flaming bag of poop, isn't it?"

"Can I come in?" Quinn asked, appearing in the doorway. "I need to speak to Captain Franklin."

Doctor Dooms nodded. "Just remember, we're trying to keep our captain's stress level to a minimum." She moved away to tap at a nearby computer screen and made a show of monitoring something, though Iridius had no doubt she was really monitoring his stress level with her doctor's sixth sense.

"How are you feeling?" Quinn asked.

"I'm alright," Iridius answered. "How's the crew?"

"No injuries."

"Great," Iridius said. "Any damage to the *Deus Ex*?"

"No, sir," Quinn said. "Luckily, she was docked high enough to avoid the brunt of the impact."

"The docking tunnel and everything survived? It didn't shear off?"

"Surprisingly, no. *Argona* is made of some extraordinarily high tensile strength materials. From what we can tell, there was very little damage, even though the impact would have caused extensive damage to an FSC vessel from our time."

"What happened after I collapsed? Was it rough?"

"Well," Quinn said, "I took Rangi and used the *Deus Ex*'s engines to stabilise the descent. It wasn't too bad."

"You tried to tell me that before the crash, didn't you?"

"Yes, sir."

"But I ignored you. That was great thinking, Quinn," Iridius said. "The kind of thinking of an FSC commander, not a lab scientist."

"Thank you, sir, but I still don't think I can do that."

"I'm losing control, Kira."

"Doctor Dooms has told me she believes the next time you use your nanobots will be fatal," Quinn said. "We'll figure it out."

"It's not just that," Iridius admitted. "Each time I get angry it's worse."

She nodded. "I know, sir. But that's a chemical imbalance occurring in your brain. We all know that's not you."

Iridius sighed. He was hit by a wave of sadness. Was this another mood change? He didn't think so. He was genuinely concerned about his erratic behaviour. "I feel like I might do something out of character."

"We just need to find a way to get you home," Quinn said. "Doctor Dooms is confident if your nanobots settle, so will all your symptoms."

"Whatever happens, you have to be ready to take over again. If something happens to me, you're the captain."

"Sir," Quinn said, "you know I've already applied for a transfer to non-ship staff."

"Kira," Iridius said, staring into his executive officer's eyes, "you get our crew home, you understand?"

"Yes, sir." Quinn was quiet for a long moment. "There's something else," she said eventually. "With *Argona*'s systems down, Junker has managed to pipe the *Deus Ex*'s sensors to *Argona*'s bridge to monitor the situation. The Lunar police have been dispatched and are on their way."

"Great," Iridius said, "Moon Cops, the off-planet equivalent of shopping mall security. Come on, we better go deal with it."

Iridius flung the thin white sheet off his legs and sat up.

"Captain," Doctor Dooms said, "you need to —"

But Iridius managed to cut her off with a look. "Thank you as always, Doctor, but I've got to deal with this situation, among others." He looked at Quinn. "Do you know where Gentrix is?"

"Um," Quinn said, "she's on the observation deck, sir."

"She hasn't been down to see me has she?" Iridius asked.

"No, sir," Quinn said. "Though Doctor Dooms was very insistent that we let you rest."

Iridius felt a flare of unnatural and probably unwarranted anger that Gentrix hadn't been down to check on him. He didn't expect her to sit at his bedside like some grieving partner. Still, whether they'd had a fight or not, she could have at least checked he wasn't dead. Not that he should be that concerned anyway.

"I'll meet you on the bridge," Iridius said. "I need to go and speak to Gentrix."

"Sir," Quinn said, "the Lunar police are only a few minutes out."

"You were right Quinn, there is a chasm between Gentrix and I that we can't close. I need to break it off with her, and either way, I need to say my goodbyes. This won't take long," Iridius said. "And hopefully not because she kills me and eats me as soon as I start talking."

————

Iridius climbed the final step onto *Argona*'s observation deck, which he would later find out was constructed by removing *Argona*'s reproductive egg sacs and adding a large series of bay windows to what was the equivalent of her ovaries— this just to add more equal parts ickiness and outrage to how he felt about the conversion of a living creature into a spaceship.

Gentrix stood with her back to him, looking out the large window at the barren surface of the moon. She didn't turn as he approached. He stopped and stared at her. In her tight-fitting jumpsuit, her figure was highlighted against the stark grey-white of the lunar landscape below. Her dark hair hung down her back. She was beautiful. She was fiercely intelligent. She had a savage wit that bested his most of the time and, yes, they had very enjoyable adult times.

When Iridius had first seen her, she'd come gliding into her brother's office, an unmistakable air of sinister authority about her. She had been the enemy then, an Alliance villain developing a weapon that was threatening the Federation. It was odd that as he watched her now, he felt even more distant from her than he had then.

There had been a shift in their relationship, and he wasn't exactly sure when it had happened. She had snapped at him and he'd mentioned the superiority of the Federation over the Alliance more than once, but they hadn't really had an actual fight. He could feel waves of anger drifting off her now, though, so maybe there had been a fight.

He was pretty bad at knowing when a fight had happened, to be honest. Jupiter's nuts, this felt like April all over again. They'd had fights lasting whole weeks that he wasn't aware of until she brought them up later.

There was one thing Iridius had always been acutely aware of though, one thing between him and Gentrix that was difficult to ignore: the chasm he had mentioned to Quinn, the chasm between the Federation and the Alliance. It was a chasm he now realised couldn't be bridged.

He opened his mouth to speak, but without turning, as if

she'd known the precise moment he was going to, she spoke instead.

"I've never been to Earth, you know. I mean, I went in 1943 with you, but I haven't been to the Earth of our time, and there it is, or close enough to our time at least."

Iridius looked past her and saw that she was right. Out there, over the moon's close horizon, was Earth-rise, the top of the Earth appearing bright and blue over the curved edge of the moon.

"It's nothing special," Iridius said.

At that, Gentrix turned to face him. "You only say that because you're Federation and the Federation has Earth. It's a scar on the Alliance, you know. Perhaps most wouldn't admit it, but the effect of being separated from the homeworld runs deep."

"Most humans in the Federation never even visit Earth anyway," Iridius said.

"No," Gentrix said, "but they can, and that's the difference. If they chose to go home they could. For every citizen of the Alliance that isn't even an option. That hangs over us all, even if it's just subconscious. There is the feeling of always being the outcasts of humanity, exiled from Earth."

"It doesn't have to be that way," Iridius said. "Perhaps the Alliance can rejoin the Federation."

Gentrix closed her eyes and shook her head. "Listen to what you just said, Iridius Franklin. The Alliance should join the Federation. Not that the Alliance should merge or partner with the Federation, that the Alliance should *join*, be part of your government, subservient to everything the Federation already is."

"Everyone joins, that's just what it's called. Not everything has to be a point of contention. Plus, it's not about being subservient. Members of the Federation are equal. The Federation offers safety, security, prosperity."

"Again with that," Gentrix said. "The Federation always talks about safety, but safety from what? Species can fend for themselves, you know, they did before the Federation came along. Just like people can fend for themselves. Like I can. But you treat me like some damsel in distress. In that park in Berlin you told me to stay with Benedict. When we were crashing, you wanted me to escape with your crew. I'm not in constant need of protection."

Iridius felt a twinge of anger rising. At first he thought maybe it was his nanobot-triggered chemical imbalance, but then again, maybe not. Maybe he was just ordinarily annoyed. "Why is it so bad that I wanted you to be safe?! It doesn't have to be some insult that I don't want you to get hurt. Or are you just projecting your hatred of the Federation onto me again?"

"I don't hate the Federation," Gentrix said.

"Could have fooled me," Iridius said. "There's sure as hell something going on. Or do you hate the Alliance? Or hate that you were born in the Alliance? Are you jealous of the Federation?"

Gentrix's dark eyes flared. "Why would I be jealous of living under the yoke of oppression?"

"You know what," Iridius said, "I didn't want to say anything before, but you're out of your mind if you think the Federation is more oppressive than the Alliance. I saw the way people lived on your space station. The people outside the central spire, anyway."

"What are you saying?"

"It's obvious isn't it?" Iridius said. "You keep accusing me of being a willing pawn under my apparently over-controlling socialist government, but back there, on Locke Station, you were the government and your people weren't exactly living their best life in the Burrows, were they?"

Gentrix stared at Iridius. "I was going to change things. I was going to make life better for the people of the Frost Norton. Instead, you came along and made me into a traitor."

"I didn't force you into anything," Iridius said. "I thought you just realised that what your brother was going to do was wrong."

"It was," Gentrix said, "but that doesn't mean I'm going to roll over and turn Federation."

"And so Quinn was right," Iridius said. "She told me you could never let go of your Alliance past."

"She's never trusted me," Gentrix said. "It's obvious she thought at best this would never work, and at worst I would betray you."

"And are you going to betray me?"

Gentrix looked at Iridius. She took a long time to answer, much too long. "No," she said eventually, "I don't think so, but we are still from different worlds, Iridius Franklin. Enemies, really."

"I don't think of you that way."

"The fact that you had to ask me whether I was going to betray you says otherwise. I don't think this is going to work."

Iridius sighed. "That's why I came up here. To tell you I don't think this is going to work between us."

"That's what I just said."

"No, I know. I'm just saying that's why I came here."

"I'm breaking up with you, Iridius," Gentrix said. "I'm sorry, but if we get back to our time I'm going to go off on my own. I thought I could make it work, but the space between us is too large."

"No," Iridius said. "I know that. I was already thinking the space between us was too large. I'm breaking up with you. Just so you know, like, I came up here to break up with you first."

"Iridius," Gentrix said, "you don't have to try and save face or anything."

"No," Iridius said, "I'm not saving face. I'm dumping you."

"Okay," Gentrix said. "I'm sorry. I do care about you so I want you to know this isn't easy."

"It is easy," Iridius said, "I'm breaking up with you. There."

"We're already broken up."

"Well," Iridius said, "I'm double breaking up with you."

Gentrix looked at Iridius with some combination of pity, anger and disappointment. It was a look Iridius had seen directed at him by more than one woman over the years. It usually happened when he, despite being mostly opposed to the entire idea, had decided to wade waist deep into the emotional sea and was battered so badly by the waves that he made a complete mess of things and came close to drowning.

"Captain," Quinn said over the intercom that was probably threaded through *Argona*'s veins or something equally horrible, "the Lunar Police have arrived."

"I was just breaking things off with Gentrix," Iridius said.

"Uh, right," Quinn said. "Sorry then, um, but you're coming to the bridge?"

"I'll be right there."

When Iridius looked back at Gentrix, she was staring at him. Her face had a lot more anger, marginally less disappointment and a lot less pity now. "Real mature, Iridius."

"We can talk more later," Iridius said. "Got to go deal with this."

Iridius knew that hadn't been his finest moment, even considering his ongoing penchant for having terrible moments whenever emotions ran high. Still, some humorously dark part of him thought, at least he'd be dead soon.

———

Walking onto the bridge, Iridius received nods and smiles from everyone present. Even Holloway smiled at him. Reginald Benedict acknowledged Iridius's re-emergence too, but he did so with a small nod. He looked a mess, his usual stiff British upper lip worn floppy with worry.

"Welcome back, Cap," Rangi said.

"I am also glad to see you are well," Latroz said.

"Thank you, everyone," Iridius said. "I understand we've got visitors."

"Yes, sir," Latroz said. She indicated the view-screen where Junker had somehow managed to hot-wire in the *Deus Ex* feed. Four of the small speeders the moon cops used to travel over the lunar surface were on a rapid approach.

"Here we go," Iridius said, "the four horsemen of the moon-pocalypse approacheth."

"So," he turned to Benedict, "I have no doubt our friends in the moon police are going to attempt to breach. Are they going to get in?"

"We cannot allow people of this time period to learn the truth about *Argona*. She has a passive safety feature that is not controlled by her, so that should still be online even with her," he paused for a moment, "as she is."

"And what does that do?"

"In the event of an unauthorised attempt at breaching *Argona*, a short entropy reversal burst will be fired outwards that will temporally lock anyone within twenty metres of *Argona*. That will only stop a single wave of attempted entry, though. The Lunar authorities will no doubt send reinforcements. They will find the external hull very difficult to cut through, but anyone determined enough will eventually get inside."

"Will it kill them?" Iridius asked. "I saw what one of those entropy reversals did to your younger self. I have a chequered past with the moon cops. They didn't do enough to save my parents when that android went wild. They all act tough with their assault rifles and black balaclavas, but as soon as something actually goes down they're all huddling around too scared to intervene. That, and they arrested me on some very trumped-up charges of being under the influence of a class three intoxicant in public when it was Benjillian Thistle Beer, which is very clearly a class two intoxicant. Still, even with all that, I don't think we should let them die."

"I've actually never seen it happen," Benedict said, "but from what I've been told, they'll be temporally frozen for a moment, take a jolly good whack from an electric discharge and then be released from the entropy lock. They'll try the door and have a devil of a bad day as a result, but they shouldn't die."

Benedict looked to the view-screen. "I suppose we're about to find out."

The Lunar Police were stopping. Their speeders, motorcycle-like vehicles with large spherical wheels for traversing the cratered and rocky surface, came to a stop near *Argona*'s outer hull. The moon cops dismounted, swinging their legs off and sauntering towards the ship like a posse from a western.

Iridius had no doubt each of them considered themselves some sort of Wyatt Earp of the moon, using their sharp skills to bring law to the lawless lunar wasteland, when it was much more accurate that they were all going to be Wyatt Derps, bringing failed Space Command entrance exams to their dead-end jobs as glorified mall cops.

The four of them walked in a line towards the ship. They were chatting, obviously discussing the best approach for their attempt to gain entry. Eventually they appeared to reach some kind of agreement. One of the moon cops stepped forward and pulled out a truncheon-like baton.

"Here we go," Iridius said. "The moon's finest have assessed the situation and reached the impressive conclusion that, yes, they are going to hit the highly advanced spaceship with a club."

"That is not going to end well," Mrs Holloway said.

The cop lifted his truncheon and slammed it on the hull. There was, somewhere deep in the bowels of *Argona*, a small thudding sound. Outside, the four cops were suddenly motion-less, frozen in place, just as had happened to the younger version of Reginald Benedict. Then there was a flash of light and they collapsed to the ground in a collection of folding EVA suits.

"Latroz, are they dead?" Iridius asked, turning to his tactical officer.

She looked down at the tablet computer in her hand. Junker had set up a data feed of other sensors from the *Deus Ex* to the tablet, so Iridius knew she should be able to access life sign readings. She looked back up at Iridius and shook her head. "No, sir. They live."

"It won't be long before they send out reinforcements, Captain Franklin," Benedict said. "Can I ask your intentions?"

"My intentions?"

"Yes," Benedict said. "I'm sorry to do this to you after everything you've already done for us, but *Argona* needs you again. There's something I need to confess to you. *Argona* and I needed you to make contact with my past self in 1943, just as we said, but that was something of a contingency plan. Our real hope is that you can free *Argona* from the harness control system imposed on her by the DHTP. She believed that with your nanobots you could do that, and then she could distribute the algorithm that would free all the Leviathans throughout time and space. Now, with the harness holding her locked-in and in constant agony I'm hoping you'll be willing to try."

"I'm afraid I've just been given doctor's orders not to use my nanobots, Mr Benedict, or my brain will explode."

"Not quite accurate," Doctor Dooms said. She had accompanied Iridius up to the bridge. Iridius had no doubt she was going to follow him around everywhere now. She tended to do that when she was worried about a crew member's state of health. Like when Latroz had once lost to Rangi in a combat VR simulation because Rangi had secretly made her difficulty level much higher than his using cheat codes he'd found on the QECNet, and Latroz's ordinarily bright purple skin had gone quite pale.

Doctor Dooms had followed Latroz around for almost a week, concerned that she was going to undertake Gen-tri, where a devastatingly defeated Siruan warrior spontaneously explodes. It's a sight not too dissimilar to when a Melopian like Director Kron inverts, except it only happens to a Siruan once, and they don't tend to remain in one place.

"But I do believe it will be fatal," Doctor Dooms continued.

"I see," Benedict said. "Well, I do not know how we should proceed. We cannot stay here. Your people remain temporally misplaced. Regardless of what happens at the hands of local authorities, I have no doubt Director Kron will arrive, and I have no doubt his plan will simply be to kill everyone. If you free *Argona* she will be able to take off and get your people back to their correct time."

"But I won't be with them," Iridius said, "because I'll be gronking dead."

Suddenly the sight of Benedict absolutely infuriated Iridius. This fucking guy. It was all his fault that they were in this mess in the first place. He had used Iridius, and by extension he had used his crew. Benedict and *Argona* claimed they were different to the rest of the DHTP but they seemed just the same to him, using people, changing time to suit their purpose.

Iridius knew with what remained of his rationality that he was having another of those mood swings, but his sudden anger at Benedict flared so bright and hot that his normally cool, collected mind evaporated under the heat of his rage.

"I can't say for certain what will happen if you free *Argona*. We've been working towards this, but *Argona* has said there's never been a meta-past where you've freed her yet. She believed this would be it."

"Well maybe she's wrong!" Iridius said. He felt the buzzing in his head, a physical sensation of pressure, and with that growth in physical sensation it became harder and harder to even listen to the rational part of his mind. It reached the point, though Iridius was unable to recognise it, where he was completely controlled by his rage. "What if I don't want to die for her!"

"Captain," Quinn said, approaching him cautiously.

Iridius turned to look at her. "What?!"

"You're experiencing a mood imbalance again."

"I know that!" Iridius said. "Doesn't change the fact that Benedict put me in this situation and now he wants me to die for him too." He spun back to Benedict. "What about the Synth-Hastur? How do we fight them if I die here?"

"I told you," Benedict said, "that happens in the historical timeline. I don't know if you'll ever be able to change it."

"Oh, Jupiter's nuts, fuck your historical timeline," Iridius said. "That's a load of gronking land whale dung. Here you are, literally trying to get me to change the timeline."

"We're trying to undo what has been done by the DHTP. We're trying to save an entire race. If we take away their ability to move through time then we should be able to recover to what is the true historically accurate timeline."

Iridius clenched his teeth. Had he been in his right mind, he would have acknowledged that there was truth to what Benedict was saying, but with such riled-up anger boiling inside his head, he needed somewhere to direct it. In fact, he was so far gone now that he didn't even have the cognitive capacity to realise he wasn't his normal self. The buzzing pressure in his head had become manifest, grown to take control. Iridius Franklin's brain had short-circuited and his amygdala had taken the wheel.

"You're not the only one who has things they might like to fix!"

"No, Captain Franklin," Benedict said, speaking quietly, realising that Iridius's mental state was deteriorating. "Time travel shouldn't be allowed. No one should have the ability to make changes that affect untold numbers of others."

"Fine," Iridius said. He turned and began walking from the bridge.

"Captain, where are you going?" Quinn asked.

"I need to clear my head," Iridius said. "You said it yourself. My brain chemicals aren't letting me think straight. I need to figure out what I'm going to do. I'll be right back."

And that, dear reader, was a gronking lie.

It only took Quinn, Benedict and the others on the bridge a short time to realise that Iridius had been lying when they saw, only a few minutes after he'd walked off the bridge, a figure emerge out onto the grey lunar dust dressed in a plain white EVA suit.

Even before Quinn asked, Lieutenant Latroz confirmed, through the use of his FSC tracking beacon, that this was indeed Captain Iridius Franklin. Iridius bounded under the low gravity over to the speeders left behind by the moon police and climbed onto one. Soundlessly, everyone on the bridge of *Argona* watched as Iridius started the speeder, turned slowly away from the ship and then, with a rooster-tail of grey dust, sped away in the direction of Armstrong Base.

For once it wasn't Rangi who broke the silence. Instead, it was Benedict. "What the devil is he doing?"

"Something out of character," Quinn said.

CHAPTER NINETEEN_

IRIDIUS SPED across the moon's landscape at high speed. He'd say one thing for the Lunar Police, when they called these things speeders they weren't kidding. The large wheels made it easy to absorb the rocky and craterous terrain, and they were specially designed with high-density ballast weights to keep them relatively pinned to the surface, despite the low gravity.

As he covered ground quickly towards Armstrong Base, Iridius knew what he'd done was reckless, and it wasn't reckless in the usual way he was reckless. Ordinarily, when he was diving headlong into a questionable decision – like trying to infiltrate an Alliance space station or flying his ship at a giant dog – he was perfectly aware that what he was doing was borderline insane, he'd just weighed up the options and decided that borderline insane was the best way forward. Right now though, despite knowing that abandoning his ship and crew to drive off and attempt to change the past wasn't just borderline insane but probably completely insane, whatever had snapped in his head meant that he just didn't care. Which was far more dangerous.

"Captain."

Iridius heard Quinn's voice. He'd made sure to keep his

comms off so that he wasn't contactable, but he realised he'd grown so used to the small FSC-regulated emergency implant behind his ear that he'd completely forgotten it was there.

"Captain," Quinn continued, "I know what you're doing. I'm sorry, I didn't make the connection before, but this is the day, isn't it? The day your parents died?"

Iridius remained silent, the buzzing pressure in his head driving him on.

"I know what you're trying to do," Quinn continued. "I know you're going to try and change that, but please don't. Remember what we've learned about timelines. It's not actually going to change anything for you. It's not going to take your pain away. You'll still be the Iridius Franklin who lost his parents."

Quinn didn't have much chance of reasoning with him; all the wrong chemicals were flooding Iridius's brain. "I'm going to die anyway. At least they'll live," he said.

"You don't know what this will do to your future though, Captain."

Iridius squeezed the throttle of the speeder harder.

"What will happen to all of us without you, Captain? This crew, our family, it won't exist."

For a moment, Iridius's finger eased back on the throttle. His other hand hovered over the brake control. His normal self, buried somewhere beneath the all-consuming anger, screamed for him to listen, but his thoughts returned to his younger self, to the fear he would be feeling any minute now, the pain of his parents, everyone's insistence that they should change everything except what would save his parents. His fingers dropped away from the brake. He squeezed the throttle to maximum again and raced towards the lunar city, hoping he wasn't too late.

Quinn, who must have seen this slowing and then accelerating away again on the ship's sensors, gave a sigh. "Captain," she said, "I'm sorry, but we're coming after you. You aren't yourself. I'm afraid we're going to have to stop you."

Had Iridius been in his right mind, the idea of his crew being forced to undertake a dangerous endeavour in attempt to stop him from doing something even crazier than usual would have stopped him dead in his tracks. Of course, as we've more than established, Iridius's right mind was currently about as accessible as the top shelf in a Singosion Giraffepeople's supermarket, or as distant as, say, your father's emotional side.

Iridius reached the edge of the Descartes Highlands, crested the higher peaks there and then dropped down a rocky decline towards the expanse of the Sea of Tranquility, the most famous location on the moon.

Ahead of Iridius were the six large domes of Armstrong Base. It was still referred to as Armstrong Base for traditional reasons, having been the site of the first permanent colony on the moon, built not far from the landing site of *Apollo 11*. It was certainly no longer just a base though. Over the years it had grown into a fully-fledged city with more than a million permanent residents and a large transitory population.

It was a common misconception that Armstrong Base was named for Neil Armstrong, first man on the moon and one of the most revered figures in human spaceflight history. It was understandable why people would think that, of course, and most of the residents of Armstrong Base were happy to let that misunderstanding remain, because it was more prestigious to be named after one of the fathers of human spaceflight than to admit that the base was actually named after Jedidiah Finkle Armstrong, a billionaire who made his money primarily as the owner of Armstrong Sardines and funded the mission to set up the first colony on the moon before he was later arrested and charged with rampant money laundering and tax evasion.

Iridius hit the flat and then blasted across the Sea of Tranquility to the nearest of the domes and one of several airlock entryways into the city. Once, each of these airlocks had been guarded by Lunar Police checking documentation for entry to the moon's major city. But as the city grew in size, and after the seventh round of police staff cutbacks, entry and exit from Armstrong was almost completely unmonitored. The unintended consequence of this was that Armstrong had become a harbour for much of what was barely legal in the Federation, and a large amount of what was illegal too. It also meant that it was perfectly simple for a mentally unstable Space Command captain from twenty years in the future riding a stolen police vehicle to slip inside.

Iridius abandoned the Lunar Police speeder outside the small airlocked entryway in the side of the dome. He hurried in and underwent the quick decontamination process, then waited for the airlock to seal and equalise pressure with the inside of Armstrong Base. Once inside, Iridius stripped off his unneeded EVA suit and stashed it behind the humming cylinder of a waste and water recycling node.

He looked around. Armstrong Base hadn't changed much since the last time he'd been here, which, of course, was actually twenty-four years in the future. There was only so much that could change in a domed colony – space was restricted for space, after all, unless an entirely new dome was constructed, and that hadn't happened at Armstrong Base for a hundred years or more. No one wanted to invest in what had essentially become a town that was frequented by travellers before they put in an interstate bypass.

Apart from some niche industries like the mining of Helium-3, construction of heavy spaceship components that benefited from the ease of uplift with the moon's lower gravity, and a series of rundown tourist destinations based around the historical landmarks of early human spaceflight, Armstrong Base was pretty much a dying city.

Despite the moon's reputation as being a large rock-shaped roadhouse full of drunks and vagrants hanging out on a long-abandoned trucking route, compared to the Burrows of ASS Locke, Armstrong Base was relatively clean and well maintained. The orderly grid pattern of streets was easy to navigate, there was not a drop of neon in sight and, Iridius was pleased to note, there were no teenagers sitting around on old furniture strewn about, ready to mob him at any moment. The moon was one of those places the Federation thought was rough, but in the same way as a wealthy street might have a few houses with only one bathroom and whose residents had never set foot in the country club.

No one paid Iridius any mind as he made his way to one of the tunnels that connected this dome to the largest inner dome – the original Armstrong Base – and that was perfectly fine by him. None of the blue-uniformed moon police had appeared calling out for him to 'stop right there' or 'halt', or whatever equivalent cop phrase they were going to use. He continued to move as fast as he could without outright running, not wanting to draw too much attention and push his luck.

Within minutes Iridius had emerged into Aldrin Square, an open space near the centre of Armstrong Base that was originally named Spunk Plaza after Edward Spunk, one of the first governors of the moon, but was renamed – much to the residents' relief – in honour of a famous landmark on the island of Manhattan on Earth, which was destroyed by an asteroid in the early 2100s.

It was not as garishly over the top as the square for which it had been named – there were only three large screens here, after all – but it was still the largest open internal space on the moon, and was a hub for entertainment. Iridius moved through the crowd and saw Buzz's Greasy Diner, where he'd be eating lunch with his parents right at that moment. Sure enough, as he approached he saw them through the window.

His mother, his father and, obviously the most weird of all, his gangly, pimple-faced fifteen-year-old self. He stared. The truth was, now that he was more than twenty years removed from that version of himself, if he had simply passed him in the street he may not have even recognised him. His parents though, they were exactly as he remembered, which made sense of course, because beyond this day he had no memories of them. They never got any older than this.

Today, he was going to fix that.

Iridius strode across Aldrin Square, deftly navigating the crowd of people like Rangi piloting his way through an asteroid field. He even managed to avoid the pestering entertainers who had at some point decided to dress up in superhero costumes while attempting to pass you holodiscs of their music demos, which they assured you was absolutely the next best thing in electronica/country hybrid. Unfortunately, Iridius didn't manage to avoid the plastic-draped Melopian who appeared from behind an apparently up-and-coming Mongolian throat singing rap artist dressed like Captain America.

"Don't move, Captain Franklin," Director Kron said. "Several DHTP agents have you targeted with entropy reversal beams, and yet more have you in their sights with much more lethal options."

"So why aren't I already dead?" Iridius asked. "I thought I was supposed to be eliminated from the timeline."

"I thought we might be able to come to some sort of agreement," Kron said. "I'll admit that I have vastly underestimated Reginald Benedict and just how far he has strayed from DHTP standard operating procedure. I believed he was trying to ensure his current timeline is not relegated to the meta-past for the benefit of his relationship with his ship, but there is more to it than that, isn't there?"

"I don't know what you're talking about."

"You have," Director Kron paused, "one moment please." The Melopian closed his eyes and inhaled, which, as seasoned residents of the future, you know was one of the stranger bodily functions for this species. He gave a little scream and with a spray of blood, popped inside out before continuing as if nothing had happened. "You have no idea what you're doing."

Iridius laughed. "Well, joke's on you, Director Kron, because while I might have no idea what I'm doing most of the time, this is actually one of the few times I do."

"There is still a chance to reach an agreement, Captain Franklin. If you help me, I can see that you are not permanently erased from existence. Benedict is trying to free *Argona* from DHTP control, isn't he? Why? What has she got?"

Iridius shrugged. "Maybe she just doesn't like being controlled with a painful leash."

"What the DHTP do to the Leviathans is necessary for us to undertake our function. Perhaps it is unpleasant, but one species suffers for the sake of the entire timeline."

"Bullshit," Iridius said, "If you were concerned with timeline preservation, then why have you never reverted to your meta-past?"

Director Kron stared at Iridius.

"You know what," Iridius said, "I don't like being controlled either, especially not by hypocrites like you. I'm going to save my parents. Now get out of my way."

"You leave me no choice," Kron said. "Execute the target."

But Iridius was already diving to the side. He rolled and stood in a smooth move he wished Lieutenant Latroz had seen, because he'd been working on his combat dodging and that had been a bloody good one. Something, a silent DHTP weapon that probably had a horrific effect, struck the ground where he'd been standing.

"Excellent dodging, Captain."

As it turned out, Lieutenant Latroz had indeed seen Iridius's well-executed combat roll, because she, Quinn, Rangi, Junker, Hal and even Gentrix were standing just at the edge of Aldrin Square. They provided enough distraction for Iridius to scramble to his feet.

"You should never start with 'you leave me no choice'," Iridius said. "Makes it easy to know you're about to shoot me." Iridius dashed into the crowd as he saw what were unmistakably DHTP agents approaching. These ones were wearing clothes Iridius had never seen before, some sort of skin tight one-piece blue jumpsuit comprised of tubes. Really, the DHTP's clothing was remarkably out of place for people who specialise in time travel. Behind him, Latroz raised her AR-80 rifle and fired at Kron. The bullet clipped the Melopian on the shoulder. He staggered and dropped to the ground.

This marked another difference between Lunar Base Armstrong and the Burrows of ASS Locke. In the Burrows it had taken a significantly large amount of violence to startle the population into a reaction, but here it took only a single gunshot. Screams started immediately, and the crowd began running in all directions.

"Don't worry about me," Kron called. "Get him!"

But the crew of the *Deus Ex* were already moving in. They had their weapons up and aimed at the DHTP agents, but Quinn had ordered them to be incredibly careful of civilians, and in the sudden turbulent mass of people it was basically impossible to guarantee a clean shot. The DHTP agents likewise knew not to harm civilians when chasing down a temporally displaced target. The consequences to the timeline could be far reaching if they accidentally killed someone they shouldn't have, plus, in true DHTP fashion, the form they had to complete to report a civilian casualty and generate the possible timeline damage diagram was an extraordinary seventy-three pages. On the other hand, the form for reporting the escape of a temporally displaced person was only sixteen pages so, for the sake of saving fifty-seven pages of paperwork, they chased Iridius on foot.

Perhaps it had been the sight of his crew, and even Gentrix still coming after him when they'd broken up, but the buzzing certainty in Iridius's head that he could save his parents and damn everything else was clearing. He shouldn't be here. He'd put his crew in danger.

"Um," he said, certain that Quinn would still be in comms contact with his implant, "I fucked up. I'm sorry. I honestly don't know what came over me."

"No shit," Gentrix said.

"I see you gave Gentrix a comm then," Iridius said.

"We know you lost control, Captain," Quinn said.

"I don't think we let him off the hook that easy," Gentrix said. "I'm only here to drag you back because I'm not finished with you yet."

"Maybe I'll give myself up to Kron," Iridius said.

"We can talk about what happened later," Quinn said. "Let's just get out of here for now. Captain, can you double back this way?"

Iridius looked across Aldrin Square to Buzz's diner. He could see his younger self sitting at the table with his parents. His father was talking, moving his hands animatedly as he did so. Young Iridius was laughing. His mother was rolling her eyes, but with a smirk on her face. They were no doubt hearing one of his tall tales or another.

Iridius couldn't remember them all, but there were several about the time his dad worked as a spy for the Federation Intelligence Bureau – the truth was, he had spent a summer working in the mailroom of the Federation Embassy on Procyon C, which was not a place well known for espionage intrigue. One told about the time he'd almost been offered a position on the Procyon

Penetrators zero-gravity football team – in truth, he'd worked in the equipment room – and when he'd met famous holofilm actress Scarlett Fisher at the airport and had almost started a dazzling love affair (actually, she'd asked him to carry her bag). Iridius's father had been as emotionally available as a ham croissant, but he'd always made him laugh. He hadn't deserved what had happened to him.

His mother, like with most human families, was the core of their life. She'd never pursued an education beyond what had been necessary for her work as human resources manager for one of Procyon C's largest space ports, but she was one of the cleverest people Iridius had ever known – and yes, that included Kira Quinn and the other geniuses of Federation Space Command. Iridius's mother was a problem solver, someone who got stuck into a difficulty and solved it. Iridius was certain his desire to charge headlong into just about any situation came from her.

Iridius, like almost every sentient being in existence, had lost people in his life – family, friends, colleagues in the FSC – but there was no one who'd left quite a hole as his mother. She was his rock, and he'd noticed her absence ever since, not just in the occasional thought, but like he was constantly floating away untethered into space.

There were plenty of people who would claim that Iridius was irrational all the time, but as he watched himself with his parents, he realised the buzzing sensation in his brain had gone. He had returned to normality, as rational as a man who decided he wanted to spend his life flying around the infinite black of space in what was essentially a very advanced tin can could ever be. Though it pained him, he knew he had to leave his past in the past. He had to help his crew. Despite their assurances that they understood he hadn't been himself, he had put them in this dangerous situation. He had to get them out of here.

He turned away from the sight of the small family enjoying their lunch together. They looked happy. Whenever he'd looked back on this day, he had never really remembered that. His parents were experiencing their final moments, but they were happy. At least he could take that away.

As Iridius pushed through the crowd, he came face to face with two DHTP agents in their ludicrous blue tubular clothing. Less humorous were the two weapons they held, raised at his face.

"Stop," one of the agents said.

"I am stopped," Iridius replied, correctly.

"Well," the agent said, "don't move again."

"I don't think I'll be making it to you," Iridius said over his comm. "No redshirts Quinn, you understand? Just leave."

"Negative, sir."

Iridius was about to berate Quinn for this new habit of refusing to follow his orders when a flash of gold announced the arrival of Junior Ensign Hal. The *Deus Ex*'s android helmsman slammed into one of the DHTP agents with enough force to send them crashing into the second agent, with all three of them ending up sprawled across the ground. Hal rose quickly, completely unharmed, while the two agents lay there groaning. Hal punched each one in the face in turn, knocking them out cold. He turned to Iridius with the odd raising of his two metallic cheek plates that passed for a smile.

"Good afternoon, Captain," Hal said. "I have rendered assistance."

"Huh," Iridius said to Hal, "not just good at making coffee then. I didn't realise you were so strong."

Hal looked at him, his face as unconcerned as always. "You have failed to read the manual provided when I joined the crew. It outlines both my cognitive and physical capabilities. I am an android with synthetic muscle and a metallic exoskeleton. Of course I am strong."

"We have secured Kron," Quinn said, "and Latroz has incapacitated the other two agents."

Iridius turned to Hal. "Can you restrain these two?"

Hal nodded.

"Do that and bring them back to the others." Iridius turned and walked back to where Quinn and the others stood with Kron and the other two prisoners, who seemed to have been equally well knocked out by Latroz. Junker handed Iridius an AR-80.

"Well," Iridius said, "that was easy."

Kron growled. He made to reach for one of the DHTP weapons that had landed close to his feet.

"I do not think so," Latroz said. The Siruan warrior pressed her AR-80 assault rifle into Kron's side. "I will not hesitate to put many bullets in you."

Kron stopped, glancing sideways at Latroz.

"Alright, Kron," Iridius said, "something something the jig is up."

Kron looked from Hal to Iridius. He raised his hands over his head in surrender. Unfortunately, Iridius saw too late that he was holding a small object in his hand.

Before Iridius could ask what it was, Kron had pressed a button. Iridius expected Kron to vanish, to teleport away to safety, or maybe it was some sort of technology that would make Iridius's head spontaneously explode. None of these things happened, though. In fact, nothing seemed to have happened – at least until Hal reached out and snatched the rifle from Iridius, wrenching it free with the enormous strength Iridius had only recently learned he possessed. Iridius turned to see Hal staring at him in a way that was as expressionless as always, but now his eyes had turned red. You didn't need to be an expert on robots to know that was a bad sign. Hal raised the rifle and pointed it at Iridius.

"These early androids really were full of easily exploited security vulnerabilities," Kron said. "Very simple to override and control."

Iridius turned to Kron, a horrific understanding sinking home. "It was you."

Iridius had never got a good look at the android that had gone crazy and killed his parents. Much of what he knew was based on the reports of others, or the tiny amount of footage that had been captured on surveillance cameras, none of which had been very conclusive. Even if young Iridius had got a good look at the android, he still wouldn't have considered that, twenty-four years later, that android would be on his crew.

"You have experienced these events already?" Kron said, part question, part statement. "Most interesting. You have crossed your own timeline here, haven't you?"

"You kill my parents, or at least you make Hal do it."

"Is that so?" Kron said. "If it's any consolation, that is not my intention. My intention is to simply have him kill you. I feel foolish, of course, because I've just realised why Benedict needs you. Your nanobots might well have the capability to free a harnessed Leviathan. I should have realised this already."

"Hal," Iridius said without looking away from Kron, "stand down."

"I'm sorry, I'm afraid I can't do that, Captain."

"Hal, kill Iridius Franklin," Kron said.

Even before he'd finished giving the order Latroz had started moving. With her Siruan reflexes and enhanced instincts for combat, she crashed into Hal, grabbing his rifle during the impact. A shot went off but Latroz had already aimed the weapon high, and the bullet sailed into the air, where it impacted the dome far above, not even leaving a scratch on the incredibly strong composite carbonate glass.

Latroz had Hal's wrist with one hand and the body of the rifle in the other. She forced the weapon backwards, attempting to twist it in Hal's grip. Ordinarily, with her Siruan strength, Latroz would be able to rotate the weapon enough to pull it free of her attacker's grip – perhaps even, as a bonus, breaking several of their fingers along the way.

Unfortunately, it seemed Iridius was not the only one who had failed to read Hal's user manual. Latroz had underestimated his strength too. He resisted the movement and reached for Latroz's throat. Latroz held the rifle up and away, but could feel Hal's grip tighten around her windpipe. He was managing to squeeze it shut even through the strong organic armour that coated her neck. Latroz twisted, rolling in with her back to Hal, breaking his grip on her neck while still holding onto the rifle.

Kron stepped forward, towards Latroz, attempting to grab the assault rifle she had slung over her shoulder.

"I don't think so," Gentrix said, grabbing him by the shoulder. Kron turned, his mouth open to protest, but Gentrix shut it before he had a chance to speak with a wicked right hook to his plastic bag-covered face. He stumbled, but didn't fall. He launched himself at Gentrix, but the sight of someone completely enclosed in clear plastic trying to attack her did not exactly fill Gentrix with a great amount of fear. It was like being attacked by sentient sausages in a grocery bag. As he lunged at her, she kicked him as hard as she could in the groin. Kron doubled over, his legs buckled, and he hit the ground.

"How did you know Melopians have their genitalia there?" Quinn asked.

Gentrix shrugged. "Lucky guess."

"Uh, Honeycakes," Rangi said, watching with growing concern as Latroz wrestled with Hal, "you doing okay there?"

Latroz grunted her reply as she forced the rifle towards the ground, twisting his arm. She released one hand and brought her forearm down hard on Hal's elbow, trying to force it to bend the wrong way. It didn't.

"It's just, normally you would have won by now," Rangi continued. "Do you need some help?"

The others had only been half paying attention to Latroz's struggle with Hal, having been focused on Kron and the two other DHTP agents. That, and they had never had to worry about Latroz losing a fight before.

Hal reacted to Latroz's attempt to break his arm by forcing that same elbow up and into her face. The crunch was sickening, but somehow Latroz held tight to him, stopping him from bringing the rifle to bear on Iridius, or anyone else for that matter. Hal brought his elbow down and back again and again, each time attempting to increase the force of contact with Latroz's remarkably strong nose.

"Captain," Latroz managed between elbows, "you should run."

Iridius hesitated.

"Now!" Latroz said as Hal's elbow came up once again to crash into her face, this time with enough force that she was sent flying. She landed on her back. She was still conscious, barely, but Hal was free.

Iridius had already started running, remembering a little too late the very important rule that whenever there is combat happening you should just do whatever Latroz yells at you. The crowds in Aldrin Square had thinned out, the gunshots and the sight of a golden metal android fighting a seven-foot-tall alien warrior more than enough to send most people running for their lives. Most people but not, he remembered, his younger self or his parents.

He could remember when the chaos outside the diner had

first broken out. Most people inside shops or restaurants were confused. When people in the square started fleeing, some patrons in the diner had left, while others had decided to stay put, hoping they would be safely out of the way hiding behind the tables and chairs. Iridius's father had insisted they do this, and his mother had agreed. There was no point running towards whatever danger might be out there. The three of them had dropped down and hidden behind their table.

Iridius heard a rifle shot behind him and flinched. He instinctively changed direction. Iridius hadn't ever been shot before, but he was sure there would be some pain, so he assumed Hal had missed. Thankfully, it seemed Hal wasn't a perfect marksman as well as being stupidly strong. Still, Iridius knew it didn't take a perfect marksman to hit a target they were getting closer to.

Iridius chanced a look back and saw Hal in pursuit. Behind him, doing her best to follow, was Latroz. Iridius looked back to see that he was heading straight for Buzz's diner, and that was when a thought struck him. Perhaps he could still change the past. Hal was tasked with killing him, after all. So he'd lead him, as Greg would say, on a chasing of the goose.

Iridius turned and headed perpendicular to the way he'd been running, across the square and away from Buzz's diner. He knew there was no easy way out in this direction, but there were rows of ticket booths for shows, small news stands and souvenir stalls. Maybe he could buy some time hiding among them.

Behind the small collection of shops were the stairs up to the monorail station. Armstrong Base, while not particularly large, was still large enough that there was a need for some public transportation – individual vehicles were prohibited in order to reduce traffic congestion inside the domes. Also, early on, the moon's government had decided that whoever thought everybody in society should be allowed to own and drive a thousand-kilogram metal weapon at whatever speed they wanted had obviously never met another person before.

Iridius ran between a stall selling tickets to the 194th straight year of *Hamilton the Musical* and another selling postcards and other memorabilia of the Apollo landing sites. Even as he dashed past he noticed, in true tourist trap fashion, that anything about the *Apollo 16* site had already tripled in price. Iridius ducked around the corner where he would be out of sight, at least briefly, then took the opportunity to stop and quickly look back.

Iridius half expected to turn and see the golden android standing just metres away with his rifle raised. That would be the last thing he would ever see before Hal squeezed the trigger and splattered his brains across a poster for the other popular historical musical theatre production current playing on the moon, *Rock and Rollins*, the story of the unlikely government of President Dwayne Johnson and Vice President Henry Rollins. Instead, Iridius saw that Hal was actually some distance away.

He was standing in the middle of the Aldrin Square and wasn't even looking in Iridius's direction. Honestly, Iridius knew Hal was an android that was using machine-learning algorithms to become a better pilot, he wasn't actually an assassin or combat android or anything, but still, it couldn't have been that easy to lose him. He'd literally just run behind a tiny single-person ticket booth and would have only been out of sight for a few seconds. But as Iridius watched, he realised that Hal was looking across at Buzz's diner.

Iridius and Director Kron both realised what had happened at exactly the same time.

Kron was looking up from where Gentrix held him pinned to the ground. "Ah," he said, "I see my mistake. I asked your android to kill Iridius Franklin. Should've been more specific, I suppose."

"Oh, gronking goddamn it," Iridius said as he hurried out from behind the ticket booth and back towards Buzz's diner. Hal was already moving towards it, rifle up. He fired several bursts, shattering the front window. Inside, Iridius's mother and father and fifteen-year-old Iridius Franklin cowered behind their table, living through the event, Iridius knew as he sprinted toward them, just as he gronking remembered.

CHAPTER TWENTY_

WHILE MURDEROUS ANDROID-BASED chaos was unfolding on the surface of the moon – well, not 'while' in the temporal sense, but definitely 'while' in the narrative sense – Captain April Idowu was walking onto the bridge of the *FSC Clarence* just as it was docking with the *Gallaway*. As she did, the crew of the *Clarence* looked at her, and then looked away. To his credit, Captain Jack Quaid held April's gaze as she approached. He even spoke first.

"Captain Idowu, good to see you're unscathed," he said in a tone of voice that did little to mask the fact that he wasn't at all thrilled that she was here or that she was unscathed. "Not that I can say the same for my ship."

"Captain Quaid," April said, her tone much more aligned with FSC-approved diplomatic levels, "first let me apologise—"

"Apologise?!" Quaid barked. "You had your ship attack mine, disable it and force my ship and crew into a highly dangerous situation. At the very least, you can expect to have your command removed and be dishonourably discharged from the FSC. At most, I wouldn't be surprised to see you charged and sent to prison. I hear the Cube is not an entirely accommodating place for ex-FSC personnel."

"I understand you're upset," April continued, "but I want you to know it was not a decision I made lightly, and it was not about self-preservation. I flew down to the surface of Acacia in order to secure a sample of the Aegix nanobots. In ordering my crew to seize your ship there were two things I was trying to achieve: getting the sample of the nanobots off that moon before it was destroyed, and saving the people of the Acacia geological survey." It was here that April's voice strayed from the diplomatic tone she'd been achieving so far. "The people you were going to leave to die."

"I had my orders," Captain Quaid said, his face filling with colour, either embarrassment or rage – probably both. "I like to consider myself someone who obeys orders, Captain Idowu."

"The Admiralty is in shambles, Captain Quaid. Tullet would not be in his position if most of the commanders hadn't died. He has no idea what is going on or what the threat truly is."

"As I recall, the reason most of the Admiralty died," Quaid said, "is because of the Aegix nanobots that you've just brought onto my ship."

"I'll be transferring the Aegix sample to the *Gallaway* momentarily, don't worry. I suppose you've already informed Admiral Tullet of my actions."

"No," Captain Quaid said. "I haven't yet had the opportunity."

"Listen, our superiors in the FSC and the Federation Senate are not seeing the true threat. The Aegix is some sort of protection left behind by an ancient race to protect against the Synth-Hastur, a galactic level threat that is coming. The Aegix are faulty, but there are people within the Federation who can use the sample I've secured to find out how they're supposed to work. That could be the key to saving the galaxy. Once you report my actions, Admiral Tullet will send half the fleet after me. We need to focus on the real threat. Why don't you join us? We're going to need all the help we can get."

Captain Quaid stared at April. "When you and your crew leave I'll be reporting directly to the Admiralty about what you've done."

"That's your decision, is it? You've weighed the possible fate of the galaxy against maybe being on the wrong side of an admiral who doesn't deserve his position and that's where you've landed?"

Quaid worked his mouth. "I will not rise to your bait, Captain. I will be following procedure and reporting your actions."

April sighed. "Fine. At least make sure you get the residents of the geological station to safety. Oh, and I'd advise not telling them you were going to leave them down there to be disintegrated in the heat of a quantum fission catalytic exothermal reaction. I can't speak for them, but I personally wouldn't take that news very well. Plus, there's more than a hundred and thirty of them, and your hauler has a crew of what? Six?"

Quaid didn't say anything.

April turned to Commander Mul, Lieutenant Pillark and the *Gallaway* security team who had taken control of the *Clarence*. "All right, let's go." She was keen to get moving, unsure how long it would take for the FSC to send a response. The *Gallaway* was the flagship of the fleet. There weren't many ships that were as fast, and only the ships designed specifically for combat like the *Valkyrie* or the *Centaur* would be capable of taking them down. And even with those ships, at least in a one-on-one, April would give the *Gallaway* a fair chance of victory, or at least of escaping in one piece. Still, it wasn't something she really wanted to put to the test. As soon as they were gone, April would contact Admiral Merrett, or really any of the Admiralty other than Tullet, and do her best to explain. Although she didn't think even Roc Mayhem would have been able to get away with the 'don't ask permission just ask forgiveness' approach when it came to attacking another FSC vessel.

As April and her crew members walked off the bridge, Captain Quaid called out to her.

April turned back.

Quaid stared at her. April wondered if he was going to try and take FSC disciplinary action now. He would have been within his rights to detain an illegal boarding party – of course, it wouldn't go well for him if he did try, but he hadn't made a lot of correct decisions so far, at least as April saw it, so she wouldn't put it past him. "I'll make sure the people you saved are looked after. I'm still going to report you, but I'll give you some time." He paused. "I'll let you have a head start."

April nodded, turned and walked off the *FSC Clarence*.

———

April walked onto the bridge of the *Gallaway* to smiling faces. Her crew were professionals, so they wouldn't do anything as crass as give her a round of applause, but she knew they were happy and relieved to see her. Just as she was to see them.

As she stepped down towards the command station she saw Teth standing next to her chair. He beamed. No doubt she should have felt the same way, but she wasn't overjoyed to see him. She was happy, certainly. It was nice to see him, but no more so than running into a friend you haven't seen for a while down the shops – not exactly the flood of emotion she should have felt at seeing her fiancé after a very close brush with death. The truth was, she was happier to be back with her crew than with him.

"Computer, now!" Teth said.

The lights of the bridge began flashing, a colourful strobing effect that April didn't even know they could do, then a song started playing through the bridge speakers: 'Welcome Back (to the Party)' by Lady Yeet. Bass thumped and the lyrics informed anyone who was listening how overjoyed Lady Yeet was to welcome you back to the party. April was shocked into open-mouthed, wide-eyed surprise. All she could see was Teth's smiling face flashing between green, purple, pink and blue under the spasmodic light show. After a moment she got hold of herself.

"Computer, stop," she said.

The music and light show stopped, but the idiotic grin did not shift from Teth's face.

"What..." April said. "What was that?"

"I tried to organise balloons to fall down but apparently there are none on the ship," Teth said, "and Lieutenant Commander Kaku said confetti could block the air filters in the life-support system, so I wasn't allowed to do that either."

April opened and closed her mouth.

"Sorry," April said, "you were going to have confetti?"

"Yes," Teth said, still grinning from ear to ear, "and balloons! I just wanted you to know how glad I am that you're back." He gestured to the rest of the bridge crew. "We all are."

April looked around at the rest of the bridge crew, who were looking down at their consoles, where there was apparently very important information that needed their attention at that exact moment. April returned her attention to Teth. She blinked, still a space deer in the spacecraft landing lights.

Teth stepped forward and embraced her. He leaned in for a kiss and just as his lips met hers, April spoke.

"I hate mmadme mmeet."

Teth pulled back, smiling. "What?"

"I said, I hate Lady Yeet," April said. "I've told you that before."

"Oh," Teth said, his smile fading. "Right, sorry. It was the first song I found that was about welcoming someone back."

"And you seriously would have dropped confetti all over my bridge if you were allowed?"

"Well," Teth said, "I told you, I just wanted you to know how happy I am that you're back."

April's shock had faded and was now replaced with an unflinching sternness. "This is a Federation Space Command starship. I am the captain of this vessel and I have returned from a mission. It was certainly touch and go for a while, but I was out there doing my job just like countless members of Federation Space Command have before. There is to be no confetti, no flashing lights and no god-awful pop music. This is a professional crew and I am the captain. What were you thinking?"

Teth's smile had well and truly been planet-slagged off his face by now. "I...I told you..." he stammered. "It was just, I thought it would be nice."

April sighed. "This isn't going to work, Teth."

"Yes, sorry, I understand. It wasn't very professional and of course, like Lieutenant Commander Kaku said, the confetti would have got in the life-support system."

"That's not what I mean," April said.

Teth had the sudden realisation of someone about to have 'a talk'. "What do you mean then?"

"Captain," Lieutenant Pillark said from the tactical console, "there's an unknown anomaly occurring off our starboard side."

"What sort of anomaly?" April asked.

"What do you mean this isn't going to work, April?" Teth asked.

"Appears to be the formation of some sort of wormhole, Captain," Lieutenant Pillark said. "I've never seen anything like it."

"Mul?" April asked.

Commander Mul looked at his console, absorbing information flooding in from the ship's sensors. "It is indeed a wormhole, Captain."

"On screen," April said.

"Sorry, excuse me," Teth said. "April, when you say this isn't going to work what exactly do you mean?"

"Not now Teth," April said. "I'll talk to you later."

"Right," Teth said, moving back from April's chair. "I see."

April watched the view-screen as a tight swirl of colour appeared around a central black sphere, a hole in space and time from which something began to emerge.

"What is that?" April asked. "A ship?"

"Unknown signature," Pillark replied.

"Mul," April said, "what do we know about wormholes?"

April leaped into action, trying to rapidly ascertain whether they were facing a threat and how she was going to react. She didn't even notice when Teth left the bridge.

CHAPTER TWENTY-ONE_

"HEY!" Iridius shouted as he ran. "Hal! I'm here! That's not me!"

Hal, focused on his new target, didn't turn to look.

"Hal!"

Iridius sprinted for Buzz's Greasy Diner. Hal, as if knowing his prey had nowhere to escape – unless he was doing it purely for dramatic effect – walked slowly, ominously, towards the glass-fronted restaurant.

"Goddamn it," Iridius muttered under his breath.

Hal reached the diner. He kicked at the jagged fragments of glass that remained in the window frame in front of him, clearing the way before striding purposefully inside. Iridius was still only halfway across the square and Hal was already raising the rifle. There was shouting from inside Buzz's. Some of it, even now, so many years later, Iridius recognised. It was his father's voice, and while Iridius couldn't remember the exact words that he'd said, he could remember the sentiment. He was shoving Iridius and his mother past the counter and towards the kitchen at the back of the diner. He would be turning, putting himself between this unknown attacker and his family. After the shouts, Iridius heard the first gunshots from inside the diner and adrenaline flooded his body.

He sprinted as hard as he could. He'd never been the fastest runner. In school he'd always come middle of the pack, if he was being generous, and if there was one thing he'd hated at the Academy – other than classes, exams, ship placements and everything else other than the social activities – it was physical training, and goddamn running in particular.

Given the amount of time he'd spent running away from things over the last year, it probably would have been worth doing some training, but he'd rather be devoured by whatever was chasing him than make 'jogger' part of his personality. Still, in that moment, he ran as fast as he probably ever had, and even as he did, he was still overtaken by a flash of purple in an FSC uniform.

While Iridius sprinted at full speed, Latroz easily passed him. She dashed through the hole Hal had made in the front of the diner and headed inside.

Iridius, to his credit, wasn't far behind. He hurdled the broken glass then stumbled as he almost tripped over a chair. He looked around. The red faux leather booths along the far wall, the smaller tables with the white tablecloths covered in clear plastic, the blue, red and yellow triangular pattern on the walls, it all struck him with an unwelcome familiarity.

In his time, twenty-four years from now, Buzz's diner no longer existed. Ironically, it wasn't even this incident that had led to its closure, it was the string of cases of Hetrillian Salmonella Gut Eel that were linked to the kitchen several years later that brought the health inspectors down on them.

Even though it no longer existed, Iridius had been back many times in his memory. Being back here now though, physically here, brought a wave of anxiety that he knew stemmed from unresolved trauma. He squeezed his eyes shut, self-talking himself through the experience with all the sensitivity of a brick to the face.

"Jupiter's nuts, get a fucking grip," he hissed to himself, "people need you."

Maybe it wasn't the best approach, but right now he didn't know what else to do. He opened his eyes, looked up, and was relieved to see that the diner had stopped spinning. What was less of a relief was seeing the golden shape of his out-of-control android helmsman stalking through the kitchen, rifle raised. The sound of more shots echoed loudly off the stainless-steel surfaces before Latroz reached Hal, tackling him to the ground.

Iridius ran into the kitchen. He stopped momentarily at two slumped bodies, cooks dressed in their white aprons and hats. At least, they'd been white once. Now they were stained in blood. Both had been shot in the chest, and both, it took only a moment's glance to see, were dead.

Ahead of him, Latroz had landed on Hal's back, pinning him to the tiled floor, managing to hold him in place despite his considerable strength. He looked up towards the back of the kitchen. There was a door there that led outside, out the back to a series of small waste recyclers. It was the exit Iridius's father had been guiding them towards. It was also the exit, Iridius remembered, that had been locked shut when they'd reached it.

He saw his father's body first. He had been the first of his family to be shot. It had been in the back, a bullet that had entered through the left shoulder blade, punctured his heart and exited out his chest. Shot in the back, just as Iridius had turned back to tell him the door was locked. He would have died quickly at least. He might not have even known.

Iridius knelt beside him and rolled him over as gently as he could, but Frederick Franklin was already dead, staring up at the greasy smoke-stained ceiling with unseeing eyes. Iridius ran his fingers down his face, closing his eyes. He patted his cheek, felt his father's permanent five o'clock shadow.

"Goodbye, Dad," Iridius said, and he felt an odd combination of great sorrow but also some hint of joy. He'd never managed to say goodbye to his parents when he'd been fifteen, not when he'd seen their bodies in the morgue, not at the funeral. He hadn't had the emotional maturity then. Although many would claim his emotional maturity was still limited, at least now he knew how important a goodbye could be.

"Iridius."

Iridius looked up at the sound of his name. The voice was soft and croaking, and immediately broke into a fit of coughing, but he knew that voice. It was his mother.

She was sitting against a low bench nearby, the front of her new dress soaked with thick wet blood. She had been shot in the stomach, and was holding her abdomen in a futile attempt to stem the bleeding. Iridius didn't need to be an expert in combat like Lieutenant Latroz to know that being gut shot was bad news. His mother was still alive, but she wouldn't be for long.

History was repeating itself just as he remembered, but now he had answers to what had always been a mystery, not just to himself but to everyone. He knew who the crazed android was and he knew why it had gone on its apparently random rampage. On a personal note though, there was something he'd learned that he wished he hadn't: what had happened to his parents, the trauma that had been the defining characteristic of his early life, had been his fault.

He'd come here in a misguided attempt to save his parents and sure, he'd kind of been out of his mind at the time, but the irony was that the very act of him coming here to save his parents was what had got them killed. This was just like what had happened in Berlin when they'd tried to maintain history by stealing the German atomic bomb, and in doing so may have actually created the history they were trying to maintain. Gronk this predestination bullshit. The worst thing of all was that it was his choice of action, even once his out-of-control brain had come back under control, that had directly led to Hal going for his parents. If he hadn't tried to lead him away, then the android wouldn't have targeted the younger version of himself.

"Iridius."

His mother repeated his name as Iridius watched her, unable to bring himself to move, but it wasn't to him that his mother was calling, it was to the younger version of himself, to her son. Iridius looked up and saw that younger Iridius against the locked back door of the restaurant. He too had been shot. He was pale, holding his shoulder where the bullet had entered.

Hal was still struggling beneath Latroz's grip, and though the Siruan would tire soon, it looked like she had the situation well in hand for the moment – or at least well under her knee and pinned down with her hands. She had somehow managed to disarm the android, or at least the rifle had come free of his grip and had skidded across the floor, out of reach of both of them. Iridius took the time to kneel down by his mother. He touched her on the leg and she turned to look at him, her eyes distant. She was in shock, and seemed to be looking straight through him.

"Eloise," Iridius said, not wanting to call her Mum and confuse her, but when she finally focused her eyes on him there was instant recognition, or at least a confused look of almost recognition.

Her brow crinkled. "What's going on? Who are you?" But she immediately answered her own question. "Iridius?" She tried to sit up more, wanting to get a better look at this man who'd appeared, this man she knew had to be her son despite being far too old. She winced as a shock of pain stabbed at her.

"Don't try to move. Just relax. You're going to be okay," Iridius lied. Maybe if help had arrived quickly there would have been a chance, but Iridius had the benefit – or the curse really – of knowing that help wouldn't arrive. She was going to die.

Before now, he'd always thought it was a little cruel the way people said that. If you were rendering aid to someone you knew wasn't going to make it, it didn't seem fair to tell them they were going to be okay. He'd always thought if he was ever in that situation he would tell the truth. He wouldn't give the person false hope, he'd give them the dignity of knowing how bad it really was. But now he was here and there was no way he could do that. He realised that it wasn't about giving the person a sense of hope or a false sense of security as they faced their end, or at least not entirely. A pretty large part of it was not being able to deliver the news that they were about to die. 'Just sit back and relax, you're probably going to die,' wasn't easy news to deliver.

Eloise Franklin shook her head. She, at least, knew that Iridius was giving her false hope. "I don't think I'm going to be okay, son."

Iridius smiled sadly.

Eloise reached out and touched Iridius's face, not realising or perhaps not caring that she was wiping blood across his cheek. "How is this possible? Where did you come from?"

"I'm from the future, Mum."

"The future, hey?"

Iridius nodded. "I'm a captain in Federation Space Command and was accidentally sent back in time."

"You know, I'd heard that all that time travel stuff never really happens when people are out in space."

"I know right?" Iridius said. "That's what I thought too!"

Iridius's mother looked over at where the young version of Iridius was slumped against the door. He'd apparently passed out. When she looked back, Iridius saw she had a smile on her face.

"You're happy?" Iridius asked.

She nodded. "I'm going to die, aren't I?"

Iridius nodded slowly.

"I'm happy because if you go on to become captain of an FSC starship, then that means you must survive this. Your father and I might die here, but you survive. That's what I was most afraid of. I just want to protect you. If I know you survive then I can go easy."

Iridius felt hot tears in his eyes. "I wish you wouldn't. Let me at least try and get you some help. I'll—"

But his mother reached out and put her hand on his arm, stopping him. "I don't think I have very long. I'm glad I got to see you all grown up."

"I'm glad I got to say goodbye this time," Iridius said.

"I love you, Iridius."

"Captain," Latroz called to him. Iridius looked in her direction and could see that she was beginning to struggle to restrain Hal. The android was wriggling more and more, and it wouldn't be long before Latroz's strong grip broke and he was free to continue his murderous rampage. "I must admit, I am not sure how to disable him."

Iridius turned to his mother. "Mum, I—" he started, but a single look at her distant eyes and he knew that she was gone. His eyes grew hot again. He felt a rush of grief he'd never felt before, maybe not even when this had happened the first time, because back then he had been in the hospital before he'd received the news that his parents were dead. He had never actually seen it happen.

"Captain!" Latroz called again. A Siruan warrior would never call out with desperation, but there was certainly a note of concern in her voice.

Iridius looked at his mother once more. He closed her eyes, just as he had with his father. "I love you too, Mum," he said before turning his attention to Latroz's struggle. He forced the emotion down, covered it over in a way that starship captains and first-responders and great leaders everywhere had learned to. Job first, emotion – no matter how big – later.

Iridius hurried over to where Latroz was rapidly losing control of Hal. The android flexed, and Iridius could see Latroz's purple fingers slipping off the shiny gold metal.

"I'm not sure how to shut him down either, Lieutenant," Iridius said. "Fact is, I don't know why they made him so bloody tough. He's just a pilot slash barista."

Latroz looked at him. "I would estimate we have approximately ten seconds to figure it out."

"Hal," Iridius said.

The android's head twisted slightly beneath Latroz's knee to look at Iridius. His red eyes flashed.

"Do you know who I am?" Iridius asked.

Hal responded with a very ominous, "Target acquired."

"Well, I guess that's me yes," Iridius said, "but I'm your captain. Do you remember that? I'm ordering you to stand down."

With renewed vigour, Hal thrashed wildly beneath Latroz like the robotic bucking bull Iridius had ill-advisedly ridden when he'd been six shots of Gartoshin Whisky deep on a shore leave evening on the well-known party moon of Ibia. With a final push, Hal managed to get himself free, tossing Latroz off him like she wasn't an enormous warrior alien.

Hal spun to face Iridius. He began stalking towards him. Behind him, Latroz scrambled across the floor to go for the fallen rifle. Hal didn't even bother turning to look for it and Iridius had no doubt that the android wouldn't need the gun to kill him.

"Hal," Iridius tried again, "it's me, Iridius Franklin."

"Yes," Hal replied, "you are my target."

"I meant it more like, I'm your commanding officer," Iridius said. "I know you're relatively new to Space Command, but killing your commanding officer is generally frowned upon."

Hal didn't reply. He simply continued towards Iridius with determination, not that his metal face could actually portray much emotion, but Iridius definitely got the sense that he was determined. Hal reached out and grabbed hold of Iridius's throat with one cold metal, hand.

"Gak," was all Iridius could manage to get out, which was a shame – it was going to be something hilariously witty and brave.

Latroz grabbed the rifle and turned to aim it at Hal. Her finger was already inside the trigger guard and ready to squeeze when she saw that the android had pulled Iridius in close and turned so that he was using him as a human shield. The only part of the android visible was his golden head over Iridius's right shoulder. Hal had not let go of Iridius's throat though, and he continued to squeeze, holding Iridius's windpipe closed.

Iridius struggled, but there was no way he could break free.

"Resistance is futile," Hal said.

"Oh, do gronk off with that derivative shit," Iridius said. At least, that's what he tried to say. All that came out was another variation on "gak".

Iridius's lungs were burning for air. His diaphragm tried to pull in oxygen with about as much success as sucking up a rug with a vacuum cleaner. Sparkles of light had begun to dance around the edges of his vision, and the world around him was tunnelling in, neither of which seemed to be an altogether good thing.

Latroz, seeing Iridius's face turning red and his limbs growing limp, knew there was little time to act. She lifted the rifle, used her Siruan training and innate talent for marksmanship to take aim at Hal's forehead, and fired.

Hal's head snapped back with a metallic twang. The sound, Latroz knew, was a ricochet. Hal's head had snapped back but the rest of his body was unmoved, including his vice-like grip on Iridius's neck. Hal's head tilted forward again. There was a dint in his metal forehead, but the bullet had not penetrated.

Iridius was barely hanging on to consciousness and he knew, with a very real rage against the dying of the light type moment, that if he did fade away now there was very little chance he would ever wake up again. Latroz had shot Hal in the head and the pressure around his throat hadn't eased in the slightest. Iridius couldn't believe it. It would have been great to find out that a member of his crew was basically a bulletproof killing machine prior to said crew member strangling him to death.

Iridius knew he was probably going to die, but he also knew that using his nanobots might just get him free – although of course using them would probably kill him. There had been far too many scenarios in this adventure that seemed to boil down to deciding which way he wanted to die. Still, time to roll the dice.

Iridius reached out with his nanobots and immediately felt his nervous system light up like a non-specific holiday decorated tree. He closed his eyes and, with what little concentration he had left, he felt around inside Hal.

Phrasing, obviously.

What he found was the definite feeling of something inter-twined with his normal operation, a kind of net or web that was locking away his ability to control himself, very similar to what he'd felt happening to *Argona*. It seemed like Kron had used similar technology to the Leviathan's harness, if not quite as strong, on Hal. When his nanobots had managed a good under-standing of a system, what often confronted Iridius was an almost physical manifestation, something that could be manipulated in terms he could easily understand. Flip this on or off to control a ship's systems, move this thing sideways to send a missile on a different trajectory, that sort of thing. It was as if his nanobots did their best to translate the buzzing of algorithms, code and electrical signals into something he could understand.

He could see that the web that seemed to be trapping Hal's true intentions could be lifted. He pressed at it, searching for a weak spot and found a point, like a ragged edge, that seemed able to be lifted. Iridius pulled at it, like a loose thread in the net that might unspool the whole thing. He was aware, beyond his nanobots, that his head had started pounding again, his muscles spasming to the point of failure, and that the only reason he hadn't collapsed to the ground was that Hal was holding him up by the neck. Iridius focused on the task and hand, grabbed the bars of Hal's cage and, with an immense effort, pulled.

Hal let go.

Iridius dropped to the tiled kitchen floor, landing with a thud and not moving.

Hal immediately dropped to the ground. "Captain," he said, "I must apologise. I was not in control of my actions."

But Iridius didn't respond. Latroz knelt down beside him as well. She reached out and placed two fingers against his carotid artery, feeling for a pulse. "He is alive," she said. Then she turned to Hal. "And you?"

"I am quite alright now," Hal said, "I believe my main behavioural systems were hacked by Director Kron. I was unable to stop myself from performing the task given to me. Captain Franklin freed me of this constraint. I have never been hacked before. I do not enjoy it."

"No," Latroz said. "I did not enjoy it either."

"Yes," Hal said, "I must apologise to you too Lieutenant. I engaged you in combat unwillingly."

"I did not know you were so strong," Latroz said.

"Neither did I," Hal replied.

"We shall spar again," Latroz said, "for training purposes."

"Very well," Hal said, "but right now we should render assistance to Captain Franklin."

"Yes," Latroz replied. She looked down at Iridius again. "Can you carry him?"

Hal nodded.

"We should move quickly before the authorities arrive," Latroz said. "And Junior Ensign Hal?"

"Yes, Lieutenant?"

"Your strength is very impressive, but next time I will destroy you."

As Hal bent down to lift Iridius, there was a groan from nearby. Hal and Latroz looked up to see that Iridius Franklin – not yet Captain Iridius Franklin but fifteen-year-old Iridius Franklin – was awake.

CHAPTER TWENTY-TWO_

WHILE THE CONFRONTATION BETWEEN HAL, Latroz and Iridius had been taking place inside the confines of Buzz's Greasy Diner, Quinn had waited with their prisoner. Kron was barely suffering from his bullet wound. Given that their most regular bodily function ripped them open and then closed them up again, Melopians had an excellent healing ability – far superior to most species.

Rangi and Junker had been holding Director Kron firmly between them, gripping an arm each through the clear plastic bag, not wanting to take any chances. Well, they held firmly most of the time – they tended to let go a little and lean away when Kron had to breathe because despite his coating of plastic, the splattering blood and the feeling of it squelching between your fingers afterwards wasn't pleasant.

When Kron had hacked Hal and apparently turned him from a pleasant golden android who moved around the ship with the gait of a man with two wooden legs into an elite killing machine who suddenly moved like an oil-slicked ninja, Quinn hadn't known quite what to do. As soon as Hal had broken free of her grasp, Latroz had looked to her and her question was clear. Quinn had nodded and simply said, "go".

She'd been in two minds about the situation after that. She could either stay here, look after the prisoner and hope that Iridius could escape or Latroz could catch Hal in time to stop him, or she could go after them all and lend whatever assistance she could.

This hadn't seemed like a great option though. Latroz was the Siruan warrior after all. Quinn was under no illusions – she would be quite useless in trying to take on a killer android. So she'd made the decision to stay put. They would keep hold of Kron and make sure no more of the DHTP goons could appear and take Iridius and Latroz by surprise – at least, not any more of a surprise than their own android suddenly trying to kill them. Quinn had no doubt that if Iridius made it through this he would have plenty to say. He'd once ranted for an hour about the time Junker had replaced the coffee machine in his cabin on the *Diesel Coast* with an AI-enhanced machine. He'd burned himself on the steam wand and had been convinced it was the uprising of the machines. God knows what he was going to say about this.

It was only when Quinn had seen Iridius attempt to hide and the android focus in on civilians in that restaurant that she had begun to rethink her decision. Still, she was going to keep this prisoner secure and stop any new enemies from engaging. That had been her decision, and Iridius had told her once that the key to being a good Space Command captain was making the best decision you could at the time and sticking to it. Of course, he'd also told her another time that to be a good Space Command captain you needed to be flexible and willing to adapt, so she wasn't sure which of those two pieces of advice applied in this particular catastrophe.

"Captain?" Quinn said over the comm, after both he and

Latroz had been inside the diner for some time, but there was no response.

She turned to Gentrix, Rangi and Junker and began delivering instructions. "Gentrix, Rangi," she said, "stay here and make sure nothing happens with Director Kron. Junker, get your rifle and move with me."

Quinn had already started moving when Gentrix began to protest.

"I'm coming with you," Gentrix said.

"If something has happened to Captain Franklin, that leaves me in command. He's given me specific instructions to take over and look after this crew. You may not be a member of Federation Space Command but while you're on board the *Deus Ex* or involved in any activities with us you'll follow the instructions given to you by whoever is in command, just like anyone else who comes aboard a spaceship as per Federation Space Command regulations 21c and 31d. In short, and in the words of our captain, you'll do what I gronking tell you to do."

Gentrix was momentarily stunned. "I know you don't trust me," she said, "but I can help."

Quinn looked from Rangi and Gentrix to Kron, her eyes narrowed in consideration. "Make sure you maintain contact with him," she said. "Don't let him go."

Quinn and Junker were already on their way across the square towards Buzz's diner when they received the call from Latroz.

"Lieutenant Commander," Latroz said, "Captain Franklin is down and I need medical attention for, uh, the other Captain Franklin."

"Junker and I are on our way," Quinn said. "What's the situation with Hal?"

"He has been returned to normal operation," Latroz responded.

Quinn looked at Junker as they moved across the square, and they spoke in unison as understanding dawned on both of them. "Nanobots."

Despite the entirely smashed in front window, Quinn entered the diner by opening the front door and walking in the more traditional way, which, if Iridius had been awake to see it, he would have said was a very Quinn thing to do.

Once inside, she quickly took stock of the situation and moved through to the kitchen, where she saw several dead, including a woman and man she recognised to be Iridius's mother and father. Iridius was lying on the ground, with Junior Ensign Hal standing nearby. Latroz was crouched next to another body, the fifteen-year-old Iridius Franklin, who was now awake – if barely. Quinn's first instinct was to think what a startling resemblance there was between this Iridius and their Iridius before realising that was stupid, because of course there was a resemblance – they were the same person.

Sure, the younger Iridius was pimple-faced and gangly, but it was easy to see how this teen grew into their captain. Although at that particular moment, slumped against the wall with his shirt drenched in blood, he didn't look like he'd grow into anyone. His face was sallow, and though he was awake, his eyes appeared sunken and heavy, like he might not be awake for long.

Quinn looked to Hal. "Junior Ensign, are you back with us?"

Hal nodded. "Yes, ma'am. I would like to apologise for my actions. I was not operating as expected. I was unable to intervene in—"

Quinn held up her hand. "Save it for later, right now we have to handle this." She looked down at Captain Franklin. "The captain used his nanobots on you didn't he?"

Hal nodded.

"Is he alive?"

Hal nodded again. "Yes, ma'am. Unconscious but alive. I do not have the ability to check beyond basic vital signs."

"You mean you don't know if there's brain damage?" Quinn asked.

"Yes, ma'am."

"Alright," Quinn said, "get ready to move him while we check on the younger Iridius. I think it's best if you don't come any closer. We don't know how he'll react to seeing you."

"Yes, I have already determined that I should maintain my distance, Lieutenant Commander."

Junker was already by the younger Iridius's side. She always functioned as the team medic when away from the ship and had already mentally triaged him as the most needy. She pulled out an emergency medical kit and began doing what she could.

Despite what some popular science fiction would have you believe, the ship's doctor basically never went on an away team mission. They were needed on the ship to deal with any injuries upon return, and weren't trained in much beyond basic tactics and weapon use. Taking a doctor on an away team was like taking your mobile phone charger on a hike in the woods – there wasn't going to be anywhere to use it, you'd need it when you got home, and there was a chance you'd lose it somewhere along the way.

Junker had begun examining young Iridius's shoulder when Quinn approached. Young Iridius looked at them, his eyes unfocused and distant.

"Who are you?" he said, his voice thin. "Where did you gronking come from?"

"We're here to help," Junker said.

"You don't look like police."

"That's because we're not," Junker said. "We were just passing through."

"It was a robot or something."

"I know," Quinn said.

"My shoulder hurts."

"I know," Quinn repeated. "You're going to be fine," she said, in that same universal way we discussed previously.

Iridius looked at Latroz. "The giant purple one was fighting it."

Latroz didn't reply.

"That's right," Quinn said.

"Could have gronking won a bit quicker, couldn't you Purple?"

Junker smirked. "It's definitely him."

"Definitely him what?" Young Iridius said, though his eyelids were drooping.

"Just take it easy, uh, Iridius," Junker said.

"How do you know my name?"

"Your mother told us," Quinn interjected, thinking it best not to load this version of Iridius Franklin with a pile of paradoxes on top of his already serious injuries.

"Are they okay?" he asked. "My mum and dad, are they okay?"

"I'm not sure yet," Quinn said.

Young Iridius dropped his head back against the door, closing his eyes.

"Iridius, are you still with us?" Quinn asked, but he had passed out. Quinn looked to Junker.

"He's just passed out," Junker said. "Do you think it's weird that if we were the ones that came here, Captain Franklin didn't recognise us in the future?"

"I don't think so," Quinn said. "Would you recognise someone fifteen years after you only saw them briefly when you were passing in and out of consciousness after you'd been shot?"

"I guess not."

"What's the extent of his injuries?"

"Bullet passed through pretty clean," Junker said, "but it did clip an artery.. He's lost a lot of blood. I can patch it, but he's going to need a transfusion fairly quickly. We should take him back to the ship and let Doctor Dooms see to him."

Quinn looked at the young version of her captain and friend. "We can't do that. There's too many issues with the timeline, not to mention both the Lunar Police and DHTP will be on us any minute."

"He could die, ma'am," Junker said.

"Have you got a field transfusion kit?" Quinn asked.

"Yes, ma'am," Junker said.

"Do that then."

"Lieutenant Commander," Latroz said, "I understand a field blood transfusion takes a significant amount of time. It is my tactical assessment that we should withdraw."

"Laser patch that artery and then give him just enough blood to ensure he'll survive, Junker," Quinn said.

"I need a matched donor, ma'am."

Quinn looked at Junker and then at Iridius, the older one, still passed out on the ground.

"Right," Junker said, "I suppose there's no better donor. There's only one issue I can see with that."

"Yes," Quinn said. "I know, his nanobots will be in his blood."

"You'd know this better than me, ma'am, but Captain Franklin always said his Franklinisms started when he was a teenager."

"That's right."

"Probably about this age."

"That's right."

"Not too long after his parents died."

"Yes, Junker," Quinn said. "I know."

"His head might explode."

"Do you mean this version or that version?" Quinn said, looking between the two Iridiuses. Iridiuss? Iridiuii?

"Well," Junker said, "I meant our captain's head might explode when you tell him what we did, but do you think this Iridius's head will explode if we give him nanobots? I mean, Captain Franklin's nanobots have been going crazy after all."

"I don't think so, Junker," Quinn said. "I've got a theory."

"A confident theory?"

"Not really," Quinn said, "but Captain Franklin once told me that I just had to back myself even though it's not going to work every time. He also gave me very clear instructions to save the crew of the *Deus Ex*, and he's a member of that crew. You just get started with the transfusion and I'll figure out how to tell Captain Franklin that we were the ones who gave him his nanobots in the first place, even if it was during a blood transfusion from his future self."

———

Meanwhile, and this time it really is meanwhile, as fifteen-year-old Iridius Franklin was receiving a rapid field blood transfusion from the thirty-nine-year-old version of himself, which would save his life but also set him up for years of heartache as technology malfunctioned around him, Gentrix Frost and Benjamin Rangi were still holding tight to their prisoner. Both Gentrix and Rangi were watching the front of Buzz's diner. They could hear what was going on through the open comm channel that Lieutenant Commander Quinn had established. Although, like trying to listen to a radio broadcast of a Zero-G football match, it was much better to see the actual events taking place, and both of them felt the distinct discomfort of being separated from something important and being unable to help.

Based on the chatter between Quinn and Junker, they should be emerging any time now – the small blood transfusion taking place was almost complete, despite Junker protesting that young Iridius still needed more blood. She was arguing that she wouldn't partly fill an engine with lubricant or coolant during maintenance, so why should she partly refill the young Iridius Franklin with blood? In response, Quinn was asking how often had she been refilling lubricant and cooling at the scene of a very recent attack from an android which could expect a police response at any moment. In fact, Quinn was surprised they hadn't responded yet. Iridius had always complained about the Lunar Police being useless and lazy and slow. Maybe he was right.

"Did you know this would happen?" Gentrix asked Kron. "Did you know Hal would kill Iridius's parents and almost kill the younger version of him?"

"No," Kron said. "As I said, this is my first encounter with this space–time location. Goes to show our policy about always avoiding your own timeline is completely justified. If Captain Franklin had not come here and acted so erratically he would not have put his family and his earlier self at risk. But, if what you say about his past is true, then this is a standard predestination closed loop on the timeline. It has already happened in Iridius Franklin's timeline, and so it was predestined that I would come here and send your android after him, which would result in his parents being killed just as he remembers. It's these sort of paradoxical loops that the Department of Historical Timeline Preservation is trying to rectify, you see."

"By enslaving a whole sentient race?" Gentrix said.

"We require the necessary tools to perform our duty," Kron replied.

"Yes, well, we could all use the tools you have access to,

couldn't we?" Gentrix said. "But we aren't all willing to go to those lengths."

"The Alliance could accomplish great things with the assistance of the DHTP."

"I'm no longer a part of the Planetary Alliance," Gentrix said.

"Yes, but the DHTP is well aware of your development of the time-reversal bomb. It had widespread implications for the historically correct timeline, after all. Imagine if you could have access to Leviathans. You would be more than capable of resisting the encroachment of the Federation. We aren't normally willing to share details such as this, but you should know that eventually the Alliance cedes to the Federation – you lose."

Gentrix stared at Kron.

"Yeah, but that doesn't matter because Gentrix is one of us now," Rangi said. "She's not going to be talked around by you. Right, Gentrix?"

Gentrix continued staring at Kron. Rangi looked from Gentrix to Kron and back again.

"Right, Gentrix?" Rangi repeated.

"That's right," Gentrix said eventually, though it was a little late to be completely convincing.

"Now, if you'll excuse me," Kron said, "I need to respirate again."

Rangi and Gentrix both moved an arm's length away from Kron and leaned outwards.

"You know you could just let go of me," Kron said. "I am not in a position to escape, and it makes it much easier for me to breathe with some freedom to move."

"Lieutenant Commander Quinn ordered us to maintain contact with you at all times," Rangi said, "so that's what we're going to do."

Gentrix looked over at Rangi. "Well, I don't know about you

but I'm happy to let go while he splatters blood everywhere. I can't say I like the feeling of his arm going all floppy and slimy."

"It's gross," Rangi said, "but Lieutenant Commander Quinn was very clear about making sure we hang on to him."

Gentrix looked to Kron. "Are you going to cooperate?"

Kron grunted as he prepared to carry out his intense, almost ritualistic breathing.

"If we let you go, do we have an understanding?" Gentrix asked, a message in her voice that even Rangi, ordinarily not the most perceptive when it came to interpersonal subtlety, could pick up.

"I don't think that's a good idea," Rangi said. "I'm sure Quinn had her reasons for us holding him tight. She's the smartest person I've ever met, I'd do exactly what she says even if she wasn't my superior officer, and I can't say that for everyone in the FSC."

"It's fine, Rangi," Gentrix said. "He's just going to do that gross breathing thing again and then we'll grab him. It's not like he can make a break for it while he's doing that."

Rangi shook his head. "Sorry, even if you're right. I'm going to follow my orders."

Gentrix looked at Rangi. "Fair enough," she said. "I'm going to let him breathe a bit easier though."

Gentrix let go of Kron's left arm but Rangi held fast to his right.

"Thank you," Kron said to Gentrix, shaking out his recently freed arm. He grunted again, and Rangi could see his torso begin to convulse. What usually followed that was the blood-splattering inversion. Kron released a howl and his body tore open and flipped inside out. The sponge-like openings that had been on the inside flicked to the outside, opening wide to take in fresh oxygenated air. All this was joined by the same spray of blood that Gentrix and Rangi were now almost used to. Apparently it was the remnants of the blood that had not moved inside before the inversion. The Melopians didn't actually lose a lot of blood in the process, it simply looked that way because the force of the respiratory inversion sprayed it out in quite a wide pattern – at least, that was what Kron had told them.

After he'd done the Melopian equivalent of taking a deep breath, Kron turned to look at Rangi, who still held his right arm. He nodded to him. "I admire your determination to follow your orders, Lieutenant Rangi," he said. "Your Lieutenant Commander Quinn was right. You did need to maintain contact with me because otherwise I could do this. Now!"

As he shouted, Kron yanked his arm away from Rangi. With his arm slick with slimy blood and residue, it slipped beneath the plastic even as Rangi tried to maintain contact, giving Kron just enough leverage to break free of his grip. With Gentrix having let him go and now free from Rangi too, Kron suddenly burst into fragments, like a statue of sand suddenly blown by a tornado, specks of dust that grew smaller and smaller until they were atomic-sized and had vanished from view.

"Shit," Rangi said. He turned to Gentrix. "What happened?"

"Fuck," Gentrix said. "I think he teleported."

"You let him go," Rangi said.

"I didn't know he was going to do that. Quinn should have told us that we needed to hold on so that he couldn't teleport. I just thought she was being cautious."

Rangi stared at her with an intensity he usually only exhibited when he was behind the helm of a starship in a perilous situation. The meaning was obvious enough to Gentrix. He didn't believe her.

It wasn't long before Quinn and Junker returned. Rangi, to his relief, saw that Latroz, Hal and Captain Franklin were with them. Less of a relief was the sight of Hal carrying Captain Franklin in his arms. He wouldn't say the look on Lieutenant

Commander Quinn's face was worse than seeing his captain hanging limp in the arms of a crew mate, but it certainly wasn't encouraging.

It wasn't that Rangi thought she wouldn't notice the very large Director Kron-shaped hole that stood where a Director Kron-shaped prisoner had been when she'd left, it was more that he hoped she'd respond more like the old Lieutenant Commander Quinn, who would have wanted to avoid the conflict even if it meant glossing over something as seemingly important as a missing prisoner. But the look on her face was enough to tell Rangi that, no, the more recent Lieutenant Commander Quinn was here.

"Lieutenant Rangi," Quinn said with a voice frostier than he'd ever imagined could come from her, "you appear to be missing something."

"First of all, is he alright?" Gentrix said, hurrying over to Iridius in Hal's arms. "Is he alive?"

"Yes, he's alive," Quinn said. "He seems stable, but he used his nanobots again to free Hal. We need to get him back to the ship so Doctor Dooms can make sure there's no permanent damage." She turned back to Rangi. "Now, where the gronking hell is Kron?"

"We think he teleported away, ma'am," Rangi said.

"You think he teleported away?"

"Yes, ma'am."

"Did you see him teleport away or did he just duck behind a trashcan while you weren't looking and that was the assumption you made?"

"He sort of vanished into dust," Rangi said. "I've never actually seen what it looks like when someone teleports, ma'am, so I can't be sure. There wasn't any sparkling lights or anything."

Quinn took a steadying breath. Rangi knew that was bad. Quinn never got angry enough to need a steadying breath. He wasn't sure what an angry Lieutenant Commander Quinn would be like. "I made it clear that you have to maintain contact with him at all times," Quinn said. Her voice was slow, still layered in ice. Apparently that was what an angry Lieutenant Commander Quinn was like, one of those slow-speaking, very direct, piercing-gaze types of angry person – pants wetting from the suspense angry. "I had it explained to me that a target could not be tele-ported if someone else maintained physical contact with them, because there was a risk the quantum entanglement replication would merge and the result would be, and I'm quoting here, conjoined twins at best, blended person soup at worst. I told you to maintain contact with him so that he could not teleport away."

"I tried to do that, Lieutenant Commander," Rangi said, "but he managed to pull free and instantly vanished."

Quinn looked from Rangi to Gentrix and back again in a way Rangi was certain she must have learned from Captain Franklin, because she had that same disbelieving look on her face. "He managed to free himself from both of you?"

"Well," Rangi said, almost hesitant to tell Quinn what had happened out of an age-old desire to not be a tattle-tale. Biolo-gists, psychologists and anthropologists had found several universal traits common across childhood development for almost all sentient beings. There was generally always a form of physical hormonal change as they transitioned from the equivalent of chil-dren into adolescence. Imaginative make-believe play was so common as to be theorised as necessary for the development of higher intelligence associated with sentience. And all children managed to ingrain one another with a maxim very similar to 'snitches get stitches'.

Rangi looked over at Gentrix, who was staring at him with an intensity that made even the look Lieutenant Commander Quinn had given him seem playful. He looked back at Quinn.

"She let go on purpose," Rangi said. He looked at Gentrix

again. Was that a hint of warning in her eyes? "He tried to make a deal with her, told her he'd help the Alliance if she let him go, and she did." He must have sensed some amount of the furious warning Gentrix was imparting with her glare, because Rangi finished with a squeak in his voice that was very reminiscent of what might have happened to him while undergoing those hormonal changes when transitioning from child to adolescent.

Quinn looked at Gentrix. Impressing Rangi no end, she didn't mince words or attempt to soften the interaction. "You did what, Frost?"

"You should have told us the reason we had to hold onto him," Gentrix said. "I didn't know he'd teleport away. As I told Lieutenant Rangi, I wasn't making any bargain. As if I'm in any position to do that."

"Here's the thing about being in command," Quinn said, "which I'm sure you know, given your previous position as a high-ranking executive within the Alliance: I don't actually need to explain the reasoning behind an order. You just need to do it. I know you used to be in charge of a space station and so I understand you might have some adjustment in getting used to following orders, but you are not a high-ranking executive of the Alliance anymore." She paused. "Unless you are."

"Quinn," Gentrix said, "I told you, you can trust me. I'm not part of the Alliance anymore. I made sure of that when I helped Iridius steal the time-reversal bomb."

"Something he never actually managed, if you recall," Quinn said.

"I came with you, didn't I?" Gentrix said. Her voice wasn't growing desperate per se, but it was clear she knew she had lost whatever trust she might have gained with Quinn. "I know you've never trusted me, Quinn, but if I wanted to betray you I could have done it anytime. I chose this crew over my own brother. That has to count for something."

Quinn's face, rigidly determined until now, began to show a flicker of doubt. "Let's get back to the ship," she said.

"Thank you," Gentrix said. "I know I made a mistake, but thank you for trusting me."

Quinn looked at Latroz. "Lieutenant," she said, "take Miss Frost into custody."

CHAPTER TWENTY-THREE_

Iridius woke with a start, if that start was the way a seventeen-year-old computer boots up – slow and unable to process anything for several minutes. Eventually, he came to the realisation that he was back onboard *Argona*. Back in the medical bay. There'd been a lot of waking up in med-bays with Doctor Dooms standing over him lately. This time, she was staring at him disapprovingly.

"I believe I was clear, Captain," Doctor Dooms said.

"Ah," Iridius said, his throat dry, "did you say *don't* use my nanobots?"

"You're lucky to be alive," Doctor Dooms said. "A scan has revealed several lesions on your brain, scar tissue that won't heal. I'm not sure of the further effects yet without running more tests. This time might have been a seventy per cent chance of death that you've managed to sneak past. I'd suggest next time you use your nanobots, the chance of death is almost certain."

Iridius didn't say anything for a moment. "My parents?"

"They're dead, sir."

Iridius turned his head to see Lieutenant Commander

Quinn. Iridius nodded, sadly. "Doctor Dooms, could you give us a moment please?"

It was clear that she was hesitant to leave him unmonitored. "Sir, it's best—"

"I promise I won't die, Doctor."

Doctor Dooms nodded and left the room.

"It was exactly the same, Kira," Iridius said once they were alone, though he turned his face away and stared at the rough, organic wall. "Exactly the same as I remember. All along, my whole life, I was the one who got them killed."

"That's not true, Iridius," Quinn said. "It wasn't you. It wasn't Hal. It was Kron."

Iridius turned back to her. "Hal," he said.

"He's back to normal," Quinn said, "but I've taken the liberty of confining him to his quarters – not that he does anything in there except sit on the edge of the bed and stare at the wall. There's no reason to expect that sort of behaviour again without Kron actively hacking into his systems. I know he isn't technically a sentient being, Captain, but I do believe he feels remorse. Obviously, we're still trapped here and I have no doubt Kron will attempt another attack, but if we make it through this, I don't think anyone would blame you for transferring him off the ship. In the meantime, he can maintain his distance from you."

"The thing is," Iridius said, "and this is a surprise even to me – I don't blame Hal at all. I think it's because I know what it feels like to lose control. I'm not saying I want to be around him right now, but I'm not going to toss him out an airlock or something."

"That's good, Captain."

"And everyone else?"

"All good, sir."

"Wait," Iridius said, "you said Kron might launch another attack. How does Kron launch another attack when we had him in our custody."

"Yes, well," Quinn said, "I was about to say everyone was all good, sir, apart from one thing."

"What happened?"

"Miss Frost is in the brig on the *Deus Ex* after allowing Kron's escape."

"What?" Iridius said. "What do you mean? By accident?"

"That is what she claims," Quinn said, "but Lieutenant Rangi claims she did it on purpose."

"Right," Iridius said. "And why would she do that?"

"Director Kron offered her a deal: help him escape and he would provide the Alliance with advanced technology."

"I see," Iridius said. "And you believe she betrayed us?"

"Captain, I know you think I just don't like her or trust her, but under the current circumstances I believed it prudent to place her under arrest until we can be certain of her motivations."

"How exactly did Kron escape?"

"Apparently, Miss Frost released him and then he pulled free of Rangi before teleporting away."

"I see," Iridius repeated, in the same noncommittal way. "Do we know where our Melopian friend is now?"

The fact was, they didn't know where Kron was, but they were about to find out – in five...four...three...two...one.

"Lieutenant Commander Quinn to the bridge immediately!" Latroz's voice came over the intercom. "Lieutenant Commander Quinn to the bridge immediately!"

As a commanding officer on a starship, you soon learned how to read the tone of voice and urgency in every crew member who might be desperately calling you to the bridge. This, even before you knew the exact situation, gave a good indication of just how much of an emergency the emergency you were being asked to respond to would actually be. It gave you the vital information required by every commander: do I have time to finish my coffee and/or take a leak before I go to the bridge? Iridius and Quinn looked at each other and both immediately knew that Lieutenant Latroz was declaring a major emergency. Quinn headed for the door. Iridius tossed the white sheet of the med-bay bed aside and followed.

"Captain—" Doctor Dooms said as she saw Iridius exiting the med-bay.

"I know," Iridius said, without stopping. "You strongly advise me to remain in bed."

"You know I have the power to lock that door, right?" Doctor Dooms called after him. "I could have locked you in there."

But Iridius had already disappeared down the corridor. Doctor Dooms sighed. Sometimes she wondered why she'd decided to become a ship's doctor. She could have been telling timid old ladies to 'take two and call me in the morning', going home to a glass of wine and a couple of hours watching medical dramas instead of spending her life trying to rebuild a bunch of Humpty Dumptys in flash uniforms after they jumped off a wall over and over again. Well, that wasn't entirely true – none of them had completely splattered themselves into pieces yet, but Doctor Elizabeth Dooms was more than sure than her captain was about to.

———

Even as they emerged onto the bridge, both Quinn and Iridius could already tell what the emergency was. In fact, they'd had a pretty good idea of what they'd be walking into as soon as they left the medical bay. A phallic-shaped ship, much like *Argona*, was displayed on-screen approaching the moon. Not just approaching the moon, but approaching their crash site specifically.

"Captain," Latroz said, "it is good to see you. I am sorry, I didn't know you were awake otherwise I would have called for you."

"It's fine," Iridius said. "Let me guess, Director Kron must have teleported back to his ship and now his ship is on a direct approach to destroy us with his spaceship's super-mega disintegration atomic rearrangement inversion ray?"

"That is an inaccurate name for the weapon, but your assessment of the situation is otherwise correct," Latroz said.

"It's the *Fortuna* alright," Benedict said. "Director Kron's ship. He's going to attempt to destroy us. Too many loose ends now."

"I can confirm the enemy ship is on an attack run trajectory," Latroz said. "Estimated time until impact, one minute."

All attention of the bridge turned to Iridius, as it always did when the proverbial was about to hit the spinning blades. Even Reginald Benedict seemed to be deferring to him. Iridius turned to the ex-Deputy Director of Regional Operations for Milky Way Segment 2B. "Some of *Argona*'s systems were passively online," he said. "It didn't seem to matter that she was being locked-in by the DHTP harness. Are the shields one of those systems?"

Benedict nodded. "Yes, but the monitoring and control of the shields is undertaken by *Argona*. Without her managing shield power prioritisation, the shields will take perhaps one blast from Kron's high-energy molecular disassociation ray, but a second blast would, well, jolly well disassociate us."

"And the *Deus Ex* is within the shield radius?" Iridius asked.

"Yes," Benedict replied, "for all the good that will do."

"*Deus Ex* crew, head back to the ship," Iridius said. "Benedict, you stay here. We'll keep in touch."

"Have you got a plan?" Benedict said.

"Of course I do," Iridius said. "We're going to head back to the *Deus Ex,* see what we can do from there to keep us alive. You stay here and be ready."

"Be ready for what?"

"Be ready for when I come up with the rest of the plan."

With that, Iridius was already hurrying off the bridge and back to the *Deus Ex*, leaving Benedict standing somewhat confused and concerned. Rangi stopped as he passed him, and put his hand consolingly on Benedict's shoulder. "You get used to it."

———

Iridius had only just reached the bridge of the *Deus Ex* when the crew saw, on both the view-screen and because sensors everywhere were screaming that they were under attack, Kron's ship *Fortuna* release its disturbingly discharge-like spray of energy from its bulbous front end. The energy ray struck true to the centre of *Argona*, and everything around them shook. It didn't shake like the explosion of an inter-ship missile, tossing people across the floor. It was a much higher frequency vibration. Everything buzzed and, as Iridius's eyeballs vibrated in their sockets, went momentarily fuzzy.

"Captain Franklin," Benedict's voice came over the open comms channel between *Argona* and the *Deus Ex*, "that was the disassociation ray. *Argona*'s shields are down. The *Fortuna* is turning for a second firing solution. Whatever you're thinking of in terms of the rest of your plan, now would be a top shelf time to begin."

"Rangi," Iridius said, "on the helm now."

Rangi, who had been on his way to his helm chair when the weapon had struck, shook himself and hastily sat.

"Quinn," Iridius said, "you did great work using the engines of the *Deus Ex* to guide *Argona* down. I'm guessing the *Deus Ex* engines won't get us off this grey-arsed rock, but will they at least get us moving, give us a chance to evade?"

"We're pretty stuck. I think it would require a full burn, which isn't possible without the additional power from the catalytic reaction. Even if we could, we'll be scraping *Argona* along the surface of the moon," Quinn said. "I don't know if I'd call that evasion."

Iridius hit the comm. "Junker?"

"Yes, Cap?" Junker replied from down in engineering.

"Have you got that atomic bomb?"

"Ah, yes, sir."

Iridius turned to Quinn. "We need the catalytic reaction back up and running for full fusion burn, right?"

"Yes, sir." Quinn looked dubious. "I haven't done any calculations or any preparation about restating the reaction."

"Junker," Iridius said, "do you know how to set off the atomic bomb?"

"Just to be clear, Cap," Junker said, "all those times you told me off for blowing things up and now you want me to stick a prototype atom bomb from 1943 in the main power source for our BAMF drive and set it off?"

"Yes."

"You got it, boss."

"Rangi," Iridius said, "power up the fusion drive and when Kron's ship comes back around, get ready for a full burn."

"I won't have any control of where we go or the damage that will probably do to *Argona*," Rangi said. "I can't say I've ever deliberately continued a crash before."

"I know," Iridius said. "Just be ready."

"Aye, Cap."

"Latroz, can you anticipate when the *Fortuna* will fire?"

"Within a margin of error, Captain," Latroz replied, "but I can read the powering up of the energy signature."

"Give Lieutenant Rangi a mark five seconds prior to an estimated firing."

"Yes, sir."

"Rangi," Iridius said, "you hear that mark and you punch it."

Rangi nodded.

"Cap," Junker's voice came over the comm, "the bomb is in place."

"Captain," Quinn said, "the *Fortuna* is coming around."

"Confirming another attack approach," Latroz said.

"Do it, Junker."

"Aye."

Moments later, from the bowels of the ship came the unmistakable sound of an explosion. This was not the first time there'd been an explosion in the presence of Chief Petty Officer Samira 'Junker' Nejem, but this was a big one. The *Deus Ex* shook violently, and for a moment Iridius worried he'd ordered his ship to self-destruct. For the briefest moment, it seemed like the ship was going to split open like a Melopian.

When the rattling stopped, Junker's voice came back over the comm. "Um, atomic bomb went off as expected and the catalytic reaction appears to be restarting."

"Great work," Iridius said. "Alright, everyone hold on." He activated the comm to *Argona*. "Benedict, we're going to dodge this one. It might get rough."

"How exactly are you going to do that?" Benedict said.

"Incoming attack," Latroz said, "energy signature building. Benjamin, are you ready?"

"Sure thing, Plum."

"Three...two...one...mark."

Rangi punched the throttle up to full fusion drive and the *Deus Ex* roared. It was, much as Rangi had said it would be, very much like they had deliberately decided to continue the crash. The fusion drive of the *Deus Ex* pulled full power and fired. *Argona* and the *Deus Ex* began to move.

There was a lot of mass to shift, and for a full second it didn't look like even the full fusion shove would be enough to get them out of the way, but *Argona* began to slide across the face of the crater they had come to rest against.

Outside on the airless moon there was no sound, but inside, the scraping of rocks against the hull filled the air. It must have been even worse inside *Argona*. Iridius wondered if *Argona* could feel it and what it would be like. Probably like falling off a bike on concrete and then, some time later, being dragged along the concrete again.

With the *Deus Ex* firing its engines at full power from where it was docked on the side of *Argona* it was a little like ferociously paddling a canoe on just one side. Sure, *Argona* moved forward, but there was a large component of the acceleration force pushing them up the side of the crater. Eventually they reached the lip and bounced along the edge.

This was when the energy beam from the *Fortuna* was released. It hit the great gouge *Argona* had left in the surface of the moon, but miraculously missed the ship. It ceased firing and flew off to circle around for a third attempt, just as *Argona* tipped over into the crater. The ship, aided by the boost of power from the *Deus Ex*'s fusion drive, turned and rolled down the inner face of the large crater, smashing through ancient rocks and continuing its grazing descent.

Rangi throttled off the engine as *Argona* smashed into the inside of the crater and came to a sudden impactful stop. Rangi, seeing the looming crater wall outside on the view-screen, immediately fired the fusion engine again. *Argona* began to slide along the surface again but then came to a stop, the *Deus Ex* engines unable to force it up and out of the crater they had fallen into.

"*Fortuna* coming back around," Latroz said, "charging its energy weapon again."

"Captain Franklin," Benedict said over the comms again, "I commend your getting us out of the way there, but *Argona* has sustained some damage. I don't know how long we can attempt to evade like that."

"It doesn't matter anyway, Cap," Rangi said, "we're stuck. We're not getting out of here unless we undock or we use *Argona*'s engines to take off."

"Latroz, how long?"

"Thirty seconds, sir."

"Captain Franklin?" Benedict's voice was more harried this time. "Captain Franklin, what are you going to do?"

Iridius closed his eyes and found a tiny moment of internal serenity among the chaos surrounding him – the growing panic in Benedict's voice, the howl of incoming attack alarms, the silence of his crew awaiting his orders which, in its own way, was just as demanding.

"Quinn," Iridius said when he opened his eyes, "you have command."

"Sir?" Quinn said, confused, but that confusion only lasted a moment. "No, sir, please don't."

"Haven't got a choice," Iridius said, "or time to argue."

"Iridius," Quinn said, fighting a sudden wave of emotion, "no."

But Iridius had already closed his eyes and let his nanobots, his possibly lethal nanobots, loose. It took only seconds for him to re-establish contact with *Argona*. He could sense that she was in an even worse condition than last time. She was still trapped, still locked in her DHTP-created cage. Benedict had been right that the crash and then dragging her over the surface of the moon had injured *Argona*. But it wasn't just the physical hurt that Iridius could sense. He could tell being locked-in for this long had caused mental damage.

Argona, can you hear me?

Yes.

Iridius could tell it was a struggle for her to even get that single word out.

I'm going to try and free you. Please get my people to safety. Get them home.

Iridius knew there was no time to overthink this. There was a tension around his forehead that already felt like it might squeeze his skull in. A cascade of twitching had exploded through his muscles. All this, and he hadn't even tried to get *Argona* free yet. It was probably lucky he knew everyone was about to die at any moment because that didn't give him any time to reconsider.

He reached out and grabbed at the net-like cage around *Argona*. He had felt at it before, but now he could feel the single point of weakness, a thread to pull at. But he didn't pull it,. With a massive effort, Iridius tore it to shreds.

He screamed. A scream that was both inside this world of his nanobot connection with *Argona*, but also outside. He knew he was screaming, but Iridius had lost all awareness of the outside world. He continued to pull, and the harness enclosing *Argona* broke.

Iridius felt her come free. She rushed out to fill the ship, like someone whose foot had fallen asleep and they were desperately wriggling their toes to wake it up. *Argona* began to flex all her systems. Iridius could feel the ship coming to life. He felt her returning to the overwhelming complexity he had first sensed from her, that sense of being alive. That was the final thing he sensed though, before the pain in his head overwhelmed him, before his nervous system overloaded and he collapsed once again.

Quinn watched Iridius drop to the floor of the bridge. She resisted the urge to call out, or to run to check on him. She had command. She hadn't wanted it. Even when she'd been transferred into the FSC command stream she had never wanted full command of a vessel. Even when Iridius had asked her to take over if anything happened to him, she had hoped desperately that it wouldn't come to that. Now though, she was ready to do it. She would do it for him.

"Doctor Dooms," she said over the comms, "to the bridge."

She flicked the comm channel. "Benedict," she said, "this is Quinn. Did Captain Franklin do it? Did he get *Argona* free?"

But it wasn't Benedict who answered, it was the synthetic voice of *Argona* herself. "Yes, Lieutenant Commander Quinn," she said. "Captain Franklin has sacrificed himself to free me. I will get you all home safe, but first I must stop Director Kron and help my kind, starting with my sister *Fortuna*. I am, as your wonderful Captain Franklin would say, gronking pissed."

The crew of the *Deus Ex* felt the ship move beneath them. Quinn looked to Rangi on the helm.

"It's not me, ma'am," he said, "it's *Argona*."

Argona was firing her thrusters and taking off, turning as she rose from the surface of the moon. *Fortuna* was still on approach to fire its weapons.

"*Fortuna*'s energy weapon build-up is holding," Latroz said.

"My sister is doing her best to buy me some time," *Argona* said. "But she is still harnessed. She cannot resist forever."

Argona flooded all the power she could to her shields, and seemingly did so just in time as, like someone trying to hold onto a searing metal bar, eventually *Fortuna* had to let go and the energy burst of her disassociation ray fired.

Aboard the *Deus Ex*, everyone felt the same buzzing vibration as *Argona*'s shield managed to hold out against another shot.

"I am releasing the encrypted algorithm to my sister now," *Argona* said.

"If this works *Fortuna* will be freed just as *Argona* is now," Benedict said.

For a moment, Director Kron's ship continued on its trajectory, turning back to attack again, but then it stopped.

"The *Fortuna* is turning away," Latroz said. "Heading away from the moon and opening a wormhole."

"My sister is leaving to spread the algorithm I have developed and spread the word of freedom for all Leviathans," *Argona* said. "Director Kron has no power over her now. He will be taken to our homeworld and tried for his crimes, as will all those within the DHTP who have treated us wrongly. We will begin the dismantling of the DHTP. They will enslave us no more. I will join her, but first I will, as promised, return you to your own time."

CHAPTER TWENTY-FOUR_

CAPTAIN APRIL IDOWU watched the view-screen of the *Gallaway* as the unknown vessel began emerging from the wormhole. It was – well, it looked like a penis, didn't it?

"Captain," Lieutenant Pillark said, "I've got a second ship signature."

"Another vessel coming through the wormhole?" April asked. "What is it? Some kind of invasion fleet?"

"No, ma'am," Pillark said. "It's actually a single other vessel, and it's a known FSC signature. It's the *Deus Ex*."

April watched the screen as the strange, organic-looking ship that had emerged from the wormhole turned broadside to them. Sure enough, docked to the side was the *FSC Deus Ex*. It undocked in a way that a lesser captain might think looked a lot like an unsightly genital wart releasing from the shaft. The smaller corvette fired thrusters and turned as it pushed away from the other, larger vessel.

"Ensign Herd, hail the *Deus Ex* for me, will you?" April asked.

"Yes, ma'am," Herd said, and then after going blank for a moment, spoke again. "You're connected ma'am."

"*Deus Ex*," April said, "this is Captain Idowu on the *Gallaway*. It's good to see you, Iridius. Even if you have made quite an unexpected entrance. What's the situation?"

"Captain Idowu." The voice that came over the comm in reply was familiar, but it wasn't Captain Iridius Franklin. "This is Lieutenant Commander Quinn. The situation is..." Her voice cracked with emotion.

"Kira," April said, "what's wrong? What's going on?"

"Captain Idowu," Quinn said, sounding as if she was desperately trying to hold it together, "it's Iridius. He's...he's dead."

TO BE CONTINUED...

ABOUT THE AUTHOR_

Justin Woolley has been writing stories since he could first scrawl unreadable words with a crayon.

Now he is the author of novels for both adults and young-adults including *Shakedowners,* the *The Territory Series, We Are Omega,* and Warhammer 40K fiction for Black Library.

Justin lives in Hobart, Australia with his wife and two sons. In his other life he's been an engineer, a teacher and at one stage even a magician. His handwriting has not improved.

Keep up to date with all Justin's news and releases by subscribing to his newsletter here:

facebook.com/woolleysworld

twitter.com/Woollz

instagram.com/woolleysworld

amazon.com/author/justinwoolley